"Go back t room now, Toby.

"Go to the table and pick up the matchbox with the name Aaron Horowitz on it. Do you have it?"

"Yes."

"Tell me about the memory."

"I'm on a big boat. Someone's kneeling in front of me. My mother and father. They're crying."

"Why are your mommy and daddy crying?"

"They are crying because I am leaving."

"Where are you going?"

"For a ride on another boat."

"Are your mommy and daddy going with you?"

"No. They cannot go. They are staying."

A flash of fear stunned Mike into cold silence. It all started to make sense. Terrible sense.

"Do you know the year, Toby?"

"It is 1912."

"My God," Mike wept softly.

"The name of the ship—what is the name of the ship you are on?"

"The *Titanic*."

_____

ANCESTORS

ANCESTORS

ROBERT Y. KLINE

PAGEANT BOOKS

PAGEANT BOOKS
225 Park Avenue South
New York, New York 10003

Cover artwork by Tim Hildebrandt

Printed in the U.S.A.

First Pageant Books printing: November, 1988

10 9 8 7 6 5 4 3 2 1

ANCESTORS

Chapter One

※※※※※※※※※※

"DEOXYRIBONUCLEIC ACID."

He pronounced the words slowly and distinctly, hoping that they might sink in.

"It's known in the trade as DNA. It's really neat stuff. Hard to imagine what life would be like without it. Everybody has gobs of it—O'Neil might even have some."

The lanky boy wrinkled his nose at the gentle dig but showed no other sign that he was paying the slightest attention to the teacher.

Mancini walked to the front of the classroom, blew a puff of chalkdust from his fingertips, and rapped his knuckles on the blackboard.

"Di–ox–i–ri–bo–nu–cle–ic–a–cid."

Each syllable was punctuated by a rap on the board and a new puff of dust. "Even a chimpan-

1

zee ought to be able to remember that. Want to give it a try, O'Neil?"

The boy rolled his eyes and slumped languidly behind the desk. He pondered for a moment, then grinned triumphantly at the girl to his right.

"Su–per–cal–i–fra–gi–lis–tic—"

O'Neil postured proudly, scanned his classmates for approval, but got only weary groans. Tyrone Williams caught his eye and flipped him the bird under the desk.

"That's very funny, O'Neil. Truly amusing." Mancini loosened his tie and sat in the old spring-back rocker with the ancient rubber wheels. He leaned back, propped his feet on the desk, and clasped his hands behind his head. "I'm not in any hurry, O'Neil. The bell's due to ring in a couple of minutes but I can stay here all day if I want to. You just take your time. We'll all wait till you get it right."

A chorus of moans flooded the science class. Mike Mancini shrugged and closed his eyes, scratching absently at an itch behind his ear. He heard a whap and a muffled cry of pain but he didn't bother to investigate.

O'Neil rubbed his head where the eraser connected and stuttered haltingly. "Dox, diox, doxy—" He finally threw his hands up in surrender. "Aw yo, Mr. Mancini, who gives a rat's rectum anyway?"

A wave of giggles replaced the moans. The biology teacher glared menacingly from his perch behind the desk. "Well, I do for one, O'Neil," he countered. "And I'm sure that some of your classmates do too. Cindy, why don't you try to help Mr. O'Neil out."

The girl at O'Neil's side wore a pair of bulky

horn rims as thick as storm doors and braided pigtails that went out about the time that Dorothy trod the Yellow Brick Road. O'Neil called her "Frog Eyes" and she was happy to get the attention. She stood by the side of the desk with her heels together and her hands folded sensibly in front of her.

"DNA, deoxyribonucleic acid." She gloated. "It's a substance found in the nucleus of all living cells. It contains the chromosomes and genes that determine physical and other characteristics." She glared through her thick glasses at Tim O'Neil like he was something she'd just scraped off her shoe. "People with defective genes often have the mental capacity of a newt."

"And the dong of a donkey." He grinned triumphantly and made a mildly obscene gesture.

Blushing a flaming crimson, Cindy sank back into her seat.

"Thank you very much, Cindy. You're absolutely right." Mancini interrupted the scholarly discussion before it took an even worse turn. With a kick at the desk, he propelled the chair toward the board and gave it another reinforcing rap. "As you pointed out, genes are the structures that determine heredity. They're the stuff of life itself, the keys to blue eyes and blond hair."

"My old man sho 'nuff must'a misplaced dem keys," Tyrone Williams announced. The class had recently read *Huckleberry Finn* for a social studies assignment and Tyrone was still mimicking the dialect.

Even Cindy had to smile. Tyrone was black as midnight, with hair like steel wool and flashing eyes like chunks of anthracite.

"Not true," Mike Mancini corrected. "In fact, Tyrone, you possess the classic characteristics of a West African tribal king, regal genealogy undiluted by rampant hybridization. You are a true thoroughbred, Tyrone, unlike most of your mongrel classmates of questionable background."

The beaming student posed like a peacock and hooked his thumbs under an imaginary set of lapels. With a flash of superiority he grinned at his friends. "Now maybe I'll be treated with the dignity and respect properly befitting my regal genealogy."

"Hey, Tyrone," O'Neil called out. "You know what they get when they cross a gorilla with an Italian?"

Tyrone shrugged.

"They get a smarter Italian."

"And do you know what they get when they cross a wise guy with a bad joke," Mancini said over the laughter.

"What do they get, Teach?"

"They get an ugly Irishman who's going to spend half the weekend writing a thousand-word paper on recombinant DNA."

"Aw yo, Teach, gimme a break. It's June. We only got one more week of school. You can't do this to me."

"Have a good time writing your paper, Donkey Dong," Cindy said, snickering.

O'Neil curled his lips and snarled and the bug-eyed girl cowered in the corner of her desk.

Mike Mancini thought he had just about the best job in the world. He loved his field of study and he loved kids, especially this irreverent bunch from the Saint Paul suburbs. They were in many ways the only family he had. He had never made an effort at a serious romance, always being too busy researching, studying, teaching, counseling. The few times that a serious affair threatened to flare up, he'd squashed it on the spot with a monologue about the reproductive apparatus of a gibbon or something equally breathtaking. Mike figured that any person who could stand living with him would have to turn on to his genetic fascination, and he didn't think he could live with anyone that kinky. There was no way out. So the twenty-three kids in his science class were his family and he loved them. And though they'd never admit it, they felt the same about Mancini.

Ever since he'd taken a razor to his first clammy frog over thirty years earlier, Mike had known how he wanted to spend his life. His specialties were genetics, the study of the hereditary process, and eugenics, the use of this genetic knowledge to improve life. He knew his stuff. When researchers at the university hit a wall trying to identify a rare genetic disorder they called for Mike Mancini.

The King of Genes his associates nicknamed him. The Prince of Protoplasm. While his friends were on the course knocking strokes from their golf scores, or chucking their grandkids under chubby cheeks, Mancini was chasing genetic clues, looking for the keys to open the doors of information for future generations.

"Things don't have to be like this. These kids could be well and normal," he confided to his close friend, Dr. Clancy Kendall. It was six months earlier, during the annual Christmas break, and they were helping out at a party at the children's home, surrounded by the innocent faces of a dozen handicapped kids. "You're too young to remember what the polio scare was like, Clancy. God, what a killer that one was. But we licked it. We licked a whole bunch of them. Smallpox, TB, typhoid—they're all on the run."

Mike had a missionary approach to anything he undertook and he zealously poked his finger into the imaginary gut of the diseases as he ticked them off. "Today you guys sew in new hearts and kidneys the way your mamas used to sew cotton patches on your blue jeans." He scanned the room, staring sympathetically at the hopeful faces and twisted limbs. "This is the next frontier."

Mike squatted in front of a wheelchair and hiked up the pillow in the baggy Santa suit. The stringy beard made his face itch and he fought the urge to scratch. The boy's eyes sparkled like stars and his toothy smile flooded the ward with love.

"Thank you, Santa." His eyes glowed like Christmas tree lights as he took the present in his clawlike hand.

Mike choked back a fist-sized lump as he watched the boy struggle with the wrapping. He looked into the young doctor's eyes. "It's not fair, is it, Clancy?"

Dr. Kendall couldn't answer.

Chapter Two

✦✦✦✦✦✦✦✦✦✦

"MOMMY, COME QUICK. He's doing it again. He's staring! Toby's staring at nothing again!" Tina Horton's urgent cry shattered the stillness and rattled the house with a measure of eight-year-old melodrama.

"For goodness sake, Tina, you don't have to screech like a tomcat. I'm right here in the kitchen." Jan Horton wiped her doughy fingers on her apron and stalked into the den. "Now what's the trouble?"

"It's Toby. He's doing it again. Look!"

Toby Horton sat primly on the flowered couch, oblivious to the commotion. He had the waxy look of a department store mannequin, a little plastic boy dressed in razor-creased blue slacks and a starchy plaid shirt. The TV vibrated to a music video but he couldn't hear it. He heard nothing as he gazed at some meaningless point in space.

"Toby! Toby, can you hear me? Look at me, honey. Are you all right?"

Jan Horton knelt on the soft shag rug and rested her hands on Toby's knees. Her voice was soft and calm, betraying none of the anxiety that welled inside her. How beautiful he is, she thought. His cheeks were like pink porcelain covered with a fine down. The soft, full lips and straight nose had been carefully molded by a thoughtful hand. And the steel-gray eyes, normally alive and penetrating, cast a dreamy gaze at some undefined target.

"Why is Toby doing that, Mommy? It scares

me." Tina crouched behind her mother and wrapped her arms around the apron-draped waist.

"It's okay, honey. The doctor said it's nothing to worry about. Sometimes Toby just likes to stop everything and think about things, that's all." She twisted around and took the little girl's round face into her hands. A dusting of flour clung to her flushed cheeks. "And do you remember what the doctor told us? What does Toby do when he wants to think about his special things?" She spoke as if Toby weren't even in the same room with them.

Tina screwed her face into a mischievous smile. "He turns himself off like a lightbulb," she said with a giggle. She craned her neck and snuck a peek at Toby over her mother's shoulder. Her blond bangs hung like a curtain over wide, curious eyes. "But why does he do it? What does he like to think about?"

"Oh, I don't know," Jan mused. "Maybe he's thinking about Santa Claus. Or maybe the Easter bunny."

Tiny poked her head higher, cocked it to one side, and grinned impishly at her older brother. "Do ten-year-olds still believe in Santa Claus?"

"If they want to," Jan answered carefully. "But it doesn't really matter. I think I know what Toby's thinking about today and it probably isn't Santa Claus."

"What then?"

"The baseball game. While you and I go shopping tonight, Gramps and your dad will take Toby to a Twins game. I bet that's what he's thinking about."

"I don't know," Tina said doubtfully. "I bet

Toby's thinking about something different. Something really different." She stretched out r-e-a-l-l-y until she ran out of breath.

"Well, if he is, you can bet he won't tell *us* about it." Jan swung around onto the couch and sat next to Toby. She wrapped an arm around his thin shoulders and pulled him close. "Will you, sweetheart? You're not going to tell us anything that you dream about, are you?"

Jan winked at the dazed boy conspiratorially. It helped her if she could treat his behavior lightly, as if that would prevent his condition, whatever it was, from being serious.

"Is he being like a cat again, Mommy?"

"A cat?" Jan frowned and reached for the little girl's hand. "I don't know what you mean, honey."

"I heard Daddy say that Toby's cata—cata—"

Jan smiled indulgently. "Catatonic, honey. That doesn't mean that Toby's like a cat. It means that he—well, it just means that he's thinking about things a lot, that's all."

"I'll kill him. I'll kill that son of a bitch."

The boy mouthed the words mechanically, and a cold finger of fear touched his mother's heart. There was no emotion in either his voice or face, just hollow words, meaningless but brutal.

"I'll kill him. I'll kill the dirty son of a bitch," he repeated monotonously.

"There he goes again," Tina scolded. "He's saying the B word again." She pursed her lips and shook her tiny finger back and forth reprovingly.

"He'll be all right now," Jan said, sighing. She had seen it all before. It was strange, a little scary, but so far his mysterious spells had been chalked up to growing pains and puberty. Those twin ailments covered a lot of ground. "You just watch, honey. In a couple of seconds he'll stop thinking his secret things and watch TV with you."

"I know. That's what he always does," the little girl said. "I think it's funny."

"Well, maybe not funny but there's nothing wrong with it," Jan said. How she wished that she was sure.

"You did it again, you did it again, you did it again." Tina clapped her hands and bounced up and down on her little legs as she scolded her brother. "And you said the B word again. You're going to get in trouble."

"Did I, Mom? Did I really do it again?" he asked. He searched his mother's face pleadingly, seeking the denial that he knew wouldn't come.

Jan held Toby tightly. "Yes, honey. Just like the other times. Do you remember anything?"

"No," he answered matter-of-factly. "I was just watching television all alone and all of a sudden you and Tina were here with me. I don't remember falling asleep. I'm not even tired. And I don't remember you coming in."

"It doesn't matter," she lied. "Dr. Wiberg said it's nothing but growing pains." She didn't bother to mention that puberty was another suspect, because it would unleash a flood of unanswerable questions from Tina.

Toby shrugged. "What's for dinner?" He had already dismissed the incident from his mind.

"Spinach and broccoli and cauliflower and liver." Jan ticked the questionable delicacies off on her fingers. "And if you finish all of those, then you can have some nice fresh brussels sprouts."

"No way, José," Toby said, laughing.

"How about some soup and sandwiches then? Something light before the baseball game. Which reminds me, get out of those good clothes and put on your jeans. If you spill mustard on your good clothes, I'll have to whack your bottom."

"Toby's sloppy, Toby's sloppy," Tina kidded.

He scrunched his face into an angry grimace and shook his fist threateningly. "I'll bop you one in the nose," he warned, barely able to suppress a smile.

"Mommy, Mommy! He said he's gonna bop me." Tina giggled playfully and ran behind her mother and hugged her legs. Jan winked and Toby smiled knowingly. He enjoyed the role of the put-upon older brother. It made him feel grown-up, and Tina had fun thinking that she was getting his goat.

A few months earlier, shortly after the trance-like occurrences began, Dr. Wiberg had given Toby a head-to-toe physical and pronounced him a perfectly healthy ten-year-old.

"Then how do you explain these—these funny spells that he has?" Steve Horton asked.

Jan and Steve had watched him with mounting concern as the spells became more frequent. The intensity and duration hadn't changed at all. They usually lasted a minute or two and always ended with the same oath.

I'll kill the son of a bitch.

But they were happening more often lately. At first they'd notice it only once or twice a month, at dinner, watching television, no real pattern. They were concerned, but dismissed the spells as some sort of deep daydream. Steve used to have similar spells himself, his father had reminded him. Now, however, the boy fell into the dazelike state a few times a week that they were aware of and God knows how many more times that they weren't.

Dr. Wiberg fiddled nervously with the end of his stethoscope. "I can't find a thing wrong with the boy," he assured them. "Everything checks out just fine."

Toby busied himself with the red rubber hammer while his parents conferred with the doctor.

"Then how do you explain the spells?" Jan repeated. "It just isn't normal."

Dr. Wiberg shrugged evasively. "Who knows?" he said with guarded professional lightness. "There's no unusual brain-wave activity, chemically he's a textbook case of a good example, his reflexes are superb for such a knothead." He released the stethoscope and mussed Toby's jet-black hair. "This kid's as healthy as a horse."

"Wheeeey," Toby neighed, picking up the cue.

"I'm inclined just to blame it on growing pains for the time being," Dr. Wiberg suggested. "As long as the boy feels as well as he does, I don't see any harm. But I do think we ought to keep a close eye on it. If you'd like to consult a specialist, though, I'll be glad to set it up for you." He looked inquiringly from Steve to Jan.

The worried parents searched each other's faces. "I guess not, Doctor," Jan finally replied.

"I'll kill him."

Dr. Wiberg jerked reflexively and dropped the stethoscope as Toby uttered the dread warning in a dead, flat voice.

"I'll kill the son of a bitch."

The doctor quickly shone his light into the blank gray pupil. It shrank to a tiny point.

The spell passed seconds later and Toby smiled brightly as he left the office. "Wheeeey," he whinnied.

Dr. Wiberg's parting smile was clouded by a question mark.

"Who's doing the pitching tonight?" John Horton asked from the back seat. He was perched in the middle so he could keep up a running commentary with his son and grandson.

"Blyleven," Toby answered, twisting to meet Gramps's eye. "He's five and two."

"Five and two, you say. That's not too bad for a young whippersnapper."

"You think everybody's a young whippersnapper, don't you, Gramps?" Toby laughed. He wiggled around and grinned over the seat at the older man.

"Well, I don't know about everybody, but I know for sure that you're one," he answered.

Three generations of Hortons rode contentedly toward the Minneapolis ballpark. Toby loved the new bulbous Metrodome. He liked the way it looked, like the giant mushroom in *Alice in Wonderland*. And he liked the way it felt, like he was inside a big silver balloon, and he imagined it floating off someday into the summer sky.

His grandfather didn't share any of his enthusiasm for the new structure. "Who ever heard of playing baseball under a roof?" he snorted disgustedly. "It's not natural. Hell, there isn't even a fence to climb over if you want to sneak into a ball game. What kind of a baseball game is it if you can't even sneak into it?" He caught his grandson's eye and flashed a sardonic smirk. "Can't even spit without getting yourself arrested," he complained.

"I bet you were a real whippersnapper when you were a kid, weren't you, Gramps?" Toby joked.

"And where are the hitters anymore?" he chided. "There's not a one of 'em around who could carry Ted William's jo—his baseball cap."

"You were going to say his jockstrap, weren't you, Gramps?" Toby accused with an impish twinkle. "Besides, how about Kent Hrbek? I bet he bangs them out the way old Ted Williams used to."

"And where's the defense?" the older man pushed on undaunted. "The kids today play on plastic grass and rubber outfields. They don't even know what grass stains are. And there's never any bad hops. Your grandmother, may she rest in peace, could play center field today."

"You just wait till you see Kirby Puckett play the outfield," Toby challenged. "He runs into the wall and catches the ball over his shoulder and all those things."

"Sure. And I'll bet that his glove's about as big as a manhole cover. Your Aunt Tillie could shag flies with the mitts some of these kids use today."

"But I don't even have an Aunt Tillie."

"Maybe you don't, but if you did she could catch any of the powder puffs those boys hit."

Steve drove in pleasurable silence, his heart bursting with the shared love of his son and father. Sometimes the three of them would lounge on the porch or fish off the dock or putt around the lake for hours at a time, and Steve would say barely a word while son and father traded jokes and ideas and love. He was content just being the biological link between the ten-year-old boy and the sixty-year-old man, and he sometimes felt a comfortable pang of jealousy when he watched his father grow younger and his son grow older as they shared each other's company.

There was an amazing resemblance among the three of them. Toby was lean and casually erect. His straight black hair was severely parted on the left and hung gracefully across his sloping forehead. Steve was a mature version of his young son. His six feet were filled out and well proportioned. Age had lent him extra pounds but he carried them with dignity. The facial similarity was remarkable. His nose and mouth had lost some of their youthful softness and taken on the sculpted lines of a carved warrior, but it was the same face that would someday belong to the boy.

Gramps at sixty was an aging photograph of Steve Horton with the same strong features, the same disciplined military posture. A few unwanted pounds had gathered around his waist too, some lightning bolts of laugh lines crinkled at the corners of his eyes, and the midnight blackness of his hair had been replaced by snowy whiteness, but he was unmistakably the father of Steve who was undoubtedly the father of Toby.

The years had worked their undeniable magic into the flesh and bones of three generations, but there was one thing the years could never touch. The steel-grey eyes were as piercingly clear and striking in the aging face of John Horton as they were under Toby's softly arched brows. The eyes were identical. Interchangeable. And the physical bond was reinforced by the wave of love flowing among them like a raging river. Steve Horton was thinking these pleasant thoughts as he approached the intersection.

The battered pickup raced through the stop sign to his right. Steve saw the sudden flash of color from the corner of his eye an instant before the bone-jarring crash. The pickup hit the station wagon by the right front tire and the impact sent both vehicles spinning crazily. The truck skidded backward across the street, bounced over the curb, and came to rest on the manicured lawn of a white colonial two-story. Steve jammed at the brake pedal and jerked the wheel to the left. He felt the sickening lurch as the tires lost their grip on the concrete and the wagon teetered on two wheels before landing heavily on its right side—roof—left side—wheels—right side—roof. It happened quickly but with agonizing slowness and he watched helplessly as Toby bounced around the wagon's cabin like a stuffed puppet. The station wagon rocked one last time before finally coming to rest on its crushed roof. Then all was silent.

The stench of burnt rubber filled the car like evil incense. A hubcap leaving the scene of the accident rattled halfway down the block. A ray of late-afternoon sun blazed through the window and bathed Toby's pale face as he lay against the ceiling of the wagon. A thin trickle of blood seeped from his nose. His eyes were closed. He looked like he was sleeping peacefully.

Steve hung upside down from his seat belt. A low moan escaped from the back seat. Then the deathly silence was shattered by the scream of sirens and the screeching of brakes.

Chapter Three

❖❖❖❖❖❖❖❖❖❖❖❖

ESAU WASN'T TOO surprised when God spoke to
him. He knew that he was worthy, there wasn't
any question about that. Didn't he pray his heart
out and spread the Lord's word to anyone willing to listen and to many who weren't? So when
it came, he was ready for the divine tap on the
shoulder. What he didn't expect was that it
would happen on Highway 35E a few miles north
of the Centerville cutoff. But the Lord works in
mysterious ways.

The sun baked the pickup with the pleasant
glow of early summer. The wind whipped
through the open window, filling the cab with
the roar of passing farmland and muting the bit-
ing smell that dripped from the farmer's sweat-
soaked shirt. He was heading south on the four-
lane with a cord of green firewood in the bed of
the pickup. The Lord provided the trees and he
provided the chain saw, a fair partnership Esau
felt.

He cruised at a steady fifty-five in the left lane,
side by side with a blue Buick. The woman driving the other car clutched the wheel with a death
grip. She had blue hair and white knuckles, and
looked straight down the highway, not chancing
a glance right or left, not wanting to catch the
eye of the driver of the pickup. She had looked
over when he first pulled alongside her. Stringy
beard, battered pickup, not well-mannered
looking—a threatening man, not at all her kind,
not one for church bazaars or doubles bridge.

Esau had been cruising at her side for the better part of five miles but had no idea that he was upsetting her. He was doing fifty-five and she was doing fifty-five and that just kept them side by side. He was hardly aware of her. The line of cars strung out behind him like a freight train didn't bother him either. Why should it? He was driving at the legal speed limit. Speeders were no better than any other criminals. They disobeyed the law and they deserved to be punished for their transgressions. Of course, they weren't quite as bad as adulterers or pornographers or fornicators or the host of other biblical lawbreakers for whom Esau had no time, but the law was the law and Esau did his part to uphold it by maintaining his steady fifty-five.

The carload of fishermen was steaming. Two days of pouring rain, a leaky cabin full of dirty jokes and wild-card poker and farting and beer and only a half-dozen decent walleye for their trouble, and now some goddamn farmer in a pickup was dogging down the highway in the passing lane. The driver finally had his fill. "Hang on," he shouted, "we're gonna head this simple bastard off at the pass."

With a twist of the wheel, the car angled onto the grassy median and the driver pressed the pedal to the floor. With tires spinning and gravel spitting they shot past the line of fuming drivers and pulled next to the battered pickup.

"Hey, asshole!"

Esau was startled by the shout and the car that came from nowhere.

"Get in the right lane, you stupid son of a bitch." The man glared angrily through the window and screamed in Esau's face.

Esau glared back in outrage at the lawbreaker

who bounced recklessly through the roadside weeds. Then the fisherman committed the final affront. With the vehicles dangerously close, he took a can of beer from the floor of the car, thrust it through the window, and tugged at the pull tab. An amber stream jetted between the vehicles like a foamy fountain and Esau was showered with the evil brew. He jerked the wheel convulsively, crossed the center lines barely missing the blue Buick. He took his foot off the gas, and the carload of fishermen shot ahead, bounced back onto the roadway, and sped away. With the logjam broken, a steady stream of cars pulled to the right and cut sharply in front of him, screaming references to his ancestry and waving clenched fists through their windows.

Esau pulled a stained handkerchief from his pocket and wiped at his beard. The cab stank of warm alcohol and the farmer felt the bile of anger and disgust rising in his throat. He wasn't aware of the cars whipping around him or the shouts of anger. He was too full of his own outrage. That was when Esau Manley first heard the voice of God.

It began as a muffled hum, a buzzing as if the cab had suddenly filled with a swarm of honeybees. A burning belt of steel encircled his chest and was pulled tight by powerful hands until the breath was crushed from his body. A wave of pain shot through him. A constellation of lights flashed in a kaleidoscopic display, horns honked in furious symphony, bees buzzed, a mighty roar exploded inside his head, and Esau heard the booming voice.

"Destroy the transgressor. Display My wrath to the trespasser. Lift up thy fist in anger and take up

*arms in My name. Esau Manley, I command you
to lead My earthly army to victory and to bring
down My judgment upon My enemies. Lead My
people along the path of righteousness. Do this,
Esau Manley, in My name and in the name of My
son, Jesus Christ."*

At the sound of His name, Esau was charged
with a furious energy, one that urged him to get
on with the quest. The tightness left his chest
and he felt an inner peace. He looked about him
and was surprised to see that he had pulled to
the shoulder of the highway. He had no recollection of doing it, further evidence of God's hand at
work.

What was it that had snapped him from his
reverie? Then he remembered. A flashing light
invaded the cab. In the mirror he saw a tan se-
dan with no markings. An orange light spun on
the roof, attached by a wire that ran into the
driver's window. A highway patrolman caught
Esau's eye in the mirror. He was talking into a
microphone. He hung the mike on the dash,
donned his wide-brimmed hat, left his car, and
cautiously approached the pickup.

"Are you having car trouble, sir?" Darkened
sunglasses lent a menacing air to the lawman.

"No," Esau answered. "Felt a little funny back
there. Needed to rest for a spell."

The trooper sniffed suspiciously. "Smells like
you might have been drinking, sir. May I see
your driver's license?" The trooper took the card
and returned to his car.

Esau watched through the mirror. *Drinking!*
What an outrageous accusation. He had never
even tasted alcohol. Probably the closest he had
ever come was the soaking spray from the fisher-

man's beer can. He would have been humiliated
and angry but nothing could spoil his elation. He
was the captain of Christ's earthly army. A surge
of pride radiated through him, made him warm
and content. He knew it was all part of the plan,
perhaps a test of his humility or patience.

The trooper was on the radio for less than a
minute before returning. "Thank you, sir." He
handed the license through the window and took
another dubious sniff. A look of doubt crossed his
face but he shrugged and backed away from the
pickup. "Drive safely, sir."

Esau nodded and attempted one of his rare
smiles but it was hidden behind his beard. The
trooper wouldn't have seen it anyway. He was
already halfway back to his car.

Esau pulled cautiously back onto the highway. He edged immediately over to the left and
drove at a lawful fifty miles an hour. The
trooper pulled alongside him, glanced to his
left, and lifted the mike from the dash. "If
you're going to drive that slow, you should be
in the right-hand lane."

The voice boomed from a speaker in the
trooper's car. Esau had never heard of such a
silly rule, but the patrolman backed off the gas
and waited until Esau drifted back into the
right lane. Then the tan car swung to the left
and blew by the pickup at seventy miles an
hour. Esau drove steadily until the police car
became a spot in the distance, then he pulled
back in the left lane and went forward to do
God's work.

He followed Highway 35 into downtown Saint
Paul and swung off the ramp at the University
Avenue exit. The lengths of cut wood tumbled

around the truck bed as it bounced over the winter potholes. The State Capitol rose like a monument to justice on his right and the Cathedral of Sts. Peter and Paul was God's beacon to the left. Another sign from on high. He parked on a quiet street where the homes were much like his own, not quite as nice as his East Side neighborhood but he knew that the people who lived here were trying. It wasn't their fault that the devil chose this neighborhood to set up his evil shop. A police car drifted by and Esau found himself turning his head away. Then he thought of Christ's own confrontation with the so-called law of His day and he was filled with disgust at his cowardice. He turned to face the cruising police car but the driver paid no attention.

The summer sky was striped with rainbow color as the sun fought a losing battle with the horizon. Esau walked the quiet neighborhood, the click of his heels the only violation of its tranquillity, until the final patch of orange surrendered to the gray of night. The falling curtain painted a cleansing coat of darkness over the neighborhood's imminent squalor. He sniffed at the coolness, folded his hands in front of him, and gazed at the early stars. With a prayer of thanks he turned toward the hazy glow.

The block stretched in endless shame past bars and bookshops, peep shows and movie houses. Esau grimaced.

Adult Entertainment!

Esau was an adult. Why not call it what it is?

Abomination!

Neon hucksters flashed their gaudy beckoning in the dusk. He was rooted to the hot sidewalk, staring in disbelief at the life-sized poster.

"Whores! Adulterers." He hissed the accusations at the naked images.

"You thinkin' about havin' somethin' like that for yourself, mister?"

He spun sharply. A sick sweet haze of cheap perfume stung his nose. The girl was tall but still only came to the farmer's bony shoulder. Pale blue cutoffs were wedged into her most private places and a thin pullover confirmed the hardness of her tiny breasts. She had a pretty face beneath the heavy makeup and she looked clean. That surprised Esau. He equated cleanliness with godliness.

Esau fought for words but nothing worked. Hand on hip, head tilted provocatively, she stared him in the eye the way no woman should.

Brazen harlot!

"I can make you real happy, mister. Won't cost you very much either."

She had a childish voice that rang with expectation and a simple, innocent smile, a real person hidden within the accoutrements of her profession. She touched his hand and Esau jumped as if stuck with a cattle prod. He could feel the hot blood flood his face. Was it embarrassment or excitement? He was glad for the dusk.

"I bet you're real good-looking behind that old beard, aren't you, honey?" She turned off the innocent and switched to practiced sultry. Full pouting lips, heavy-lidded eyes, words breathed rather than spoken. She hooked her fingers over his thick belt and pulled close to him, tilted head, liquid eyes gazing seductively. She ran her pink tongue over her perfect teeth. An invitation.

Esau felt a raw stirring in his crotch and was angry.

Hussy! Harlot! Tempt not the captain of His earthly army.

Then she touched him—there!

She didn't grab him like a barroom hooker. Nothing like that. It was a furtive gesture, maybe an accident, no more than a casual brushing of knuckles across the embarrassing bulge. He felt a stirring, an electric shock. Then she did it again, no accident. Esau felt the bottom drop from his stomach. His heart banged against his rib cage like it wanted to escape. He gulped short gasps of air. He smelled her hair, clean. Her perfume, intoxicating. Herself, disturbing. Her nearness angered him, frightened him, excited him. And he was further angered by his own excitement.

"C'mon, Mr. Quiet Man," she teased. "I got me a real nice place down the street. Got a great view." She pointed her chin at the movie poster. "Betch'a I can make you forget all about those girls in no time at all."

Esau felt her hand entwine his own and he fell obediently in step. Numb and speechless. The swelling in his pants throbbed like a migraine, bursting. Images attacked him from each passing storefront.

Sex aids! Breasts! Wanton leers! Women embracing each other! Long milky thighs! Firm rounded buttocks!

Her hand lightly squeezed his and she ran her fingernail idly around his palm. Esau cursed the devil for his work but didn't pull his hand away. He had never been this hard. He had a crowbar in his jeans.

She led him to a narrow flight of stairs between two store fronts. Lights from a passing car bathed the entrance in a buttery glow. He passed a window full of auto parts; spark plugs, headlights, jumper cables. The stairs were steep and worn and creaked resentfully. They ended at a solid door smeared green with tired enamel.

It was a large, single room that had seen an endless parade of miseries. K-Mart prints hung at erratic intervals, concealing the thoughtlessness of past occupants. It reeked with the stench of warm bodies and cold pizza. The only inside door led to a small bathroom. That door was open, revealing the room's private parts. From where he stood at the doorway, Esau could see the stove and sink tucked into a tight corner, a round table and two chairs for dining, a small leather couch and a portable TV on a stand for relaxation, and a king-sized bed that filled one side of the room. The bed was neatly made, covered with a fading quilt. A stuffed panda slept with staring eyes.

"Don't you go away now." She stepped back and studied his bearded face. "You know something, mister. I don't even know your name. Now, we don't exactly have to be pen pals or anything like that, but it is nice to know a person's name." She smiled pleasantly. "I'm Candy." A pause, another smile. "Good to eat."

"Esau," he croaked.

"You can talk," she said with a shriek of amazement.

She gave his beard a playful tug and hooked her hands over his thick belt, again pulling him close.

"You wait right here, Esau, while I get myself spruced up nice and pretty. Think about what I'm doing behind that door. Think about what you're going to see when it opens."

She pushed away and faced him, challenging him with eyes that smoldered like hot coals. Then she hugged herself, licked her lips, and ran her fingertips over herself in a way that built a fire in Esau's jeans. She stretched like a cat and floated across the room to the bathroom, gently closing the door behind her.

Esau's heart raced wildly. His mouth felt dry. He ached in a way long forgotten.

Lead my earthly army—bring down my judgment—destroy the violator.

A blinking stoplight pulsed a pink tattoo on the window that looked down on the busy street. A trickle ran down the farmer's sides. There was a tinkle of laughter from the street below. The toilet flushed.

Do this in my name—display my wrath to the trespasser.

"Esau."

The voice was full and husky, not the child's tinny sound she had used on the street. He looked up and his mouth fell open. The doorway framed her naked body. Her arms stretched high above her head and gripped the top doorsill. Her legs were slightly spread, the backlight from the bathroom's glow painting her lithe silhouette. Esau swallowed and gasped. His eyes traveled the long lines of her slim body. Small hard breasts pointed accusingly and Esau gazed hungrily.

"Do I look good?" She cupped her breasts in her palms and toyed with her nipples. A soft

moan escaped her and she closed her eyes and
ran her moist tongue over her lips.

It was a cool night, but beads of sweat ringed
Esau's forehead. In slinking steps Candy crossed
the room. She took Esau's hands and put them to
her breasts, then she worked loose the heavy
buckle of his belt.

*Destroy the violator—display my wrath—lift thy
fist.*

Esau's work pants slumped around his ankles.
He wore no underwear. Candy touched him gently, exploring, and a jolt of electricity charged
his veins.

Esau exploded mentally and physically.

"Esau," she said, laughingly. "We haven't even
started yet."

But her next words were cut short by viselike
fingers circling her delicate throat.

Chapter Four

∞∞∞∞∞∞∞∞

"THEY'RE ALL RIGHT, Mr. Horton. Believe me.
Nobody's hurt badly. Your son's got himself a
nasty bump on the head. He probably has a
slight concussion, but he'll be okay in a little
while. He's sleeping right now. You'll be able
to see him in just a few minutes." The doctor
probed a not-so-gentle finger under Steve Horton's ribs. "Your father's just about as uncoop-

erative as you are, but aside from that, he's fine, too. What I don't understand is why you two so-called adults had your seat belts on but the boy didn't?"

"No excuse, Doc. We always use them. This time I must have forgotten to check on Toby. He can be absentminded at times, too. I guess this was just one of those times." He grimaced when the doctor touched another tender spot. "He was pretty keyed up about going to the ball game."

The accident had drawn out most of the emergency resources of the Roseville Fire Department, and they had the Hortons on the way to Ramsey Hospital before the station wagon's tires stopped spinning. The driver of the pickup was a kid coming from "double bubble" hour at Yuppie's and he flunked the breath test from twenty yards away. They stuffed him in the police car where he guffed up a six-pack of Coors and half a sausage pizza all over the back seat. Gramps and Steve walked away from the battered wagon, sore but otherwise none the worse for the wear, but Toby was too dazed to stand on his own and he was ferried to the hospital with tires screeching and sirens blaring.

"Ooooof!"

"Does it hurt when I press you there?" Dr. Kendall asked unnecessarily.

"No, Doc. I always bellow like a cow in heat."

"You're going to turn some pretty fall colors where the seat belt grabbed onto you. Too bad you won't be able to show them off."

The space was well lit, hospital green, a ten-by-ten exam room with shower curtain privacy that left a corner open for the curious to peek in. It smelled of antiseptic and clean sheets. The young doctor poked around Steve's bruised hips and waist. "I heard about a guy once who got his pecker caught in his seat belt in the same kind of accident you had. You don't know how lucky you were," the doctor joked.

"How did they write that one up in your medical journals?"

"Dickus detroitus, they called it. But it's better than the alternative."

"What's that?"

"Cranius decapitus. That's what happens when you do a Wilbur and Orville through the windshield."

Dr. Kendall smacked Steve on the belly with an open palm. It cracked like a rifle shot and Steve tried unsuccessfully not to wince. "You're okay. I'll go get your old man before he tries to make a move on one of the nurses, then we can go visit your boy. Get yourself decent, you're a disgrace." He breezed through the curtain, leaving it gaping open so three teenage girls walking by could get the giggles, Steve's penance for not hooking up Toby's seat belt.

Toby made soft rasping sounds as he slept. The starchy sheet was pulled up to his chin and the bed lamp cast a soft white glow across his face. His lips were parted slightly and made barely perceptible movements, as if he were whispering a childhood secret. Jan sat in the leather guest chair next to the bed and held his hand beneath the sheet. Tina gripped the metal rail around the bed and gaped in admiration at the egg-shaped bump on Toby's temple.

He was in a semi-private room but the other bed was empty. The curtains had been drawn back from both beds to give the tight room an airy feeling. Steve and his father looked at the sleeping boy with mild concern.

"He looks like an angel, doesn't he?" Jan swept her eyes across Toby's face and looked up at the two men. She always marveled at the family resemblance but this time she was stunned by the similarity. She brushed Toby's hair into place.

"Except angels don't have big bumps on their head, do they?" The little girl perched on tiptoes, her chin hooked over the guard rail on the hospital bed.

Jan glanced at Tina and saw the frown of doubt and realized that the question was sincere. "Probably not," Jan answered with a smile.

"And they don't use the B word, either," she reminded her mother.

"No. I'm sure they don't do that, either," she said with a laugh. She'd have to remember to tell Toby about his sister's observations.

"So we're all in agreement that the boy's not an angel," Dr. Kendall said as he took Toby's pulse. "If heredity has anything to do with it, then I'm not surprised. Any descendant of Battling John Horton already has his genes pretty well stacked against him in the sainthood department."

Gramps looked only mildly embarrassed by the rebuke. He appeared worried, even more so than Steve and Jan. A grandfather's prerogative.

"When can he come home, Doc?" Steve asked.

"We'll want to keep an eye on him overnight. I'm sure that he's fine, but it's always a good precaution to watch for a little while to see if there's been a concussion. I'll probably let him go after morning rounds tomorrow. We'll keep him here for one of our sumptuous hospital lunches, then he ought to be ready to go." Dr. Kendall pulled back Toby's eyelid and peered at his pupil. "But you might as well be on your way. We gave him some of Clancy Kendall's heavy-duty knock-out drops and he'll stay zonked like this for a couple more hours at least."

The doctor turned to the older man. "There's still room for one more in the other bed if you change your mind. You know, you might think that you're a spry young kid, but nobody bothered to tell your bones about it. Tomorrow morning you're going to think a freight train ran over you and then backed up again."

"Don't worry about me, Sonny. You just give your pills to the sick people—"

"I know. And leave you he-men alone," the doctor finished. "Everybody out now." Dr. Kendall shooed them toward the door.

He had just entered the hallway when he heard Toby's flat voice. A cold shiver shot through his spine.

"I'll kill him. I'll kill the son of a bitch."

"What was that?" he asked.

"A dream. Toby's been having this same dream over and over again. It's been going on for months," Jan said. "We've had him looked over but they say there's nothing wrong. Growing pains, they call it."

She gave the doctor a quick rundown of Toby's symptoms and he fretted his brows doubtfully. Kendall was a gangling six and a half feet and his every gesture was magnified by his own proportions.

"And that's where it ends?"

"Always. First he says 'I'll kill the son of a bitch,' and then he wakes up a few moments later."

"Not this time, he won't," the doctor countered. "Not with all that kickapoo juice we squirted into him."

"And he always says the B word, too," Tina added. "I don't think that's nice."

"I'll kill him. I'll kill the son of a bitch. He killed Pinky and I'm gonna kill him. I'm gonna take my .22 and shoot him in the stomach and I'm gonna watch him squirm the way he made Pinky squirm."

The words began as usual, flat and lifeless. Then the voice became booming and triumphant, finally trailing off in a quivery rattle. Toby lay in the dimness, his face twisted in a mask of rage. Then his anger melted and a faint smile of contentment crossed his childish features.

Jan flew back into the room and wrapped her arms around the sleeping boy. Fear choked at her throat. "What does it mean? Why is he talking like that?" she jabbered convulsively.

Tina began to cry softly.

Steve Horton felt his legs start to tremble. A sheen of perspiration coated his blood-drained face. He felt light-headed.

"Are you all right?" Dr. Kendall asked. He took Steve by the arm and lowered him to the edge of vacant bed.

"Yeah, I'm okay," he muttered breathlessly.

"You look like you've just seen a ghost," Kendall said. He tried to sound light but the look on Steve Horton's face left little room for levity.

"Not seen a ghost, Doctor—heard one. Toby

just repeated something that I said over twenty
years ago. Something I never told him about—
something I never told anybody about."

They all stared at the peacefully sleeping boy.

Chapter Five

❖❖❖❖❖❖❖❖❖❖❖❖

"DOES ANYBODY use cream?" Dr. Kendall shouted
the question across the hospital cafeteria to the
table full of Hortons. Gramps waved in the affir-
mative. Jan and Steve shook their heads no.
Tina, absorbed in a root-beer float, didn't respond.

Clancy Kendall had invited the family to the
cafeteria after the disturbing incident in Toby's
room. He was genuinely curious about Toby's
condition, and he liked the Horton family. He
was a little weary of the doctor worship exhib-
ited by so many of his patients and the disre-
spectful familiarity of the Horton men was a
welcome relief.

"Three blacks, one with cream." He dealt the
steaming cardboard cups around the table from
a white Styrofoam tray. He burnt his fingers on
one and said "damn" under his breath but Tina
picked it up and shot him a reproving look.

It was late and only a handful of people were
still in the cafeteria. A few nurses about to go off
their shift lounged in a far corner, and a wor-

ried-looking mother and her young daughter silently sipped Cokes near the door. Clancy sat between the two men and across from Jan and Tina. He took a sip of coffee and smiled apologetically at Tina.

"Now please tell me if it's none of my business, okay?" He searched their faces for any objections but there were none. "So why don't you start at the beginning and tell me what's happening here. Toby's condition has my curiosity antenna tingling." He glanced expectantly at Jan.

"You know just about as much as we do, Dr. Kendall," she began.

"My name's Clancy."

"Dr. Clancy," Tina said and giggled.

"Just plain Clancy," he corrected.

"Anyway, Doc—I mean Clancy, Toby's been having these strange dreams—at least we think they're dreams—and they always end the same way. We've seen it a hundred times. It never changes. It usually happens when he's quiet, like when he's reading or watching TV. Sometimes it happens when he's sleeping. At first he seems relaxed and he gets a calm expression on his face. Peaceful."

Clancy nodded thoughtfully.

"Then he seems to be staring right through things, like they're not even there. This goes on for about thirty seconds then he comes out with the same lines. You heard them. First he says 'I'll kill him,' then, a few seconds later, he says 'I'll kill the son of a bitch.' It's always been the same." She turned to Steve with a worried frown. "Until tonight, that is."

Steve didn't respond. He hadn't said a word

since Toby's outburst. A sheen of sweat still filmed his face but his color had returned. He took a sip of coffee and stared into the cup. It gave him a queasy sensation. He swirled the coffee around his cup until some splashed over the side. It embarrassed him when he looked up to see they were all watching him, waiting for an explanation. Even Tina had stopped fiddling with her straw and looked at him with wide, questioning eyes.

He spread his hands in an evasive gesture. "You're going to think I'm crazy," he said faintly.

"Try us," Clancy challenged.

"Well, like Jan said, the boy's been saying that 'I'll kill the son of a bitch' stuff all along. It didn't mean anything to me—to any of us."

Steve's father eyed him sympathetically as he groped for an explanation. Tina looked up with a shocked expression when her father said "the B word," but she refrained from her usual disapproving remarks.

"But tonight was different. Tonight he continued the dream past the part where he used to wake up. And when he did, he talked about Pinky and he almost knocked me over."

"What's this about Pinky?" Jan asked. "You don't know any Pinky, do you?"

Steve threw the question at his father. "How about you, Pop? Do you remember Pinky?"

The older man looked pensive and uncertain. "Can't say that I do, Steve. Should I?"

"I guess not, Pop. I guess Pinky was only important to me and nobody else."

Suddenly John's eyes came alive with recognition. "Pinky! You don't mean that rabbit you used to keep in your bedroom, do you?"

Steve smiled at the recollection. "That's the one, Pop. Do you remember what happened to it?"

"I'm afraid I don't. You had more smelly animals around that house than they've got at the Como Zoo."

Steve nodded in agreement. "But Pinky was the first," Steve reminded him.

"So?" Steve's father looked at him curiously.

"The point is, Dad, I was real broken up when that silly rabbit died. When it got killed, I should say. It was one of the worst days of my life. It's funny how some of the tragic things stick in your mind."

"What does that have to do with Toby's behavior?" Dr. Kendall asked.

"This is probably going to sound completely ridiculous," Steve warned, "but some things seem more important when you're a kid."

Kendall nodded his understanding. "The loss of a pet can be as traumatic as the loss of a loved one under certain conditions," he said sympathetically.

"It wasn't only that it was my first pet," Steve continued. "It was the way the rabbit got killed that really upset me. We used to live across the street from some old guy who kept a mongrel dog chained up in the front yard. I think he was a little whacko."

His father nodded his agreement.

"I remember it like it happened yesterday. I was sitting on the curb in front of our house doing whatever it was that kids do when they are bored. My rabbit was on the lawn behind me tethered to a tree with a piece of clothesline. The mutt across the street saw the rabbit and started growling and tugging at its chain. It was the ugliest dog I ever saw. All the kids were afraid of it; part boxer and part shepherd along with half a dozen other breeds. The next thing I know, the chain snaps and the dog's across the street in two leaps. Before I can even move, it's got its teeth clamped around Pinky's head like a vise, shaking the poor rabbit like a rag doll."

Tina's eyes glittered like two pearl buttons as she held her breath and listened attentively.

"Now I remember," Gramps said. "Your mom told me she heard a commotion in the yard and found you whacking that dog with a tree limb till it could hardly walk."

"And did Mom tell you what I said, Dad?"

"Now I do," he reflected. "You wanted to kill the dog, didn't you?"

"Right. And I recall exactly what I said. It's one of those things that's imbedded in your brain. I said 'I'll kill him. I'll kill the son of a bitch.' They were my exact words. I remember them like I remember my own name."

"That's not surprising," Clancy added. "Most of us have deep-rooted memories going back to our childhood. I remember my first day at summer camp at Smedley Park. I must have been four or five years old. I was playing on the bank of a creek and it was covered with sumac. I slipped on a rock and tumbled into about six inches of water and thought that I was drowning. Now, whenever I smell sumac I start to sweat and my heart races a mile a minute. It sounds like your experience had the same effect on you."

"He couldn't sleep right for a week," Gramps volunteered. "It's coming back to me. He even had nightmares over it for a while."

"But what does all of this have to do with Toby's dream?" Jan asked.

"Maybe nothing," Steve said. "But I'd be willing to bet that he's having the same dream that used to wake me up in the middle of the night. I can't explain why but I'm certain of it."

"When did you tell Toby about it?" John asked.

"That's just the point, Pop. I never told Toby. I never told anybody. It's a memory I never discussed. Even Jan didn't know about it."

"He's right," she admitted. "It's news to me."

"Did you say the B word when you were little?" Tina asked, wide-eyed.

Clancy reached over and ruffled her shiny bangs. "Sometimes the B word isn't so bad," he soothed.

"Like when your rabbit gets ate?"

"Right, Pumpkin. At times like that."

"But that still doesn't explain how Toby knows about it," Jan said weakly.

"Maybe it's something completely different," Steve lied. "Nothing at all to do with my old dreams."

"Maybe," she said doubtfully.

They finished their coffee and soda and went their separate ways. The next day Toby got a clean bill of health and went home after lunch.

Chapter Six

❖❖❖❖❖❖❖❖❖❖❖❖

"HOW IS THE 'Sultan of Sperm' tonight?"

"Well enough to suck warm Jell-O through a straw," Mancini said, sighing wearily. "And how is the famous healer of running sores and other oozing maladies? Copped any good Medicare checks lately?"

"I had a great day at the plant today," Dr. Kendall said proudly. "I performed two tonsil transplants, delivered quads to a three-hundred-pound welfare mother who didn't know she was pregnant, and found a cure for the heartbreak of psoriasis. Top that, Sperm Brain."

The banter was standard fare at their Wednesday night get-together. Neither doctor nor teacher could recall when the tradition began, but it had been a ritual for years, missed only during emergencies or an occasional vacation. In earlier days they alternated among the finer restaurants around the Twin Cities, but eventually they had zeroed in on Lindey's Steak House for a predictably succulent piece of beef. Cholesterol City, Clancy Kendall called it, but Mike Mancini argued that nothing so delicious could possibly do harm to the human body. They clinked their glasses together and smiled warmly.

"To mankind!"

"L'chaim!"

"You medical types think that you have a lock on good deeds," Mancini chided. "I bet you didn't know that Khadafy was a med student before he studied terrorism. It seemed like such a natural transition." He twirled a cube with his little finger. "And of course it's common knowledge that Hitler was a gynecologist in Vienna."

Clancy rolled his eyes blandly.

"On the other hand, we in the teaching profession dedicate our every waking hour to the development of fragile young minds, molding formative bits of pubescent clay into the leaders of tomorrow."

"If you didn't, the little shits would mug you."

After a week of harping patients and adolescent students, the homey cheeriness of Lindey's provided a welcome outlet for their anxieties. They could slosh down one too many old-fashioneds and scoff up an extra potato and neither would feel the guilt as long as they left some of their "mind monsters" behind with the dirty dishes. Mind monsters were an invention of Mancini's that justified youthful behavior by "pre-seniors," another term that he coined.

"Going out with the boys again, are you?" Clancy's wife accused when he left the house that evening. "More mind monsters, no doubt."

"Who else can keep the old guy from chasing broads?" he joked as he pecked her on the cheek.

Mancini was a regular Sunday guest at the Kendalls' and Nancy Kendall loved him like an older brother. Her gripes were only a front because she welcomed Wednesday night for the change of pace it brought both Clancy and herself. She knew Clancy was good for Mike. The teacher had been alone most of his life with no one to care about but his students. He was almost twice Clancy's age when they met but a bond of friendship had formed between them that didn't recognize age as a barrier. Their

Wednesday night rituals ran the gamut from insulting banter to broad philosophical discussions.

They sat in their usual booth in the No Smoking section by the window overlooking the parking lot. The perfume of sizzling steaks tantalized their taste buds but they tested their willpower by dawdling over a drink. All the tables and booths were packed with casual diners and the hubbub of chatter forced their voices a few decibels higher.

"You guys ready for another round?" The waitress was classic Minnesota, big jugs, silky blond hair, innocent blue eyes, a grade-school sweetheart smile, and ankles just a tad thicker than sexy. Her plastic name tag said "Angie." They ordered another round of old-fashioneds and a matched pair of king-sized New York strip steaks.

"How's your meat tonight, Angie?" Clancy asked suggestively.

"All that you can handle," she said and winked back.

"Your move, Clancy." Mike grinned. They both watched admiringly as Angie hip-swung between the tables on her way to the kitchen.

When their new drinks arrived, Clancy took a sip and twirled a wet ring on the table. "I had a real strange one tonight," he began.

Mike looked up expectantly.

"I had three generations of Hortons in the emergency room at the same time."

"Oh, wow!" Mike Mancini took a long pull on his drink. "That's utterly amazing," he deadpanned.

"I thought of you as soon as I saw them," Clancy continued, undaunted by his friend's rebuff. "There's a ten-year-old boy named Toby, his thirty-some-year-old father named Steve, and sixty-year-old John, the grandfather. They were in a minor traffic accident."

"Is that what made you think of me?" Mike asked.

"No," he said with a chuckle. "I thought of you because when I looked at those three generations, all I could think about was genes. They looked like a set of triplets who'd been delivered twenty-five years apart."

Mike set down his drink and tugged his earlobe. "That is unusual," he agreed. "Usually some traits from the X chromosome will show up in each successive generation and chances of the mother's genetic contribution being that recessive are very low, but it does happen. I'd like to meet them someday. Maybe they can add a footnote to what we've learned since Mendel started playing with his pea plants."

"I'm sure they wouldn't mind talking to you, Mike. But their physical resemblance wasn't the only thing that was unusual. It was something that Toby did. He's the ten-year-old."

Clancy described Toby's sleep-talk at the hospital. Then he related his conversation with Steve in the cafeteria. Mike listened attentively, interjecting an occasional question to clarify a point. When Clancy finished, Mike rubbed his chin thoughtfully.

"Now I'd really like to meet them. When do you think you can arrange it?"

"Any time at all. But why the sudden renewed interest?"

"Maybe nothing," Mike answered. "But then again, it just might be a key link in a theory I've been working on."

"Another new theory? Are you about to blaze fresh trails through gooey rivers of sperms and eggs?"

"Something like that," the teacher said with a mysterious smile. "Something like that."

Angie arrived and the hungry pair attacked their sizzling steaks.

Chapter Seven

◇◇◇◇◇◇◇◇◇◇◇◇

"WHY DOES HE want to see us?"

"Actually, Jan, he never said he wanted to see you," Clancy apologized. "I think he wants to see your assorted menfolk. I never said that this guy was logical."

The last days of spring had tiptoed out with a shy wink and June burst hot and unseasonal across the land of ten thousand lakes. Late May rains had raised the lake levels and early summer fishing was disappointing. The Twins had lost three out of four in their home series with Kansas City. And Toby had been having severe headaches accompanied by fearful dreams that he couldn't recall when he woke up. Jan decided to bring him in for a checkup by Clancy Kendall. Dr. Wiberg had agreed a second opinion was a good idea.

"He's a good friend of mine. His name's Mike Mancini. He teaches biology at Kellogg but he's also done some postgrad studies in genetics. He's regarded as the leading authority on the subject in the Upper Midwest."

Toby was stripping in the examination room while his mother talked to Clancy. "I had dinner with Mike the night your clan came to the hospital with their assortment of bumps and bruises, and I happened to mention the striking family resemblance among the three generations of Hortons. I'm sure you've heard that before," he said with certainty.

"Wait till you see Greatgramps Aaron," she said with a laugh. "He's an apple off the same tree. We have pictures of him as a little boy and you'd swear you were looking at tintypes of Toby in lederhosen."

"There's another?"

She nodded and smiled guiltily.

"My God! Mike will go off his cork when he hears there's another one in the chain. Anyway, when I mentioned the family similarity to Mike, he showed an interest. And when I told him about Toby's dream, he almost spilled his drink. I hope you don't mind that I discussed this with him. I think of him almost as another physician."

"No, not at all," Jan replied.

"I'm sure you'll like him. So will Toby. Mike loves kids. I think that's why he's teaching high school instead of using his degrees elsewhere. So it's okay if I set it up?" He smacked his palm on the desktop to punctuate his question.

Jan nodded her agreement.

"Great! I'll ask Mike to call you at home to make a date. Now let's go see what's bothering the littlest clone."

Mike had arranged to visit the family after dinner on Friday night. He stood in the brightly lit foyer feeling rather sheepish, but Jan's warm smile made him welcome. "It's kind of you to let me intrude on you like this, Mrs. Horton. I hope you don't mind." Jan escorted the teacher through the house to the screened-in porch overlooking the calm suburban lake.

"This is Mike Mancini," Jan announced. "Mike, this is Tina."

"Pleased to meet you." She curtsied daintily and Mike thought of flower petals.

"And this is Toby."

"Hello, sir." The boy extended his small hand. The shake was firm and unexpected. Mike was taken by the intensity of the deep gray eyes set incongruously in the boyish face.

"And this is my husband, Steve."

"Hi, Mike." He shook hands with the handsome young man. Same shake, only the hand was larger.

"And this is John Horton, more affectionately known as Gramps." Mike thought he saw a special smile reserved for the older man.

Now Mike understood what Clancy was talking about. Like peas in a pod, he thought. Mendel's peas.

"And this," Jan announced with a flourish, "this is Aaron Horton, aka Greatgramps."

Clancy had purposely neglected to mention the fourth generation to Mike. He wanted it to be a surprise. "Another one," Mike exclaimed with delight. "This is even more than I bargained for."

"Didn't Dr. Kendall tell you about Greatgramps?" Jan asked.

"Clancy likes to play tricks," Mike said caustically. "I'm pleased to meet all of you."

They seated themselves in canvas lawn chairs arced in a tight-semicircle facing out over the lake. Jan poured coffee. Mike's eyes worked their way around the porch, focusing on each of the four Horton men in ascending order. He estimated a seventy-five-year spread between Toby and Aaron Horton but there was no denying the lineage. Aaron was trim and erect with the same steely eyes but his features had been softened by the years. His once black hair was now as white as angel wings and was complemented by an old-world goatee that lent an air of intrigue to his otherwise gentle face.

"I hope you don't mind," Mike said apologetically. "I mean, this isn't something that I do every night of the week, barging in on people like this. I feel a little foolish."

"No need to feel that way," Steve comforted. "Dr. Kendall explained your interest. I've always suspected that we were a little unusual, looking so much alike the way we do. So what do you think? Do we have something special going for us? Maybe we're ready for a spot on Johnny Carson," he kidded.

Mike shrugged the question off. "I don't know how much Clancy told you about me," he began, "so I'll go back to the beginning. I'm a biology teacher at Kellogg High School. That's no excuse for invading your home," he admitted. "But I also have the dubious reputation of being somewhat of a local expert in the field of genetics."

"What's that?" Tina chirped. She had decided that Mike's visit was a special event and used the occasion to dress up in her prettiest yellow frock. Her corner of the porch blossomed.

Mike welcomed the question.

"Well, Tina," he began, "did you ever notice how some of your friends look a lot like their parents? If their mom has freckles on her nose then they have them, too. Of if their dad is as tall as a basketball player, they're tall also. That's called heredity. It means that some of the physical characteristics of parents are passed on to their children. And when those children have children of their own, they keep passing along these same traits."

Even though he was answering Tina's innocent question, Mike was using the opportunity to cover the basics of heredity for the benefit of the entire family. "So if somebody tells you that you have your mother's nose, they're not kidding."

Tina's eyes grew wide and she touched her nose without realizing it. The teacher coughed lightly and glanced at the other Hortons, indicating that he was speaking to them all.

"And then there are those traits that aren't visible but are also passed along. For example, some people have natural artistic ability. It just seems to happen for them. Nobody ever has to teach them to paint or to draw—they're just able to. Well, if they check back in their family tree, they'll usually discover that one of their parents or maybe even one of their grandparents had a similar talent. Or they may have to go back even further. It's possible for a number of generations to be skipped before a trait reemerges. But unfortunately most of us don't know very much about our great-great-greats."

Aaron nodded and smiled indulgently.

"Athletic ability is something else that can be inherited."

As Mike spoke, a runabout with a skier in tow raced across the lake. The young man leaned back as he cut sharply behind the boat and a wall of water cascaded over the dock. Mike pointed at the departing wake.

"That boy's a good example. He appears to be well coordinated. I wouldn't be surprised if his dad was a good athlete also."

"That must be what my problem is." Toby snickered.

"You're flirting with trouble," Steve threatened with a playfully cocked fist.

Mike saw in the repartee the qualities that had impressed Clancy about the Horton family in the first place. "So you see, Tina," he continued, "each one of us is a reflection of those who came before us. You asked what genetics is. Genetics is the study of genes and genes are tiny parts of a cell that carry all these traits from one generation to the next. So it's safe to say that the reason you're so pretty is that your mom passed you some 'pretty' genes."

"And it's probably safe to say that your dad was full of the old Italian malarkey, too," Gramps accused with a twinkle in his eye.

"That he was, John," Mike admitted. "I'm a slice off the old ham, so I'm told."

The powerboat roared past again and the skier slalomed back and forth across its foamy wake but none of the Hortons paid attention. Mike's gaze roamed over the four males. "So what makes the Horton clan so different?" he asked rhetorically. "You recall that I said that children inherit the characteristics of their parents. Obviously that means both the mother and the father. But for some unexplained reason, the Horton boys seem to inherit only the traits of their fathers. There's either some unknown biological reason for this or the law of averages has broken down completely."

Tina had lost the thread of the explanation, but the others hung on to every one of the teacher's words.

"When you consider that there's only a fifty-fifty chance of a given trait coming from the male parent, the passage of four generations of males who could have been quadruplets at the same age carries astronomical odds. That's what piqued my curiosity when Clancy first described you. And that was before I even knew about Greatgramps," he added wryly. "So that's the reason I wanted to meet all of you. To chat with you to see if there's anything to be learned that would add some information to the body of knowledge called genetics."

Mike looked at Toby and met the boy's serious stare. "You see, Toby, the study of genetics is much more than idle curiosity. Every time we learn something about how our bodies work, we have another clue about how to make them work even better. That's really what it's all about. You know, Toby," he stressed, "most truly great discoveries happened accidentally. It's called serendipity. Like when Pasteur discovered vaccination while he was experimenting with bacteria. That's how science works," he admitted. "We just stumble along and poke around the edges of ideas and sometimes that brings us new information. From that new information we develop theories. When we gather enough information and we piece it all together, we can finally call something a proven fact. Well, I have some theories about genetics that I'm trying to prove and I have a hunch the Horton men might be a valuable link in the knowledge chain."

Mike took a deep breath and squirmed self-consciously. "Wow! That was some speech, wasn't it? Make sure you stop me if I get wound up like that again."

"Not at all. It sounds like a very interesting and worthwhile pursuit." Aaron Horton spoke for the first time. His voice was deep and strong, hinting of an accent that Mike couldn't place. "I for one will be pleased to cooperate, as I'm sure we all will be." With a small sweep of his manicured hand, he involved all of the Hortons.

Mike noticed Aaron wore his years with considerable grace, not surrendering to the throes of time. Only slight clefts and wrinkles acknowledged his decades of existence. And, as promised, he provided an enormous amount of family information.

Jan refilled their coffee cups three times as Mike probed into the Horton family history. He learned that for as far back as Aaron could document, each generation had produced only one son. Mike asterisked the point on his yellow notepad. How fortunate, he thought, that the fragile chain hadn't been broken by sickness or accident.

He learned that they were unusually healthy—rarely incapacitated by common colds or annoying viruses. They did have a family history of headaches—no real pattern and not very intense but abnormally frequent. All four male Hortons had them but Tina displayed no such problem. They all had excellent teeth. Even before the introduction of helpful chemicals, neither John nor Aaron experienced the usual childhood tooth problems. And at eighty-five, Aaron's teeth were white as Chiclets and strong as tombstones. Toby mentioned that he hated red beets. So did the others, although Steve ate them to provide a good parental example.

Mike had filled three pages with scribbled notes and still hadn't found any significant differences among them. The family was a mother lode of hereditary coincidence—or a path through uncharted chapters of genetic knowledge.

"Clancy told me that you were interested in Toby's dreams," Jan said. "Does that have something to do with your theory?"

"It has a lot to do with it," Mike replied. "But right now the theory's too weak to even discuss it intelligently."

Jan cocked her head quizzically.

"Remember what I said about theories and facts? Any idiot can have a theory. But bringing it to life requires research and a lot of digging. That's what I'm doing tonight," he explained.

"Do you think we have genes?" Tina blurted.

"I wouldn't be surprised," Mike said with a laugh.

Chapter Eight

❖❖❖❖❖❖❖❖❖❖❖

"AND HEED YE the powerful voice of the Lord who sayeth, 'Whoever harkens to the message of the false prophet shall burn in everlasting hell.'"

"Amen!"

"And let not the glitter or promise of worldly things distract thine eyes from His mighty word."

"Amen!"

"And fear ye not to raise thy fist in anger to strike down the bearer of Satan's evil message."

"Amen!"

"And let thy rage seek out and punish the worshiper of false gods, the liar, the thief, the pornographer, the fornicator, the adulterer."

"Amen!"

"The Lord is merciful and the Lord is just. He showers His faithful with divine grace. He opens His loving arms to the repentant and He strikes down His detractors with a blow from His earthly army."

"Amen!"

"Who has the Lord appointed to be the soldiers of His earthly army?"

"We are the soldiers of the Lord."

"Who has the Lord chosen to lead His earthly army?"

"He has chosen you to lead His earthly army."

"With His divine help I will lead His forces against the traffickers of evil and against those who would defile His earth and the blessings He hath bestowed upon us and I promise this in His name."

"Amen!"

Esau Manley posed at the head of the plank table, eyes blazing in ecstasy as his message fanned the flames of his listeners. He was a craggy stick of a man, taut skin stretched over a knobby skeleton, a tombstone face with sepulcher cheeks. He seemed to duck when he entered a room but that was an illusion. Behind his scraggly beard, bubbly hives of spittle clung to the corners of his mouth and a fiery spark smouldered in his haunting eyes. His bony hands flailed the air as he spoke, punctuating his sermons with wild exclamations.

Hattie Manley sat to his right, her piggy eyes downcast throughout the oration. Her mammoth rear spread like putty across the hardwood bench, and a housedress stiff with food and sweat draped her hoglike shoulders and bulged over her balloon breasts. Small lifeless eyes peeked through folds of her flesh and thick dark hairs decorated a mole on her chin. The bench groaned beneath her, sagging like the leaf spring on their crumpled pickup.

Amos and Abel sat on the bench opposite their mother, heads down and eyes closed as Esau led the family in nightly prayer. The twins had neither Esau's ranginess nor Hattie's fat and their bright red hair gave cause to wonder whether Esau did indeed probe her folds of flesh or whether her impregnation was the result of some other divine diddling. But both boys did wear the same frown that stiffened Esau's face into a mask of dread and they appeared to burn with some of the same fiery zeal, but then who can say that a groundhog wouldn't become a zealot under such a constant bombardment of godliness.

Their faces were identical but lacked the character that marked Esau, whose face burned with newfound faith and radiated his rage at the world full of defilers. Esau was vital and dangerous while Amos and Abel were mirror images of dullness.

Esau spread his arms wide and stared holes through the stained ceiling. "Bless this food, Lord. Let it provide the strength Thy earthly army needs to fulfill Thy mission. I ask this favor in Thy divine name."

"Amen!"

Esau dragged his bench from beneath the table and sat to his meal. His body wasn't designed to fold in the normal manner, and when he sat he became a stick puzzle of angles and joints bent in unseemly directions, like plumbing under the sink of an old house. He plowed through the simple meal, fork in the left hand and knife in the right, never looking up except to reload.

No one spoke.

Amos and Abel also attacked their food without mercy, but their eyes darted about nervously as they speared a boiled potato or raked a knife through the defenseless piece of beef. All three of the Manley men chewed noisily, mouths open and gasping for air as their swallowing competed with their breathing for throat use. Hattie ate steadily, without the sound effects or the urgency of the menfolk but with a strong sense of purpose. Eating was the highlight of the day and the table was an assembly line, a fuel depot.

Neighbors knew little of the Manleys. They came and went at respectable hours. They were neither noisy nor nosy. They said little if anything at all. They kept their house neat enough,

not as nice as most on the block but respectable.
But there was a time when folks in the close-knit
neighborhood were fearful of the newcomers. A
few months earlier when the old pickup chugged
down the street and three bearded strangers and
a blimp of a woman clambered out there were
concerned whispers. But, giving the benefit of a
doubt, folks grew accustomed to the dour-faced
man and his quiet sons who nodded a greeting
only when necessary. They minded their own
business and you could tell they preferred others
to do the same.

Esau mopped up a puddle of gravy with a crust
and pushed his plate across the rough boards. He
shoved the last morsel through his beard and
patted his spindly stomach. "Thank the Lord,"
he announced.

"Thank the Lord," the others repeated.

Esau thanked the Lord for just about everything. He thanked Him for his family's health,
which had always been good. He thanked Him
for their food, as well he should since the Manleys plowed through chow like a bunkhouse full
of starving field hands. He thanked Him for their
wretched income and he thanked Him for their
little house with its patchy lawn and cracked
steps. Esau Manley was a man at peace with his
Lord, a man fulfilling the assignment the Lord
had personally handed down to him. But Esau
had no peace with the rest of the world and the
godless heathens who peopled it.

"They even flaunt their bosoms in the food
store," he ranted before dinner. Just that afternoon he had attacked the magazine rack at Super Value with a can of Cool Whip. Shoppers
abandoned their carts and hid behind stacks of

canned goods. Pressed into action, the store manager stuttered, "Now see here—" But Esau threatened him with the frothy weapon and the manager joined the shoppers behind the Campbell's Soup display while the madman sprayed a fluffy icing over the exposed female skin. He finally flipped the empty weapon aside and walked away unmolested, and he felt a welling of pride when a white-haired old woman stepped creakily forward and applauded.

"It's about time someone had the gumption to come forward for the Lord," she harangued the cringing crowd.

The magazine attack was an impromptu affair, but it was no less a response to God's command and some evils were best smitten on the spot, met with an outpouring of instant anger like the money changers in the temple. Pictures of naked women by the frozen vegetables—an outrage. But there were so many outrages, so many transgressions. Esau sometimes wondered how his small earthly army could cope.

Priorities!

The word just popped into his head. God must have sent it. Of course he had to have priorities. Cut off the head and the body dies. Stamp out the nests of evil. Kill the roots and the branches wither and fall to the ground. But the creeping tentacles of Satan were everywhere. Lawless speeders shouted obscenities and sprayed beer on God-fearing men. Men wagered their families' food money on games and races. Healthy young people parked their cars in spots reserved for the handicapped. Women flaunted and sold their bodies, and men paid for the illicit pleasure. Schoolyards were flooded with cigarettes and dope. Men held hands and kissed each other on city streets. Neighborhood stores rented pornographic movies. Grocery stores sold books with filthy pictures. Blasphemers borrowed Satan's power to foretell the future.

Priorities!

Hattie munched on the last piece of potato. The twins fidgeted on the bench. Esau sat hunched like a folded scarecrow, eyes clamped shut in silent prayer, contemplating the immensity of the work that lay ahead.

Amos and Abel were God-fearing but they feared Esau's rage even more. They cringed at the crack of the rod but the sting from their father's tongue delivered greater pain. When Esau gathered his family around the table and told them about his highway encounter with God, Amos appeared skeptical. He regretted it immediately.

"You dare to doubt the word of the Lord," Esau shouted, and he lashed out a stinging backhand that left its scarlet print on the boy's cheek.

There was no more discussion. The boys were conscripted into the earthly army.

Hattie cleared away the dishes, angling delicately around tables and chairs in the small dining area. She moved lightly for such a wad of a woman. The twins moved to the couch and turned the TV on low.

Esau flashed a glare of annoyance. "Keep that thing low." He despised the modern miracle of television for the corruption that it spread, but it did have its moments. Sunday-morning *Gospel Hour* was a family event. And he also needed it to keep up with the news. Part of his assignment was to know where in the land the sick head of evil was rising.

Know thy enemy.

Esau grunted his disapproval at the television then resumed his chat with the Lord.

The sun sank low, sending a watery bar of light across the plank table. The TV droned a senseless mumble. The twins stared vacantly at the flickering picture, like identical bookends on either end of the couch. The lingering aroma of the roast mingled with the late-day scent of the Manleys. Esau's eyes blinked suddenly open. He spread his arms, palms up, as if trying to embrace the world. He raised his head, looked at the spotted ceiling, through it. He had made a direct contact.

"Lord, look with kindness upon Your earthly army. Guide us to Thine enemies. Grant us the wisdom and the strength to deliver a mighty blow in Thy name."

"Amen," echoed from the couch and kitchen.

Amos snapped off the TV and grabbed a handful of pamphlets from the coffee table. Hattie wiped her hands on her housedress and held open the door. Esau led the small army into the dusky evening.

He drove with Amos at his side and Abel slouched in the back of the pickup leaning against the cab. The truck coughed noisily down the street, and Hattie turned the TV to a game show, cranked up the volume, and finished the dishes.

Hennepin Avenue shone a sickly yellow as it streaked along the edge of downtown Minneapolis. Violent reds turned to muddy browns in the neon glare and flocks of jaundiced strollers lined

the block. A banker in tux and his wife in fur
strolled arm in arm, drawing curious glances. A
frizzy old lady with a knobby cane inched down
the middle of the sidewalk. The crowd flowed
around her like litter on the highway. Snakes of
red neon flashed Girls! Girls! Girls! and strollers
turned from red to orange as they were washed
with the glow. Blacks, Mexicans, American Indi-
ans, and Puerto Ricans mixed with the Scandinavians and strutted or shuffled down the block,
meeting, greeting, buying, selling.

Some just leaned.

Esau glared in angry disapproval at the girl
with the black lipstick and spiky blue hair. Her
boyfriend had a shaven head and was trussed in
leather and chains.

A horn blared behind him. "Move it, Pops. Get
that piece of crap out of the street."

Abel stared uneasily at the car full of teenagers, and Esau crept slowly around the corner.

The pickup rolled to the curb in front of a
bookstore. Sun-shielding plastic sheathed the
windows and a heavy mesh screen filled the
doorway. Abel scrambled over the side and Amos
shouldered open the door. Each was armed with
a stack of pamphlets as they rounded the corner
in search of a likely spot. Esau watched them
briefly before pulling back into traffic.

"Will you join His earthly army? Sir, will you
join the Lord's earthly army?"

Regular visitors to the strip learned to ignore
the orators and pamphleteers of Hennepin Avenue. They were part of the scene, like the junkies
and the punkers and the grinning men who
strolled hand in hand. It was all part of the show.

"Sir, will you join His earthly army?"

A burly youngster in a U of M sweatshirt took the proffered literature and stuffed it in his pocket. Farther down the block another hawker gave him a flier for "The Pink Pussycat—Girls! Girls! Girls!" and the boy shoved that next to the crumpled recruitment pamphlet.

Esau felt frustrated in his efforts to stamp out evil with his tiny earthly army. He needed help, people who believed, people who were as committed as he was. He hit on the pamphlet idea when he opened his monthly mailing from the power company and had to wade through offers for luggage and jewelry while he searched for his gas bill.

"Join His Earthly Army" the pamphlet shouted. "Join His legions of soldiers on earth." The message stopped short of advocating violence but the implication was clear.

"Raise your fist in anger and stamp out those who defy the will of God."

Those wishing to join the troop and receive literature and future notices could send their name and address to "His Earthly Army, P.O. Box 1286, Saint Paul, Minnesota." No contributions were required, which was just as well since none were received.

Amos and Abel played no favorites as they went about their mission. Old and young, black and white, people of curious sexual persuasion and attire, all were offered the opportunity to join the earthly army.

"Will you join His earthly army, sir?"

"Fuck off, creep!"

But the boys weren't deterred nor were they intimidated. They believed the message. Though they lacked some of Esau's fire, a lifetime of his example was impossible to ignore. They handled the occasional physical threats by turning the other cheek, but these times were rare. A lifetime of farm labor had broadened their bodies and few of the pedestrians were anxious to confront the pair. Any would-be attacker had numerous more vulnerable targets along the strip. Their stacks of pamphlets dwindled as the walking traffic thickened.

Esau swung back to the freeway and headed east. The glow of the IDS tower faded to a sparkle and a row of spiky antennas twinkled like birthday candles in the northern suburbs. The *Saint Paul Pioneer Press* lay open on the seat beside him. Yellow highlight marker circled the classified notice.

"Fortunes told, palms read, speak to departed loved ones."

It gave a phone number.

It was an abomination and the Lord wished it to be removed. Esau had called the number from a booth in Rosedale Mall and made the appointment. He wasn't sure what category fortune-tellers fit into but there was no question that they violated God's order of things. Idolaters maybe? Fornicators? Blasphemers? It really made no difference. There were no degrees of evil.

It was a once elegant mansion, a *grande dame* basking in the fading brilliance of past grandeur. Wrought-iron shafts with hammered spearheads formed a painful picket atop a low brick wall. The metal barrier was woven with ivy. A lone street lamp cast a pale complexion on the stone front. A rounded turret with a snug patinated cap was silhouetted against the night sky. Esau knew the neighborhood. He had done some handyman work there. It had once been Millionaires' Row, the stately homes of the early barons—lumber, livestock, railroads. F. Scott Fitzgerald lived and wrote right down the block, he had once been told. Esau had nodded absently at that tidbit of Saint Paul minutia, wondering who F. Scott was but not so curious as to ask. But taxes and heating bills had taken their toll on the once privileged community. The homes that had once been stately queens were now dotty dowagers waging an endless battle against the wrinkles of time.

The gate creaked like a kitten when he swung it open, and his boots clicked a tattoo on the flagstone path. He cast a long steeplelike shadow across the lawn, over the shrubs, and up the stone facing. The door was imposing, thick panes of cut glass set into massive oak. It opened into a dim vestibule with a door to the left, one straight ahead, and a third to the right. There were no bells but three mailboxes were hung in a column between the doors. A business card was tacked to the door on the right.

"Mme. Chetret—Readings and other experiences."

It gave her address and phone number.

"Come in."

Esau hadn't knocked and the announcement startled him. The command wasn't spoken loudly but he heard it clearly. It was husky, like an amplified whisper through the dark wooden door. The doorknob was a glass diamond that filled his palm. Esau turned it cautiously and pushed inward. The door opened halfway before sticking.

"Come in quickly and close the door, Mr. Christianson."

Esau didn't think it would be wise to use his real name. The one he chose seemed fitting. He pushed harder and the door stuttered against the bottom frame before swinging free.

He could see very little as he stepped inside, only gloomy silhouettes without shape or form. Once inside, he paused and waited for direction but none was forthcoming. There were no lamps turned on, but an eerie luminosity seeped from around the baseboards. A dry smell hung in the air like a powdery mist, dusty with a pinch of spice. Curtains, dark and colorless, draped the wall. There was a muted hissing, sibilant, like compressed air escaping through the cracks.

"This way, Mr. Christianson."

The voice was crisp and brittle. There was an accent, a back-of-the-throat sound with rounded edges.

Esau followed the sound to an archway. He came to a cube of a room, ten by ten by ten, with a round table in the center. Points of diffused light sparkled like mist-shrouded stars from the walls, but there was no other source of light. Wisps of white smoke curled from an iron pot in the farthest corner. The spicy smell was stronger here. There were two high-backed chairs across from each other at the table. Mme. Chetret sat in the chair facing the archway.

"Come in and sit down, Mr. Christianson." It was a command.

She wasn't young but it was hard to pin down her age. She was somewhere between fifty and infinity. A gauzy veil masked her features. She looked very small.

Esau walked uncertainly into the room. He didn't look directly at the woman, staring instead at the dark tabletop with the strange markings that seemed to waver and glow. Stars, swastikas, zodiac signs.

Symbols of Satan.

He felt suddenly light-headed and folded himself into the chair. The stars on the wall began to blink and the smoke curled thicker from the iron pot. It hung in a cloudy layer near the ceiling.

Destroy the blasphemer.

The room was cool but Esau felt runnels of sweat trickle down his sides. His chest was tight and ached dully. The gloom, the incense, the flickering lights, the smoke—it all disoriented him. It wasn't what he had pictured. What had he pictured?

"I am Mme. Chetret." She stared at him sharply but didn't offer her hand. "I presume that you are Mr. Christianson." It wasn't a question.

Esau met her gaze and nodded.

"You weren't very clear on the telephone. I'm not sure what you want, Mr. Christianson. If you want to speak to someone who has passed through, I won't be able to help you tonight. I need more time to prepare."

A bead of perspiration rolled between Esau's eyebrows, caromed down his nose, and splashed on the tabletop. He had heard about these people, read about them. Wizards and gypsies! Charlatans! Blasphemers! Now he actually faced one across three feet of sacrilegious tabletop. He sat in the nest of Satan, sniffed his evil incense, was mesmerized by his symbols and flickering lights.

"I am, however, prepared to discuss your future, Mr. Christianson. Is that what you wish?"

How does one speak to the devil? Esau's eyes finally adjusted to the gloom and he could define her features through the diaphanous veil. Her face was small and pinched like a hurt sparrow. Her eyes met his and they burned with intensity, red-hot nail heads blazing in a wrinkled old face.

"My future. Yes, that's what I want," he blurted out.

"It will cost fifty dollars." She looked at his work shirt questioningly but not disdainfully.

Esau reached for his wallet, peeled out two hard-earned twenties and a ten. He slid the money to the center of the star. A surprisingly delicate hand came from beneath the table and pulled the bills into the folds of her gown. He noticed that the gown, like the tabletop, was covered with symbols.

"Put your hands on the table, Mr. Christianson."

Esau stared blankly.

"Like this."

She laid her hands on the table, shoulder wide, palms down, fingers splayed. Esau hesitated. She looked at him queerly, then he did as she instructed.

"Closer to the center of the table," she commanded.

He slid his hands farther until his fingers touched the tips of the pointed star. The table felt warm. For an instant he thought he felt it move.

"I don't use crystal, Mr. Christianson."

Another blank stare.

"Crystal balls, objects! I don't use things like that. They're artificial. They're only used by amateurs and frauds."

Esau nodded dumbly. He was bewildered. He came to deliver the vengeance of the Lord upon the blasphemer and the wispy old woman was engaging him in conversation about crystal balls. He was confused.

"Many people think that this is witchcraft, Mr. Christianson. That's why they resort to props. People come to expect them. But they're mistaken. The gadgets do nothing without the gift. And I do have the gift, Mr. Christianson, the gift from God."

Esau felt as if he'd been slapped in the face.

"You look surprised. Don't worry. You needn't worry where my gift comes from. Just be thankful that you came to someone with a true gift, not one of the filthy gypsies with their blasphemous hocus-pocus."

Esau's mind reeled. He knew goodness. Goodness meant seeing things his way, which was through the eyes of God's captain on earth. And he knew evil. It reeked and there was no way to disguise it. But what was Mme. Chetret? She spoke of evil as if it were her enemy. Would a messenger of the devil speak in that manner?

"Give me your hands, Mr. Christianson."

Yet another blank stare.

She reached for his wrists and pulled his hands closer to her. Then she covered his outstretched fingers with her hands. His hands were twice the size of hers. Another drop of sweat ran down

Esau's nose and exploded on the tabletop. Mme. Chetret pretended not to notice. She closed her eyes and pressed lightly on his fingers.

It was quiet. Esau had never heard such silence. Even the hissing had stopped. The spicy smell was cloying and the star lights on the walls grew dimmer. The smoke layer dropped lower and wispy tendrils snaked above the table-top.

Mme. Chetret finally spoke but it wasn't with the same voice. It was thin and hollow like a flute. "You're deeply troubled, Mr. Christianson. Something happened to you recently. Something very important."

Esau felt a stab in the center of his chest and his sweat ran freely.

"Someone spoke to you and changed your life."

His hands trembled and she felt their dampness. "It was the Lord," he whispered viciously. "It was not 'someone.' It was the Lord Himself who commanded me to lead his earthly army."

Mme. Chetret looked up. Esau's face was a mask of pain and rage. Drops of sweat raced over his cheekbones and disappeared into his beard. His eyes blazed feverishly. She wrapped her slim fingers around his callused hand and squeezed. Her strength surprised him. "Yes," she said quickly. "It was the Lord. Your Lord and my Lord. He has commanded you."

His eyes blazed with madness and Mme. Chetret felt her own heart race with fear.

"Heed His word, Mr. Christianson. You are truly His instrument." She reached back into the folds of her gown and produced the bills he had given her. "We are both instruments of the same Lord, Mr. Christianson. He would want you to use this to further His work."

He took the bills. "The future," Esau gasped. "What is the future?"

The old woman stood and leaned forward with her hands flat on the table. She leaned close to Esau, heads level, faces only inches apart. "You will lead His earthly army, Mr. Christianson. You will do His will and you will succeed. Now go! Go and do as the Lord has commanded. Hurry!"

She reached under the table and flicked a switch. Harsh light flooded the room and Esau blinked as he scrambled to his feet. Mme. Chetret scurried around the table in quick choppy steps, took Esau by the arm, and pulled him to the front door.

"Bless you for your work of the Lord, Mr. Christianson."

She held the door open and Esau rushed through. The door slammed shut behind him and he heard the heavy bolt slam into place.

Mme. Chetret went to a cabinet, took out a bottle, and poured four fingers of Black Label.

Esau lurched down the flagstone path to the pickup holding a fist to his chest as if that would still the pain, feeling like he had failed his mission but not knowing why.

Chapter Nine

❧❧❧❧❧❧❧❧❧❧

"YOU'RE NOT EXPECTED to understand anything this complex, Dr. Kendall. After all, you're a mere physician, not a biology teacher."

They were at Lindey's for their regular Wednesday-night dinner and Clancy was anxious to hear Mike's reactions to his meeting with the Hortons. Mike addressed the doctor as he would a dull-witted tenth-grader at Kellogg.

"You do recall learning that the human body, every living thing for that matter, is made up of cells?"

Clancy toyed with his old-fashioned and regarded his friend with a scornful gaze.

"In fact, your own body has over one hundred trillion of the little fellas, give or take a few. And smack-dab in the middle of each one of these little buggers is a tiny ball of goo called the nucleus. Inside each of these goo balls are a bunch of squiggly things called chromosomes. Are you with me so far, Doctor?"

Clancy waved at the waitress for a refill.

"Listen up," Mike continued. "Now we're getting to the tough part. These chromosomes are made from DNA. I don't think you're ready to handle what that stands for, so you'll just have to trust me. Now this DNA looks like a long necklace, only instead of beads this bauble is made of genes, and the way these genes are strung together controls heredity. It's called the genetic code. All living things from the lowliest medical student all the way up the ladder to the pomegranate have their own specified number of chromosomes. In human beings and doctors that number happens to be forty-six."

Clancy waited patiently for Mike to get to the point.

"Except that certain cells have only half that number. Those cells are called gametes or sex cells. You probably call them sperms and eggs. Now listen closely to this part. It gets tricky. When a man does a dirty deed to a woman, the little sperm goes swimming merrily upstream until it finds an egg, then—bingo—they get together and make a new nucleus with the original forty-six chromosomes."

"Ain't nature wonderful," Clancy said with a groan.

"The new cell formed from the sperm and the egg is called a zygote and it's the start of a little bitty baby."

Clancy smiled up at the departing waitress who had delivered their drinks. "She's got some big genes."

Mike became more serious. "Everything that we know about heredity has been discovered within the past hundred and twenty years." He pondered thoughtfully for a moment. "You know, when I started teaching I used to tell my students that everything we knew was learned in the past ninety years. On a chronological scale, we're still in the Dark Ages as far as heredity is concerned. That's probably why I enjoy it so much. There are still a few frontiers to crack."

"And you might have found one?"

"Maybe."

"Where do the Hortons fit into the scheme of things? Are they that different?" Clancy asked.

"They're different, all right. Remember how those gametes each contained twenty-three chromosomes from each parent, and those chromosomes contain the genes that determine appearance—straight or curly hair, blue or brown eyes, tall or short, fat or thin—thousands of physical and mental characteristics? By and large, these traits will be randomly inherited and the offspring will show traits from both the male and the female parent. You recall Mendel's law regarding dominant and recessive genes?"

Clancy nodded. "One gene more or less overpowers the other in the formation of a new being."

"Crude but close enough," Mike conceded. "With that concept in mind, look at what we have here with the Hortons. Four generations, maybe five, where each generation produces no more than one male offspring and those four or five individuals appear to be physically identical. What happened to Mendel's law? Where are the mothers' traits? More important, is this an aberration, a freak one-in-a-trillion chance, or is it the key to yet another genetic door?"

"What kind of door?" Clancy asked.

Mike chewed thoughtfully at his inner lip. He met Clancy's eyes and locked them contemplatively. He fretted with his glass, deciding whether or not to share his thoughts. Clancy was his friend—his best friend—but he was still a doctor, a man of science by training, not predisposed to flights of fancy. Certainly he wasn't one to jump at the wispy straw upon which Mike's theory was hinged. But Clancy was also a good sounding board, an open mind to ideas of sub-

stance. Mike had bounced numerous ideas and
problems off his agile brain before. They usually
pertained, however, to the physical or mental
health of his students—nothing so speculative as
his theory about the genetic conveyance of memory.

"Clancy, do you believe in the occult?"

The doctor eyed his friend curiously, then he
stopped to ponder. "Not really," he said. "If you
probe deeply enough, everything has a logical
explanation. I especially don't believe in those
out-of-body experiences that seem to be so popular in the OR's nowadays, the kind where peo-
ples' spirits float around the ceiling of the
operating room and watch the surgeon whacking their lifeless body with electric paddles. Is
that the kind of occult you mean?"

"Something like that, but that's only one
example. How can you logically explain some
of the other unusual phenomena, things like
automatic writing? There are numerous docu-
mented examples of people, usually under hypnosis, who all of a sudden write in a language
that they never learned—were never even exposed to."

"I'd have to see it to believe it, and even then
you'd have a hard time convincing me it wasn't
a hoax."

"A hoax? Why would someone go to all the
bother? What would they have to gain?"

"I'm a medical doctor, not a psychiatrist,
Mike. People do a lot of strange things for reasons I'll never understand. Like that nut from
Dallas a couple of years ago. Do you remember
the one with the cocker spaniel that made stock
market picks? He was the darling of Wall Street

until they found a little electronics package from Radio Shack implanted in the poor mutt's throat. You figure it out."

"I agree, Clancy. There are a lot of whackos out there. And that's the problem. Whenever a truly unexplainable event takes place, people automatically scream fraud—guilty until proven innocent."

"Exactly as it should be," Clancy admonished.

"Maybe," Mike agreed. "As long as the doubters have an open mind and are willing to judge fairly."

Clancy held his palms up in a gesture of surrender. "Okay! I'll give you the benefit of the doubt. I'll even pick up that rag at the supermarket to study up on the subject, the one with the headline: Co-ed Gets Knocked Up by Ghost of Archduke Ferdinand."

"That's part of the problem, the sensationalism and exploitation. The people who read that crap are the same ones who want to make tractor pulls and mud wrestling into Olympic events."

"Aren't they?" Clancy asked with a look of mild surprise.

"Most unexplained psychic phenomena aren't so dramatic. They wouldn't sell papers."

"Such as?"

"Such as the little girl from Iowa who slipped into a trance during her school's Christmas pageant and began speaking what sounded like gibberish. Only at the time, the school was videotaping the play and they recorded every word she spoke. One of the parents worked at the university in Ames and he played it for the head of the language department. It took him three weeks but he finally figured it out. The girl was speaking a forgotten tribal dialect of Middle Europe that eventually evolved into Hungarian. It was a dialect that hadn't been spoken in a thousand years." Mike searched the doctor's face and said pleadingly, "She was only eight years old, Clancy. She had never been outside of Iowa. Her parents are fourth-generation Scandinavians. Nobody in the family has a trace of Hungarian as far as they can determine. It wasn't a hoax, Clancy. The whole thing only lasted thirty seconds at the most. The little girl snapped right back to her lines in the play and didn't even realize that she'd skipped a beat."

Clancy shrugged expansively. "Chalk up one for the true believers."

"Just one of many," Mike corrected. "Try this one on for size. About four years ago an old black woman in Memphis was hit by a car while she was pulling her shopping cart across the street. She had major head injuries and went into a coma. She became a vegetable and they put her into a nursing home to die. But she took her time dying—two years to be exact. And during that time she slipped in and out of the coma nine times. Nine times that they knew of."

"People don't just slip in and out of comas," Clancy argued. "It's not like they're taking a nap."

"Pardon my ignorance. Maybe coma's not the right word. Anyway, she lay in that nursing home with her eyes closed, tubes poking in and out of every hole in her body. You could stick her full of pins and tickle her feet and she'd never

know it. Call it a coma, deep sleep, unconscious—call it a Fig Newton if you want to. The
point is that the old lady was out of it for two
years." Mike stopped and fixed the doctor with a
sober stare. "Except for the nine times that she
sang the Bopanissi."

Clancy put his hand to his throat and faked
choking on his drink. "You're kidding," he sputtered. "Not *the* Bopanissi?"

"C'mon, Clancy. This is serious," the teacher
scolded.

"I'm sorry. Tell me about the Bopanissi,"
Clancy apologized.

"In Ghana, about two hundred miles inland
from Accra, there's a tribe called the Obatis.
They've been around since dinosaurs but
there's only a handful of them left. They're still
living in the bush but they're getting old and
dying off fast. The young ones leave for the big
city as soon as they're able. Give it another
thirty or forty years and the Obati will be history. They've always been isolated from other
tribes. They aren't migratory. They just stay in
their little corner of the world and grow barely
enough food to survive, maize and roots and
God only knows what other delicacies. And like
so many tribes in Africa, they have their own
language. Also, they have their own customs.
One of these customs is to lament a parent's
death by chanting their ritual song."

"The Bopanissi?"

"The same. And that's what this old lady from
Tennessee sang to the walls of the nursing home.
She never once woke up. Never! She never even
opened her eyes, just sang the sad words of an
old song that hadn't been heard on this side of

the Atlantic. No hoax, Clancy. What would be the point?"

"Okay, you win. There are some psychic phenomena that can't be easily explained. How did we get onto this subject anyway?"

"You have the attention span of a doughnut. I asked you whether or not you believed in the occult."

"Idle curiosity?"

"Not at all. It has to do with the theory I'm working on."

"Let me guess. The theory has something to do with the family Horton."

"It has everything to do with the Hortons. When you described the family similarity, it interested me much as it would interest any serious student of genetics. But when you mentioned Toby's strange soliloquy, you hit my theoretical nail right on the head."

"Your theory is about these so-called psychic phenomena?"

"Exactly! Except that if the theory proves true, some of these strange rantings won't be considered psychic phenomena anymore. They'll be just as explainable as your brown eyes or your ugly nose."

"I think we need some heavy-duty fortification. I get the distinct feeling that you're about to embark on a lengthy diatribe." He signaled the waitress to bring a couple more drinks and settled comfortably back in the heavy oak captain's chair. "I'm ready to be amazed, Professor."

Clancy saw the excitement light up his friend's face as he prepared to launch into his theory. Mike folded his hands together, put his elbows on the table, and rested his chin on his thumbs. He was leaning halfway across the table, as if to share a dark secret with a co-conspirator.

"Think about this for a minute, Clancy. What does Toby Horton's case have in common with the other two cases I just described?" Mike sat back and watched intently as Clancy chewed pensively on a thumbnail.

"Two things come to mind right off the bat," he offered. "All three people were in some stage of loss of consciousness when they spoke and all three spoke about something that happened in the past."

"Excellent." Mike was pleased by Clancy's grasp. "There's a third similarity also, but I'll have to finish one of the stories if you're to catch it. The little girl from Iowa, the one who spoke old Hungarian—I never told you what it was she said."

Clancy waited expectantly and without his usual flipness. "That's right, you didn't."

The waitress arrived with their fresh drinks and Mike waited patiently while she tidied up. They declined the opportunity to order their meal and she left.

"It took the language department at the university a few weeks before they felt entirely confident with their translation." Mike reached into his inside jacket pocket and pulled out a typed copy. He carefully unfolded it and held it at an angle to catch the light from the wall-mounted lamp. He began to read.

" 'She is dead. My beautiful Markya is dead. The terrible raiders from the East rode their brutish horses into our village and snatched my darling from my breast! Then their leader threw her tiny body into the air and caught her on the end of his spear. Her cry of pain still wakes me from my sleep at night. Why does this happen?' "

Mike read the words slowly and he looked his friend in the eye as he spoke the poor woman's unanswered question.

"Powerful stuff," Clancy whispered.

"Do you see the third similarity among the cases?" Mike asked.

Clancy responded instantly. "Death. They all involve death. A pet, a parent, and a child."

"Right again. All three cases involve death. But if my theory is correct then the fact that they all involve death is coincidental. The similarity that I see is shock, in these cases brought on by the death of someone or something loved. If my theory is correct, at the same time they happened, these three incidents were the most traumatic events to have taken place in an individual's lifetime."

"What individual?" Clancy asked, even though he was sure that he already knew the answer.

Mike spoke softly and precisely, watching Clancy for any flicker of understanding—or of scorn.

"An ancestor. An ancestor of the old black woman's, an ancestor of the little Iowa girl's, an ancestor of Toby Horton's."

Chapter Ten

❖❖❖❖❖❖❖❖❖❖

THE SUN BEAT kindly on the silver surface of Big Bass lake, spreading its warming touch over the fishermen and skiers and boaters who basked in its pleasant grip. The low rumble of passing outboards was absorbed by the lapping wavelets. A soft breeze billowed the blue and white striped canopy of the pontoon boat that purred effortlessly under the power of the twenty-five-horse Evinrude.

Toby sat proudly in the swiveled captain's chair and guided the twenty-foot float boat skillfully along the edges of the dappled water lilies. A long table hooked over the front railing and extended down the center of the boat, stopping a few feet short of the steering console. Clancy, Mike, and John sat along one side of the table and Tina, Jan, and Aaron sat across from them. Steve was taking orders for soft drinks and beers and sorting through the red plastic cooler for the makings of a snack.

"How's the old head bone been?" Clancy shielded his eyes against the setting sun and smiled at the youngster sitting proudly behind the oak boat wheel.

"I'm still getting some headaches but they're not so bad," Toby answered.

"And he hasn't been staring at nothing and saying the B word, either," Tina added.

"Really?" Clancy said. "It sounds like that bang on the head was just what the doctor ordered. When do your headaches come?"

"Almost any time. I have a little one right now but it's no big deal."

Clancy took the cold Stroh's that Steve offered and leaned back in the padded deck chair. He took a frothy sip and wiped his lips with the back of his hand. Mike Mancini accepted a cold Coke and coughed lightly to get everyone's attention.

"It seems that every time we meet I'm thanking you for letting me impose on you. I should warn you, if this discussion turns out the way I hope it will, this won't be the last time. The reason I asked that we get together again has to do with a conversation Clancy and I had the other night." He had to raise his voice as a ski boat swept a wide path nearby. "I'm convinced that your family could provide some valuable insights into a theory I've been researching for some time now, a theory that could have significant implications in many areas of science and medicine. Until I had the opportunity to observe your family, I hadn't discussed my theory with anyone." He glanced toward the doctor. "Aside from Clancy here, you'll be the first to hear it."

Toby took a wide turn around a lazy canoe without taking his eyes off the teacher. All of the Hortons sat in hushed expectation as Mike led into his explanation.

"Let me begin by saying that I'll understand if you don't want to be bothered with going ahead with my idea. I'll be disappointed but I'll understand."

"We've been through all of this," Steve said, dismissing Mike's concern with an impatient wave of his hand. "We'll help you no matter how crazy your theory is, right, Toby?"

Toby grinned and made a circling gesture around his temple with his index finger.

"Okay, then," Mike continued. "I'll start with a little more background. In our mini genetics lecture last week I told you about DNA and chromosomes and genes and how the structure and composition of these genes determines characteristics that are passed from generation to generation."

He looked around for confirmation and received cautious nods of understanding.

"The males in your family are proof positive of the concept. We know, for example, that a person's genetic code is determined by the type of DNA units in addition to their number and arrangement. We know that a child inherits twenty-three pairs of chromosomes from each parent." Unconsciously he looked from Steve to Jan to Toby. "One of these chromosomes determines the child's sex, and certain traits, some good and some not so good, are known to piggyback along with it. Color blindness is a good example. Hemophilia is another. Through experimentation and observation, in some cases we've been able to pinpoint which characteristics are carried by which chromosomes. Which means that it may be possible in the future to correct deficiencies before they begin by altering the genetic structure that causes them."

Aaron raised his eyebrows as the implications of genetic reseach became more apparent.

"But for every piece of hard information we have," Mike continued, "there are still hundreds of unanswered questions. That's why genetics is such a popular field of study. It's a new frontier. It's like space in a way—right there for us to see but still slightly out of reach. And every new door that we unlock opens onto new corridors each with another hundred locked doors."

"Wow!" Tina breathed.

Mike laughed softly at his own fervent eloquence. "There I go again," he confessed. "My students are always telling me that I get carried away whenever I get on the subject."

"He's a born romantic," Clancy interjected. "The Christopher Columbus of Kellogg High School."

"Please go on," Aaron insisted. "It's very interesting."

Mike smiled appreciatively. "Like any science, genetics is very complicated and it's made up of many individual fields of study. Some of these specialized fields are well-traveled paths supported by thousands of hours and millions of dollars. Others are fledgling ideas or theories that are no more than a gleam in the eye of a curious scientist." He winked at Toby. "Betcha can't guess which kind mine is."

Toby regarded the biology teacher with a thoughtful gaze. He throttled the Evinrude down to a quiet gurgle and allowed the pontoon to drift with the breeze toward the center of the lake. His response showed an intuitiveness beyond his years that both surprised and pleased the teacher. "You're a curious scientist, aren't you, Mr. Mancini? And your theory has something to do with my dreams."

"You're right on both counts," Mike said admiringly. "Do you remember our conversation about eye color and hair color and all those other traits that you inherited from your dad and he inherited from your Gramps?"

"Sure. That's why we all look so much alike."

"Right. But those are only the physical traits. They're the easiest to identify. But there are other characteristics that also pass from generation to generation, some that aren't quite so obvious. Creativity, for example. Artistic ability seems to run in families. That's just another way of saying that it's inherited. If one of your parents can draw, there's a better than average chance that you'll be able to, also. Technical ability is another. The children of engineers are more likely to pursue and excel in a technical field than are the children of social workers, for example."

"Doesn't the home environment play an important role in that?" Steve questioned.

"Undoubtedly," Mike agreed. "And it wasn't too long ago that it was assumed that environment accounted for all such predisposition. But recent studies of adopted children who were removed from their biological parents at birth prove conclusively that certain personality traits and skills are carried in the genetic code."

"Like athletic ability." Toby recalled the conversation of the previous week. "The reason I'll never play for the Twins is that my dad's too clumsy."

"But you'll probably win the Nobel Prize for good looks instead," Steve parried.

"Fat chance," Toby said, giggling.

"You've got the idea," Mike said. "Now stay with me just a little longer. I'm working up to my theory. Okay, we know that the way we look can be inherited."

He looked around the table and waited for the

nods. "And we agree that, to some extent, the way we think and act can be inherited."

Another round of positive nods. "Then what does that leave?" he wondered aloud.

Tina was distracted by the rooster-tail spray of a passing speedboat. Toby leaned against the wooden spokes of the steering wheel, his boyish features wrinkled in a questioning frown.

"I think maybe you speak of the way that we remember."

It was Aaron's crisp voice that broke the silence. His gray eyes shone with understanding, two bright beacons of knowledge and experience that spanned both the years and the continents. He looked a little the scientist himself with his intelligent face sandwiched between his wind-blown white hair and his neat goatee. "I think your theory is that we can inherit our parents' thoughts. Am I correct?"

Until the dinner with Clancy, Mike hadn't divulged his controversial theory to anyone. And now, to hear an eighty-five-year-old man hastily fit together the loose pieces of his puzzle fueled his excitement.

"Exactly!" Mike exploded. "The genetic transference of memory."

He rose from the bench seat and gripped the canopy support that spanned the boat. His face glowed evangelistically. "I want the Horton family to help me prove the theory that we can inherit the memories of our parents."

Steve looked up at Mike questioningly. "Are you saying that when Toby dreamed about my pet rabbit and how it died, he was digging up an old memory that he inherited from me?"

"That's precisely what I'm saying, Steve. And

if I recall, Gramps said that you had similar experiences as a child."

John nodded. "He used to stare into space and say strange things—like he was talking in his sleep, just like Toby does. Except that I never recognized anything he said as coming from my past."

"I've had the theory for years," Mike continued. "But it was built on such a fragile base. Actually it wasn't much more than supposition supported by unusual and sometimes sensational reports of unexplained psychic phenomena. But then the expression 'psychic phenomena' itself is a question, not an answer."

The teacher was in front of a class now, probing, explaining.

"So I sorted through reams of documents, hoping to find those that supported my idea, but I kept running into brick walls. I was looking for people who'd had experiences like Toby's but, for a variety of reasons, none of my leads amounted to anything."

"What makes you think that this one will be any different?" Steve asked.

"Well, for one thing, you're right here in the Twin Cities," Mike said with a look of relief. "Remember, I'm just a poor biology teacher. No big university research grants are backing this study. But even more important than that, I've never run into a situation that combined the type of subconscious experience that Toby has along with the rare family resemblance that the Horton family has. I'm not really sure why I feel that's so significant but I'm convinced it's a piece of the puzzle. Add a third ingredient, your willingness to cooperate, and I see a once-in-a-lifetime opportunity for a poor biology teacher."

"How would it work, Mike, this memory inheritance?" Steve asked.

"I wish you hadn't asked," Mike said with a laugh. "That's another one of those long corridors behind one of the locked doors. First we have to answer an even more basic question, 'What is memory?' How does it work? Is it animal, mineral, vegetable? Is it chemical, electrical, spiritual? What is it in your body that enables you to remember what happened last week, last year? How do you even remember what I just finished saying?"

"An interesting question," Gramps agreed. "I never gave it a second thought."

"Maybe it's something like a computer," Toby volunteered excitedly. "I use a Macintosh in school and it remembers things."

"Maybe it is something like that," Mike conceded. "But I doubt it. The computer only knows a bunch of zeros and ones, yes and no, stop and go. Give it a logic path to run on and it sends a mild current through a silicon chip or reads tiny speckles of magnetized oxide. But can you compare that with the human brain?"

Mike stepped to the front of the pontoon and pointed across the lake. "Let's try something. Follow my finger. Take a look at that dock, at that house, at that boat, at that water-skier." He pointed at each item mentioned, then turned back to the Hortons. "Now close your eyes and form a mental picture of what you just saw. Picture the dock—the house—the boat—the skier."

He paused while they obediently followed his instructions. Even Clancy sat docilely, eyes closed, a hint of a smile tugging at the corners of his mouth.

"There's not a computer in the world that can begin to do what you're doing at this moment," Mike announced excitedly. "All of the bits and bytes of the largest mainframe computer in existence couldn't duplicate that feat." He looked at Toby. "Now, Toby, close your eyes again. Try to picture the dock. What do you see now?"

"I kind of forget. It was there just a moment ago but I can't picture it too well now."

"Exactly. But where did it go? Like you said, it was there just a few moments ago. Computers don't do that. Computers don't forget things. And, for computers, no single memory is more important than another. Not so for us human types."

Mike motioned to Aaron. "Care to be part of this experiment?"

"Of course. This is all very interesting."

Mike sat back down and studied the old man. "Tell me, Mr. Horton, where were you at this time of night three weeks ago?"

The old man stroked his goatee and frowned. "On such short notice, I don't recall, Mr. Mancini. Perhaps I could figure it out given a minute or two."

"That's okay. I doubt if anyone here could pass that test. Let's try another question." Mike smiled wickedly. "Who was the first girl you ever kissed, Aaron?" Mike could have sworn the old man blushed.

"Such a devilish question, young man. And in front of the children." He indicated John Horton. He tugged at his goatee and gazed contemplatively over the side of the boat. Then he smiled brightly and turned to Mike. "Helga," he announced with a note of melancholy. He closed his eyes and tapped impatiently on the tabletop as if doing so would refresh his memory. "Helga Eisenstein," he said triumphantly. He winked at Toby. "She was such a cute little thing."

"And do you remember how old you were when you kissed Helga Eisenstein, Mr. Horton?"

"Well, let me see now. We were sitting in the old milk cart and being pulled by the brown mare. And that mare died while I was still in school. I couldn't have been more than thirteen at the time."

"Case in point," Mike said. "You can't recall where you were a few weeks ago, yet you could probably describe in detail something that occurred over seventy years ago."

"I'd like to hear some of that detail, Great-gramps," Steve said with raised eyebrows. "And I'll bet Helga Eisenstein has some tales to tell, also."

Aaron wagged his finger back and forth. "Even in those days we didn't kiss and tell," he admonished with a gleam in his steely eye.

"Let's try another memory experiment. Are you game, Gramps?"

"Sure," John answered. "I'll teach you young pups something about memory. This old bone's still as sharp as a tack." He tapped his temple for emphasis.

"How's your history? I bet you studied the Gettysburg Address until you could recite it in your sleep. Let's hear you give it a try."

"I think I'm in trouble already," John said, laughing.

"C'mon, Gramps. That's easy," Toby coaxed.

John stood in his place and tried to mask his pleasant face with a severe frown. " 'Four score and seven years ago our fathers brought forth on this continent, a new nation, conceived in Liberty, and dedicated to the proposition that all men are created equal.' "

"Go on."

"There's more?" he joked.

"That's about as far as anybody ever gets with it," Mike admitted. "You did pretty well, actually. But remember, you had the speech drummed into your head until you knew it as well as you knew your own name. But when you didn't need it anymore, what happened?" He blew on his fingers and waved his hand. "Gone! Erased like a blackboard. Now let's try something else. Let me hear you sing 'Chickery Chick.' "

"Now there's one I haven't heard in forty-some years."

"Exactly. But do you remember how it goes?" Mike challenged.

"You rascal! You knew I'd remember it, didn't you?"

"What's 'Chickery Chick,' Gramps?" Tina asked.

He lifted the girl to his lap and pulled her close. "It's one of those old songs that they don't write 'em like anymore, honey."

"Sing it, Gramps. Sing it, please." she pleaded.

Clancy shook his head and clucked sympathetically. "And this is only the beginning, folks."

"Does it get even more bizarre than this?" Steve asked with mock alarm.

"When you volunteered to put yourself in the hands of Mad Mike Mancini, you surrendered your right to privacy and dignity," he said wryly. "You might as well sing it, John. He's not going to get off your case until you do."

Gramps flawlessly croaked his way through the convoluted lyrics and they all applauded. Gramps took a formal bow at the waist. "Anybody want to hear 'Mairzy Doats'?" he asked, buoyed by his success.

"How did we get into this anyway?" Steve wondered aloud.

"Toby compared our memory to a computer memory," Mike reminded him. "These are just a few examples of how they differ. The human memory is very selective. It spits out the craziest things when you least expect them. It recalls 'Chickery Chick' from forty years ago, but the next thing you know you'll forget the name of your best friend when you go to introduce him."

Their approving smiles told him they all knew the experience.

"But back to your question, Toby. I don't know what memory is—how it works—where it disappears to—why we remember some things and forget others. But whatever that thing is that we call memory, I'm betting that somehow it hitches a ride on a chromosome. And that's what I'm hoping you'll help me prove."

"What do you want us to do?" Steve asked.

Mike turned to Toby. "You won't have to do anything except sit and watch, Steve. Toby's going to be the star in this show. Do you know what hypnosis is, Toby?"

"Like the magicians use?"

"And like the medical profession uses," Mike corrected. "With the help of hypnosis, we're going to try to tap that memory gene that's bouncing around your old head bone."

"When?"

"Soon. I want to pull some things together first. I'll be back in touch in a few days."

"I want to help," Toby said.

Mike stood and shook the young boy's hand warmly. Then they let the subject fade as the sun did the same, and they drifted lazily, enjoying God's light show in the summer sky.

Chapter Eleven

◈◈◈◈◈◈◈◈◈

"JUST WHAT IS IT you want me to do, Mr. Mancini? I don't think I understand. After all, I'm a journalist, not a physician or a geneticist."

"That's precisely why I want you there to observe, Mr. MacBride. You've read the summary of my findings, and while it's not a certainty, you have to admit that the theory is plausible."

Mike felt a pleasant sense of claustrophobia in the cluttered little office cubicle. The wall to his left was draped ceiling to floor with book-laden shelves sagging under the weight of Grolier, Britannica, Webster, Roget, Tolstoy, Kesey, Ludlum, Keillor, Asimov, next to a collection of Garfield, Guindon, and Gary Larson cartoon books. A pair of mismatched shelves on the wall to his right boasted of athletic prowess with a disjointed display of bowling and charity golf trophies. It also provided a home for a few executive doodads of spinning chrome, a dented globe, and a rogues' gallery of photos of Teddy MacBride shaking hands and smiling with an impressive array of personae. Harmon Killebrew's boyish grin was matched by Teddy's own hero-worshiping expression in one of the earlier photos. Gerry Ford wrapped a comradely arm around Teddy's shoulders in another oldie. In a third shot, he stood casually beside a stern Anatoly Dobrynin at a Washington press party. Written in Cyrillic script in a cartoon balloon emanating from the Russian were the words, "If I defect, must I live in Minnesota?" And a pixyish Hubert Humphrey beamed with genuine pride at the young journalist who treated him so roughly yet so fairly.

Teddy MacBride's desk screamed of unharnessed energy with only an occasional maple-stained peek of wood finding its way through the jumble of papers, books, and office paraphernalia.

Teddy himself seemed to be a product of his own environment. Strutty as a fighting gamecock, he brought to mind a bag of laundry that needed folding. He was about the same age as Mike Mancini but his unkempt crop of wiry gray hair added ten years to his age, an asset that endowed him with an undeserved aura of maturity. Teddy MacBride had to report on the serious, the horrible, and the seedy, but he didn't have to let the worries of the world cost him a moment's sleep. And he didn't. He ran his fingers through the bristle of his head as he regarded the earnest teacher.

"I still don't understand. What do I know

about genes or hypnotism or bad dreams? I report on crime in the streets and corruption in the courts and in government. We have a staff science writer who would enjoy this type of assignment. She'd do it justice. Why don't you contact her?"

Mike tapped the sheaf of papers with a stubby index finger. "You've looked at these papers, Mr. MacBride. Please tell me honestly, what's the first thing you thought of when you read them?"

The newspaperman smiled shrewdly at the entrapping question. "Something between Ray Bradbury and *The Twilight Zone*," he answered honestly.

"And that's exactly my point. If it strikes you that way, just imagine how it will be perceived by others. I need you to help me present an unslanted viewpoint, a serious look at the implications if the theory proves valid. What I don't need is righteous ridicule and a lot of hocus-pocus sensationalism. I'm sure your science reporter is excellent but right now I'd feel more comfortable if you checked the story out yourself and then decided who if anyone should cover it." He shuffled nervously at the papers. "To tell you the truth, Mr. MacBride, I'm afraid of success. If my research progresses as I hope it will, then every crackpot in the country will want to exploit it and the next thing you know it'll be in all the supermarket newspapers." He shook his head sadly. "I can see the headlines now. 'Duluth Housewife Was Ghengis Khan's Mistress.' I want to avoid that, Mr. MacBride. I'd like you to help me."

Teddy MacBride had a nose for honesty as well as a nose for a good story and he saw both in the fervent high school teacher and the boy with the strange dreams. He leaned back in his spring-loaded chair and steepled his fingertips as he looked over the top of his half-rims. He breathed a deep sigh of defeat.

"Okay, Mike. I'll sit in at the session but I'm not making any promises. You said it yourself in your letter. I have a reputation for truth and diligence and the preservation of the American way of life and a lot of other very important bullshit, and I can't let my readers down. In a nutshell, Mike, if your theory proves to be true, it's top news and I'll treat it like the discovery of penicillin. If nothing happens then I'll slip quietly out of the house and that'll be the end of it. But if this *is* some kind of a hoax, then I'll do as big a hatchet job on it as the next guy. They're the ground rules if you still want to play."

Mike stood and extended his hand to close the pact. "I couldn't ask for more, Mr. MacBride."

"Teddy," the journalist corrected.

"Tonight then at seven o'clock at the Hortons'."

Teddy MacBride stood and came around the desk. He only came to Mike's shoulder but his handshake jangled the bones of Mike's hand.

"I'll see you tonight, Mike. Who knows, maybe someday I'll have a new celebrity's picture on my shelf. A hometown biology teacher even."

The evening sun was slanting into the western sky and it shot an angry barb of light across the surface of Big Bass Lake. An aluminum canoe hissed along the water's edge, sending a mother and her dozen ducklings scurrying to the safety of the cattails. The rattle of an ancient Toro echoed through the trees as a neighbor took advantage of the twilight coolness to trim his property. The soft smell of evening drifted lazily, encompassing all that it touched with its gentle caress.

Mike Mancini introduced the little man to the group sitting in lawn chairs by the water's edge. Steve Horton winced at the journalist's viselike grip.

"We're very pleased that you could come, Mr. MacBride. Toby's dreams seem to be getting as much attention lately as the Twins' five-game winning streak."

"We just want to make sure that any attention this study receives is the right kind," Mike cautioned. "That's why I asked Mr. MacBride to join us."

"Just joking, Mike," Steve said easily. "I understand why Mr. MacBride's here." He turned to the journalist with an approving smile. "I read that piece you did on the efficiency of the mayor's office. I bet it lit a fire under a couple of complacent butts."

"One of the few fringe benefits of the job," the journalist replied with a knowing grin. As he spoke, his swift gaze took in the full range of Hortons from the elfin girl to the goateed patriarch.

"Are you going to write a story about Toby?" Tina's question ended on an upnote as if such a thought were absurd.

"I might," Teddy said. "If I do can I mention your name, too?"

"Ooooh, would you?"

Already there was no question in his mind that this wasn't a put-on but then he hadn't expected deception. Still, the absence of a hoax was a long way from a story and he cautiously reserved judgment. He looked from face to face and finally stopped at Steve Horton.

"I hope that Mike warned you about the possible consequences of a little publicity."

"We talked about it," Steve replied. "I'm not worried. Anyway, it's Toby who will be the focus of any publicity. He's the one you ought to ask."

Teddy met the boy's steady gaze and arched his brows in silent question.

The boy's answer rang with the innocent simplicity of youth. "It's okay with me, Mr. Mac-Bride. Mr Mancini told us that we might learn things that will help save lives. Not too many kids get the chance to do that."

Teddy pulled a yellow lined notepad from his jacket pocket and scribbled a few notes. "You're right, Toby," he said without looking up. "Not many kids do."

"Well," Mike said expansively, "let's talk about how we're going to go about this." He stood in the middle of the grouped lawn chairs and squinted against the setting sun. "First I think a few words about hypnotism are in order."

Clancy slumped in his chair and began to snore loudly.

"And I promise not to lecture too long," Mike said in response to the doctor's implied accusation. "Like so many misunderstood ideas," he began, "hypnotism has gotten a bum rap. It delves up images of mad scientists in black capes waving coins in front of unwitting subjects. It's not like that at all. In fact, in 1958, the American Medical Association officially approved the use of hypnosis in the practice of medicine."

He glanced toward Clancy for confirmation but the doctor's eyes were tightly shut against the fiery sunset.

"The dictionary description of hypnosis tells us that it's a psychological state of altered awareness where the subject is extremely receptive to suggestions. The word comes from the Greek word *Hypnos*, which means sleep, but it really isn't sleep."

"Does that mean I'll be awake when you do it?" Toby seemed surprised.

"Well, it's not exactly awake either, Toby. It's really somewhere in between awake and asleep. Do you remember when Clancy tapped your knee with the little rubber hammer and your knee jerked?"

Toby nodded.

"Well, that reflex doesn't happen when you're asleep, but if you were under hypnosis, your knee would pop up the same as it does when you're wide awake. And there are other ways of measuring the activity of your brain. The brain waves of a person in a hypnotic state are more like those of someone who's awake."

Clancy erupted in a rumbling snore, a signal that the lecture was becoming tedious.

"Will I remember what happens?" Toby asked.

"Probably not," Mike admitted. "I'm going to try to put you in a deep trance and that's usually associated with total amnesia. There are three levels of hypnotism. In a light trance the subject appears to be asleep and he'll usually follow simple posthypnotic suggestions. It's fairly easy to achieve. That's what you usually see amateurs do at parties. It's quite harmless."

The topmost arc of the sun flamed through the trees across the lake before flickering out like a spent candle, and a lone speedboat roared through its fiery footprint. Mike removed his sunglasses and put them in his shirt pocket.

"The next level is called a medium trance. When this is achieved the subject can be induced to have simple hallucinations and he often won't remember what happened. But what we're after," he advised, "is the third and most complete stage, the deep trance. Not everyone is capable of reaching that stage but I have a feeling that Toby will be an excellent subject."

Steve formed the question that preyed on all of their minds. "Is there any danger?"

"Not at all," Mike assured him. "Today you'll regularly find hypnosis used in simple surgery and dentistry to achieve anesthesia. Someday it might be as common as novocaine. Psychiatrists use it to probe the minds of their patients for painful memories that might be the key to mental problems. I'll be using similar techniques tonight but for a different reason."

Clancy opened his eyes and sat forward in his chair. "What Mike says is true, Steve. Under proper supervision hypnosis is as safe as an aspirin. If I thought there was any risk, I would advise against it."

"I don't know what everybody's so scared of," Toby insisted. "I think it's going to be fun. I'm not worried."

"Then what are we waiting for?" Mike clapped his hands together and pushed himself from the lawn chair. With Steve leading the way, the Hortons, the doctor, the teacher, and the journalist filed across the back lawn and into the house.

Chapter Twelve

❖❖❖❖❖❖❖❖❖❖

THE HORTONS' FAMILY room was wainscoted with dark wood paneling that hinted at an air of casual opulence. Rustic boards of rough-sawn cedar added a touch of English Tudor. An eclectic display of sports memorabilia adorned the walls and a leather-padded bar dominated one corner. The shelves of the back bar were of the same cedar and they bristled with a variety of exotic liqueurs, traditional whiskeys, and a scattering of airline miniatures.

The group was spaced evenly about the room on the roomy sofa, an easy chair, and a few high-backed bar stools. A leather covered card table and two folding chairs were set up in the center of the room. Mike Mancini sat in one chair and Toby sat across from him. The teacher felt exhilarated, like he was poised on the brink of discovery, like Pasteur and Curie and hundreds of others before him must have felt when they finally put their theory to the test. A battery-run tape recorder hummed evenly between them.

The sun had dipped over the edge of the earth, leaving only a few ribbons of impossible pink violating the darkening sky, and it was this light that now bathed the family room. Teddy Mac-Bride's pencil hung poised over his pad in the muted dimness. The tension was palpable. No one spoke as Mike shuffled soundlessly through notes on the table in front of him. Toby's eyes glittered like hot coals but he felt a warming calm envelop him like a comforting blanket. Tina huddled against the safety of her mother's breast with none of the fidgeting that was her trade-mark. The doctor felt an unusual wave of excite-ment flush through his veins, the excitement of discovery. Jan noticed for the first time the loud ticking of the clock that hung behind the bar.

The teacher cleared his throat and looked into the unwavering eyes of Toby Horton. In a low-pitched voice that caressed the boy, he explained once again the purpose of the session. The others had to strain to hear the soft words.

"Toby, I'm going to put you into a deep sleep. I want you to relax. Sit back and get comfort-able. While you're resting, I'm going to ask you to remember some very old memories. I want you to tell me everything that you see when these pictures come to your mind."

He folded his hands in front of him and stared deeply into the boy's steely eyes. Toby showed neither fear nor excitement. Mike began without further preamble.

"Your eyelids are getting tired, Toby. They feel heavy and it's difficult for you to keep them open. Just relax and feel the heavy weight of your eye-lids. It feels like a curtain is closing in front of you. You're having trouble keeping your eyes open, Toby. They're starting to close and you can feel yourself falling into a sleep, a very deep sleep. Your hands feel heavy. Very heavy. You can't lift them. You feel like you're floating in space, comfortable and asleep, resting, your mind is free, you're in a peaceful sleep."

Toby sat perfectly still. His eyes were closed. Not squeezed shut but draped in heavy-lidded submission to Mike's simple suggestion. Outside, a neighbor's dog kicked up a ruckus over the trespass of an unrepentant squirrel that left the duped spaniel baying frantically at the base of a skeleton oak. But Toby acknowledged the interruption by ignoring its existence. He sat like a sleeping sphinx unfazed by the unwelcome disruption of its peaceful sandhill.

"Wow!" Tina's wide-eyed adulation expressed the sentiments of all the watchers. "Is he hypnotized?"

Mike made a gentle shushing gesture, finger to lip, and returned his attention to Toby. The back bar clock ticked loudly, a metronomic disruption of the dim silence.

"Your eyelids are still too heavy to open, Toby, but you'll be able to open them soon. When I tell you to open your eyes you'll be sitting in your family room. You'll be able to look around you and you'll see your family and Dr. Kendall and Mr. MacBride and me."

Toby sat rigid yet relaxed with not a flicker of recognition to indicate that he heard or understood the teacher's words. Darkness was falling rapidly and Mike motioned for Steve to turn the rheostat to take the dull edge from the dimness of the room. A boat droned somewhere on the still lake.

"When I tell you to open your eyes, Toby, I want you to look at the TV. And when I tell you, the TV will turn on and you'll be able to see movies of the stories that are in your mind." Mike had thought earlier that using a familiar device like the TV would make the boy more comfortable.

Tina glanced expectantly at the twenty-one-inch Panasonic.

"You can open your eyes now, Toby."

The boy's eyes opened with a snap, not the slow, cautious reaction of one awakening from a peaceful slumber but the startled response to a bone-jarring phone call. But his face was in repose and his eyes betrayed no emotion as he contemplated the blank TV screen.

The onlookers watched reverently, not knowing what to expect but feeling as if they were part of an unfolding drama. Only Toby seemed to be detached from the events, like a saintly figure in devout communication.

"Toby, I want you to look inside your mind now. I want you to go to the place where you store your memories. Can you see it, Toby?"

The boy stared vacantly, a confused expression clouding his usually alert face.

"Look on the TV screen, Toby. Can you see it there? Look around. Take your time, Toby."

Toby cocked his head and stared at the empty screen. He studied its lifeless rectangle with the intensity of a first-time visitor to the Louvre examining the surprisingly small Mona Lisa.

"Have you found the place, Toby?"

"Yes."

Mike felt his heart bang against the wall of his chest. "Describe it for me."

"It's a room. I keep the memories in a room. It's very big."

"How big, Toby?"

"It's too big."

"Could you throw a baseball the length of the room, Toby?"

"No. It's too big."

Tina curled into a small ball on the plaid sofa and tucked tightly into her mother's side. Steve shuddered involuntarily as he felt a cold wave roll across the room.

"What does it look like, Toby?"

"It's big. Like a church. But there's no altar. And the walls are high and covered with curtains. They're red. I think they're made of velvet. The floor's made of slate. Big pieces of gray slate. Everything looks so clean."

"What does it remind you of?"

"It's like a picture from a storybook. It's like Camelot in King Arthur's court."

"Is it pretty?"

"Yes. It's beautiful."

Toby spoke softly and Clancy had to lean forward in his chair to pick up the boy's words. Everyone watched in silent fascination. Teddy MacBride scribbled on his pad. The lake was silent and the last hint of radiance deserted the western sky. The Hortons' family room was cloaked in the dimness and drama of the teacher and the ten-year-old.

"What do you see inside the room, Toby?"

"It's almost empty except that there's a table right in the middle. There aren't any chairs or anything like that, just the table. It has a shiny wood top like our dining room table and it has fat wooden legs like a pool table."

"Is there anything on the table?"

"No."

"Where are the memories, Toby?"

"I'm not sure. I think they're nearby."

"Now listen carefully. I want you to search the room for them. Look everywhere. Somewhere inside that room the memories are hidden, some very old memories. Look for them, Toby. Find the old memories."

The ticking of the bar clock seemed to shake the room. For the first time since the session began, the youngster betrayed an emotion other than boredom. His delicate eyebrows arched and a quizzical frown shadowed the perfect little face. His head tilted slightly to one side and Jan recognized the gesture, a contemplative move, one that Toby often assumed as he pondered his ten-year-old's dilemmas. The clock cracked out each second like a rifle shot but no other sound spoiled the perfect silence.

"Have you found the memories, Toby?"

The room was charged with electric anticipation. The muscles of the teacher's face quivered as he anxiously clenched his jaws. He watched the boy closely. A trembling at the corners of Toby's lips hinted at a smile.

"Yes," Toby whispered.

The teacher's shoulders slumped in relief and he allowed himself a triumphant sigh, removed his glasses and roughly massaged the reddened bridge of his nose. He glanced toward Teddy MacBride and nodded, but the newspaperman didn't notice as he busily penciled notes on his lined pad. He noticed Aaron off by himself in a corner, his expression a mixture of impassivity and something else—fear? He caught Aaron's eye but the old man didn't acknowledge or respond. He turned back to Toby.

"Where are they, Toby? Where are the memories?"

"They're in a closet near the back of the room."

"Is the closet open?"

"Yes."

"Then take them out, Toby. Take the memories from the closet and put them on the table in the middle of the room."

"What's he doing?" Tina whispered. "I don't see the closet."

Jan hushed the little girl with a gentle gesture and hugged her tightly to her side.

"Are they on the table now, Toby?"

"Yes."

"What do they look like? Describe them for me?"

Toby stared wordlessly at the blank screen. Suddenly a spark of light danced in his eye. "Matchboxes. There's a stack of matchboxes in the center of the table. They have a rough black strip down both sides—the place where you strike the matches—and there's red and white writing on the tops. The inside is like a little drawer that pushes in and out. That's where the memories are."

Mike decided to take a giant step. Toby's trance was deep, as was his level of suggestibility. "Put yourself into the TV picture and try to take the top matchbox off the stack. Can you do that?"

Toby's expression didn't change. "Yes," he acknowledged.

In his own mind's eye, Mike formed the picture of the small boy stretching across a heavy oaken table and delicately lifting a tiny matchbox from atop a wavering pile. He wondered if

Toby's perception of the same activity took the same ten seconds—or was it only a millisecond?

"Do you have the matchbox, Toby?"

"I have it in my hand."

"What does it look like up close, Toby? Does it have writing on it?"

"Yes."

"Can you read it? What does the writing say?"

" 'Steven Horton.' It says 'Steven Horton.' That's my father's name. The matchbox says my father's name."

Steve felt a cold drip of perspiration run from his armpit and a clammy mask wrapped itself around his face. Mike Mancini sat motionless across from the boy with his head in his hands. He felt himself walking the razor's edge of a precipice. On one side was success, the verification of the theory that had monopolized his thoughts for so many years. But the other side was failure and the ridicule and depression that would accompany it. And the answer was—of all places—in a tiny matchbox in the hand and mind of a ten-year-old boy who sat so peacefully across the table from him. Mike Mancini took a deep breath and surveyed the expectant faces of his colleagues and the Horton family. They offered no help, only fearful curiosity.

He turned to Clancy with a wry smile and whispered. "Top of the ninth, three and two, bases loaded, tie game and two out. Time to throw the pitch."

The timbre of the teacher's voice was steady and resolute when he once again addressed the boy. "Are you still standing there at the table, Toby?"

"Yes."

"Good. Now I want you to open the matchbox that you have in your hand and let the memory spill out and fill the TV screen. After you've released the memory, I want you to come back into the family room and watch it on the TV. Can you do that?"

"Yes."

Reflexively, everyone's eyes flickered toward the empty screen, but only Toby could see the vivid colors that streaked its cool surface. Mike felt a moment of fear and uncertainty when he saw Toby's fists clench and his small body tighten as he watched the spectacle of his mind.

"What is it, Toby? Tell me what you see on the TV."

Beads of perspiration broke out across Toby's forehead in the cool room. A haunting expression glazed his eyes and his breathing quickened as he began his monotone narration. But the voice was distant. It was Toby's small voice but it rang with an unfamiliar resonance. It haunted.

"It's a street. My feet are in the street. I'm sitting on the curb and my feet are in the street. There's a car parked off to my left. It's new. Looks like a sixty-five Olds. There's a dog tied up across the street—ugly son of a bitch—it's tugging at its chain and yapping like hell."

"What's the dog barking at, Toby?"

"Pinky. The stupid dog goes crazy whenever it sees Pinky. Pinky's not bothering anybody. He's tied up to the tree behind me. That dog's just crazy."

Toby suddenly jerked upright in his chair. "Oh no, no, he's coming, he's coming. Let go—let go, you son of a bitch. He's killing Pinky. Oh, no!" A silver tear sparkled on his cheek. "The ugly son of a bitch killed Pinky. I'll kill him. I'll kill the son of a bitch. I'm gonna take my .22 and shoot him in the stomach and watch him squirm the way he made Pinky squirm."

Toby sat motionless on the chair but his face was frozen with sweat and grief. He stared vacantly at the blank TV screen and breathed heavily, almost hyperventilating, as he related the traumatic event.

"Close your eyes, Toby," Mike said quickly. "Close your eyes and turn off the TV. The picture's gone now. Tell me where you are."

Toby spoke once again in his little boy's voice as if nothing had happened. "I'm in the memory room."

"Where's the matchbox with your dad's name on it, Toby? Is it back on the pile?"

"No. The matchbox is gone. It's gone for good. It won't ever come back."

"How do you feel, Toby?"

"Very well, thank you."

"Good. I want you to do one more thing before we finish, Toby, then I'm going to wake you. Take the next matchbox from the top of the pile."

Mike waited another few seconds. He looked at the faces around him. They all showed concern and a hint of fear.

"Do you have it, Toby?"

"Yes."

"Look at the top of the matchbox. Does it have writing on it like the other one did?"

"Yes."

"What does that one say, Toby?"

The boy answered without hesitation. " 'John Horton.' This one has Gramps's name on it."

Mike Mancini put his face in his hands and

raised his eyes to the ceiling as if in prayer. He had to restrain himself from shouting "Eureka" as he heard the first evidence of his theory's viability from the lips of the innocent child. The newspaperman scribbled furiously. Clancy Kendall's mouth hung open in wonder. The Horton family all wore the glazed expression of one stunned by an unexpected blow. Mike stared thankfully at the boy's beautiful face.

"I'm going to wake you in a moment, Toby. When I snap my fingers I want you to wake up, but of course you won't remember any of what happened. But keep it handy because we'll be coming back to the memory room again. Do you understand?"

The boy nodded.

Mike Mancini snapped his fingers loudly. Tina jumped. Toby opened his eyes and stared curiously around the dim family room.

"When are we going to start?" he asked innocently.

Chapter Thirteen

◇◇◇◇◇◇◇◇◇◇◇◇

THE TWINS WERE back at their corner post on Hennepin Avenue. It was probably the best spot in the Twin Cities, a midwest miniversion of Times Square. Esau had already received half a dozen replies to the pamphlets. Three of them expressed legitimate interest in joining the earthly army, another asked for money, one had a clipped-out crotch from a *Playboy* centerfold, and the most recent was a number-ten envelope stuffed with dried cow dung. On balance, he considered it a success. He dropped the boys off and headed back to the Saint Paul side of the Mississippi.

Esau parked the pickup by a meter. It was free parking after six so he felt no moral obligation to feed it. He was close to the State Capitol, not too many blocks from where he met Candy. Esau thought about that night occasionally—and the important event that preceded it. It was the day God called out to him, made him captain of His army and gave new meaning to his life. Esau needed that. Having the farm sold out from under him had thrown a gloom-filled shadow over his life. The labors of five generations of Manleys slipped through his gnarled fingers like dust bowl topsoil, and he could do nothing but watch helplessly from the sidelines while the auctioneer sold piece by piece his life's possessions to the highest bidder. His head hurt whenever he thought about it. But soon after, God had spoken to him and Esau knew that it was all part of His plan. He had to grieve so that later he could rejoice.

The plan!

He could handle it. He even smiled behind his beard when he thought of the trick that he and God had pulled on the state trooper on Highway 35. The stupid cop thought Esau had been drinking. How wrong could he be? That was God's idea. He didn't want the world to know about Esau's appointment. Not yet. That was okay with Esau. He could handle that. He could live with the anonymity. He always had.

Occasionally, the night with Candy stabbed through his thoughts. Something kept the memory from being as joyful as it should be. But why was that? It was the first blow struck in His name, but for some reason it was an imperfect memory. Esau wondered about it whenever he thought about that evening, but he didn't let it prey too deeply. Everything was part of the plan and he found comfort in that.

Esau felt sickened as he looked at the scene surrounding him. Seedy! That's the word that came to mind. The neighborhood itself wasn't run down. It was the tenants who made it seedy, the filth peddlers who set up shop there.

Peep Show flashed in angry red neon. Esau wondered what a peep show was, and he pictured a row of derelicts lined up in front of a row of keyholes.

"How 'bout a quarter, mister? Can you help somebody down on his luck?"

Esau jerked reflexively. The fellow had come up from behind and stood at his elbow. His eyes pleaded and his hand was poised expectantly. He could stand a haircut and a bath. He didn't look much older than the twins.

"If you want to improve your luck, then go out and find a job," Esau spat.

"Ain't much honest work around this town for a good farmer," the boy answered earnestly. He was more apologetic than angry.

How Esau understood that plight. His face

softened and he reached in his jeans and pulled out a wrinkled dollar. He gave it to the young man along with a pamphlet. "Have faith in the Lord and ye shall be saved," Esau advised him.

"God bless you, sir," the boy called after him but Esau was already on the way down the block.

"High School Hot Pants—double—double—double—Teen Temptations."

The marquee blazed in the night like a faulted ruby in a string of tasteless gems. The sidewalk was bathed in its red tint. It reminded Esau of the outskirts of hell. He felt dirty, as if its aura would coat him with indelible grime. The box office was a glass octagon, its sides ringed by steel bars. A narrow slot allowed for the passage of money and tickets. The woman inside looked like everybody's grandmother. Esau was embarrassed to approach her. He shuffled nervously to the window and slid five dollars through the slot.

"You'll have to do better than that, honey."

He looked at the price taped to the glass and had to choke back his anger. People paid more than the price of a meal to disobey God's will. An abomination. And he didn't like speaking to these people. Fortune-tellers, harlots, beggars, porn peddlers. It made them too real. It covered them with hair and skin and made them breathe the same air that kept him alive. Esau found it easier to view evil from a comfortable distance. Then he remembered that Christ Himself went face to face with the devil. He could certainly do no less. He slid another bill through the slot and the woman pushed back some change. She wore a gold cross around her neck and Esau felt like smashing the glass and ripping it from her throat.

She looked up and caught his angry glare. "Something wrong, honey?"

Wordlessly, he snatched the ticket and stalked into the theater. The lobby was dim and smelled like wet wool. The word *seedy* came back to him. A poster was mounted on the wall to his left, a slave trader with a whip standing over a trussed-up black girl. She was naked and screaming. A glass door had once covered the display but only the metal frame remained. A candy machine stood alongside the poster, but instead of dispensing peanut chews and jujubes this one dropped sex aids and photographs into the tray. The dull ache returned to caress his chest with angry fingers. He squeezed the bottle in his pocket.

Esau hadn't been inside a movie theater for years, not since taking Hattie and the twins to see *Sound of Music*, but the boys had fussed and they had to leave early. He looked around for an usher but the lobby was deserted.

The flicker from the screen was enough to light Esau's way down the side aisle. There were only a handful of people inside. They all appeared to be men, spread randomly around the theater. Most were alone but a few were paired up for reasons Esau couldn't understand. He walked to the front, in the far right corner of the theater. A deep voice said something and another giggled as he passed but he didn't look around. He selected the corner seat and settled into it. The bottle thunked against the armrest and he looked guiltily around. He finally turned to the screen and gasped audibly. He quickly looked away.

A door marked Employees Only was off to the right where the wall jutted in before dropping away into the orchestra pit. It appeared to be open a crack. Because the wall was facing away from the screen, it was in deep shadows. He glanced around but no one was looking his way. The dull light from the screen lit the faces in a ghostly glow as they gazed zombielike at the unfolding abomination. A slurping sound boomed from the speakers. Esau looked up and was horrified. He had heard about the practice but didn't believe that it occurred in real life, thought it was one of those things that was invented for dirty jokes. He turned away. The sound was loud, too loud for the small theater, but that would work in Esau's favor. The slurp was interrupted by a series of moans and a loud cry and Esau chose the moment to slide low in his seat. His arms and legs bent into impossible positions, but he stayed down until the moans and cries reached a crescendo, then he slid to the floor and inched to the nearby door. It creaked rustily as he pushed it open, but the noise was smothered by a man's grunts amplified to seventy decibels.

The chamber behind the door wasn't intended as a room. It was more like a corridor, long and narrow, except that it towered to the roof of the theater, thirty feet above Esau's head. It bent to the left after about twenty feet and a faint glow from a red lamp high on a wall provided enough light to move without walking into the walls. Esau reached out carefully and touched a stack of cartons leaning against the right-hand wall. Then he touched the wall to the left. He made his way carefully down the corridor, touching and stepping, touching and stepping, until he came to the break.

Esau arrived in a storeroom, a cemetery of

billboards and posters. Another red light shone dully. This one read Exit and burned above a metal door on the far wall. An American flag on a tall pole with a gold eagle on top leaned disrespectfully in the corner. Esau went to the door. It had a waist-high push bar. He leaned against it and smelled the night air even before he realize that it opened into the parking lot behind the theater. He poked his head outside. The lot was full of cars. Some teenagers huddled in the shadows at the farthest corner of the lot. They seemed to be passing something between themselves but Esau couldn't make it out. They didn't see him. He shut the door softly and looked around the storeroom.

The building was old, prewar, built when such places looked forward to a century of service. Its architect would shudder in his coffin to see its current state.

The thick plaster and lath walls would be a deterrent to Esau's plans but lumber and framing from long-forgotten sets littered the room and piles of mildewed curtains were crammed into cardboard cartons. The wood and the boxes would serve his purpose quite well.

Esau took the bottle from his jacket pocket. It once held a pint of Jack Daniels and Esau smiled at the irony. It was finally being put to good use. He unscrewed the cap and sniffed at the neck. He liked the smell of kerosene. It was clean. It didn't gag his throat like the heavy fumes of gasoline.

The old man on the floor was having trouble focusing. His head ached and his ears buzzed and at first he blamed the booze for his hallucinations. It had happened before. He lay sprawled in a crumpled heap, indistinguishable from the pile of old curtains that he used for a bed. In the dimness he thought he saw an awesome figure inching past, tall and gangly like a praying mantis on tiptoes. He shook his head to clear his vision but the figure remained. Then he heard the dull click of the door and smelled the fresh evening air and he knew it was real. He curled tightly into the curtain, an aging chameleon blending with its environment. But he could still watch the movements of the visitor through half-opened eyes.

Esau selected the most likely spot, a row of two-by-fours leaning against an inside wall next to a stack of cartons containing posters and old programs. He stretched to his full height and poured the kerosene against the stack. It ran down the sides of seven cartons and splashed into a puddle around the two-by-fours. He took a wooden pencil from his shirt pocket and punched a hole in the side of the bottom box. Then, from the same pocket, he took a light blue birthday-cake candle and forced it into the hole. It stuck out an inch and a half.

Perfect.

The old man watched in fascination. His eyes were used to the dimness of the murky store-room and he saw the activity quite clearly. But he was afraid to do anything about it. Years of alcohol and fitful sleep in cold doorways had left his body weak and his mind nearly useless. He felt the stirrings of panic. He began to feel nauseous and was afraid he would barf up a pint of Jack Daniels.

Esau rose and put the empty bottle in his pocket. He looked around one last time before setting God's plan into motion. The scratch of the wooden kitchen match sounded to the old man like a pistol shot and the blaze of its flame lit the storeroom like a flashbulb. Esau's eyes were glued to the tip and the explosion of flame shrank his pupils to fly specks. He was staring directly at the old man but all he saw was a phosphorous flash. Careful not to come too close to the kerosene, Esau touched the match end to the stringy wick of the candle. He watched for only a second, making sure it was lit before making for the door.

Chapter Fourteen

"WELL, WHAT do you make of it?" Mike Mancini asked as they got themselves settled.

The teacher, the journalist, and the doctor were squeezed into the Leatherette booth at the Perkins Pancake House. Except to arrange the morning meeting, few words had been spoken since the dramatic events of the previous evening. Toby and Tina had padded off to bed without complaint, and the rest of the group, numbed by Toby's revelation, broke up in thoughtful silence, drifting apart like witnesses to a holy event, not wishing to despoil its sanctity with senseless prattle.

"I'm a believer," Clancy admitted. "Not that I

ever thought it was a hoax. It's just easier to believe once you've witnessed it firsthand."

"What do you think, Teddy?" Mike pressed.

"About the same as Dr. Kendall here. I'm sure that what I saw last night was spontaneous. I don't question that at all. And it appears that everything Toby related under hypnosis supports your theory. But it's not enough to go too far out on a limb for. Not yet at least."

"Of course it isn't," Mike agreed. "Not yet. It's only the first step. But I hope now you understand my reason for wanting you to cover it. The thing is ripe for exploitation and abuse. I just want to make sure that it doesn't end up in the supermarket newspapers. It's just too important to be trivialized like that."

A sleepy-eyed waitress came by to refill their coffee and take their orders. They waited for her to shuffle off before resuming their discussion.

"You must be very pleased with the way things went last night," MacBride said by way of congratulations.

"It was perfect," Mike agreed. "Everything ties in exactly with the theory that memory's transferred genetically, and I couldn't ask for a more responsive subject than Toby."

"Didn't you suspect that all along?" Clancy asked.

"Yes, I did. The way you described how he slipped in and out of his self-induced trances indicated he'd be a good subject."

"You sure impressed the hell out of me," Teddy said. "Where did you learn hypnosis?"

"Self-taught with a little help from the psychology department at the university. It's not really difficult, especially with such a willing subject."

"Now that you have our undivided attention, what's the next step? Or did you just bring us here to buy breakfast?" the newspaperman chided.

"I thought this would give us a chance to debrief," Mike said. "And to plan for tonight. I'd like to take a peek into the next matchbox. I checked with Steve early this morning, got him out of bed actually, and he gave the green light for another session tonight. He's a little concerned but I assured him there's nothing to worry about. And Toby's none the worse for the wear. He's ready to go."

"Is there any danger whatsoever?" the journalist asked. Now that he was committed he seemed a little worried. "That's one of the first things readers will jump on if anything goes wrong. They love to rake over the coals anybody who disturbs their comfortable set of beliefs, and they'll be looking for an excuse to crucify the bunch of us."

"There's no history of hypnosis being harmful when properly used," Mike responded simply.

"But neither is there any history of it being used to prove a theory such as yours," Teddy MacBride cautioned. "How did you describe it? The genetic—"

"Transference of memory." Mike completed the phrase for him. "And after tonight, we should have a better idea whether or not it's fact or fancy."

*   *   *

Everyone sat in the same location as they had the night before, either to bring good luck or as if the experiment would be jeopardized by any deviation. Toby had slept well and had gone the entire day without a headache. That hadn't happened in quite a while. Mike made a note of it as did Teddy MacBride. The boy remembered nothing of the previous evening's revelation and, at Mike's request, nobody shared the results with him. Mike wanted a clean slate.

"Look at my hand as I raise it up and down, Toby. It's difficult to do because your eyelids are so heavy. They're getting so heavy that you can't even keep your eyes open any longer. Your eyes are closing and you're getting so sleepy. You can't raise your hand, can you, Toby? That's because you're asleep, Toby. You're in a deep, deep sleep."

Mike marveled at the boy's susceptibility to hypnosis. They were starting earlier in the evening, around eight o'clock, and the dimness that had haunted the room the previous night was replaced by a flood of blazing rays from the setting sun. Toby was dressed in a Twins T-shirt and a pair of ragged cutoffs, a latter-day Huck Finn, not looking anything like the subject of a psychic experiment.

"Toby, I want you to open your eyes now and look at the TV screen. I want you to turn on the TV and tune in the memory room again. I want you to return to the place where you found the memories last night."

A glimmer of recognition brushed across the boy's face as his eyes locked on the lifeless screen.

"What does the room look like, Toby? Is it the same as it was last night?"

"Almost," he answered. "The pile of matchboxes is still in the center of the table except that there's one sitting all by itself near the edge."

Mike glanced knowingly at John Horton, and Gramps responded with a hesitant smile and a palms-up shrug that said "Might as well get it over with."

"Are you in the memory room, Toby?"

"No. I'm watching it."

"Go into the room. Put yourself next to the table like you did last night, Toby." Mike waited a few seconds. "Now pick up the loose match-box. Is the writing still there?"

"Yes. The writing says 'John Horton.' "

"It's time to open the box, Toby. Open the matchbox and step out of the picture. Let the contents of the matchbox fill the TV screen. Sit back and relax and tell me what you see."

The tape recorder whirred silently and the clock ticked loudly as the boy stared at the gray screen. Tina leaned forward on the sofa, not exhibiting any of the apprehension of the previous evening. Gramps sat impassively with his hands folded on his lap but his twirling thumbs betrayed his poorly concealed anxiety.

"It's dirty."

Gramps's eyebrows rose at Toby's opening line.

"It's a dirty place and it's hot as hell. There are men sitting around me eating out of mess kits. It's not the usual C rations. It's some kind of stew. McCarter shot something in the bush and dressed it down for stew but he wouldn't tell us what he killed. He told us we'd have to eat it and guess. Smitty guessed it was dog and I said snake but McCarter just smiled and shook his head. If you ask me it tastes like moose shit."

Tina raised her eyebrows in alarm. Gramps didn't talk like that. Toby stopped for a moment as if to gather his thoughts. Clancy glanced at John and was afraid the man was going to be sick. The blood had drained from his face and a film of perspiration broke out on his forehead.

"Are you okay?" Clancy whispered across the room.

John waved off the doctor's concern with a trembling hand. Then they all looked back to Toby, who sat and stared at the screen in stone-faced silence.

"Where are you?" Mike asked gently.

"That shitty little island," came the reply.

"What's its name?"

Clancy was still watching John Horton and saw his lips silently form the word as Toby spoke it aloud.

"Guadalcanal."

"And who are you?"

"Corporal Horton. Corporal John Horton of the 25th Division. The Lightning Division," he added proudly.

"What's happening now, Corporal?"

"Just a little grab ass. We flushed a handful of Japs out'a the woods a couple hours ago, but they must have given us the slip. So McCarter decided to kill some time and give us one of his special treats. Tastes a little like the south end of a north-bound skunk."

The remark brought smiles to the group and lightened the mood. Teddy MacBride smiled across at John but froze when he saw the look of terror spreading across the man's face.

"Watch out!"

Gramps's shout brought Clancy to his feet and

the rest jumped in fright. The man dove headlong from his chair and sprawled across the
room, crashing into the card table and sending
the tape recorder spinning across the room before it shattered against the brick fireplace. He
landed on his stomach and curled into a tight
ball, oblivious to the shocked stares of the others. Clancy rushed to his side. Then he heard the
brittle cry that bellowed from the frail boy.

"It's a Jap grenade. Watch out!" A tear rolled
over Toby's downy cheek and splashed on his
bare leg.

"Turn off the TV, Toby. Do it now." Mike ordered.

The boy stared straight ahead, at Mike and
through him, ignoring the sobbing man who
lay at his feet. Steve knelt next to his father
and gently gripped the man's quaking shoulders.

"Pop, it's okay. Pop, listen to me. Everything's
gonna be okay."

With Clancy's help, Steve lifted John Horton
to his feet and returned him to his seat.

"What happened? What's going on?" John
was completely disoriented as he surveyed
the tangled scene. The card table lay upside
down across the room with one leg buckled.
The tape recorder was in several pieces on
the brick hearth. Except for Toby who stared
straight ahead, all eyes in the room were riv-
eted on John Horton. He didn't know what to
make of it. Then the memory came flooding
back.

"Oh, my God. It was Guadalcanal all over
again, wasn't it? It was Guadalcanal and that
Jap grenade." John Horton put his head in his

hands and rubbed his forehead roughly as if to exorcise the memory.

"Are you all right now, Mr. Horton?" Clancy knelt alongside him and automatically counted the beats as he held the man's wrist between his sensitive fingers.

"Yes, I'm okay, Doctor. It's just something that I've always tried to forget."

Steve reached down and took his father's hand. He brimmed with love and pride. "You always told us the Silver Star in your dresser was for saving someone's life, but you would never tell us how you did it. You never told us you jumped on a live grenade."

"It was a dud," John corrected. "Anyway, it was no big deal. The whole thing happened before I had a chance to think about it. Anybody would have done it. I must have been crazy," he said with a grim smile. "How's the boy?"

"He's fine," Mike answered. "Let's get this place organized before we bring him around."

Steve flipped the card table onto its three good legs and propped the fourth one on a book to keep it from wobbling. Clancy took the broken tape recorder from the hearth and pushed the pieces beneath the couch. Everyone tried to erase the shock from their expressions as Mike readied himself to resume. Tina shook in fright but was comforted by Jan's loving caress.

"Where are you now, Toby?"

"I'm back in the memory room."

"And where is John Horton's matchbox?"

"It's gone."

"How many matchboxes are left, Toby? Can you count them?"

"Ten. There are ten boxes left."

"Can you reach the top box, Toby?"

"Yes."

Mike looked toward Steve Horton and waited. Steve turned to Jan and she nodded imperceptibly.

"Okay, Mike," the boy's father said uncertainly.

"Take it down, Toby. Take it and read the name on top of the box." Mike waited but the boy didn't respond. "Can you read it, Toby? Read the name on top of the box."

"It says 'Aaron,' " he said stonily.

Everyone's eyes shifted to Greatgramps, who sat stiffly in the corner of the room. He stared at the floor. Mike thought he looked ten years older than he had at the start of the session.

"It says 'Aaron,' " Toby repeated. " 'Aaron Horowitz.' "

Chapter Fifteen

❖❖❖❖❖❖❖❖❖❖

Saint Paul Pioneer Press and Dispatch
Wednesday, June 18, 1986

MacBRIDE'S MUMBLINGS

I've had a truly marvelous week. Big deal, you say. Who gives a fig? Well, one of the fringies of writing a weekly column is that I'm allowed to indulge myself on occasion, and I'm going to tell you about my good fortune whether you like it or not. If you don't like it, then read the funnies, airhead.

Do you want to know what made my week so great? No? I'll tell you anyway. Two things made my week great; first, I met some very nice people, and second, I got a lead on what could become a very large story. The whole thing started with a letter and a telephone call from a biology teacher from Kellogg High School in Roseville. The guy wanted to talk about genes and chromosomes and dreams and somebody's pet rabbit named Pinky that had been dead for almost a quarter of a century. Another typical whacko citizen with a story that was burning to be told. Anyway, that's how I met Mike Mancini, a man with a curious mission.

Mike, as it turns out, has a theory that's burning to be proved. Remember how your Aunt Hilda used to tell you that you had your mother's complexion and your father's nose and your Uncle

Elmer's jug ears? Well, Mike Mancini goes a step further. He's willing to bet that you also have your grandfather's memories—his big nose, his freckles, his curly red hair along with the thoughts that puckered his freckled brow a century ago. Heavy stuff, what? And the craziest part about it all is that he has me half believing this stuff. You see, this teacher's a pretty persuasive guy. Not only did he talk me into watching a little exhibition of hypnosis, he also conned a reputable member of the medical community, one Clancy Kendall, M.D., to observe the proceedings with me.

Clancy, by the way, is another nice person whom I met last week. That makes two nice people so far, well above average, but wait, I'm not through yet. Mike, the biology teacher from Roseville, and Clancy, the reputable (is there any other kind?) medic from Saint Paul, introduced me to the family Horton, also of Roseville. This gathering turned out to include a veritable plethora of nice personae, all of them unaccountably constructed in the image and likeness of one another. Try to imagine a great-grandfather, a grandfather, a father, and a son who, except for some snow-white hair and a sprinkling of wrinkles, could be quadruplets, peas from the same pod, birds of the same feather, chips off the old block, and so on. According to biology teacher Mancini such an unlikely event is a zillion-to-one shot, genetically speaking, that is. Add to that breakdown of the law of averages the fact that the youngest chip from the block had a strange recurring dream and you have the stuff that stimulates the curious juices of biology teachers from Roseville.

For reasons too deep to go into, given the well-below-average IQ of my faithful readers, this bio teacher thinks that Toby Horton, the ten-year-old with the strange dreams, might possess the key to unlocking his favorite theory. And that's where the hypnotism comes in. I sat in the comfortable home of the family Horton for two consecutive nights (one of them being mixed doubles bowling night) and watched in wonder as Mike Mancini mesmerized the lad into revealing that he was in a roomful of memories, each one tucked neatly away inside a little matchbox. At Mike's suggestion, Toby opened two of the matchboxes and watched as the memories unfolded on the blank TV screen, blank, that is, to me and the rest of the uninitiated.

By this time, those of my readers with an attention span beyond that of a turnip, approximately fifteen percent of you, are rising as one from your sweaty recliners, spilling cracker crumbs all over the floor, and shouting, "Hoax, charlatan, imposter, a pox be upon you." And, as usual, you would be wrong. I'm not quite ready to lay my dubious but hard-won integrity on the line and say without fear of contradiction that Mad Mike Mancini's improbable theory passes muster, but I will bet my autographed picture of Prince that Toby Horton and his family are on the level.

So far Toby has watched the flickering images of two painful memories, memories of which he had no previous knowledge. The first was the tragic demise of Pinky, the aforementioned little white rabbit that belonged to Steve Horton, Toby's dad. Said rabbit gnawed its last crunchy carrot twenty-five years ago before it met its gruesome fate in the jaws of a depraved canine. The second memory was a heretofore untold tale of bravery that occurred in the South Pacific during World War II.

Toby retold the true story with sufficient detail to cause his startled grandfather, John Horton, to relive the agonizing episode.

According to Toby, there are many more matchboxes where those two came from. So, dear reader, yours truly has been enlisted in the effort to either prove conclusively or to debunk the wild theory of the impetuous bio teacher from Roseville. Do we each have within us some of the stuff of the past? I'll let your own turbid imaginations mull that one over as you sip your beer and munch your Fritos in front of a *Three's Company* rerun. Don't forget to tune in next week to the second installment. Frivolity aside, methinks that we might be on the threshold of discovery. And to think that it's happening right here in River City.

Chapter Sixteen

◇◇◇◇◇◇◇◇◇◇◇

TEDDY MACBRIDE SLOUCHED in his sway-backed chair amid the clutter that he generously described as his files. Most of the papers and notes were the same ones that graced the desk a week earlier when Mike Mancini paid his visit but, since then, they had been strewn about into new piles or positions. Teddy MacBride didn't put or place things—he strewed them. He chewed absently at the crumbly eraser of the yellow number 2 pencil, the point of which he had earlier used to pick at an itch deep within his auditory canal.

"Concentrate, Fleabrain," he mumbled absently to himself. He was trying unsuccessfully to put the final touches to the outline for his weekly Minnesota Public Television show, but his thoughts were no more focused than his desktop.

Teddy MacBride's greatest strengths were also his most annoying flaws.

Curiosity!

Curiosity and instinct!

Curiosity, instinct, and impulse!

These were the traits that separated the Teddy MacBrides of the industry from the drones who plugged away uninspiredly at the typewriters perched on top of their tidy desks. But these same creative gifts became organizational albatrosses when it was time to mold the chunks of ideas into something recognizable.

Teddy's weekly TV show was the basic Sunday morning public television *Issues and Commentary* format where the worldly but genial host sits in a sagelike posture of relaxation amid the rustic props of the ersatz den and babbles idiotically with the local intelligentsia about earth-shattering issues of the day; things like who does the dishes in two-worker families or gay clergy. But Teddy's show was more than a few cuts above the standard fare of the genre and it was surprisingly popular due to his—well, due to his curiosity, instinct, and impulse.

Teddy first gained local prominence, along with a reputation for no-nonsense wisdom, during a live interview with the governor. The governor postured theatrically and orated eloquently about his dramatic new proposal to revolutionize the state's already incomprehensible tax structure. Teddy listened attentively, head cocked to one side, brow appropriately furrowed as the red-eyed camera framed the two men within its unforgiving stare. As the governor rambled on, small crinkles began to radiate at the corners of Teddy's bright eyes and a barely perceptible twitch started to tug at his tightly compressed lips.

This man is certifiable, Teddy thought as the governor elucidated another of his nonsensical schemes. And as he thought these thoughts, he brought a concealing hand to his mouth, fighting a losing battle against the overwhelming urge to explode in laughter.

Why, he wondered, do these things always happen to me? Am I so damn immature that I still giggle like a schoolboy? But there he was, a fledgling host in front of a stern Sunday morning audience, interviewing the state's chief executive and about to erupt in uncontrollable laughter.

An experienced, big-bucks cameraman might have anticipated what was about to happen and pulled a close-up on the governor's powdered face. Or, giving the cameraman the benefit of the doubt, perhaps he *did* anticipate what was to follow.

Teddy tried to block his mind but nothing seemed to work. The most alert of his viewers could have seen the eye crinkles deepen and the mouth twitches increase their frequency. Then he tried to think of something serious, or depressing, or downright morbid. He finally settled on his mother's funeral.

While the governor droned on monotonously, Teddy pictured the gunmetal casket, lid tightly closed, housing the last earthly remains of his beloved mother. It rested on its wheeled dolly at the foot of the steps leading to the dramatic stone altar where the satin-draped priest stood, back to the congregation, exhorting a benevolent God to accept this sinful servant into His kingdom.

It was beginning to work. The twitching ceased and the mischievous spark deserted Teddy's eye. A mask of solemnity shrouded his impish face. Then the priestly image made a sweeping sign of the cross, intoned a crystal-shattering *dominus vobiscum*, and spun slowly around to face the grieving friends and family of Mary Ellen Mac-Bride.

And there stood the governor in a wide-lapeled suit of pink and green plaid, twirling a yo-yo and grinning idiotically.

Theodore Francis Xavier MacBride came apart at his loosely sewn seams—on camera—in front of his new audience of Sunday-morning watchers—in front of his friends, family, and employer. Tears streamed unchecked down his cheeks as he tried unsuccessfully to cap the gusher of laughter, and the probing red eye of the camera caught every irreverent convulsion.

The governor froze in mid-oration and glared incredulously. "Mr. MacBride, I fail to see anything humorous about the state's financial situation."

The camera finally responded and pulled in tightly to the angry chief executive. His normally vapid stare burned with indignation. But the protest was lost in the growing hysteria taking place on both sides of the camera. The soundman had to run from the studio and fell to the floor in the corridor, tightly holding his sides to still the racking sobs. The show's producer stared in horror but couldn't check her own infectious giggles. The governor's head bobbed up and down like a bouncing beach ball on thousands of TV screens in rhythm with the cameraman's quaking body.

Teddy finally recovered sufficiently to wipe the tears from his eyes with the back of his hand and, through sheer force of will, to bring his rebellious emotions to a semblance of self-control. "Governor," he sputtered, "no disrespect intended, but that is without a doubt the most inane proposal I've heard from your office in over a week."

The governor turned a flaming crimson and the cameraman caught the changing of every colorful shade. The chief executive harrumphed indignantly, rose from his chair, and stalked from the studio, tripping on a cable and knocking a lighting prop to the floor in his haste.

MacBride's Sunday Mumblings became an overnight sensation and Teddy himself earned the fitting reputation of a "cut 'em down to size" investigative reporter. The coming Sunday's offering would present the views of the community's homosexual community. Teddy refused to call them gay. But his heart wasn't in Sunday's show. It wasn't just the homosexual thing. It was really his preoccupation with Toby Horton's visions and Mike Mancini's theory. He slammed the pencil to the desktop and ran his stubby fingers through the wiry crop of hair.

"Sheila," he called to his assistant. "Has the mail come in from Wednesday's column yet?"

Reader opinion usually arrived two days after a column appeared, and Teddy was curious to feel the public pulse about the family Horton. Sheila whisked efficiently into his office and frowned instinctively at the clutter. She wore her blue-white hair short and stylish and her trim figure belied her sixty-plus years.

Teddy leered lecherously. "God, if you were only twenty years younger you'd think you fell into a pool of piranhas."

"Teddybear, you couldn't handle me if I was twenty years older. Clean up this mess and make some room."

Teddy swept a pile of papers aside and Sheila dropped the stack of mail into the clearing. "From the looks of this batch I'd guess that you've piqued the public's interest. It might not be a bad idea for one of the Sunday shows."

"As always you're reading my mind, dear heart. What're the chances of cutting out the fruits and nuts this week?"

"Teddy MacBride, you know you shouldn't talk that way," she scolded. "But I'll get the head cashew on the phone and feel him out—figuratively speaking, that is."

Teddy chuckled as Sheila swept from the office with a coy wiggle of her girlish hips.

There were about thirty letters, twice the usual number, and Sheila had opened and flattened them into a neat stack. It was Friday, two days after the column, and most of the letters referred to Teddy's experience with the Hortons, although there were some late letters about last Sunday's TV show with the chief of police. Sheila had a paperclip around the small stack. Teddy flipped the short stack to one side of his desk and took the top letter from the larger pile.

Dear Teddy,

    I knew it was too good to last. You finally got as kookoo as the people who read your column. Memories in genes— come on! Next thing you know the kid will tell you that he used to be Alexander the Great—and you'll probably believe him. Stick to governor bashing. It made you what you are today.

Purvis Shea

Teddy shoved aside a larger clearing and put the letter on the left side. Compliments and agreeable letters went to the right. Complaints and disagreements went to the left. Teddy's idea of statistical research was to see which stack looked higher at the end of the morning, which didn't matter anyway since he wouldn't allow the rabble to change his mind on an issue.

The next letter was neatly printed on pale blue stationery with tiny flowers adorning the corners.

Dear Mr. MacBride:

    I read your column in Wednesday's *Dispatch* and I want to tell you that I think your theory of memory inheritance is fascinating, so fascinating that I would like to meet with you to discuss the possibilities of collaborating on a book about Toby Horton's experiences. The attached sheet contains my professional credentials. I'll be contacting you in a few days to discuss a business proposition.

Sincerely,
Rebecca Smith-Lowry

Teddy didn't bother to read the second sheet. He crumpled the papers into a baseball-sized wad and launched a one-handed set shot toward the wastebasket in the corner. He hit the wall about a foot too high and the projectile bounced across the floor, joining a number of other wads which had suffered similar fates.

Teddy zipped through the letters and directed them to the appropriate piles. He had a hard core of regular readers who wrote religiously, a collection of bored retirees, a few lonely widows, and at least one would-be philosopher who could be counted on to take the opposite stance from Teddy no matter what the issue. Many of his readers were also steady contributors to the paper's Letters to the Editor.

The column about Toby, though not especially controversial, struck a popular chord among his readers. For the most part, the letters were neither critical nor laudatory. Instead, they carried a uniform tone of interest and curiosity, the same elements that had attracted Teddy in the first place. And there was a thread of sympathy, a kindred-spirit kind of statement that tried to say, "Yeah, I know what you mean. Something like that happened to me once."

The next letter was printed in a childlike scrawl on yellow notepad paper.

Mister MacBride,

Your column about the boy who has the strange dreams causes me great concern. When man meddles with visions from the past, how far can he be from pretending to be able to see into the future? And when that happens, he is doing the devil's own work like the fortune-tellers and other blasphemers. Stop this godless quest before an innocent boy becomes an instrument of Satan and calls down the wrath of His earthly army.

His Appointed Captain

A new whacko in town, Teddy thought. Such letters comprised a predictable percentage of his mail, but their writers were all part of his public so their vote counted along with the rest. He flattened the yellow lined sheet in the left-hand pile.

The next letter was neatly typed on embossed letterhead.

Dear Mr. MacBride,

I read with interest your column of Wednesday, June 18, regarding the youngster with the unusual revelations while under hypnosis. I applaud Mr. Mancini and all involved in this important line of research. In my lifetime, man has begun to unlock the secrets of the universe, probed the atom and the stars, but has remained woefully ignorant of matters of the mind. What is the mind—what is thought—what is memory? We take these wonders for granted, accept them as our just due, thinking that they are simply things that the brain does.

Yet man in his self-proclaimed wisdom can't begin to duplicate such feats through artificial means. All of our whirring computers strung end to end couldn't emulate the workings of the fist-sized brain of a three-year-old.

But my instinct tells me that this may be about to change. Stay by the side of your persuasive friend and add your journalistic muscle to his dogged determination. I wish you continued perseverance and success.

Yours truly,
E. C. Dunwoody, Professor Emeritus
University of Minnesota School
of Medicine

"Sheila," he shouted, "wiggle in here."

"I hear and obey, Your Messiness."

"How did you make out with your phone call to the flighty folk?"

"He said something like *Que sera, sera*. I think that means no problem." Sheila automatically cast an inquisitive glance at the two stacks. The pile to the right was noticeably higher. "The ayes have it, right?"

"In spades. Get Mike Mancini on the phone. See if he can organize a meeting at the Hortons' at seven tonight. Then you can wiggle off to lunch."

"TV, wow!"

Tina Horton eloquently expressed all of their views. They sat at ease around the screened-in porch, more comfortable with each other than the first time they had met there. Clancy was half an hour late so they chatted casually until he arrived. Toby sat quietly in the corner. He didn't react to Teddy's announcement that he might be on television.

"I'm not sure I understand," Steve said. "I'm not saying I'm against the idea, but I just don't see what Toby's going on television will bring to the party."

"Steve, I'd be insulting you if I said trust me," Mike acknowledged. "I know that you trust me or you wouldn't have gone along this far. If I thought that TV exposure would have any negative effect, I wouldn't condone it. But I do think that the upside potential far outweighs any slight downside risk. I don't think any of us have any doubt that Teddy will treat both the subject and Toby with dignity."

Steve shrugged, as if such a possibility hadn't entered his mind.

"And the credibility of the research will increase dramatically. It's one thing to read about Toby in the newspaper, but I defy anyone to doubt his credibility after they've seen him on television."

Teddy shifted in his chair to face Steve Horton. "Mike's right, Steve. Seeing Toby face to face is what hooked me. To see him is to believe him. But I understand your concern and I'm not going to try to talk you into anything. I'm only the chronicler of this event; Toby is the star. You and Toby and the rest of the family will have to decide if this is right for you." He spread his hands in an apologetic gesture. "If you're on TV, there's no doubt that you and the family will be in the limelight. That usually means a few crank phone calls, people wanting interviews, a certain loss of privacy."

The newspaperman looked to Toby, but the boy sat quietly and stared at the rough porch deck. "It's like what happens to Kent Hrbek, Toby. If he has a good season, then everybody's a fan, everybody loves him. But let him go 0 for 4 and he becomes an instant bum. The same thing could happen here. Either way, you can count on a certain amount of fame and notoriety. It goes with the package."

Steve glanced around the porch at the anxious faces of his family. "Jan, what do you think?"

The slight woman hesitated and looked uncertainly at her son. Toby was sitting beside her with his head down. She laid her hand on his thin shoulder and the boy turned and smiled weakly. "I'm a little nervous about the whole thing, I admit, but I trust Mike and Mr. MacBride. We can handle a few curious stares or a couple of crank phone calls. As long as I'm convinced that Toby won't be in any danger physically or emotionally, I'll agree to the TV idea." She pulled the boy tightly to her side. "But I'm not the one to ask. Like you said, Teddy, Toby is the star. If it's all right with Toby, then I think you can count on the support of the rest of the Horton family."

Toby didn't wait for the question to be asked. "I'll do it, Mom. It'll be fun being on TV and everything."

"Then it's settled," Steve said. "We go public."

"Not quite," Mike interrupted. "I said that I agreed with the idea of going on TV, but I didn't state the conditions that we should work under. As you know, Teddy's Sunday-morning show is live. That creates some possible problems. I think that the publicity and the exposure will be great. It will speed up the research. I'm sure there are others out there who can help support the research and the broad exposure of television will flush them out. But live TV is out."

Everyone turned to the biology teacher for an explanation. John Horton shielded his eyes from the blazing spear of light that streaked across the lake from the setting sun. "Do you think there might be danger?" he asked suspiciously.

"No, there won't be any danger. That's not the point," Mike replied.

Teddy leaned back in the deck chair and folded his arms across his chest. He eyed the teacher curiously and waited for an explanation.

"Hypnosis isn't an exact science," Mike began. "In fact, it isn't a science at all. Besides that, it's somewhat unpredictable."

"In what way?" Jan asked with a trace of fear in her voice.

"Don't get me wrong," Mike continued. "It's nothing to be alarmed about. It's just that things might not go the way we plan, and on live television you don't get a chance to take it to the editing room and recut it. For example, I might not be able to hypnotize Toby."

A gleam of understanding registered on Teddy's face. "You're saying that my hundreds of millions of fans could be glued to their TVs and we might flop?"

"That's exactly what I'm saying. But it's not the potential flop that concerns me. You can always recover from that by chewing out the governor next Sunday. What I have to worry about is the effect that a failure on live television could have on the credibility of the research. If something was to go wrong, it would be strike one, you're out. No second chance. And I'd have lost valuable ground."

Mike settled back in the deck chair. Like the others, he was dressed casually in loose, lightweight clothes. He took a sip of his iced tea before continuing. "I think that part of the reason for our success to date has been Toby's comfort in his home surroundings and I don't want to take a chance on changing that."

"What are you suggesting?" Steve asked.

"I think I know," Teddy answered, nodding his head in agreement. "We videotape the session right here, then show the tapes on Sunday. Am I right?"

"Exactly."

"I think it's a great idea. All we need are a couple of portable lights and one cameraman. It won't be disruptive at all." He looked questioningly at Steve and Jan for their approval.

"Sure, why not?" Steve shrugged. "In for a dime, in for a dollar."

"Will the dust show?" Jan asked with a weary sigh.

"*Mutti, Mutti, Ich bitte dich, bleib da. Lass' mich nicht allein. Bitte nicht weggehn, Mutti!*"

Toby sat rigidly in the deck chair. His voice was flat and guttural, conveying an undercurrent of fear. He stared blankly into the warm June twilight.

"What is it?" Clancy gasped. He made a move to leave his chair to go to the boy's side.

Steve stopped him with a shake of his head and a finger to his lips. "Let him be, Clancy. I think it's another spell, a new one."

"Matchbox number three," Mike whispered.

Suddenly Toby sat erect, full of life, the Toby that the family recognized. "What about matchbox number three?" he asked as he snapped back to reality, unaware of his brief distraction. But he suspected what had happened when he looked around and saw the curious and sympathetic stares. "I did something, didn't I?" He turned to his mother for confirmation. "What did I say, Mom? It wasn't bad, was it?"

But Toby's question wasn't to be answered. Before Jan could respond, Aaron Horton sucked in a loud rasping breath, clutched at his chest, and toppled from the chair to the sun-bathed deck. As the blood drained from his face, the tear that rolled from his steel-gray eyes coursed down his cheek and splattered into a hundred droplets on the rough fir planking.

"Don't go, Mommy," he gasped. "please don't go."

Chapter Seventeen

JAN LEANED AGAINST the front door and chewed nervously at her knuckles as the emergency vehicle sped down the driveway. Tina huddled at her side, overcome by the tragedy. Her lower lip trembled convulsively and a flood of tears stained her soft cheeks. Sickness and tragedy were foreign to the little girl. As he watched, Mike couldn't help but wonder if this traumatic event had become a matchbox in Tina's impressionable mind.

When Aaron's unconscious form had been placed in the back of the emergency van, Clancy and Steve jumped in with the paramedics and Mike followed in his car with Teddy riding in front and Gramps gently comforting Toby in the back.

Time had no meaning to the worried entourage. They waited and worried while the clock ticked without letup. The minutes crept and the hours raced, but no word of Aaron's condition was forthcoming. Clancy fielded their hopeful questions with a mixture of caution and gentle patience, trying to bridge the gaping chasm between encouragement and despair.

"The first few hours are crucial," he advised with a bedside manner appropriate to the circumstances. "Every minute that passes improves his chances; helps his system adjust and stabilize."

The paramedics' reaction time was also a hopeful omen. The sound of Aaron's fall still echoed through the kitchen as Mike Mancini dialed 911, and it seemed he had just hung up the receiver when the emergency vehicle burst down the drive with flashing lights and whooping siren. But now they could do nothing but wait and hope and pray. Funny, Mike thought, for a while there, time was the enemy. Now it had become a friend.

Teddy tried unsuccessfully to stand outside the grieving circle of family and friends so he could observe the event with a reporter's objectivity, but the emotional tug that caught at his chest when he saw the anxious faces proved too much to overcome.

"I think that Greatgramps is going to get better," Toby announced.

Steve's sad eyes betrayed his forced smile. He nodded and squeezed the boy's hand in response.

The waiting room was cheerfully decorated, as if paint and flowers and colorful pictures could neutralize the sadness and anxiety that hung like a heavy mist in its confines. There was a stack of magazines for friends and relatives to browse through while their loved ones were being probed or stitched or sent arching violently from the sterile table under a well-intentioned rush of current.

Teddy MacBride, Mike Mancini, Clancy Kendall, and the three Hortons sat quietly as the cheery room attempted to work its distracting magic, but the opposing forces were too powerful to overcome.

"He's eighty-five years old," John Horton said to no one in particular. He wrung his hands and smiled sadly. "But he sure doesn't look it, does he?"

"No more than you look sixty," Steve answered.

Gramps accepted the statement as a fact, not a compliment. "I've always felt lucky," he continued, "being able to share my dad with my son and my grandson. It sure does make it nice." His voice trailed off on a melancholy note.

"But he *is* going to be all right," Toby repeated urgently. "I know he's going to get better." He looked anxiously from father to grandfather for confirmation.

"We hope so, Toby," Gramps said. "My dad is a tough old bird. It'll take more than this to knock him off his feet for long. Remember, he's a Horton."

As if in response, the door swung open and the green-gowned resident strode in with a weary but steady gait. He was a young man but his thinning hair added years to his age and enhanced his credibility. This hiss of the slowly closing door was the only sound in the expectantly charged waiting room. The young doctor wasn't sure whom he should address as his glance surveyed the room. His eyes came to rest on Toby.

"He's sure a tough old bird," the doctor said, shaking his head in awe.

The grin that split his sensitive face told Toby that things would be okay.

"Is Mr. Horton your grandfather, son?"

"He's my great-grandfather," Toby said, choking back a sob of relief.

The doctor laid a comforting hand on Toby's shoulder as he looked at the other tense faces. "Mr. Horton's suffered a mild heart attack—but at his age, there's really no such thing as mild."

"He's going to be all right, though, isn't he?" Toby implored. The boy asked the question that preyed on all of their minds.

The doctor addressed the entire room with his response. "Yes. I think he's going to be all right. He's not out of the woods yet but his chances improve by the minute. All we can do now is wait and pray. A lot of the credit goes to all of you for getting him here so quickly." A look of surprise crossed his tired face. "I almost forgot. I'm Ernie Zack." He circled the room and shook the bevy of outstretched hands. His eyebrows rose when he came to Teddy and Clancy.

"It's Dr. Kendall, isn't it?" he asked.

"Yes. I'm a friend of the family."

"And you're Teddy MacBride, the newspaper-man?"

"One and the same. Also a friend of the family," Teddy replied.

Dr. Zack rubbed a knuckle over a tired eye and sat heavily in one of the soft chairs. "Well, it's plain to see Mr. Horton has a lot of moral support. I'm sure that didn't hurt his chances."

Clancy liked the young man's manner. He was able to convey the seriousness of the situation without spreading unproductive fear. It was an ability that some physicians never learned. "Is he stable now?" Clancy asked.

"Yes, under the circumstances," Dr. Zack answered. "It took a while to get his signs to the point where we felt comfortable. That was the reason for the delay." He said it almost apologetically. "But now he's sleeping like a baby." He turned to Steve and John. "In fact, he's more comfortable than any of you are right now. He's in Intensive Care, heavily sedated so there's not much you can do around here except worry, and that doesn't help anybody. I suggest you all go home and get a good night's sleep." Turning to Toby, he said, "In a day or two, you'll be able to visit your great-grandfather."

"That's good," Toby said tonelessly. He looked suddenly pale.

"Are you okay?" his father asked.

The spark ignited by the hopeful exchange with the doctor was extinguished and a pained expression deadened Toby's usually beaming face. "I have another headache, Dad. I think it's the worst one ever."

Toby was embarrassed by the tears of pain welling up in his eyes, but he couldn't stand it any longer and he put his hands protectively to his temples and wept freely. Dr. Zack caught Clancy's eye as if to offer help.

"Just a couple of aspirin," Clancy suggested.

Dr. Zack hurried from the room.

"I think all the tension finally caught up with him," Clancy offered. "Dr. Zack's gone for some aspirin. Just sit quietly, Toby. Try to relax."

"Something wants to get out," Toby sobbed. "My head. It feels like something wants to get out. It hurts so bad, Dad. Help me, please." As they watched, Toby's angelic face contorted into an agonizing grimace and a keening wail split the air.

Before Steve could react, Mike Mancini was out of his chair and on his knees in front of the tortured boy. "Toby, look at me, look at my eyes," he commanded.

Toby's eyes were both startled and pained as they met Mike's anxious stare. The steely gray was clouded by the unchecked flow of tears.

"Toby, watch my eyes very closely. Look at them carefully. Just looking into my eyes is making your own eyelids heavy, very heavy. Your eyes are closing, Toby. Something is pulling your eyelids down and you can't resist it." Mike spoke slowly but forcefully, concealing his growing fear. He gripped Toby's hands by the tips of his fingers, acting on impulse, instinct, not at all certain that his course of action was correct.

"Your eyes are closed now, Toby, and you're asleep. You're in a very deep sleep."

Mike paused and searched Steve Horton's worried face. He saw a slight nod that he interpreted as agreement. Clancy Kendall was at his shoulder with an expression of clinical concern. Teddy MacBride stood in the center of the room, pad and pencil poised, but he was frozen in thought, unable to make the first meaningful mark on the paper. John Horton sat with head bowed, lips moving almost imperceptibly as he mouthed a silent prayer.

"How do you feel, Toby?"

"Fine."

"And your headache? How does your head feel now?"

"I don't have a headache."

"Good. That's good. You just relax now, Toby, Just relax and let your mind float free. Let it float far away from here—let it drift away high into the clouds. I'll be back with you in a little while. Just rest now, Toby. Rest and relax."

"Here's some aspirin."

Everyone was so absorbed with Mike's ministrations they hadn't noticed Dr. Zack's hasty return. He held a flowered paper cup in one hand and a plastic bottle of generic aspirin in the other. He took a step toward Toby but Clancy laid a restraining hand on his arm.

"I'll take that, Doctor. Thank you very much."

Dr. Zack shot a quick glance at Toby and was puzzled by his tightly closed eyes and pain-free expression. "Is everything all right? Are you okay, Toby?"

The boy remained motionless, not a flicker to indicate that he had heard or understood the doctor's question. A pair of shiny streaks led from his eyes to a pair of sparkling tear drops suspended like pearls from his cheeks, but nothing about his expression indicated sadness or pain. He appeared to be in a dream-free sleep, totally unencumbered by worldly woes, not a bit like the pain-racked little boy who had cried out for help only moments earlier.

"What's going on here?" the young doctor demanded. His cold, unwavering stare hit Clancy like a slap in the face. "What's happened to the boy?"

"Take it easy, Doctor," Clancy said soothingly. "The boy's all right. He's under hypnosis. We thought it was best under the circumstances."

"What circumstances? With all due respect, Dr. Kendall, this is my turf and I consider myself responsible for the well-being of everyone here, patients or otherwise."

"My apologies, Doctor. Of course you're right."

"It's my fault, Doctor." Mike jumped to Clancy's defense. "I did it before anyone had a chance to vote on it. I couldn't watch the boy suffer."

A bolt of recognition suddenly hit the young doctor. "Teddy MacBride, Mancini, Kendall, Horton. Let me guess. This is the boy you wrote about in your column a few days ago. This is the boy with the dreams."

"That's right," Teddy acknowledged. "He's a very special little boy."

"And special boys call for special measures," Clancy added.

"We're sorry to have alarmed you, Doctor. The boy was hurting and I think it has something to do with his—unusual gift." Mike directed his words to Dr. Zack but the message was intended for everyone in the room. He turned to Steve

Horton. "My instincts have been right so far, Steve. I'd like to ask you to trust them once again."

"What do you mean?"

"Toby's headache. He said that it felt like something was trying to get out."

"So?"

"Another matchbox, Steve. Please don't ask me to try to explain it, but I think Toby has a memory that he needs to get out. It appears to be causing some kind of pressure in his skull that can only be relieved when he empties a matchbox. Remember how his headache cleared up after our first session?"

Steve looked from the teacher to his son questioningly. "You think that a memory caused Toby's headache?" He glanced to the two doctors for support but received a pair of blank stares in reply.

"I don't know for sure, Steve. But there's one quick way to find out."

A look of understanding crossed Steve's face but it was clouded by doubt. No one else spoke. Only the low hum of the air conditioner cut through the slab of silence hanging within the cheerful waiting room.

"Here?" he asked incredulously. "You want to do a session here?"

"Not exactly here," Mike conceded. He glanced at the worried resident. "Is there a room that we can use, Doctor? A meeting room of some kind where we can have some privacy?"

"A lounge. There's a doctor's lounge right down the hall. It will be empty now. But I'm not sure—"

Clancy stopped him with a peremptory gesture. "I understand and I appreciate your concern, Dr. Zack, but let me assure you that nothing unethical or dangerous is going to happen."

Teddy MacBride interjected himself into the conversation for the first time. "Dr. Zack, you've read my column so I assume that you're aware of the significance of Mr. Mancini's research."

"Yes, but—"

"Mr. Mancini's instincts have been very accurate to this point."

"Yes, but—"

"And he feels that the time is right to initiate another session, a perfectly proper and ethical session, which will move his theory one step closer to reality."

"A session," Clancy interrupted, "for which I'll assume full responsibility."

The harried doctor threw his hands up in surrender. "All right already, you win. Out this door, take a right, straight down the corridor, first door on the left. I never laid eyes on any of you before, got it?"

"Thanks." Teddy smiled. "I'll be sure to speak highly of you in my column. How do you spell your name?"

"Out, MacBride!" The young doctor pointed to the door. "You tarnish the good name of Zack in that tawdry column of yours and I'll sue you blind."

Teddy chuckled and shook the doctor's outstretched hand. "You're okay for a doctor, Ernie."

Clancy overheard the remark and hooked his finger through the journalist's collar and pulled him toward the door. Mike spoke softly to Toby and the boy followed in glassy-eyed obedience.

Chapter Eighteen

❖❖❖❖❖❖❖❖❖❖❖❖

THE FLUORESCENTS BATHED the room with a fierce glare, making the red Formica table and the plastic-covered chairs even gaudier than their maker intended. An orange ashtray bearing the message of a medical-supply distributor overflowed with the detritus of dozens of unrepentant doctors. There had been a few attempts to bring the place up to standards, at least to meet the health codes, but the doctors of Saint Paul Hospital steadfastly thwarted such well-meaning efforts to sanitize their sanctum sanctorum.

"This place is a pit," Teddy complained. "I wouldn't want anybody who hangs out in a sty like this groping my groin for a hernia check."

"That's the kind of good news that will keep the place open," Clancy quipped.

Mike shot a disapproving look at the two, like a pair of disruptive sophomores caught talking in study hall. He ushered Toby toward a cracked Leatherette chair that faced an ancient floor-model Sylvania. When he got the boy situated, he waited while the others seated themselves around the lounge.

Teddy pulled his chair close to the boy and was fidgeting with the batteries of a tiny recorder. Satisfied it was in working order, he angled his chair to be sure Toby's words were aimed in its direction.

Mike pulled his chair around so he was facing Toby but slightly off to one side, not obstructing Toby's view of the TV screen.

"How are you feeling, Toby?" Mike began.

"I feel fine."

Mike's sudden start caught Teddy unawares and he had to hurry to flick the "on" button on his recorder.

"And your headache's gone?"

"I don't have a headache."

"Where are you, Toby? What do you see in your mind?"

"It's white—and it's fluffy. It's like I'm floating high in the sky."

"Look down toward the ground. What do you see?

"Buildings and cars and lots of tiny people. And I can see the IDS Building and the Metrodome." His lips quivered in a semblance of a smile. "It looks like a mushroom from up here."

"Toby, I want you to come out of the sky now. I want you to come down and return to the memory room. Do you remember where it is? Can you find the memory room?"

"Yes."

"Are you there now?"

"Yes."

"What's in the room, Toby?"

"The big wooden table's still there. And all the matchboxes are still in a pile, except the one I took off the top. That's sitting on the table where I left it the last time."

"Go into the room and pick it up, Toby. Pick it up and read what it says on the cover."

"It says 'Aaron Horowitz,' " he said without hesitation.

Mike looked obliquely at John Horton. His eyes asked the unspoken question but John made a palms-up, eyebrows-up gesture that said "Beats me."

"My grandfather very rarely spoke about his past. The name Horowitz means nothing at all to me," Steve volunteered.

"Nor to me," John concurred. "Dad only told us that his parents died when he was very young, and he never really knew them. I never dwelt on the subject. He gave the impression it was something he'd rather not discuss. It seemed to cause him pain. But Horowitz—that's a new one on me."

"Do you suppose it might have something to do with Toby's dream?" Teddy asked cautiously, looking up from his notepad. His question drew a panorama of blank looks. "The way he reacted to what Toby said—on the porch—his attack."

He drew more blank stares.

"Look, I know that everything happened pretty fast tonight but if you ask me, I think what Toby said on the porch had something to do with Aaron's heart attack. I think Toby was watching a chapter from his great-grandfather's past and that Aaron knew it."

"Could there be something in Aaron's past he doesn't want anyone to know about?" Clancy suggested.

"Or something he'd like to forget," Teddy said. "Maybe that's what those little matchboxes are all about, capturing old memories we'd rather not think about, like John's experience in the war or Steve's painful memory about his rabbit."

"Perhaps you're right," Mike agreed. "But let's not forget that those little matchboxes filled with fearful memories could be the key to unlocking the secrets of the mind." He looked into the anxious faces of Steve and John Horton. "Besides, I don't think Toby's going to feel better until we do it. I think it's time for us to open Aaron Horton's or Aaron Horowitz's matchbox."

Aaron's son and grandson studied each other for any sign of doubt.

"It's your decision, Dad," Steve finally said. "Do you want to go ahead?"

John Horton studied the faces of the people sitting around the garish room but they offered no help. Then he looked at Toby, his slender, little-boy body sitting stiffly erect, the beautifully carved features of his immature face set serenely in place. He recalled the anguish of the same features only minutes earlier as the boy's head throbbed with pain. "Something's trying to get out," his pain-ridden grandson had sobbed.

He turned to the teacher and nodded uncertainly. "We will proceed," he whispered. "I pray that we're doing the right thing."

Mike nodded understandingly and turned back to face the boy. "Have you been resting, Toby?"

"Yes."

"Good. You can open your eyes now. Your dad's here. And Dr. Kendall and Mr. MacBride from the newspaper."

Toby's eyes darted from face to face but his head never moved.

"There's a TV in front of you, Toby. When I tell you, it will turn on and you can watch movies of the stories in the matchboxes."

Toby's eyes snapped to the blank screen.

"Go back to the memory room now, Toby. Are you there?"

"Yes."

"Go to the table and pick up the matchbox with the name Aaron Horowitz on it. Do you have it?"

"Yes."

"Open it, Toby. Open the matchbox and let the memory out. Let it fill the TV screen."

Toby's eyes came alive and Mike could see them jerk as they darted from point to point on the old Sylvania. Beads of perspiration dotted his brow and his chest rose and fell with his heavy breath and quickened heartbeat. His arms trembled and his fists clenched. But his gaze never wavered from the dull gray screen.

"Is the memory on the TV, Toby?"

"Yes, it is."

"What do you see, Toby? Tell me about the memory."

Teddy quickly checked the twirling tape. He'd had his share of stories fouled up by mechanical malfunctions. It spun slowly from left to right, about twenty minutes showing on the see-through plastic case.

Clancy, Steve, and John leaned forward, eager to hear—curious and concerned.

Toby spoke without emotion, flat and toneless, a robot drone that struck like a chill wind. "It's dark and very cold. I'm wearing pajamas with red and white stripes."

"Where are you, Toby? Can you recognize the place?"

He hesitated. "A boat. I'm on a big boat." His eyes widened momentarily as an ancient image flashed across the dull gray screen. "Someone's kneeling in front of me. *Mein Vati und meine Mutti. Und wie Sie weinen.*"

"In English, Toby. Tell me again in English."

"Mommy and Daddy. They're kneeling in front of me and they're crying. They're talking to me and they're crying."

"What is your name, Toby?"

"On the boat I am called Aaron Horowitz."

"How old are you?"

"Twelve."

"What are your mommy and daddy saying to you? Why are they crying?"

"Sei brav, Aaron."

"In English, Toby. Tell me in English."

"Be brave, Aaron. Be brave and strong. This my daddy said to me."

"And your mommy? Is she saying anything?"

"No." Toby's eyes bathed the screen with love. "She is so beautiful. She was a dancer, you know, before Daddy married her." Then a renewed sadness overcame him. "She is crying and tying something around me. It is a jacket, a brown jacket. It has writing on it."

"Describe your daddy, Toby. What does he look like?"

"He looks like my father."

"Of course, he is your father."

"No. I mean that he looks like my today father. My memory father looks like my today father."

Another look-alike generation, Mike thought numbly. Teddy wrote a few quick notes.

"What is your memory father's name?"

"Abraham Horowitz."

"And your memory mother's name?"

"Gisèle Horowitz."

"Why are they crying, Toby?"

"They are crying because I am leaving."

"Where are you going?"

"For a ride on another boat."

"Are your mommy and daddy going with you?"

"No. They cannot go. They are staying."

A flash of fear stunned Mike into cold silence. It all started to make sense. Terrible sense. He had to choke back a sob as he asked the next question.

"Do you know the date, Toby?"

"It is April fifteenth."

"And the year?"

"It is 1912."

"My God." Mike wept softly. He turned slowly to the others and felt a deeper pang of sorrow when he saw the tears streaming down John Horton's aging face. He had to grope for the strength to ask the next question. Although he already knew the answer, he needed to hear it through the lips of Toby Horton and Aaron Horowitz.

"The name of the ship—what is the name of the ship you are on?"

"The *Titanic*."

Mike slumped wearily. He pulled a handkerchief from his pocket and wiped at his tear-filled eyes. John wept unashamedly. Steve gulped at a large lump that lodged in his throat. Teddy Mac-Bride and Clancy Kendall stared at the blank screen in stunned silence.

The enormity of Toby's revelation struck them like a blow to the face. They were there—not in the tacky doctor's lounge at Saint Paul Hospital—they were there with young Aaron Horowitz and Abraham and Gisèle Horowitz and with John Jacob Astor and with Benjamin Guggenheim. They were there on the deck of the sinking *Titanic*. They were there when the blazing flares streaked from the bridge and exploded like fireworks in the dead night air, and they heard the muted words of a prayerful hymn float like a dirge across her listing bow. They were there as Gisèle Horowitz strapped the canvas life vest around the heaving chest of her only child and kissed him gently on his trembling lips. They were there as she lifted him over the rail and placed him in the arms of a matronly heiress laden with furs and pearls seated on the rough planking of a lifeboat number eight.

"What's happening now, Toby?" Mike asked in a choked whisper.

"My boat's rowing away. Mommy and Daddy are waving. They're saying good-bye." He hesitated. A worried crease furrowed his soft brow. "I'm crying."

"Why, Toby? Why are you crying?" The question gushed out with a new flood of tears. The biology teacher was unable to control it and beyond caring. He felt himself seated on the plank alongside the trembling boy in striped pajamas, sniffing the perfume from the wattled neck of the heiress mingled with the salty aroma of the black ocean, and he heard the last faint strains of a hymn in the resonant voices of the brave men and women clinging to each other on the dying ship.

"I'm crying because I'm sad—and ashamed."

"Ashamed?"

"I'm a coward. I row to safety while Mommy and Daddy die in the sea. I don't deserve to have their name. I don't deserve to be called Horowitz."

"Is there more, Toby?" Mike sobbed.

"It's almost over. I can't see Mommy and Daddy anymore. I'm too far away. The front of the boat is under water. It's standing on its nose. No one can still be standing on the deck. Mommy and Daddy are probably in the cold water." He stifled a sob. "Mommy can't even swim. It's going now. There it goes—it's gone. The *Titanic's* gone." His flat, cold voice returned and his gaze was stoic. "Mommy and Daddy are gone."

A jewel of salty tear sparkled in the glare of the harsh fluorescent before cascading over his downy cheek.

"Is the matchbox empty?" Mike asked. He swallowed hard and spoke in more reassuring tones.

"Yes."

"Turn the TV off now, Toby. Turn it off and close your eyes. Close your eyes and relax. Are you comfortable?"

"Yes."

"Good. I want you to go back to the memory room now." Mike hesitated momentarily. "Are you in the memory room?"

"Yes."

"Where is the matchbox with Aaron Horowitz's name?"

"It's gone."

"That's good, Toby. Now in a few seconds I'm going to snap my fingers. When I do, I want you to wake up but you won't remember anything about Aaron Horowitz or his memory. Do you understand?"

"Yes."

The loud snap jarred the onlookers back to the present and they jerked upright in their chairs.

Toby opened his eyes and searched the sea of anxious faces. "Where am I? Did I have another dream? Is Greatgramps okay?" His eyes suddenly lit up. "Hey! My headache's gone."

Chapter Nineteen

◇◇◇◇◇◇◇◇◇◇◇◇

Saint Paul Pioneer Press and Dispatch
Monday, June 23, 1986

MacBRIDE'S MUMBLINGS

Those of you with an IQ larger than your waist size might recall last week's column about Mad Mike Mancini and his incredible theory about the genetic transference of memory. To refresh your muddled minds, Mad Mike would have us believe that memory, like flat feet and overbite, hitchhikes a ride on a (pardon the expression) sperm and that it travels this squiggly route from generation to generation, passing on a pearl of ancient wisdom at each stop along the way. It's an intriguing concept. Imagine being able to relive those magical days of yesteryear, the Babe's sixtieth homer, Lucky Lindy's flight, Aunt Irma's wedding day.

But before you get your spongy imaginations all worked up, you ought to know that the only memories plucked from the past so far have been some pretty fearsome scenes and that's not exactly what Mad Mike bargained for. The way his theory's evolving, certain families possess the genetic clout to pass on their memories to their offspring along with their curly hair and baby-blue eyes. But hold on, there's another catch. It seems that there's only room for one such memory per generation. That's always been the problem with tiny sperms. And after that generation has told its tale through Toby Horton's eyes, the youngster pops out of his trance as if nothing at all had happened. And speaking of trances, Mad Mike took the time to lecture this humble reporter on the difference between being asleep and being in a trance. It didn't make much sense at the time but it's clear as a bell now, and I know that if I dreamed what young Toby described, I'd wake up with eyes like saucers and a pint of sweat sogging up my flannels.

I told you about Pinky's untimely demise (matchbox number 1 courtesy of Steve Horton, Toby's father) and about a World War II combat incident on Guadalcanal (matchbox number 2 courtesy of John Horton, Toby's grandfather). Since then, yet another matchbox has spewed its contents, this time in front of a blank TV screen in the doctor's lounge at Saint Paul Hospital. It was there that I relived a moment of tragic history as a young German lad named Aaron Horowitz watched in horror as his parents slipped to the ocean floor on the doomed *Titanic* (matchbox number 3 courtesy of Aaron Horton, née Horowitz, Toby's great-grandfather).

There's no question about it, Mad Mike Mancini is on to something. Your faithful scribe can't say for sure whether it's caused by bright genes or tight jeans but one thing's certain, this is no hoax. And my mailbag indicates that most of my readers agree with me, although I doubt if a survey of the bottom quintile of the IQ range carries much weight. But in spite of the overwhelming agreement, there were still a handful of doubters out there in fuzzy-wuzzy land. One such cashew threatened to roar across Roseville leading his "earthly army" if I didn't stop doing "the devil's work." I took that to be a negative vote even though I usually don't count ballots written in crayon.

If you've read this far without flipping to the comics, it's clear that Mad Mike's quest has caught your fancy. Want to hear more? If you do, it's a good news/bad news story. First the good news. Mad Mike and Toby will be quests on my Sunday TV show. Now the bad news—two parts. First, you have to get out of bed by noon. Still with me? Next, I had to bump the Minnesota Gay Coalition to make space. If you can live with those twin tragedies, tune in on Sunday morning. Now you can all go back to your funnies.

Chapter Twenty

◇◇◇◇◇◇◇◇◇◇◇◇

THE HEAT WAS wretched, the kind that made dogs' tongues hang and drip like the poor beasts were melting on the sidewalk. Newcomers to the state couldn't imagine how one place could be so deadly cold in the winter and unbearably hot in the summer and they made a good point. It wasn't natural. "Keeps out the riffraff," the old-timers would say and they were right. But on this late June day with the temperature hovering near 100 degrees, even the hardy Scandinavians whose forebears cleared the land in the first place were doubting their ancestors' wisdom.

Esau lifted his felt hat and wiped muddy runnels of sweat from his forehead with his flannel sleeve. The men around him were stripped to the waist or, at the very most, wore loose-fitting T-shirts that were transparent from dampness. It bothered him that they'd dress this way. He couldn't come up with a biblical root for his distress, but something about it didn't sit right. And the way they strutted and spat and scratched themselves and swore—it wasn't what God had intended. But Esau kept his objections to himself. It wouldn't do to lose his temper and with it his source of income, meager though it might be. A salty drop rolled into the corner of his eye and it stung fiercely but Esau had no vocabulary to express his dismay. He wiped harder with the sleeve and resumed his work.

The crew was moving heavy brush to make way for a stand of new homes. "Suckers are gonna sell for more than a quarter million," he heard one of the workers say. He couldn't contemplate that. He could have saved his farm with less than half of that but none of the big-shot bankers in their quarter-million-dollar homes would give him the time of day let alone the money that he needed. It annoyed him and he wondered sometimes how it could all be part of God's same plan.

God's plan! It worked in strange ways. Esau tried to do his small part but sometimes it seemed that wasn't enough. Like the theater that showed the filthy movies. Esau followed the plan. He did it by the numbers but, for some reason Esau didn't understand, God chose not to let it work that night. Esau had raced to the 7–11 the next morning for the early edition, expecting a front-page splash on the roaring fire that had destroyed a temple of evil.

Nothing!

He eventually found it on page 7 beneath an ad for ladies' undergarments. Attempted arson they called it. Someone was in the room in the back of the theater and saw the arsonist try to start the fire. They lie. Esau was alone back there. The box-office attendant described one particular patron as "weirder than most of our customers, a big guy with a bushy beard and wild eyes. He scared me," she told the reporter.

As well he should, Esau thought as he grabbed one end and helped to haul a sawn-off limb to a waiting truck.

"On three we'll swing this sumbitch into the back of the truck," Larry said.

The boy was young and muscular, thick like the twins but with white-blond curls and lively eyes. He stopped at the gate of the truck and waited for Esau to bring the back end of the limb around. It tortured Esau to have to even listen to such language and it tore at his vitals to have to respond. It implicated him, it implied tacit approval.

"One, two, three—oof da!"

The branch lofted through the air and settled

on top of the growing pile. Larry brushed off his hands and flashed a dazzling smile. "Teamwork," he said with a wink that Esau thought was supposed to seal a bond of some kind. Just then the crew chief's voice rang through the muggy air.

"Take ten, guys. We don't want anybody getting heat exhaustion for four fifty an hour." The announcement brought a short chorus of approval.

The boy brushed a thick curtain of blond hair back from his eyes. "That's about enough of this bullshit for a while. Let's grab some shade."

It was a young and vital group. Esau could have been any one of their fathers. They were mostly college kids working through the summer to pick up the next semester's tuition.

"You must be dying in that goddamn shirt, mister. Why don't you hang it up somewhere before you pass out?"

The advice was well meant but not well received. The boys were self-conscious working side by side with the older man who never spoke. This was the third day of the job, and none of them could recall him saying a single intelligible word. He usually grunted and went about his assigned tasks with a determination that embarrassed them. When they talked and joked among themselves, they wondered if he was short a few chapters.

"I heard people talk about it but I never saw anybody do it before," Larry told the group. The boys were laughing and joking as they waiting at the pickup point that morning. Esau always drove to the work site alone, but the other workers arrived in a stretch van that picked them up at Maplewood Mall. "The old sumbitch just jammed his finger against one side of his nose like this and blasted away. Instant oyster stew. Efficient as hell if you ask me. Saves on handkerchiefs."

"Yeccchhh!"

"Gross!"

"You ever talk to him, Larry?"

"Never. I say 'Mornin', Esau. Afternoon, Esau.' He nods and grunts and goes about his work. He's what you call the strong, silent type, I guess." He smiled wryly. "I heard him fart once. Does that count?"

"He doesn't look too strong, but I sure as hell wouldn't want to tangle with him. Did you see how he handles some of those logs?"

"No shit. I don't think he knows his own strength. He grabbed one end of a log today and waited for me to get the other. I haul on the sumbitch and it feels like it's still rooted in the ground."

Then the van came and the boys clambered aboard.

That was at seven in the morning when the first warm rays were invigorating. By three in the afternoon, most of the piss and vinegar had been sweated out.

Esau stared at the boy who suggested that he remove his shirt. 'You must be dying in that goddamn shirt, mister.' That's what the boy named Larry had said. The boy was right but Esau couldn't admit it. He was hot and he was angry. Esau wanted to work but he wanted to work on his terms. He wanted to feel the sweat running freely down his body as he did the work of the Lord. And he wanted to talk to the Lord as he went about his labors, but he couldn't do that amid the crudities and blasphemies of his brazen co-workers. The farmer muttered a silent prayer and stared blankly at infinity.

"Are you okay, mister?" Larry asked. "Christ, you can pass out from the goddamn heat on a day like today."

He stood facing the boy. Esau was tall and dark like the trees they were felling and hauling away. Larry was young and bronze and sunny. The crew were sitting in shady places watching the attempted conversation with languid interest. No one spoke. They wanted to find out if Esau could talk. He sensed their curiosity but he read it as hostility. A thin boy with a cigarette whispered to his partner and the two snickered. At me, Esau thought. They're mocking me. They're mocking me because I do the work of the Lord while they follow the lead of Satan.

Larry watched the older man's eyes and saw a fearful transformation. They were always a little on the wild side, darting here and there the way a squirrel shifts about as it hunts for acorns. But now Esau's eyes began to blaze like embers, and clusters of bubbles grew from the corners of his mouth. Larry stepped back as Esau raised his arm above his head.

"You dare to take His name in vain!" Esau pointed his finger at the sky as if indicating the object of the boy's derision. Some of the boys shielded their eyes and followed his lead, staring into the blazing afternoon sun. "You walk around half-naked in His sight and you blaspheme."

Larry backed farther away, keeping out of

reach of the wild man's rangy arms. "I-I-I'm sorry, mister," he stammered. "I didn't mean anything by it."

"Thou shalt not take the name of the Lord thy God in vain," Esau shouted.

"Hallelujah!"

Esau spun and was face to face with the crew chief. He was a big man, not as tall as Esau but wide and thick. He wore a pair of mirrored sunglasses that had annoyed Esau from the start. They reminded him of the state trooper. Rolling muscles bulged from beneath the tight yellow T-shirt. A red bandanna was knotted loosely around his forehead.

"What the hell's goin' on over here? Isn't it hot enough for you guys without kicking up more steam?"

Esau spun back to the young blond boy and pointed his knobby finger. His hand trembled. "He blasphemes," he shouted. He waved his arm in a wide sweep. "They all blaspheme." Flakes of spittle flew from his mouth as he made his accusation.

"What the fuck are you talkin' about, mister? You some kind of nut or something?"

Giant hands pulled the steel band tightly around Esau's chest. His breath was sucked from his body and a wall of flashing red lights exploded in front of him.

"Sinners," he shrieked. He swung wildly and his bony fist crunched into the crew chief's ear. Esau's breath came in staccato bursts. His face writhed in fury. Fists clenched and shaking, arms at his sides, hunched forward, Esau stared dazedly at the stunned man.

The crew chief backed off, rubbing his tender

ear. "Out!" he yelled. "We don't need no trouble around here. We don't need no weirdos, neither. Get the hell out of here. We'll send your check in the mail."

He didn't recall getting into the pickup. When the pain finally left his chest and the wall of red cleared from his mind, Esau was driving down the highway, straddling the center line with horns blaring all around him. He pulled to the left, which generated a new chorus of hoots, and he crept down the road.

"Weirdo!" The shout came from a passing car.

Esau was bewildered. He was trying. Lord knows he was trying. Why don't they listen? What's weird about performing the work of the Lord? The wracking pain in his chest leveled off to a dull ache. He had to squint against the drooping sun and that brought a new wave of pain to his head. He could smell his own rancid sweat as the pickup rumbled down the road.

Esau wasn't one to feel sorry for himself. After all, wasn't everything that happened part of the plan? But even thoughts of the plan couldn't keep something from grinding at his gut. The farm was gone. That had been tough at the time but he'd learned to accept it about as well as could be expected. And his life had been given new meaning when he was appointed captain of His earthly army. Then why didn't he feel God's blessings? Esau knew the answer. He was failing. He was given the assignment but he was failing in the Lord's mission.

In the weeks since the onset of his assignment he had rid the streets of but one sinner. Hardly the work of an army. Then he had attempted to destroy the blasphemer in her den, but he ended up on her front steps with the dead bolt slamming home behind him. Next he'd sought to destroy a temple of evil but his fire fizzled out even as his own faith sometimes wavered. And today he was chased from his employment by a blasphemous boor. It was a trying day for the captain of the earthly army. He brooded about his misfortune as he pulled the pickup in front of his house.

Hattie snapped the TV off when she heard the pickup. She was watching one of the afternoon soaps; evil idling, Esau called it. She snatched up a dust rag and fiddled with the legs of the coffee table.

"God is great," Esau said as he lurched through the front door.

"God is great," Hattie parroted as the door slammed shut. "You're home early. Are you sick?"

"*They* are sick," Esau corrected. He gave no further explanation and Hattie could see that none would be forthcoming. She went to the kitchen to brew him a cup of tea while Esau sank into a chair and picked up the newspaper. He read it daily now, cover to cover, at least the headlines. It gave him news of the enemy and led him to his lair.

The Mideast situation exploded in fat letters on the front page. Esau ignored it. Even if he understood what was happening there, he was powerless to do anything about it.

Teenage gangs were roaming the streets in Minneapolis like preying dog packs. How he wished his tiny army could rid the earth of those vermin. Wishful thinking. But he saw some hope when he read how they killed each other off as they battled over drugs and whores in the festering bars where they lurked like cockroaches.

A ship sank somewhere in India. Over five hundred people were killed. Drowned. He wondered why God did a thing like that. They couldn't all have been evil. He closed his eyes and saw a sea filled with people waving in desperation while God watched. He felt no remorse, only curiosity. Everything was part of the plan.

A man from Florida received an artificial heart and was shown sitting in bed reading a newspaper. Esau was bothered by this. It wasn't natural. Surely God didn't intend that His creations be kept alive like a windup toy, stuffed full of wires and plastic gears. Esau took his scissors and carefully snipped the article. He placed it on a stack on the end table. More grist for his mill.

Hattie brought him a cup of tea. She leaned over to place it in front of him and her blouse hung down, revealing huge fleshy breasts, pale white fingers of blue veins coursing through them.

"Cover yourself, woman!" He spat the words and she jerked back, splashing tea into the saucer. He ignored her while she wiped up the liquid and fastened the top button of her housedress.

It pained him sometimes to think of Hattie— the ripe young farm girl—the bride.

The lover!

But that was in another lifetime. Long ago. That was when there was still love and laughter, when the farm families met on Saturday nights and the men drank beer and the children drank cider and the ladies chattered about recipes and

quilts. That was when the whole town danced to
the fiddle and left before eleven to be fresh for
church on Sunday morning. That was when
young Hattie Wyckstrom met Esau Manley in
the barn where they made carefree love amid the
grunts and squeals of the onlookers.

He could never forget that memory, sinful
though it might be. The smell of dry hay mingled
with the aroma of damp farm animals—the tinkle of laughter and rhythm of the fiddle—the
wonderful warm feel of Hattie Wyckstrom's lithe
young body against his own. It made the blood
stir in his loins but that's as far as it went. The
woman whose thighs chafed each other red and
raw and whose breasts waved like feed bags
wasn't the same Hattie who stole his heart so
many years ago. That girl was long gone as was
the shy young farm boy who fell for her charms.

He stifled the thought and riffled steadily
through the pages of the newspaper. Robberies,
rapes, murders, drugs—these were all too frequent occurrences on the streets of the city, but
Esau knew that a mechanism was in place to
mete out justice for such flagrant infractions.
The blue-uniformed law that acted against
these criminals was but another instrument of
the Lord and Esau gave it its just due. His concern wasn't with these obvious violations of
man and his property. His army had other targets. They sought the violator of God's other
laws, the laws that tried to rob God Himself of
His sanctity.

As usual, he stopped at the Entertainment Section. This was the part of the paper that made
his heart race and his blood boil. This was where
the devil spewed his most vile filth. The first few

times he studied the section he shredded the paper like confetti, circling, clipping, cutting out ads for the most offensive attractions. These clippings comprised most of the stack that grew like a tower at his elbow on the end table. But he soon realized the futility of venting his outrage at every tasteless show in the Twin Cities. It was endless. But where should he start?

Priorities!

He had to learn to focus his outrage, concentrate his strike to make it felt by the masses. He was through with trapping prostitutes or fortune-tellers. His quest needed greater attention, the kind of attention that a roaring fire at the theater of sin would have created. But he had messed that up. Perhaps God didn't want it to happen. Maybe He was saving Esau for some greater opportunity. Esau took comfort in this possibility.

The Business Pages offered no opportunities to Esau and his small army. They spoke in unfamiliar terms about things he couldn't fathom. Stocks and bonds and hostile takeovers didn't have the stink of evil that he could glean from other sections. And the rows of numbers and letters that cluttered two full pages were as meaningless as ancient hieroglyphics.

Neither did the Sports Pages provide many useful leads. Certainly it wasted too much paper and ink on the trivial pastimes of grown men playing boys' games, and this annoyed Esau considerably but it wasn't the kind of stuff that fueled his rage.

The Focus Section contained editorials and letters to the editor. He had never bothered with it before, but since he began serving as captain of the earthly army, he found it to be a valuable source of information. He'd even ventured an opinion of his own regarding the exploitation of the boy who had the strange dreams. He'd sent his letter a few days earlier and checked Teddy's column each night to see if the journalist got his message.

He got it.

"One such cashew threatened to roar across Roseville leading his earthly army."

The mocking words leaped from the page like a blow to the face and Esau's mind reeled. Failure, mockery, ridicule, getting fired, heat. A blue vein writhed like a snake on his forehead and his nostrils dilated like a panting thoroughbred. He slammed his fist on the coffee table and the fragile wood shattered like a brittle pane.

"They will not listen," he roared.

Hattie raced from the kitchen and the twins hurried down the stairs.

"They dare to mock the message of the Lord." He wheeled and aimed his finger and his fury at the front door. "Then they will feel his rage; they will learn that His will is not to be denied."

"Father, what happened?"

Esau stabbed his finger at the offending article in the newspaper. "They use the mouth of a boy to do the work of the devil." His eyes blazed with the fever that the twins had grown to fear and they stayed out of his reach. Then, as suddenly as it began, his rage subsided. He looked calmly at Hattie and the boys. A hint of a smile crossed his face behind the scraggly beard.

Hattie walked to his side and took him by the hand. She tried to pull him back to the couch, but he stood rooted to the floor.

"He must be saved," Esau said.

"Who, Father?"

"The boy. The boy they use to do the devil's work. I've heard a message from the Lord. I know what it is that we must do."

The twins and their mother passed worried glances among themselves. Esau had always provided for the family and they were thankful, but sometimes they worried. He had changed. He was always a good God-fearing Christian, but recently his religion had taken on a frightening zeal. But a lifetime of obedience was difficult to turn off.

"What must we do, Esau?" Hattie asked.

Esau ordered them to sit and he told them what the Lord had commanded.

Then they prayed.

Chapter Twenty-one

◈◈◈◈◈◈◈◈◈◈

THE BOY APPROACHED the table with caution, eyes downcast, hands held shyly behind his back. He was terrified. He couldn't have been more than eight years old, maybe younger. "Mr. Mac-Bride," he stammered.

Teddy looked at him through bushy eyebrows. He tried to look kindly but his wild hair nullified the attempt.

"I see you on television every Sunday. Can I

have your autograph please?'' He produced a Lindey's napkin and a ballpoint pen embossed with the name of a local realtor.

Teddy took the items. He smoothed the napkin on the tabletop. "You here with a date?" he growled.

"No, sir."

"You married?"

"No, sir."

"You here all alone?"

"No. My mom and dad are here." The boy pointed to a young couple seated across the room. The woman smiled and gave a coy wave and the father tried unsuccessfully to become invisible.

Teddy grunted again. He wrote something on the napkin and the boy took it and scurried away.

"I'm impressed," Clancy chided.

Teddy took a chug of his beer and snorted. "I'll never get to be a big-time curmudgeon if I can't scare away kids any better than that. If that kid ever saw my show, I'll eat your socks. The parents are too embarrassed to come over themselves so they send a kid."

"I'm afraid you're just doomed to being a nice guy," Mike comforted.

"And destroy my hard-won reputation?"

"I'll keep your secret," Mike joked.

"Does that happen often?" Clancy wondered.

"Just enough to keep me from getting too humble."

"Fat chance of that," Clancy said.

"It never happened at all until the TV show started. For twenty years I wrote brilliant columns and I stayed anonymous. But then I go and stick it in the ear of one mentally defenseless governor on TV and I become an instant celebrity. All that matters is to get your kisser on the tube. It doesn't matter what it's there for—mass murder, bulimia, the Nobel Prize—it's all the same. That's the part that keeps me humble."

"I know what you mean," Mike said. "Michael Jackson got one hundred percent recognition but only one kid in my class ever heard of Albert Schweitzer."

"From what I've heard about today's high school kids, that makes your class way above average."

"Not really," Mike admitted reluctantly. "The kid thought Schweitzer was a war criminal."

"Such academic excellence calls for something moist. Innkeeper!" Teddy signaled the waitress to refill their glasses.

Mike and Clancy had invited the journalist to join their Wednesday night rendezvous and he gratefully accepted. It was a perfect opportunity to pull their thoughts together. The taping session was scheduled for Friday night and, if all went well, Teddy's Sunday morning audience would get to see a piece of the past through Toby Horton's strange gift.

"How's it shaping up?" Clancy asked.

"The crew's scheduled to show up at the Hortons' at seven," Teddy answered.

"Crew? I thought we were going to keep this small."

"Not to worry. Crew means one cameraman and another guy to handle sound and lighting. You won't even know they're around."

Mike seemed relieved. He turned to Clancy. "And how's the Horton health?"

"A little more complicated than cameras and lights, but I think everything's under control. Aaron's due to get home next week. Tests show that he suffered only minimal damage. He's a tough one."

"How about Toby?" Mike asked.

Clancy tugged his ear thoughtfully. "That's not as easy to answer. It's the headaches that concern me. I'm not sure if they're strictly physical or if they're psychosomatic."

"You mean because of the matchboxes?" Mike asked. "Opening matchboxes cures his headaches, right? Is that psychosomatic?"

"I don't know, Mike. I'm not even sure what psychosomatic is. But we all saw what happened at the hospital. You cured the boy's headache better than I could have done with a ton of Tylenol."

"And from what you've told me, we can probably expect more of the same. It seems that I opened a floodgate and now there's no stopping it." Mike shook his head sadly.

"I don't agree," Clancy argued. "I think it was the auto accident that opened the floodgate and you're the cure, not the cause."

"I only hope you're right," Mike muttered.

"How far back in history do you suppose he'll take us?" Teddy asked.

"Good question." Mike waited while new drinks were served. He pondered Teddy's question while the waitress took their empties and moved off. "Toby counted ten more matchboxes including Aaron's. That makes a total of a dozen that he had to start with." He took a sip and silently did the mathematics. "At an average twenty-five years per generation, Toby will bring us back three hundred and some odd years, somewhere in the sixteen hundreds."

"Unless some generations are skipped," Clancy ventured.

"Do you think that's a real possibility?" Teddy had pulled out his notepad and was scribbling as he asked the question.

"Sure it's a possibility," Mike said. "But your guess is as good as mine. We'll know more after Friday night but my bet is that it'll be Aaron's dad, the one named Abraham who we already met on the *Titanic*."

"Give me two to one and I'll bet that it's not Abraham," Clancy challenged.

"You're on."

Teddy looked at Clancy curiously. "Sounds like a bad bet to me. Do you know something we don't?"

"Just a hunch," Clancy admitted.

"These medicos got bucks to burn, Teddy. This dumb pill pusher would bet on the rerun of last year's Super Bowl and pick the loser if you gave him good enough odds."

"Speaking of money," Clancy cut in, "have you heard from any of the purse strings?"

"As a matter of fact I have," Mike said. "I've been flirting unsuccessfully with the university for a couple of years for a research grant, and since Teddy's column hit the street their interest has perked up. I've heard from a couple of other possible sources, too. Things are looking up."

"I have been used," Teddy wailed.

"For a worthy cause," Mike soothed. "Like I told you at our first meeting, the theory just needed a little of the right exposure."

"You're a devious Italian, Mancini."

"And that coming from an opportunistic Irish-man," Mike countered.

"Here's to a big-bucks grant." Clancy raised his glass and the three friends toasted Mike's success.

Chapter Twenty-two

TOBY AND GRAMPS were leaning against the bar at the back end of the rec room, idly watching the two-man crew set up the taping and sound equipment. Teddy introduced the cameraman as Cecil B. He was short and round and worked with precise little movements. The other man was called Art and he darted about with a light meter. He also checked the microphone pickup. In addition to the two technicians, there was a Betacam on a tripod, a recorder, a color monitor, and a floodlight bouncing its rays off a silver umbrella. Teddy said it was a bare-bones setup.

"I'm ready whenever you are, Teddy."

Cecil B. had the leather-covered card table and the two chairs set up as they had been on the first night. He didn't like working with only one camera. It lacked flexibility and hampered his creative bent, but he followed Teddy's ground rules. Be as inconspicuous as possible, the journalist had insisted.

The chairs were placed across from each other.

The camera was set up between them, about five feet from the table. That way Cecil B. could wide-angle it to get Mike and Toby in the picture at the same time or he could zoom in on either one. He would have liked to capture the reactions of the onlookers for dramatic effect but having only the single camera ruled this out.

"Makeup?" Art asked.

Teddy shook his head and waved him off. "Not today. We'll save that for Sunday when we're on live."

Toby and Mike sat facing each other across the table. Toby's hands were damp, a mild case of camera jitters. Teddy signaled to the cameraman. "Any time you're ready, C.B."

Cecil flicked a switch and a faint purr was felt more than heard. Art took a light reading by Toby's cheek then repeated it next to his checkered shirt. Teddy stepped to the table, temporarily blocking the camera. He laid a furry knuckled hand on Mike's and Toby's shoulders.

"Just ignore all this junk. Pretend it doesn't exist. Go right ahead and do exactly what you did before." He wrapped his hand around the top of Toby's head like it was a coconut and turned it around to face him. "My God, he looks just like Robert Redford. There's no doubt about it. This could be the start of something big."

Toby smiled shyly and Teddy plopped down on the soft couch. Only the monotonous ticking of the clock behind the bar shattered the silence. Mike coughed lightly and glanced at the camera's red eye. What was about to take place could spell life or death for his research, but he wasn't as nervous as he thought he'd be.

"How do you feel, Toby?"

"Fine, Mr. Mancini. I have a little headache but it's not so bad," he said.

"We'll take care of that," Mike promised. "Watch my eyes closely, Toby. Just sit back and relax. Your eyelids are getting heavy. Do you feel it?"

Toby's eyes were already closed. He nodded wordlessly.

"Your eyelids feel like they have tiny weights hanging from them. Your hands are heavy, too. Very heavy. You can't move them they're so heavy."

Toby's fingers twitched lightly but his hands stayed flat on the tabletop.

"You're getting sleepy, Toby. You're falling into a very deep sleep, deep sleep, deep sleep."

Mike spoke with a low purr. The needles on the sound equipment quivered. Mike and Toby were bathed in the soft glow of the reflected light. Cecil B. had shut off the fading bars of the setting sun with a flick of the cord on the slat blinds.

"You're floating, Toby. You're floating on a cloud high in the sky, a soft warm cloud. You're relaxed and your mind's at peace. Now you're asleep, a deep, deep sleep."

The tape whirred softly. The camera closed in on Toby's tranquil face. It revealed only a little boy asleep. Its high-tech state-of-the art electronics couldn't begin to show the fascinating turmoil within.

"We're going to use the TV again, Toby. When I tell you to open your eyes I want you to look at the TV. Do you remember how we did that before?"

"When I open the next matchbox I'll see the memory on the TV," he said flatly.

"Exactly. And then I'll ask you to describe what you see. You can open your eyes now, Toby."

The boy's eyes snapped open and he stared vacantly at the empty screen. The camera tightened on the blank screen and then pulled back to encompass Toby and the teacher.

"I want you to go back to the memory room now, Toby." Mike hesitated for only a second. "Are you there?"

"Yes."

"Describe the room for us." Mike asked for the description for the benefit of the TV audience.

"It's a big room, as big as a football field. Everything's heavy. High stone walls with narrow windows around the top. There's sunlight coming through the windows and they make squares of light in a line down the middle of the room."

"How high are the walls?"

"Higher than our house. And they're covered with thick velvet drapes. Maroon. The room seems hard and cold. The floor is laid with irregular pieces of gray slate. It feels medieval."

"Do you remember what it reminded you of the first time that you saw it?"

"Camelot. Like something from King Arthur's court. It's exquisite."

Toby spoke with his child's voice but a mature choice of words. He seemed more comfortable in his surroundings, as if they were becoming familiar.

"Is there anything inside the room?"

"There's a table. It's in the middle of the room."

"Nothing else?"

"A few doors. They're set back inside deep stone arches. And there's a torch sticking over each door but they're not lit."

This was all new to Mike. "Where do the doors lead?"

"One leads to the memory closet. That's where I found the matchboxes. That room's empty now."

"Where do the others lead?"

"I don't know."

"Go into the memory room now, Toby." Mike hesitated once again. "Are you inside?"

"Yes."

"Walk over to the table. Are you there?"

"Not yet."

Mike waited. Teddy glanced at his watch and counted off the seconds.

"I'm at the table now."

It took eight seconds. It seemed much longer. It had never taken that long before.

"What does the table look like?"

"It's big and heavy with thick wooden legs. It's kind of like our pool table except that it has a smooth top."

"Is there anything on the table?"

"The pile of matchboxes."

"How many?" There was another hesitation.

"Nine."

"Take the matchbox from the top of the pile, Toby. Take it and read what it says on the cover."

The camera moved in close and Toby's serious

young face filled the screen on the TV monitor.
Teddy and Clancy leaned forward expectantly
from their perches on the couch. Mike held his
breath.

" 'Zigmund Horvitz.' The name on the matchbox is Zigmund Horvitz."

"How is it spelled, Toby?"

Toby spelled the name and Teddy printed it on
his notepad. Clancy flashed a victory sign to remind the teacher of their bet.

"Toby, I want you to look at the memory of
Zigmund Horvitz. I want you to open the matchbox then come back to the rec room so you can
watch the memory on TV. Open the matchbox,
Toby, and tell me what you see."

Cecil B. angled the camera to frame Toby and
the TV set. The screen was dull gray. Toby's eyes
were black as coals as they flicked across the
lifeless surface.

"Es raucht so viel hier."

"Say it in English please, Toby."

"There is so much smoke. It is difficult to see
clearly."

"Where are you?"

"I'm in the forest at the edge of the village."

"Are you alone?"

"No. All of the villagers are here."

"What is the name of your village?"

"Schwamlich."

"Where is Schwamlich?"

"It is in Bavaria near Augsburg."

"You mentioned smoke. Is something burning?"

"The smoke is from the funeral fires."

"Has someone died?" The memories are still
consistent, Mike thought ruefully.

"Mother is dead, Grandfather is dead, Irena is dead, the blacksmith is dead, Mr. Steinbrecker is dead. Many others whose names I do not know are also dead."

"How did all these people die?"

"They died from God's anger."

"God's anger? Why is God angry?"

"No one knows but He must be very angry to touch so many."

"How many have died?"

"Almost half the village has been touched. The schoolteacher was the first. He died five days ago. Then the miller's babies died. After that His finger touched every house in the village at least one time. I am the only one who has not been touched in our house. I am alone."

Cecil B. checked the monitor and was pleased to see the tear sparkle as it crept down Toby's cheek.

"I am afraid that His finger will touch me also."

"It won't," Mike promised. "Believe me, it won't." He felt a wave of relief when he realized how close the chain had come to being broken, and he thought he saw another look of relief cross the boy's face.

"Do you know the year?" he continued.

"Of course. It is sixteen hundred and forty-three years since the death of Christ."

"The plague," Clancy whispered.

"Who will care for you now?"

"Now I must care for myself. I am ten years old. I am not a child, you know."

"What will you do?"

"The blacksmith had no children. Perhaps I will learn his trade. I am very strong."

Toby's face hardened into a mask of determination, and Mike realized that he wasn't talking to ten-year-old Toby Horton of Roseville; he was discussing the future of ten-year-old Zigmund Horvitz of Schwamlich, Bavaria, a future that faded into history over three hundred years ago.

Toby sat erect, hands flat on the table. Only his eyes moved as he watched the scene unfold on the darkened Panasonic. Suddenly he jerked his hands to his face and covered his eyes. "Oh no!" he cried.

"What is it? What do you see?"

"The flames. They are reaching Irena," he sobbed. "I can't watch it. I can't."

"Turn off the TV, Toby," Mike ordered. "The memory is gone. Turn off the TV and relax."

Toby's face softened and the tears seemed out of place. The tension, which had been a physical presence, fled from the room. Art tilted the lighting umbrella slightly, erasing a shadow that darkened Toby's eyes. Cecil B. pulled back into wide angle and brought Mike into the picture once again.

"Just relax for a moment, Toby. Float on your cloud for a while. Are you there?"

"Yes," he said, sighing.

"When I snap my fingers you're going to wake up. You won't remember any of the memory. I'll do it on the count of three. One, two, three." The snap popped the needle on the recorder to the far right.

"Cut and print," Cecil B. announced.

"Is it over?" Toby asked.

*   *   *

"That's the house. The green one with the long driveway."

The pickup chugged noisily down the street, slowing as it rolled past the three cars parked at the curb. Esau felt a surge of excitement as he glanced quickly down the drive. The twins stared at the house openly.

"When will we do it?" Amos asked.

"God will tell us."

Chapter Twenty-three

THE MORNING BROKE with an egg-yolk sun in a sea-blue sky, the kind of day that only allows for wonderful events. Serious fishermen were already on the lakes and rivers and early worshipers flocked to sunrise services.

Toby was the first Horton to greet the new day, unable to resist the excitement stirred by the wand of sunlight that sliced across his bed. He had gone about his A.M. rituals soundlessly, careful not to wake the sleeping household. It was like him to be thoughtful and considerate, probably another something in his genes. He was barefooting around the kitchen like a foraging squirrel, gathering milk and Cheerios and sugar and berries and bowl and spoon. He didn't hear his father approach.

"Morning, son. I think you beat the rooster out of bed this morning."

"Hi, Dad. You're up kinda early yourself."

"Get the paper yet?" Steve asked.

"Not yet. I'll go get it now." He started for the door.

Steve held him up. "Not today you won't. You're the star. Today I'll do the dirty work."

Steve walked behind Toby's chair and squeezed the thin muscles of his shoulders. "Nervous, Champ?"

"A little. I'll be okay."

"I know you will. You know, we're all very proud of you, Toby."

"Aw yo, Dad. I didn't do anything special. Mr. Mancini says that what I have is a gift. I'm just lucky, that's all."

"I know. That's not what I meant. We're proud of the way you're handling it. Not only me and the rest of the family but Mr. Mancini and Dr. Kendall and Mr. MacBride as well. We're all proud of you."

"Thanks, Dad. I want to do the best I can. I think it's real important. Mr. Mancini says it will unlock doors to the mind. It's kind of like discovering a new medicine that can help people live longer."

"It could be something like that," Steve said proudly. "It sure could be."

"I'm anxious to see the tape, too," Toby admitted. He laughed with a little-boy giggle that helped his father put things back into perspective. "I'm supposed to be the star of the show but I'm the only one who hasn't seen it yet."

Steve gave the bony shoulders another tender squeeze. "Well, today's the day you make your grand debut." He grabbed a banana from the fruit plate and used it for a microphone. "Ladies and gentlemen and children of all ages." He strode to the sink like the center-ring announcer, and Toby pictured flowing tails and top hat. "Today—for your edification—and your enjoyment—the Teddy MacBride Show— is proud to present—the tall—the dark—the handsome—"

"The hungry." Gramps interrupted the center-ring introduction as he bustled into the kitchen with Tina nipping at his heels. "Movie stars can't do a decent day's work with no more than crunchy little letter *O*'s in their gut. That's for dandies like Kirby Whatsisname. Up-and-coming TV stars got to wrap their necks around some real man's food."

Tina wrapped herself around her grandfather's knees. "When are we going to eat, Gramps?"

"Soon." John rubbed the palms of his hands together like a mad scientist. "Now, zee first sing ve need are zee ingredients."

"Uh-oh." Tina moaned. "It sounds like icebox omelet again." She raced for the door. "I better tell Mom."

Gramps intercepted the little girl and scooped her up under his arm like a toy poodle. "Now you just let your mother sleep for a little while. It'll do her good to get away from this kitchen for a couple of extra minutes."

"Fat chance." Jan wandered sleepily into the sunny kitchen and automatically took command. "I appreciate the offer, Gramps, but we'll save your icebox omelet for another day. Today it's going to be apple pancakes and bacon."

Gramps sniffed petulantly. "Well, I suppose

TV stars would eat apple pancakes if they really had to," he said.

Toby grinned and winked knowingly at his grandfather.

Mike enjoyed the drive to Clancy's house and it was even more enchanting at such an early hour on such a perfect day. The cloistered little community of North Oaks sat like a priceless jewel encrusted at the top of Saint Paul's sparkling tiara. Mike loved to cruise its winding wooded streets. Shaded strips of tar with names like Duck Pass Road and Chipmunk Lane wound like meandering snail tracks through the leafy glades and secluded homes, befitting nature's grandeur, nestled in their pastoral embrace.

"Nancy! Come quickly and see what's in our driveway. Hurry before it runs away." Clancy stood on the front step and yelled back inside the house.

"Are the deer back?" she asked breathlessly. Then she appeared at his side and saw the object of Clancy's interest. She punched him in the ribs.

"Shhhh!" Clancy admonished. He whispered just loud enough for all to hear. "Don't make any sudden movements or you'll scare it away. Go back inside and get the camera."

Nancy folded her arms across her chest and leaned against the door frame. She fixed him with a reproachful glare.

"Look at its ears and nose," Clancy whispered in amazement. "They're grossly overdeveloped. That's how you can tell an East Side biology teacher from your more normal strain. And they usually have thick thumbs from too many nights in the bowling alley."

"Hi, Nancy."

"Hi, Mike. Do you have time to stop for a cup?" she asked hopefully. She liked to spend time with Mike Mancini. He was that rare kind of friend who meant equally as much to every member of the family. He was Uncle Mike to their two preschoolers, as important a family figure as any of the natural aunts and uncles who populated the area. Nancy Kendall wasn't simply the wife of Mike's good friend, she was a good friend in her own right, and wasn't it Mike's good fortune to be able to visit two such very good friends under the same roof?

"We don't have time to stop right now," he replied apologetically. "Okay if I take a rain check?"

"How about dinner tonight?" she countered.

"I thought you'd never ask."

"Don't I even get a vote?" Clancy asked, trying to appear put out but unable to pull it off.

"Where'd that come from?" Mike jerked a thumb at Clancy as if he were something that just crawled from under the porch.

"Beats me," Nancy said, playing along. She put her hands on her hips and studied her husband curiously from head to toe. "It might have wandered in from the woods."

"Think we ought'a shoot it?"

"Might not be in season." Nancy giggled, then she tucked her blond head under Clancy's chin and squeezed him close. "Off with the two of you. Don't forget, I'll be watching both of you on television. I don't want to see you sniffing around any of those young starlets."

"Nancy, I'm shocked," Mike said indignantly. "Have you forgotten? This man's a *doctor*." He pronounced the title as if it cloaked the bearer in a shell of righteousness.

They climbed into Mike's car and Nancy blew them both a kiss as they circled the driveway. Two little hands snuck through the upstairs curtains and waved good-bye. Clancy waved back and Mike blew a kiss.

"Nervous?" Clancy asked.

"A little," Mike admitted. "I feel like the producer of a new show waiting to hear from the critics after opening night. Can you believe it? Some of those Broadway shows are years in the making. Hundreds of people pour time and talent and money into the things, then they have to stew around and wait for a handful of twerps to tell them if it's any good. It doesn't seem fair. Today's opening day for the Mike Mancini show and I don't have any doubts that the show's good—at least, I'm sure the theory is. What I'm worried about now are the critics."

Clancy and Mike both wore comfortable slacks, loafers, and open-collar blue shirts. Their ties and sport jackets lay across the back seat. Teddy told them to be comfortable, assuring them the audience would be more sympathetic to them in the casual attire.

Mike whistled to himself and glanced from the window as they wound through the leafy estates on the way to the highway. "There aren't too many AFDC checks mailed to this zip code, I'll bet."

"You're absolutely right," Clancy agreed. "And it's regrettable. It makes us look like a bunch of elitist snobs. We're thinking of building a slum on the north side to achieve some balance."

Mike had to jerk to a stop to avoid creaming a golf cart that bolted onto the blacktop. The white-haired driver smiled guiltily and tipped his North Oaks CC golf cap in embarrassed greeting.

"There oughta be a bounty on 'em," Mike grumbled.

"Even the landed gentry need to play," Clancy said, chuckling. "And don't think for a minute that all of these high rollers are right-wingers. It wouldn't surprise me if some of my own neighbors didn't pull the donkey's tail in the privacy of the voting booth. You can take the boy out of Minnesota, et cetera. I hate to admit it but I think we might have more than a few closet Democrats in this last bastion of conservatism. So you better be careful who you run over, Teacher. You might squash a fellow pinko leftist, God willing."

Mike waved back at the driver of the cart and moved ahead cautiously. He pulled to a stop next to the guard shack at the entrance to the community, then swung left on Highway 96 and headed toward the freeway.

"Do you have a prepared statement or any kind of script to work from?" Clancy asked.

"No. I got the same instructions that you did. Teddy knows what questions he wants to ask. The way he described it to me, he's going to start the show with a monologue, discuss the theory for a couple of minutes, and give some background on what's happened up till now. Then he's going to play the video of the Zigmund Horvitz matchbox. After the tape, the station runs a public service ad and we file in with Toby. That's when the curtain goes up on opening day," Mike said ruefully.

"Break a leg."

"Don't be so literal."

"Lord, bless this food. Give us the strength to do Your bidding. Show us the way to victory over the defilers. We the members of Your earthly army ask this in Your name."

"Amen."

The twins snatched up their knives and forks as if a second's delay might cost them a meal, but then they sat motionless until Esau speared his fill of the pancakes from the top of the stack and unwound his ration of bacon strips from the greasy plate. When they were certain his plate was loaded they attacked the heaping platters with the grace of a starving dog pack.

The boys deserved to be hungry. They had worked late into the night passing out a record number of pamphlets and Esau had roused them again before the morning sun peeked over the horizon. Morning prayers were part of the family's standard devotion but the duration and intensity of this morning's session set new endurance records. Esau had thanked the Lord for everything from their humble house to the chief of police, and he asked the Lord to rain His curses on liberal senators, smutty movies, nonbelievers, *Playboy*, potholes, Canterbury Downs, and Soviet imperialism. Since his appointment as captain of the earthly army he read the newspaper voraciously, forming views on subjects that were of no interest only weeks earlier.

After the assortment of thanks and curses, Esau unfolded his full plan for the first time. The twins accepted it without question. Hattie had some misgivings but she kept them to herself. No good could come from antagonizing Esau, especially in his current state, so she did his bidding. She was in the small cellar moving boxes and organizing the room according to his plan when she heard the pickup roar down the street.

Teddy's fire-engine-red 300 ZX was in the far corner of the parking lot where it was too obvious to be easily stolen and far removed from the idiots who swing their doors open like cattle gates. He called the sports car his mid-life crisis escape vehicle. Mike expected Teddy to arrive at the studio first but he was surprised to see the Hortons' station wagon already there. As it turned out, Mike and Clancy were the last to arrive. A few other cars were scattered about the lot, probably belonging to the technicians.

The lot had two entrances, one from a secondary street that ran into West Seventh and the other a narrow alley that was normally clogged by trucks making deliveries. But today, except for an occasional car rumbling by, the place was a peaceful square of patchy blacktop basking in the brilliant Sunday morning sunshine. Clancy breathed deeply of the warm air that emanated from the spongy surface. It smelled like Sunday morning and soft tar. A short flight of metal stairs tucked between a pair of handicapped-parking spots led to a rear entrance. The metal door was hissing shut behind them as the pickup rattled through the alley.

"This is where the star sits." Teddy rested his arm on the back of the cushioned easy chair. "It's from here that I engage in witty repartee and issue quotable statements."

The set was dimly lit. It consisted of a coffee table, a few chairs, part of a wall with flowered paper and a print of a largemouth bass flashing from the surface of a still lake.

"I thought we'd be in a living room," Tina said. She looked questioningly around the set. "This is a fake."

"*Bella figura*," Mike answered in the tongue of his grandfather.

"What does that mean?" Teddy wanted to know.

"Look it up, genius," Mike kidded.

"Where do I sit?" Tina wondered.

"You and your folks will sit over there behind Cecil B."

They hadn't noticed the cameraman when they entered the studio. He stepped from behind the camera and waved at Tina. A small gallery of theater seats rose against the wall behind him. They were covered with green velvet, worn bare along the front edge by years of silent observation.

"Will Toby sit here, too?" Tina continued with unabashed curiosity.

Teddy picked her up under the arms and plunked her down in his own easy chair. "No. Not today, sweetheart. Today Toby's the star of the show." He smiled impishly. "Next to me, of course. Toby will sit over here with Mike and Clancy." He ran his hand along the back of a long sofa. "This is where the guests sit."

"Like on Johnny Carson?" Tina blurted.

"Exactly," Teddy agreed. "Except that I do a better monologue than Johnny. And speaking of monologues, let's huddle up and try to get our act together."

Teddy waved everybody around him. Cecil B. joined the group and Teddy ran them through the schedule. As he discussed the monologue, the tape replay, and the guest portion, Teddy wandered around the studio with the others trailing behind him like a tour group. It was mostly for Toby and Tina's benefit but Clancy and Mike enjoyed it as well. Teddy led them through the soundproof booth and explained how the producer controlled the action from that vantage point. The producer questioned whether anybody could control Teddy. He let the kids wear the headset of the soundman and they both looked through the eyepiece of Cecil B.'s camera.

It was fifteen minutes before showtime and Teddy kept up the running commentary. It helped put his guests at ease. Butterflies were a common malady for first-timers so Teddy kept them too busy to let their nerves get the best of them. Clancy recognized the tactic. He often used it himself on apprehensive patients.

Toby was by the doctor's side looking young and fragile in his blue slacks and crisp plaid shirt. Clancy laid a comforting hand on his shoulder. "How are you holding up, Toby? Ready for your big debut?"

"I have a little headache, Dr. Kendall. I think

I better take an aspirin." He turned to Teddy.
"Where can I get a cup of water, Mr. MacBride?"

Teddy pointed to the door leading to the parking lot. "There's a water fountain in that little
hallway. Grab yourself a snoot full of fresh air
while you're out there. It'll do you good. I'll call
you when we're ready to go."

Toby smiled wanly and walked off.

"Ten minutes, Teddy," the producer signaled.

"Got'ta spruce up for my public," Teddy said.
"You guys get your coats and ties on and swab
some axle grease on your cowlicks." He walked
off through a door labeled Employees Only.

An associate producer in tight jeans and tank
top turned on the set lights and did some last-
minute flitting about. She organized the seating
in the gallery and returned to her duties in the
booth. Cecil B. and a second cameraman flicked
some switches on their equipment and took some
light readings. The producer in the booth got the
lead-in tape and the public-service spot set up,
and made sure that the tape of Zigmund Horvitz's memory was ready to roll on cue. Mike and
Clancy knotted their ties and buttoned their collar buttons. Then they pulled on their sport coats
and parked in a couple of folding chairs under
the producer's window.

"Five minutes," the producer announced.

Teddy appeared from the side door running
his fingers through his bushy hair as if to undo
any damage he might have done in front of the
mirror. He went to his easy chair and the second
cameraman took readings off his sport coat. He
pointed at Teddy's wildly checked tie and grimaced. Cecil B. shook his head in disgust as if to
agree that some people never learn.

"Where's the star?" he asked.

"You told him he could go outside for a snoot full," Tina reminded him.

"So I did. Why don't you go get him, honey, and tell him that we're almost ready to go."

Tina skipped across the tiled floor. Her Sunday shoes made little crisp clicks as she ran. She pushed through the door.

"One minute, Teddy."

"Everybody check your neighbor's teeth for spinach," Teddy said as a final announcement.

The door to the hall burst open. "He's gone. Toby's not out there, Mr. MacBride. He went for a ride with some men in a truck."

Chapter Twenty-four

POLICE INSPECTOR Einar Borg arrived at the studio bristling with spring-loaded energy. He was a small man with eyes like piercing chips of flint that scanned, evaluated, decided. Precise features, intricately carved, lent an air of thrifty efficiency to his efforts. He was a compact detecting machine who moved with the grace of a mountain cat prowling its terrain with carefully placed paws, sweeping the scene with a twitch and a flick. His tan summer suit was crisp and spotless, a uniform ready for inspection cloaking a disciplined body, hard and wiry. Tiny lines around the eyes and streaks of gray in the hair were the only harbingers of his true age. He worked officiously but with a sensitivity that helped to round the sharp edges off the panic that hung so close around him and his clients.

"Tell me exactly what you saw, Tina."

The show was canceled, the set was now brightly lit. Tina sat nervously in Teddy's soft chair while the inspector perched on the edge of the sofa. He had a kindly way when the situation called for it, the ability to slow his metabolism, soften his chiseled features, and still the child's fear.

It had all happened so quickly. Toby's strange disappearance, Teddy and his producer scrambling about to find a fill-in program, police cars screaming into the parking lot. Teddy's regular watchers, those who hadn't already tuned out, were told something about technical difficulties and were watching a documentary about the Winter Carnival Ice Palace.

Tina fidgeted under the attention and Jan gripped her hand tightly. "Tell the officer exactly what you saw, Tina. Try to remember everything."

The young girl could feel the urgency behind the penetrating stares and was frightened by their expectations. Her lip trembled and pools of tears welled in her large blue eyes, balancing precariously on her lower lid before finally flooding down her soft cheeks. "They took him away with them," she sobbed. "Some men put Toby in their truck and then they drove away."

Einar Borg took a tissue from his pocket and

gently dabbed her reddened cheeks. "We're going to help find him for you, Tina. Don't you worry." He ran his fingers across her cornsilk hair, fingers short and square and meticulously trimmed. "How about a pop?" He turned to the associate producer. "Can you find a can of something fizzy for my girlfriend here?"

Tina forced a tight little grin. The AP hurried off in search of the soda and Inspector Borg took Tina's free hand. His grip was gentle compared to Jan's fearful clutch. "You say it was a truck, Tina? What kind of truck? What did it look like?" The questions flowed conversationally, gentle inquiries rather than barked demands.

"It was like Charlie's," she answered, feeling reassured under the detective's gentle prodding.

"Charlie is a boy who lives down the street from us," Steve cut in. "He has a beat-up old pickup."

"Was that what it was?" Borg pressed smoothly. "Was it a pickup truck?"

"Yes," she whispered.

"Do you remember what color it was?"

"I don't think so. It was just dark and dirty looking."

Detective Borg penned some notes. "Tell us about the people you saw, Tina. Were they all men or did you see any ladies with them?"

"I didn't see any ladies."

"How many men were there?"

"I think there were three. I'm not sure," she sobbed as her bravery deserted her again. "They were big and they had beards."

"Did you hear them say anything?"

"They said something like 'get in' or 'hurry

up.' It was only something like that." Her voice trailed off and a new river of tears began to flow. The associate producer handed her a can of Sprite.

Einar Borg gave her hand a small squeeze before he released it. "You just sit still and relax, Tina. If you think of anything else that you saw, be sure to tell us."

The girl nodded and sipped hesitantly at the can of soda.

The inspector scanned the faces of the others. He had asked them to gather in the gallery of seats at the rear of the set and he now paced in front of the three-tiered section like a trial lawyer addressing a jury. Teddy, Mike, Cecil B., and Clancy were in the first row; Jan, Gramps, and Steve were in the second row; and Teddy's studio staff and Sheila were in the back row. As was her Sunday custom, Sheila arrived at the studio after the opening of the show to take down the rambling ideas that Teddy usually had at its conclusion. This Sunday she got more than she bargained for.

"So far we know nothing about motive." It was difficult to tell whether the detective was talking to the assembled civilians or to the cluster of uniformed policemen who hovered nearby. "We don't know if this was a random act or a planned abduction, but until we learn something definite, I'm going to go on the assumption that the kidnappers specifically sought out Toby Horton."

It was the first time that the word *kidnap* had been spoken aloud, and at its mention, Jan drew in a sharp breath.

"Mr. and Mrs. Horton, can either of you

think of any reason for someone to want to kidnap your son? Remember, it may have absolutely nothing to do with Toby. Sometimes things like this happen where the parents are the target and the child is only an innocent victim caught in the middle. Do you have any enemies? Could it have anything to do with your business, Mr. Horton? Do you have access to large amounts of money that might be tempting?"

The inspector didn't really suspect that the line of questions was going anywhere but he was anxious to eliminate ransom or revenge as a possibility. It was the way he ran an investigation; peeling away layer after flimsy layer until all that remained were the seeds that might eventually bear fruit.

"I can't think of any reason why someone would want to use Toby to get at us," Steve answered. "We have no enemies and if it's money that someone's after there are better fish to fry than us."

The detective jotted some notes on his pad, then addressed Teddy MacBride. "Do you have any ideas, Mr. MacBride? Could this have anything to do with you personally or with your television show?"

Teddy ran his fingers through his bushy hair. He was shaken by the abduction and an air of concern had displaced his cocky, strutting style. He had the uncomfortable premonition that the kidnapping was in some way related to his show, but he couldn't make any logical connection. "I'm in the public eye every day of the week, Inspector, but unlike Steve Horton, I can't truthfully say that I have no enemies. I deal in controversy and that means conflict and that creates some enemies. But I still can't come up with any logical reason why someone would kidnap Toby Horton just to get at me."

"The key word there is *logical*," the detective ventured. "Too often logic doesn't play a part. At least not what you or I might consider logic."

Teddy shrugged and turned his palms up in a gesture of dismay. A mask of concern creased his brow. "There are a bunch of whackos out there who read my column and watch my TV show, Inspector, and I'm sure that more than a few of them don't care much for me. But kidnapping one of my guests—" His face wrinkled in disbelief.

"We have to investigate every possibility, Mr. MacBride. Have you received any threats recently—phone calls, letters—anything out of the ordinary?" The inspector paced in front of the seats, hands clasped behind his back.

"Nothing unusual that I can think of, Inspector." He twisted around to catch his secretary's eye in the back row. "How about it, Sheila. Can you think of anything strange lately?"

The gray-haired assistant grieved deeply for the Horton family's plight and had been racking her brain for some connection that might lead to the abductors. "You had a call yesterday afternoon from someone representing the Gay Rights Coalition. Some of their membership were miffed at being cut from the show today, but the caller seemed reasonable. He wasn't violent or anything like that."

"What was the caller's name?" the inspector asked, pen poised.

"I have it back at the newspaper office. I can run over and get it for you."

"Later. Can you think of anything else?" he asked.

Sheila pondered momentarily. A spark suddenly lit her eyes. "There were a couple of negative letters after Teddy's first column about Toby's dreams. One of the letters accused Teddy of using Toby to do the devil's work." She shrugged uneasily. "But we've had people say things like that about almost everything the least bit controversial. There was another strange letter on Friday. That one suggested that Toby's dreams were caused by the depletion of the ozone layer from all the hairspray being used."

The inspector smiled and his crisp features blended into boyish good looks. "Do you have those letters?"

"We sure do. Teddy doesn't throw out anything," she said in mild complaint. "Maybe for once that will be a blessing."

"I'd like to send someone to your office to pick up the letters and the name of the caller."

Sheila gave one of the uniformed policemen a key to the office and told him where to find the items requested by Inspector Borg.

Borg had put out an APB for the truck immediately after Tina's tentative description but pickups in Minnesota dotted every other driveway. Slim chance. He also instigated a search of criminal files to get a list of all known sex offenders, child molesters, and people with other types of erratic behavior, but Borg didn't tell the Hortons about that part of the investigation. Not yet. Nor did he expect any meaningful results from further interrogation at the TV studio, but he hated to cut it off. It only added to the family's despair if it appeared the investigation was running out of steam.

"We've got every cop within a hundred and fifty miles looking for that pickup and Toby's picture has been wired to every precinct." At this stage the detective grasped at any available straw to try to put the family at ease.

"Is there anything we can do to help?" John Horton asked. "Anything at all?"

"I don't think so, Mr. Horton. If you've all told me everything that might be pertinent, I'm afraid all we can do now is sit back and wait."

"Wait for what?" Jan asked, trying unsuccessfully to hide the tremor in her voice.

"For one of three things," Borg said with more confidence than he felt. "Hopefully we'll get a call that Toby was dropped off somewhere nearby, none the worse for wear." He ticked off the first point on his index finger. "Or second, one of the patrols will spot the pickup and we'll get a call telling us that they found Toby safe and sound. Or third"—he scanned their expectant faces, stopped at Steve—"we'll get a call from the kidnappers and we'll find out what this is all about."

Jan winced visibly at the last alternative. "What makes you think that it's one of those three?"

The detective stepped close to Jan and laid a comforting hand on her arm. "I think I know some of the other alternatives that are running through your mind, Mrs. Horton." He could see the turmoil in her reddened eyes. "You're worried that some harm will come to the boy—physical harm."

Jan took a deep breath and closed her eyes. The walls seemed to be closing in on her. She felt faint but managed to speak. "Yes, Inspector, that's exactly what's running through my mind. I want to know why you didn't list that as a possibility. Was it just to spare my feelings or do you suspect something you're not telling us? I need to know for my own sanity."

Einar Borg squeezed her arm reassuringly. "The answer is in what Tina just told us. There were three men, Mrs. Horton. As far as I'm concerned that's a positive piece of information. I know the horrible alternatives that are haunting you. You're letting yourself be tortured by newspaper accounts you've read about other abductions and disappearances. Unless I'm mistaken, every one of them probably has one thing in common."

Jan opened her eyes and knuckled some tears from her cheeks. She looked up hopefully.

"In almost every kidnap case where physical harm occurs the abductor acts alone. The weirdos who make the headlines don't travel in groups, Mrs. Horton. They usually live deep inside themselves. They don't share their sickness with others, they're too ashamed of it." He looked up and addressed the entire group. "I don't think that we're dealing with a random abduction. I think that these men wanted Toby and I think they knew exactly where to find him. If they hadn't been able to do it today, they would have kept trying until they were successful. Toby just made it easy for them today when he went outside for air."

"And I suggested it," Teddy lamented.

The detective shrugged. "Nobody's to blame

for anything. What we need now is faith and patience."

"Would it be all right if the family went home now?" John asked wearily. "I think we'd be more comfortable there."

"I was going to suggest it," the inspector said.

"If it's all right with the Hortons, I'd like to go with them," Teddy said. Mike and Clancy expressed their desire to go along also. The inspector assigned a detective to accompany them and the anxious group filed from the studio.

The hours since the abduction droned on end-lessly and every tick of the clock without word of Toby's whereabouts sent a new stab of fear into each family member. Jan sat on the cool porch staring silently at the orange sunset. Steve paced restlessly, first across the plank deck and down the steps to the yard. Then, with head down, hands sunk deep in his back pockets, he'd pace across the yard, over the narrow strip of sandy beach and down the length of the wooden dock where he'd lean against the railing of the pon-toon boat and gaze absently across the water, studying the homes on the opposite shoreline. Then he'd reverse his steps and return to the porch.

Gramps sat stiffly in the corner of the porch with nothing to say, too heartbroken even to join in the occasional speculation among the family and friends.

Tina had been sent to bed shortly after eight o'clock. She wasn't tired but she offered no re-sistance. The little girl wasn't fully aware of the significance of Toby's disappearance, but the gravity wasn't lost on her. She knelt stiffly by the side of her bed and had a serious conversation with God. Then she lay in her bed with the bright yellow canopy and wept silently.

Sheila had found a pizza in the freezer and baked it in Jan's oven. They ate it in mournful silence, tasting nothing, conscious only of their bodies' need for fuel. It served the meager appetites of the entire group with a slice left for the detective assigned by Captain Borg. The policeman chewed the last piece of hard crust as he tried to melt inconspicuously off to the side of the porch.

The police and the phone company had worked hand in hand and were poised to trace any call that came in. A sound-actuated device was attached to the phone by Jan's side to record the kidnapper's words should they ever come.

The sky was painted with a palette of harsh brush strokes. The spires of the evergreens across the lake speared the brilliant horizon like pointing fingers celebrating the artist's excellence. It was the type of sunset the Hortons would often enjoy in the canopied pontoon boat, putt-putting around the shoreline, nodding pleasant greetings to other boaters or waving to neighbors enjoying the sunset in their bright canvas lawn chairs.

But tonight God's artistry was wasted on the Hortons. There was no room in their hearts for beauty. Such thoughts were blocked by a gnawing fear, a fear that was crystallized when the phone jangled at Jan's elbow.

The detective was by her side before the second ring. The tape machine began to whirr automatically. Jan looked expectantly at Steve. The phone rang once again and he snatched it from the cradle.

"Hello." He wanted to be calm but his voice barked shrill and brittle.

"Steve. It's Marvin. I just saw it on the news—about Toby. I don't know what to say. It's terrible. Is there anything Gloria and I can do to help?"

Steve's heart beat like a jackhammer. His voice cracked when he replied. "Thanks, Marv. No. There's nothing you can do right now. We'll let you know if there is."

"You're sure? We can come right over."

Steve fought to keep his voice even but the impatience broke the surface. "Marv, we have to keep this line open in case anyone calls about Toby. I have to hang up now. I'll talk to you later."

He hung up the phone and frowned at Teddy. "It's on the nine o'clock news. That was a neighbor calling to help."

Before Teddy could reply the phone rang again.

"Hello."

"Steve, it's Helen Sorenson. I just heard about what happened to Toby. I'm so sorry. How's Jan? Can she come to the phone?"

"Helen, we have to keep the phone lines open for the police. We'll get back to you as soon as we can. Thanks for calling."

He replaced the receiver with a trembling hand and ran his fingers through his straight black hair. "Now what do we do? If anybody's trying to contact us, they won't—"

Even before he could finish the sentence the phone rang again. Steve grabbed it.

"Hello," he snapped.

"Let me speak to Mr. Horton."

"This is Mr. Horton. Who are you?"

Jan looked up hopefully and a finger of fear stabbed at her chest. The detective held his breath. Teddy, Clancy, and Mike caught each other's eye in a silent signal, a wish for some good news.

"My name isn't important. I have your son."

"Why? Who are you? What do you want?"

"I want one million dollars, Mr. Horton. I want one million dollars in cash by the end of the week. I'll call you back tomorrow and tell you how to deliver it."

The phone clicked off and Steve stared dumbly at the silent receiver.

"What was it?" Jan shrieked. Her courage had finally deserted her. John Horton reached over to take her hand and comfort her but she pulled sharply away. "What did he say? Where is he? Where's my baby?" She buried her face in her hands and sobbed.

"What did he say, Steve?" Teddy asked sympathetically.

Steve repeated the brief conversation, surprised that he recalled it word for word.

Teddy shook his head doubtfully. "It sounds like a crank call to me."

"A crank," Jan cried. "What kind of a person would do something like that? What kind of a—"

The phone jarred them once again. Steve let it

ring twice then he breathed deeply and lifted it from the table.

"Hello."

"I want to speak to Mr. MacBride."

"Who is this?"

"I want to speak to Mr. MacBride."

"Just a moment." Steve cupped his hand over the mouthpiece and motioned to the rumpled journalist. "He wants to talk to you."

The detective nodded vigorously. Teddy pushed up from his chair and took the phone. No one else moved. Even the crickets postponed their twilight trill.

"This is Mr. MacBride." He tried to keep the anxiety from his voice. Keep calm, Teddy. Sound normal. Don't scare him off.

"You use your position to do the devil's work, Mr. MacBride. Your voice is heard by thousands and you stand in the devil's pulpit and shout Satan's evil words." There was a pause as the caller waited for a response.

"What would you like me to do?" Teddy asked. The lines on his face told the others that this was no crank call.

"And you bring an innocent child into Satan's camp to assist you in his evil work. Only the Lord has the power of revelation, Mr. MacBride. Only the Lord sees the past and the future. The Lord seeks to destroy the defilers, the fortune-tellers, the prostitutes, the blasphemous, and the idle." The caller's voice rose in pitch as he progressed through his endless list of evildoers.

Steve gestured frantically and mouthed the question, "Is it him?"

Teddy shrugged apologetically. He wasn't

ready to commit unequivocally that the caller was the kidnapper. "What do you want me to do?" Teddy repeated.

"The boy is here with me. He must be cleansed."

"Can I speak to him?"

The caller ignored the question. "He must be cleansed of the tainted seed that you planted inside him, Mr. MacBride. He must rid himself of the seed of Satan and he must cease to do the devil's work."

"Who are you?" Teddy asked cautiously. He knew that he was talking with someone who was balancing on the fine edge of reality. He was afraid to push too far.

"I am the appointed captain of the earthly army of the Lord. I do His will as He has instructed me." The man spoke with the confidence of one who *was* so selected. His perseverance unnerved Teddy.

"Did the Lord instruct you to kidnap Toby Horton?" Teddy accused.

The caller's outrage escaped the phone and its vehemence sent a spear of shock into everyone on the porch. "Kidnap," he shrieked.

Teddy jerked the receiver from his ear.

"You dare to say kidnap? At God's command I have rescued the boy from the clutches of the devil and you dare accuse me."

"I'm sorry," Teddy said hurriedly. "I shouldn't have used that word. May I speak to the boy?"

"No."

"When can he come home to his family? They're very worried about him, you know."

Teddy sensed a moment's hesitation before the

caller continued. "Why were they not worried when they allowed the devil to possess his mind and body? The boy must be cleansed. Nothing else matters. He will be returned when he is cleansed."

The phone clicked off abruptly and Teddy stared at the dead receiver. He placed it softly into its cradle and sank onto the porch chair. He could feel Jan's pleading eyes boring into him but no one spoke. A blue heron with a giant wingspan glided to the end of the dock and stood like a guarding sentinel. A largemouth bass leaped from the lily pads and snared an unsuspecting creature from the water's surface.

Teddy shook his head slowly from side to side. "I don't know. I just don't know."

He described the conversation to Steve and Jan, and the others listened attentively. A blue-uniformed policeman had been monitoring the police radio from a patrol car parked in the garage. He hurried to the detective's side.

"They missed him. They traced the call to a pay phone at Rosedale. Couldn't have missed the guy by more than a minute or two but they came up empty." His eyes met Jan's. "But they're still looking." Turning back to the detective, "Do you think he's our man?"

"Could be." He thanked the officer and sent him back to the radio car. "I want to play the tape back now. Maybe there's something on it that will give someone a clue."

The detective took the tape from the recorder and replaced it with a new one. He wanted the machine to be ready in case there was another call. Then he took a portable from his pocket and snapped in the tape. It rewound with a rapid hiss. He replayed it from the start.

Some of Jan's greatest fears were realized as she listened to the solemn, resonant voice. Her boy was in the hands of a madman and the fear in her face reflected the outrage that poured from the small recorder.

"Well," the detective asked at its conclusion, "does anybody recognize the voice?"

Jan shook her head slowly from side to side. "My baby," she muttered. "What will he do to my baby?"

"Detective." Sheila raised her hand to get the man's attention.

"Yes, miss? Did you recognize the voice?"

"Not the voice, Officer. It was the words that were familiar." She turned to Teddy. "Do you remember the crazy letter, the one after the first column about Toby?"

The journalist massaged his brow then shook his head apologetically.

"I wouldn't expect you to," she said with a smile. "Except that you even mentioned it in a later column. Do you remember the guy who was going to attack with His earthly army if you didn't stop doing the devil's work?"

A spark of recognition flashed across the journalist's face. "Of course. And those were the words he used—earthly army and devil's work—just like this guy used on the phone tonight."

"Do you have the letter?" the detective asked eagerly.

"You have it," Sheila replied. "One of the officers went to my office this afternoon and picked it up. I think he gave it to Captain Borg."

The detective squatted down in front of Jan

and gripped her trembling hands. "This is a real lead, Mrs. Horton, a good lead. We have a tape of his voice and a sample of his handwriting. Who knows, maybe somebody even saw him make the phone call from Rosedale. We're on his trail now, right behind him. We'll get him. Don't worry."

Jan forced a wan smile. Gramps reached over for her hand and this time she took it.

Chapter Twenty-five

❖❖❖❖❖❖❖❖❖❖

NOT ONCE DID Toby cry during the kidnapping. Even during the scary ride in the pickup he got no worse than a bulging lump in his throat. He never had been a cryer. Gramps liked to kid him about it. Like the time he was building a bird-house and whacked his thumb with a hammer. It puffed up like a ripe plum and throbbed like a toothache.

"If that hadda been me, I'da bawled my fool head off," Gramps had said admiringly.

But Toby just gritted his teeth like a Spartan warrior and waited for the pain to give up. It always did. He was stoic when it came to pain. But sadness was another thing altogether. He cried himself to sleep the night of Greatgramps's heart attack. Last summer he had sniffled for hours over the little yellow songbird that had flown headlong into the sliding door, sobbing silently when its tiny wings fluttered their last twitch as it lay in his outstretched hand. Sadness made him cry—pain didn't.

Fear?

He didn't know about that yet.

Toby hadn't been afraid on too many occasions in his young life. Not until the kidnapping. At first he was too surprised to be afraid. It happened so fast. He had popped a couple of aspirin for his headache and, as Teddy suggested, he stood outside the metal door and breathed in a refreshing lungful of the morning air. It did make him feel better, at least temporarily. Then the old pickup rattled into the handicapped-parking spot next to the steps and a red-haired man jumped out. Toby figured he was another technician late for the show and in a big hurry. But instead of entering the studio, the man bounded up the steps. "Toby Horton?" he asked. Toby nodded and without warning the man wrapped one hand around Toby's mouth and the other around his waist and carted him down the steps to the waiting pickup. The whole thing was over before Toby even knew what was happening, but he recalled every frightening moment. He remembered being squeezed in the front seat with the three men and how one of them pulled the itchy wool stocking cap over his eyes and wouldn't let him pull it off. And then there was the smell. It reminded him of the gymnasium at school, sneakers and underwear and armpits. There was still a musty hint of it in the air but he didn't know if it was burned in his memory or rubbed on his clothes.

The conversation was curious too, what little there was of it. No one had actually said any-

thing mean or unkind to him. The man who
snatched him from the steps said "Come with
me please," or something halfway polite like
that, not that he gave Toby any choice in the
matter. And once they were on the road the
driver grunted some kind of prayer and the other
two mumbled "amen" from time to time. It was
strange but not quite intimidating and Toby
didn't know what to make of it.

So he didn't say a word. Not during the drive,
about fifteen minutes he figured, not when he
was lifted from the truck and carried through a
door and down a flight of steps, not when he was
led into a room by a firm, guiding hand on his
elbow. Only when he heard a door click shut
behind him and felt the ominous silence did he
finally speak.

"Can I take the hat off now?"

He could see tiny pinpoints of light through
the loose knit, but he couldn't make out the
surroundings—or the company if there was any.

"Can I take it off?" he asked again.

His answer was silence. A board creaked on
the floor above him and he heard a door slam
somewhere in the distance. But no one answered.
He slid his thumb between his nose and the dark
blue wool and peeled the cap from his head. The
light was harsh and it brought back the stirrings
of his headache. He hadn't even thought about
that since he took the breath of fresh air on the
studio steps. He scratched his itchy forehead and
squinted to ease the pain.

The pale yellow light shone from a bare bulb
screwed into a porcelain ceiling fixture. The
walls and ceiling were of Sheetrock that had
never been taped or painted. The floor was bare

concrete. The place was surprisingly cool, a small room filled with a jumble of books and cartons that made it seem even smaller than it actually was. A narrow metal cot with a sweat-stained mattress was tucked into a corner next to a card table and a spindly green chair. A pair of folding chairs were set up in the middle of the room. Four stacks of sealed cartons were piled in another corner and two stacks of magazines that reached Toby's chest were next to them.

There were two doors in the room. One was open, revealing a closet-sized bathroom with a toilet and sink. An oak-framed mirror with a crack running from upper left to lower right hung above the basin like the sales graph of a bankrupt business. The other door was shut, the door that Toby entered by. He edged over to it and tried the knob. He wasn't surprised to find it locked.

The walls were cluttered with a picture pan-orama of Christianity including three crucifix-ions, a variety of saints, and two Last Suppers, one a large print over the cot and the other a framed five-by-seven. *Today is the first day of the rest of your life* was printed in red Gothic, surrounded by gold leaf and hung in a rich ma-hogany frame next to the bathroom door. The Lord's Prayer was printed on what appeared to be a dish towel hung over the desk. *The Lord is my shepherd* was carved into the wooden plate around the light switch and a large leather Bible was carefully placed in the middle of the desk.

Toby didn't know what to make of it. His brief glimpse of the men's faces hadn't terrified him. They didn't look like ogres and they didn't scream at him or push him around. If anything they were polite, almost gentle. And they believed in God in a really big way and that confused him. Really bad people didn't believe in God. At least that's what he had always thought. But if they weren't bad, then why did they snatch him away from the studio? They must know that his family would worry. His mom worried so much anyway. She must be frantic about this. And his poor dad would have to worry about Toby and his mother. And what could they tell Tina? If Toby couldn't understand any of this, what would little Tina think? And what about Gramps? He'd be worried sick by now, and then there's Greatgramps lying in a hospital bed with searing pains rocketing through his chest.

That's when Toby decided. These people must be bad. If they were good, they wouldn't frighten people that way. With the decision made, he had to decide what to do about it. He put his hands on his hips and scanned the room one more time, hoping to find a way to just stroll out—but it didn't look hopeful. The door he had tried earlier wasn't an option. His only hope was the small bathroom and he crossed the room to look inside. There was no Sheetrock here, only exposed two-by-four studs on the inside and unfinished cinderblock on the outside wall. There was a window at the ceiling level. Besides the locked door it was the only exit. The outside of the glass was coated with mud and only thin streaks of light trickled through. Toby recognized it as the inside of a basement window well. It was a possibility.

He retraced his steps to the magazine piles and glanced at the covers, picking at the top few in each stack, expecting to find *Sports Illustrated* or *National Geographic*, but they were issues of *Farmer's Weekly*, *Harvest*, seed catalogs, and a mixture of religious magazines, one unread, still in its brown wrapper. Toby saw that it had an address label and he pulled it from the stack.

> Esau Manley
> P.O. Box 1288
> Mankato, MN

He tore the white sticker from the wrapper and stuffed it in his pocket. He wasn't sure why he did it but it seemed a good idea.

The thought of escape tied his guts in a knot but he had to start thinking of a way out. Waiting around for something good to happen wasn't enough. He returned to the bathroom and studied the window. It was cheap but functional, two crusty panes in an aluminum frame with a twist lock at the bottom, too gritty to see through. Looking up made his head hurt.

Memories of Jimmy Hawkins and Long John Silver, Tom Sawyer and Injun Joe. He felt as one with his storybook heroes and imagined that their hearts raced and their mouths dried at their own moment of decision. They survived their ordeal so why shouldn't he?

He stepped onto the toilet seat and stood with feet spread, leaning slightly from side to side, testing its strength, making sure that the fixture could support him. Then he pivoted toward the cinderblock wall and reached toward the window.

It was a full-depth basement. Eleven courses of knuckle-scraping cinderblock raised the ceiling to over eight feet. The window's top was even with the ceiling and the bottom was within

Toby's grasp. He stretched toward the locking device. It was grimy and covered with rust. His hand brushed against an ancient cobweb and he recoiled, lost his balance. He had almost recovered when he heard the nearby footsteps. Waving his arms like a windmill, he tumbled backward, thudded into the studded wall, caught himself, skipped to the floor, and scurried into the room. It wasn't much exertion but he was breathing heavily and his heart raced wildly.

His courage drained through his legs, wrung from his slender body like a twisted dishrag. His knees turned to jelly as he watched the doorknob slowly turn. The door creaked partly open and he froze.

"Yoo-hoo! Anybody home?"

The door swung open and Toby stared wide-eyed at the cow of a woman who filled the frame. She was a mountain of flesh draped in a wrinkled housedress bigger than Toby's two-man pup tent. Her hair hung straight, a shiny waterfall plunging to massive mounds of shoulders and breasts. Her eyes were black buttons peeking through folds of flesh. The woman's cheeks and jowls quivered as she muscled her lips into a cautious smile.

"So there you are," she said playfully.

If Toby didn't see her, he would have thought a little girl had spoken. She waddled into the room and closed the door behind her.

"Your name's Toby."

She spoke as if she had just christened him with the name. She didn't ask it like a question and it certainly wasn't news to Toby.

"My name's Hattie."

She crossed to the desk, pulled out the spindly chair, and lowered herself onto its fragile seat. Toby expected the wood to splinter like kindling but the chair was steady as a rock as flaps of her bottom draped over its sides. Toby felt cool, almost chilly, but he noticed tiny droplets of perspiration glistening on the woman's face. She was trying to be friendly and he felt his tension ease but his legs were still rubbery. He leaned against the wall to steady himself.

"Whats'a matter, Toby? Cat got your tongue?"

Gramps often used the same line, and the familiar words released another wave of tension.

"No, ma'am."

"That's better. You hungry?"

"No, ma'am."

"Is that all you can say? No, ma'am?"

"No, ma'am."

He realized he said it again and a sheepish grin spread across his face. Hattie giggled with him and he was sure the chair would go this time. Every bit of her shook, from her earlobes to her ankles, and Toby's smile widened as he recalled Gramps's description of Jell-O. "Nervous pudding" he called it. That's what Hattie reminded him of as she giggled and shook.

"C'mon over here and let me get a good look at you."

She gestured with a pudgy finger and Toby walked uncertainly toward her.

"My Lord, Toby, I'm not going to bite you. I just wan'na get a look at you."

He moved closer but stayed cautiously out of reach.

"You're a good-looking one, all right." She put

her hands on her knees and leaned closer. "You look like you're smart as a whip, too. You do good in school?"

Toby nodded. "Pretty good, ma'am."

"I bet you do. I can see it in your eyes. They're smart eyes. That's what they are."

"Thank you, ma'am," he stammered.

"Don't thank me. Thank the good Lord. He's the one who gives out the good looks and the brains." Her face lit up and she started the Jell-O giggle again. "He gave me extra helpings of pounds. That was His gift to me. And He can take some of 'em back any time He feels like it." She laughed heartily at her own joke, too hard, as if humor came to her so infrequently that every small piece of it had to be squeezed dry.

Toby grinned shyly at the joke. There was God again. The men's prayers in the truck, the holy pictures on the wall, Hattie's frequent mentions—how could they be bad?

Hattie stopped her own chuckle and leaned closer. "You're all right, ain't you, boy? Those men of mine didn't do you no harm, did they?"

"Oh no, ma'am. Nobody hurt me."

"Good thing," she said, "I ain't so sure I care for any of this no how."

The woman's concern gave Toby a new infusion of courage. "Why did they take me away?" he asked.

He stepped closer, within reach of her pudgy hands. He heard some thumping noises from somewhere above and Hattie looked uncertainly at the ceiling. She took his small hand in her own. Subtle expression was hard to come by in her puffy face but Toby read the sadness in her eyes and it frightened him. Why should she feel sad about him?

"You'll have to ask the mister about that," she apologized.

"Is he the man who drove the truck?"

"That'd be him. He's a good God-fearin' man. Name's Esau. He's my man." The admission conveyed a sense of duty, a need to justify her being there, to justify Toby's being there.

"Then why did he take me away? Why would anybody want to take a little boy away?"

"Don't you worry none, boy. Ain't nobody gon'na hurt you. They just want to get some of them fool notions out'a your head. Soon as that's done the mister will take you home to your family." She smiled mirthlessly and looked into Toby's dark eyes. "You got yourself any brothers at home?"

"I have a little sister."

"What's her name?"

"Tina. And my gramps and greatgramps live with us, too. Except Greatgramps is in the hospital right now. He had a heart attack." Toby had trouble squeezing the last sentence around the lump in his throat.

It didn't matter because Hattie wasn't listening. "Never did have no little girls myself," she mused. "Just the twins. That's how God blessed me." Hattie's gaze was fixed at some point over Toby's shoulder in a dreamy stare. The wistful grin reappeared on her puffy lips. "They was always good boys, praise the Lord." She glanced at one of the crucifixion pictures to personalize her thanks. "Know what they used to do when they was your age?"

Toby shook his head.

"They worked the farm just like little men. Did the milkin', helped with the chores, worked the tractor with wood blocks on the pedals so they could reach they were so tiny." Her eyes misted and she rubbed at them with a fat knuckle.

Toby wasn't sure if he owed her a reply. "Yes, ma'am."

"Wasn't all that long ago, neither." Her face brightened as she reminisced. "Used to have a big white barn down south of here. Good clean farm country, a good place to raise the twins. It got kind of run-down there near the end, but when times was good, me and Esau and the twins used to keep it as spanky as a new button. Amos and Abel was about your size and each of 'em had their own bucket and horsehair brush. The mister told them that they was in charge of paintin' the low spots. Seems as if they could spend a whole summer brightening up the bottom of that barn."

"I painted our garage last summer."

"Bet'cha did a pretty good job of it, too," she praised.

"Yes, ma'am." He wanted her to know that. He wanted to stack up well against the twins.

"Them was the good times. Lots of hard work—milkin', cuttin', calfin'—didn't never seem to end but that didn't matter none." She wasn't even aware of Toby's presence now. She was stroking herself with happy thoughts from another time, a drugless high.

"Esau used to laugh a lot in them days. He used to give the boys horseyback rides, then he'd chuck them into the hay pile and they'd curl up and giggle like a pair of hamsters. He was a handsome man in them days." Her voice rose in pitch as if expecting a challenge. "When he was courtin' he used to get hisself all sparked up in his blue suit and come a'callin'. My daddy was so pleased."

A loud thud from the floor above jarred Hattie back to the present. After a moment's disorientation she took Toby's hand and gave it a squeeze. "Anyway, boy, that was a long time ago, when we still had the farm and before the mister saw his first vision." She sighed wearily and pushed herself ponderously to her feet. "Things is so different now. The good Lord saw fit to take the farm and He asked Esau to do some other work. Important work, mind you. Praise the Lord," she muttered halfheartedly.

Hattie tugged the wrinkled housedress away from her damp body and began waddling toward the door. "You sure you ain't hungry, boy?"

Toby hesitated and she dug her hand deep into her pocket.

"I thought so." She extracted an apple and placed it in his hand. "Got'ta keep up your strength. The mister will be along in a little while. He's a good man, Toby. He don't mean no harm. He's only doin' the will of the Lord."

Hattie's ominous apology didn't lessen the weight of Toby's fear but he tried to smile bravely. "Thank you for the apple, ma'am."

"The twins was real polite, too. They was such good boys." She stopped at the door and pointed toward the desk. "Bible's there if you're lookin' for somethin' to read."

The door clicked shut behind her and Toby knew without trying it that it was locked.

Toby sat at the desk nibbling small wedges from the apple and chewing out the drops of juice. Gramps said he nibbled like a field mouse and Toby would wrinkle his nose and sniffle like a cartoon chipmunk.

He leafed idly through the Bible. He liked the crisp feel of the pages but he furrowed his brow at the mystical meaning of the words. He studied Bible tales in Sunday school and delighted in the stories of parting seas and forbidden apples, but he couldn't find such tales in the pages of this ancient tome. He bit another juicy sliver and sucked it between his teeth. He wasn't hungry. He wasn't even conscious of eating. The apple was more of an activity than a snack. Like turning the pages of the Bible, it helped him keep his mind off his predicament.

Hattie had only half eased his mind. He wasn't afraid of being harmed anymore but he wished he knew what this was all about. What did she mean about fool notions in his head? He didn't have any fool notions. If she's looking for fool notions, how about snatching kids away and pulling stocking caps over their eyes? Now *that's* a fool notion. "Such good boys" she called them. Good boys didn't snatch little kids. He took an angry bite from the apple then swiveled in the chair to glance at the open bathroom door.

Why not? he challenged himself.

He snuck a quick glance at the locked door, then crossed to the bathroom.

His head hurt again, a stabbing pain over his right eye. There was no pattern to his headaches. Sometimes the back of his head throbbed with every beat of his heart. Other times it felt like a clamp steadily squeezing from ear to ear. He knew this one would get worse.

Toby was having trouble getting a handle on his emotions at the moment. Some of his fear had been assuaged by Hattie's revelations. His anger had also been tempered, and what remained was more like resentment, a deep resentment of someone Hattie called "the mister."

Esau.

What kind of name was Esau anyway? Toby wondered. Wasn't that the name of one of those old-time baseball players that Gramps was always going on about? No. That was Enos—Enos Slaughter.

It was Toby's resentment of the "mister" along with the tempered fear that fed his courage as he studied the crusty windowpane. Toby knew he could stand on the toilet seat and reach the latch, but that wouldn't be good enough. Even if he could open the window, how would he pull himself up to the ledge? Maybe if he stood on the back of the toilet.

Toby hesistated for an instant, steeled himself, then stepped up on the toilet seat. The bathroom door was to his back, the window was in front of him above his head. The back of the toilet was against the cinderblock wall. Toby stretched his arm toward the window as he had done before. His fingers curled over a lip that formed a narrow ledge at the top of the block. He needed the grip for reassurance and support for his next precarious step. With his right foot planted in the center of the white wooden seat he carefully placed his other foot on the porcelain tank top.

He wished he had on his sneakers, but his mother had insisted that he wear his dress loafers to Teddy's show. He liked how they looked but they weren't the best wall-climbing shoes. He tested his weight. He gripped the ledge with both hands now, one foot on the seat and the other on the tank top so he could shift any or all of his weight to either location. He put some more stress on his arms, dug his fingers over the lip, and lifted his foot from the seat. He pictured the tank top splitting in half like a graham cracker and his leg plunging into the cold water with all the pipes and floats and other slimy stuff. He held his breath and eased the tension from his arms, then let out a long, slow breath as the tank top held.

A trickle of cold sweat rolled down his side. He shuddered and caught his breath. The latch was now right at eye level, within easy reach, and he got a better look at the whole arrangement. With the latch released, the window would swing inward from a long hinge that ran along the side. He'd have to find something to prop the window open so he could scramble through but that could wait. First he had to make sure it would even open.

The metal latch was brown with rust, and bits of the oxidized surface crumbled against his fingers. He gripped it with one hand, used the other for balance, and twisted.

It didn't budge.

A salty drop rolled down his forehead into his eye and he blinked the sting away. The thumping sounds from the room above began again and he recognized the even cadence.

Footsteps.

Toby filled his lungs with air and clamped his jaw in a determined set. He managed to fit both hands on the latch and he twisted with every muscle in his slender young body. For a moment nothing happened, then he heard the metallic snap and felt an instant of exhilaration—until he realized that he was falling free of the wall with a piece of broken metal in his hand.

The concrete floor slammed into his back and the air exploded from his lungs. His back teeth crunched down on the edge of his tongue and the coppery taste of blood flooded his dulled senses. Lights flashed, his mouth was on fire, and his head exploded an instant before the welcome black curtain descended and separated him from the rest of the world.

"Are you okay, boy? Toby, are you all right? He ain't movin', Amos."

"He's breathin'. Look, you can see his chest movin' up and down."

The voices floated all around him, unintelligible, out of reach, peaceful.

But then came recognition. It was slow at first; a tingling of awareness, a familiar thought.

"Look! I think he moved."

"Yeah. Look at his hand. His fingers are moving."

Toby flexed his hands as he recalled the plunge. In his mind he reached for the window ledge to catch his balance and then the entire scene came flooding back.

"He's opening his eyes."

Toby blinked and the glare of the harsh light sent a wave of shock from his eyes to the back of his head. The sounds became voices and the voices became words but the words still had no meaning. Indistinct shapes bobbed and weaved before his eyes—head-shaped images crowned with red.

"You took a bad tumble."

"Yeah. We were watchin'."

"You—you were watching?" Toby's tongue was thick and dry in spite of the painful bite and steady drip of blood. Lines became sharper and features formed on the bobbing shapes. A new worry stabbed at Toby. I'm seeing double, he thought. And it seemed so real. The faces were curious and not at all unkind. High cheekbones flowed smoothly into strong jaws and carved lips. The eyes were worried and flecked with green. The hair was thick and full and as red as Toby's bicycle. Toby blinked rapidly to bring them together but the faces refused to blend into one.

"Yep," one of the faces answered. "We was watchin' you the whole time."

Twins, Toby realized. These are the twins that Hattie talked about. *Such good boys.*

"Yeah," the other face added. "You was already standin' up on the hopper when we opened the door."

"That was some tumble. Good thing you're a little 'un. It's easier to handle a fall like that if you're a little 'un."

"Like a colt," the other added. "Colts can take a little bangin' around but the mare breaks pretty easy."

Toby shook his head to clear away the last of the dust and the effort sent a new flare of pain over his eye.

"Let's get you up off that cold floor, boy. Easy does it now."

Toby didn't even help as he was plucked from the concrete and gently carried to the cot. He sank into the webbed spring and the thin mattress wrapped around him like a cocoon. It felt reassuring.

"How come you was climbin' up on the toilet, Toby?"

"You don't have to ask him that, Abel. He was tryin' to climb out that window. Ain't that right, boy?"

Toby nodded wordlessly. What was there to hide? Besides, he couldn't lie, didn't know how to. The closest any Horton came to handling the truth loosely was when Gramps spun some of his wild yarns. Toby was trying to escape and he was caught. His captors knew all that and now the ball was in their court. He wiggled his head to a more comfortable position on the pillow and waited for the consequences. From his position on the cot he looked into the patient eyes of a benevolent Jesus on the opposite wall. He was holding a long staff and speaking to a group of children who stared at Him with adoring eyes.

"We ain't plannin' on hurtin' you none, Toby. Pa just wants to help you. But you sure are a brave little guy."

The other twin nodded in agreement and admiration. Then they both smiled, revealing strong straight teeth and lively eyes that spent too much time trying to look serious.

"I'm Amos," one said.

"I'm Abel," the other echoed.

Toby liked them. He felt that he could believe and trust them, so he decided to try to find out once again why he was snatched from the studio parking lot.

"Where am I?" he began.

"You're in our basement but we can't tell you where it is. I don't think Pa would like that."

"Why am I here?"

The twins looked at each other uncomfortably. Amos finally answered. "Pa wants to get the devil out'a your head. But that won't hurt you none," he added quickly.

"Why does your pa think I have a devil in my head? I don't even know your father."

"It's those dreams you have. Pa says they're the work of the devil."

Toby didn't understand at all. Mike Mancini's lectures on genetics had convinced him of the value of the research and he didn't see what that had to do with the devil. There wasn't any connection. In fact, Toby only knew what the others told him. He didn't remember a thing about any of the dreams. "Why does your dad say that? My dreams are because of genes. That's what Mr. Mancini says and he's a teacher."

"That's not what Pa says. He thinks the devil put those things in your head."

"What do you think?" Toby asked.

The twins exchanged uncertain glances. Amos shrugged and ran his fingers through his thick waves. "I guess I think the same as Pa. The Lord spoke to Pa, you know."

"I know. Your mother told me." Toby didn't sound convinced.

"The Lord told Pa to lead His army," Abel added. "We help him," he said proudly. "We hand out pamphlets." He crossed to one of the cartons, tore open the top, and pulled out a handful of fliers. "This is what the Lord wants us to say."

He handed the single sheet to Toby and the boy glanced at the bright red headline.

Repent or Die.

It seemed rather a harsh message for such a mild twosome to be handing out.

"What do people say when they read these?" Even at his tender age, Toby could tell that this was inflammatory stuff.

"Some thank us. Some get a little nasty," Amos admitted.

"But that's when we turn the other cheek," Abel cut in. "That's one of the things the Bible tells us."

Toby scanned the wall hangings, feeling some comfort in the familiar pictures of Jesus. He pushed into a sitting position on the edge of the cot, moving warily so as not to aggravate the searing pain above his eye. He glanced at the leather-bound Bible that lay on the desktop. "Where did you learn so much about the Bible?"

"Pa taught us in school."

"Is your father a schoolteacher?" Toby couldn't hide the doubt in his voice.

"He taught us. We never went to no regular school. Pa always said that they're too full of the devil's teachin'."

"Wow!" Toby exclaimed with traces of awe and pity in his tone.

"Pa says that the Bible tells us all we need to know."

"How about math and science and social studies? Didn't you have to learn anything like that?"

"Weren't no reason to learn it if it wasn't in the Bible," Amos replied.

"Wow!"

"Don't you know the Bible?" Amos asked accusingly.

"Sure I do. I study it in Sunday school. I really like Sunday school," he added. "But I like regular school, too. My gramps says you have to know a lot of different things if you want to get a good job. And you need a good job if you want to make a lot of money."

For the first time Toby detected a note of animosity.

"The Lord will provide," Amos said sternly.

"Pa says that money is the root of sin," Abel declared with the same scolding tone.

Toby thought it was time to change the subject. "Did your pa give you grades in school?"

"Grades? What do you mean?" Amos asked suspiciously.

"If you did real good, did he give you an A? That's how my school works. And if I get a bad grade like a D, my parents have to go see the teacher and I get punished. It only happened one time," he added quickly.

"If we slouched on our Bible studies, we'd get a whuppin' with Pa's shavin' strop."

"That was before he growed his beard," Abel added with a smile.

Toby was glad to see that the mood had lightened. "One time I had to miss a Twins game at the Metrodome because I got a C in history." Toby still winced whenever he recalled that cruel punishment.

"Pa don't take no truck with sports," Amos said.

Did Toby detect a trace of discontent in the statement? "Is that some more of the devil's work?" The boy was beginning to catch on.

"For sure. It's idle and it comes to no good."

A door slammed somewhere in the house and the twins froze. The tiny spark that had stirred briefly in their eyes was puffed out like a candle, and they backed away from the little boy as if he were infected by sin and spread it by his presence. The hint of curiosity was extinguished and their handsome faces slumped to masks of dullness.

Toby could feel the fear crowding the small room as the footsteps grew closer. The knob turned quickly, the door swung open, and the doorway was filled with the cadaverous specter of Esau.

Chapter Twenty-six

JAN TWISTED AND rolled under the tangled sheets. Despite the cool breeze from the lake she was slick with a thin film of nervous perspiration. Bright red numbers blazed the time from the bedside clock. The bedroom window framed the gray dawn. An early fisherman purred across the lake and roused the morning songbirds from their sluggishness.

But Jan Horton noticed none of it. The sedative Clancy had given her the night before dulled her mental nerve endings and she passed the night in mindless restlessness. But something discomforting still nudged at her drug-muddled thoughts as she broke through the morning mist.

"Toby!"

She shouted his name and shot upright in bed, frightened by the shrillness of her own voice. Her heart beat a tattoo against her ribs until she thought her chest would explode. Why was she frightened? Was it a bad dream? But then she remembered and she wished that it had been only a dream. Toby was gone, kidnapped, held captive, terrified, and maybe in danger. Who would do such a thing—and why?

The TV studio, the police, the phone call—all the frightening memories from the night before came flooding back to haunt her. She began to sob, then she felt Steve's strong arm around her shoulder. He pulled her close without a word and they stayed like that, locked in silent prayer until the first shard of sunlight pierced the morning sky.

Inspector Borg arrived at the station an hour before his shift was scheduled. He always did. He did his best work in those dark minutes before the town rubbed the sleep from its eyes. He liked the way it felt during that quiet time after the first false dawn and before early-morning traffic sullied the smell of daybreak. It was a time for thinking and doing, a time uninterrupted by the shrill demands of the telephone or the dull proddings of the daily agendas.

He stopped by the desk of the duty sergeant as he entered. The sergeant, a man with a chopped-sirloin face and the rheumy eyes and florid nose of a whiskey drinker, had a Travis McGee thriller open on his desk and less than six months until retirement. He spent most of his shift contemplating the snowy grandeur of the north woods as he toured the macadam roads in his soon-to-be-purchased Winnebago.

"What's happening, Sergeant Jacobson?"

The burly sergeant fumbled with the paperback, tried to hide it and appear some shade of busy. "Another quiet night in the naked city, Inspector." He pulled a handwritten sheet across the desk and read indifferently. "A dog barking on Woodhill, a lawn job on Matilda, a fistfight in Mooney's parking lot, a fender bender at 36 and Dale. We've crushed crime one more time and preserved truth, justice, and the American way of life."

Was it Borg's imagination or was the grizzly sergeant becoming more flip as he neared the day when he would finally pull the rip cord? He never said that he was retiring, it was always "yank the cord" or "clear out the desk" or "hang up the old holster." Borg didn't really mind the sergeant's early-morning high jinks as long as it didn't interfere with getting the job done, and it didn't.

Einar was respected by every member of the department and liked by most. No one actively disliked him but some were afraid to get too near, fearful that his no-nonsense determination would shine a poor light on their own mediocrity. And his tireless efforts usually paid off. The department's thin log of unsolved cases was a monument to Borg's persistence and its conviction rate was a scoreboard for his thoroughness.

"Nothing new on the Horton case?" he asked unnecessarily.

Sergeant Jacobson cocked his head and frowned. "Not since you left late last night, Inspector. Hell, you were here for half the night shift. You ought'a put in for OT."

Borg smiled his tight, feral grin. He had finally left at midnight and thought he had slipped out unnoticed. Apparently Sergeant Jacobson wasn't as engrossed in Travis McGee as he appeared to be.

He went into his office and shuffled absently through the day-old paperwork. The room was a mirror of its occupant, spare and neat. An oak-topped desk with scars from an earlier, less caring occupant was centered in the ten-by-ten cube. A picture of three kids whom he visited religiously at their mother's every Saturday was propped at the corner of the oak credenza. When Borg had seen Toby Horton's picture he was reminded of his own son, but then almost every young boy reminded him of Randy. A half-filled in-basket, an empty out-basket, and a standard black telephone were on the desktop. Nothing but the bare necessities. A framed replica of the Constitution was on the wall to his right, the Declaration of Independence was to his left, and a topographical map of the state of Minnesota hung behind him.

He sat in the leather padded swivel chair and leaned back thoughtfully. Somewhere nearby a little boy was being held against his will. He was probably frightened. Einar Borg's job was to find the boy, return him safely to his parents' home, and bring the kidnapper to justice. Most men would shrink from the strain. Few could do it well. None could do it better than Inspector Einar Borg.

"What do you do for a living?"
"I'm a police officer."
"What does a police officer do?"
"I rescue lost children."
"That's nice. I'm a carpenter. I build houses." or
"I'm a bartender. I pour drinks." or *"I'm a bus driver. I drive buses."*

He rubbed his temples with his palms and breathed a weary sigh. Sometimes he envied those who could leave their jobs at work. But he knew he could never be happy with that. Somebody had to find the Toby Hortons of the world and who could do it better?

He toyed with the corner of the photocopied letter, tried to find some new meaning in the words, the rhythm, some new clue in its message. What kind of person would call himself a captain of God's earthly army? Would he be fat or thin?

Thin, Borg decided.

Would he be tall or short? The inspector couldn't make up his mind on that one. How about the color of his hair—was he married—did he sleep well last night?

Borg didn't.

The policeman smiled wryly at his rambling thought process. It was a game he always played with clues, and it had brought results on more than one occasion. It was a brainstorm process that dismissed the unlikely with a mental wave of the hand, expanded small facts into believable reality, and blended the results with experience and intuition. But it wasn't getting him anywhere in the Toby Horton case.

So far the letter from Teddy MacBride's office had been a dead end. Lined notebook paper that could be bought at any K-Mart, a ubiquitous number 2 pencil, probably Eberhard Faber, handwriting that the experts said belonged to a male. That was something. But beyond that small bit of information, the investigation had hit a stone wall.

Nobody at Rosedale Shopping Center had noticed the caller, and efforts to lift a set of prints from the phone were next to useless. Every gum-chewing teenager in the Twin Cities must have handled that receiver on the day the call was made.

What did he really have? A male religious fanatic, who lived somewhere nearby and read Teddy MacBride's column, kidnapped a little boy to cleanse his mind and keep him from doing "the devil's work."

Not a lot to go on.

They had run a list of known child abusers, psychotics, even a handful of paranoid schizophrenics, and they had come up empty-handed. No big surprise. But the worst part was still ahead, the moment he had to look Jan and Steve Horton in the eye and admit their failure, his failure.

Inspector Borg knew all too well the kind of blind trust people had in the police department at times like this and he had watched too often as the panic of despair settled its weighty chains over their shoulders. He didn't look forward to this morning's meeting. A light tap on the door snapped him from his painful reverie.

"Got a sec, Inspector?"

Nick Mandikas stood in the doorway. He was a three-year veteran; young, aggressive, and ambitious. He was the kind of cop who gave law enforcement a good name. Inspector Borg just hoped he'd stay challenged and enthused long enough to get promoted. Otherwise he'd look for greener pastures like so many of the other good ones.

"Sure, Nick. What can I do for you?"

"It's probably nothing, Inspector, but—" He shrugged and took a sheet of paper from an inside pocket. "I heard you're looking for a religious nut in the Horton case."

Borg turned his attention up a notch.

"Well, it's probably nothing but I remembered picking this up a couple of weeks ago."

He handed the paper across the desk. Borg looked at the blazing headline and chuckled mirthlessly.

" 'Repent or Die.' Doesn't leave a person a lot of choice, does it? Where did this come from?"

"A couple of young guys were handing them out on University Avenue." His chin dropped and he flushed with embarrassment. "We never got their names. They just happened to be in the wrong place during a mid-week hooker roundup. They got in the net and we just let them go. They seemed like a couple of nice guys. They were twins, I think. Strong-looking bucks with beards and bright red hair. They didn't give us any trouble or anything like that."

He waited for a response but got only a curious stare. He shrugged and started for the door. "Like I said, Inspector, it's probably nothing—"

But the inspector wasn't listening. He was too engrossed in the message that recruited people to join the earthly army of the Lord. "Where on University Avenue?" Borg asked suddenly.

"Near Dale Street."

"Isn't that near where that hooker got strangled a little while ago?"

The young policeman nodded. How could he forget the case? He was the one who broke down the door after neighbors complained of a foul smell from the apartment.

"Write up a full report on where that flier came from. Get out a description of the guys who were handing them out. Put a trace on the print job. Let's get cracking!"

Borg pushed away from the desk and shoved some papers into a leather folder as the young officer hurried out.

"Oh, Nick."

"Yes, Inspector?"

"Nice job."

The last time Mike Mancini and Clancy Kendall met at Perkin's for breakfast had been an upbeat affair sparkling with the excitement of discovery. Not so this morning. A pall of guilt and fear enveloped their booth like an evil mist. Mike usually devoured the $2.99 special but today he chewed dutifully on cardboard pancakes and leathery strips of bacon. The banter was missing too. None of the jokes and jibes that usually punctuated their conversation were being flung across the table. Their mood left no room for levity. Mike washed a mouthful down with a sip of coffee and banged the cup heavily in the saucer.

"I got him into this mess, dammit. If it wasn't for me, he'd be sound asleep in his own bed."

"Take it easy on yourself, Mike. Wearing a

hair shirt isn't going to help get Toby out of this jam."

He refilled his cup from the copper and black pitcher. He offered to put a warm head on Mike's cup but the teacher shook him off.

"That Inspector Borg seems efficient." It was a positive statement, anything to clear the air of the heavy depression. Clancy said it brightly, as if his optimism alone would help to break the case.

"I hope you're right, Clancy, but he doesn't have a helluva lot to go on."

"Besides," Clancy added optimistically, "the inspector said there's nothing to make us think the kidnapper's dangerous—that he'd do anything to hurt Toby."

"That *is* some consolation," Mike admitted, "but that doesn't make Toby feel any better. And he wasn't feeling all that well when we last saw him. In fact, if it hadn't been for his headache, he wouldn't have gone outside for air and maybe none of this would have happened. If only I'd gone outside with him, he'd be okay," Mike said, sighing.

"If my aunt had balls, she'd be my uncle." Clancy tried to crack the somber mood with his irreverence. He was partly successful.

"If your aunt had balls, you'd probably send her to six specialists and collect a finder's fee."

"Just another indication of the complexity of modern medicine."

"Is it true that the most popular course in med school is Advanced Financial Chicanery?" Mike asked.

"That's the second most popular. First place goes to Diagnosis for Fun and Profit."

Mike forced a smile and reached for the coffee pitcher. He poured, swirled the coffee around his cup, and looked at his close friend with a pained expression. "What do you really think, Clancy? Is everything going to be all right?"

The doctor reached across the table and took his friend's hand. "They're going to find him, Mike. And everything's going to be okay. You have to keep believing that."

"I'll try, Clancy. I'll try."

"Sheila, how old am I?"

"What kind of a question is that?"

"I just want to know how many years it took me to get this dumb."

"That's hard to know," the secretary mused. "You've been this dumb for as long as I've known you. Maybe you started out dumb." She winked at the rumpled journalist as she took the signed letters from the littered desktop.

"The question was meant to be rhetorical," he growled.

"So was the answer," Sheila parried.

"There's no such thing as a rhetorical answer." He looked up, scratched his head, and furrowed his brow. "At least I don't think there is."

Sheila laid the papers down and walked around the desk behind him. With practiced fingers she kneaded the aching muscles of Teddy's shoulders and he purred a long, low moan. "Just stop fretting, Teddy. All the worrying in the world isn't going to solve this."

"That's what I mean. That's exactly why I feel so dumb. All I'm able to do is worry, and here's some innocent little kid scared half to death and it's all because of something I did."

"Why don't you take the blame for the *Hindenburg* disaster while you're busy confessing to all the misfortune of the world?"

"Only you and I know about that," he said, smiling, "and I'm not telling."

She gave his shoulder a husky whack and retrieved the letters. "Now how about doing something productive and stop wallowing in self-pity."

Teddy contemplated an obscene gesture then thought better of it. It had nothing to do with chivalry, it was her eventual retribution that he feared.

Hoping to help the investigation, Teddy had plowed through the last year's letters, the complimentary ones as well as those laced with insults. He wasn't sure what he was looking for but it beat sitting around doing nothing at all. He chuckled in spite of his bleak mood as he read over the correspondence.

Dear Teddy, You are an insecure, insufferable asshole who shouldn't be allowed to—

That one wasn't the kidnapper. Teddy figured that such an astute observer of human nature wasn't capable of crime.

Dear Mr. MacBride, Your column about the school bond issue was pure genius.

This guy's a definite suspect, Teddy thought as a crooked smile wrinkled his face. But aside from a few snickers and frowns the search brought no results.

"Phone calls, Sheila. How about the phone calls that came in after the columns and the shows? Do you keep a log?"

"Sure, Teddy. It's all computerized and filed alphabetically by date and gender."

"Don't be a smartass."

Sheila appeared in the doorway looking a little older than Teddy remembered, still not anywhere near her age—just a little more mature than usual. Teddy suddenly realized that she was suffering with him and he felt guilty. He was dumping his own grief on her narrow shoulders and she piled it on top of her own without complaint. He felt like a shit.

"I'm a shit."

"You're a shit," she agreed.

"You're a sweetheart."

"So are you, Teddybear."

If Teddy was paying attention he might have seen her green eyes mist over, but he was too busy shoving papers into his briefcase.

"Anybody for pancakes?"

Gramps fussed around the cabinet, fumbling cans and boxes as if keeping his hands busy would distract his mind. It didn't work. He couldn't believe the torture. He thought he'd felt the worst of it—the Depression, the war, even the nightmare of Guadalcanal, but none of it approached the torment that tore at his gut. Was that how his own mother had felt when he went to war, worrying and wondering whether she would ever see him again? Was this the kind of pain that Aaron had felt as his only son boarded the train in his crisp khakis?

My God, but it hurt.

Baby Toby who tugged on his nose as a one-year-old and laughed at his corny jokes just yesterday. And now he was missing. Missing and scared and God knows what else. It didn't seem real. It wasn't fair, and it took every ounce of the old man's willpower to keep from falling face down on the floor to beat the artificial brick surface while crying like a baby.

"How about some pancakes, Jan?"

"Just some coffee please, Gramps." She didn't even want that but saw the need in John Horton's face. It made her feel a little better knowing she made him feel better.

"Can I have a pancake, Gramps?"

Tina felt the vibrations of fear. They echoed from the walls and ricocheted from the sink and cabinets but the full dread of their meaning eluded her. Toby was gone and Mom and Dad and Gramps were upset about it and that was bad, but her mind couldn't wrap itself around the fearful potential of the episode.

"Just one pancake, honey?"

"Well, maybe two," she said with her impish grin.

Gramps moved slowly around the kitchen, keeping the social breeze stirred with a minimum of words and motion.

Of the two parents, Jan was doing the better job. At least she was able to make occasional eye contact with the rest of the family, but Steve was too far gone for such niceties. The strain of comforting Jan in the early-morning hours had worn his crust away, laying bare the raw nerve endings that pulsed and throbbed with each tortured beat of his heart. He sat in his usual place, head in his hands, red-eyed from the endless night.

"Somebody's coming," Tina announced loudly but with half the lung power she normally employed.

Gramps glanced at the clock in the wall oven. Nine o'clock. Time everybody was arriving.

Inspector Borg was the first on the scene. He spent a few minutes in the driveway debriefing the patrolman who had spent an uneventful night in the Hortons' living room, then he entered the house through the garage. Mike Mancini and Clancy Kendall were next, closely followed by Teddy MacBride.

They sat informally around the dark trestle table in the Hortons' country kitchen. Gramps filled coffee cups and greeted everyone politely. He was relieved to be finally able to share the chore of keeping the deadly silence broken.

The inspector started right in as soon as they were all seated. He searched for just the right tone. It wasn't easy to describe a temporary lack of positive results without making it sound like defeat, especially to the sensitive ears of Toby's loved ones. His eyes darted from face to face, finally settling on Steve, who stared blankly into his empty coffee cup.

"Last night was uneventful," he began without prelude.

No one seemed shocked. They hadn't expected otherwise.

"Toby's photograph has been shown to hundreds of people in three states with concentration on the five-county metropolitan area. This hasn't turned up anything so far."

"How about the letter?" Teddy asked.

"The paper and pencil are common. We have nothing to go on there. The handwriting was done by a male, but that's no surprise. For what it's worth a handwriting expert is going to give us his analysis of the writer's personality today if you believe in that stuff."

It was obvious the inspector didn't.

"Also, copies of the letter have been distributed for handwriting comparisons with samples on file but I'm afraid that's another long shot."

"What about the phone call?" Steve spoke for the first time, and the inspector winced at the torment that seeped from the dull, red-rimmed eyes.

"A dead end too, I'm afraid." He regretted his choice of words immediately. "Steve, we never held out too much hope that those early leads would pay off. But neither are we pessimistic. As I told you yesterday, there's no reason to think that Toby's in any kind of physical danger. I won't try to kid you and pretend that he's not scared. Of course he's scared. But from everything I hear, Toby's not an ordinary little boy. He's smart and he's resourceful."

The inspector forced a tight smile and glanced at Gramps, who was brewing a fresh pot of coffee. "Let's not forget about the Horton genes. They got us into this and they can get us out." He thought he saw a trace of life in Steve's eyes, a flickering spark that extinguished before it could flare.

"You're right, Inspector." Gramps's eyes sparkled too, but it was a spark of hope and anger. "Toby won't give up and neither will we."

Jan forced a pained smile and covered Gramps's hand with her own and the old man burst into tears.

Chapter Twenty-seven

◇◇◇◇◇◇◇◇◇◇

TOBY KNEW IT was only a dream but he couldn't crack the brittle shell that separated it from reality. He watched like a spectator as he raced up and down the school hallway.

Raced?

No. How could he call that racing? He plodded with leaden legs past the olive lockers and the jeering faces that sneered and smirked at his dilemma. Tommy Mendel stuck out a sneakered foot and tripped him, but Toby windmilled his arms and managed to keep his balance.

He wore only his underwear and that embarrassed him, tight Jockey shorts with a little bulge in front like a ripe plum and all the girls in the hallway stared at it as he slogged past and Vicki Wilson whispered something to the girl at her side and both girls laughed out loud.

He was embarrassed—and terrified.

The hall full of students parted before him and closed behind him, not hindering his progress but certainly not supportive. Fortunately, they made progress just as difficult for his pursuers. He could see their heads above the throngs of children, bright red heads bobbing and weaving, getting closer then falling back, never quite close enough to reach out and grab him.

The end of the hallway was only steps away, then down a long flight of stone stairs where he would burst through the heavy door to freedom. The last of his schoolmates parted before him, and as they did, the lead drained from his legs and he flew down the stairs barely touching the smooth wooden bannister. He glanced over his shoulder one last time. The stairs were empty— no one was in the corridor—no schoolmates, no red-haired pursuers, only long rows of olive lockers lining the walls as far as the eye could see. His heart sang as he pushed against the door, flooding the grayness with blazing sunlight. Then it crashed and shattered when he saw the tall, angular man in a long black robe blocking his way to freedom, pointing accusingly with a knobby finger.

"Evil," he shouted and Toby's heart fluttered wildly.

"I'm not evil, I'm not evil." With flailing arms Toby declared his innocence until his clenched fists slammed into the wall, sending a framed picture of John the Baptist crashing to the floor. Toby's eyes snapped open and he stared wild-eyed into the unfamiliar gloom. Where was the school, the red-haired men, the tall man with the black robe? Where was Toby?

He could feel his heart chugging in his spindly chest, as if fueled by the runnels of sweat that streaked his face. He blinked his eyes once, twice—trying to focus and break free of the gripping terror. Gray dawn seeped from a doorway, filling the room with its gloomy presence. That's the bathroom, he remembered. That's where I fell. He pushed himself up and threw his legs over the side of the cot, arms trembling and head pounding as he reoriented his thoughts.

Memories came tripping back in pieces, disjointed slugs of thought, parts of a puzzle that, even when complete, made little sense.

TV studio, headache, aspirin, parking lot,

pickup truck—it came in staccato bursts. The stark room with its stacks of books and its walls covered with holy pictures. The cubbyhole of a bathroom with its tempting window. Big fat Hattie with her puckered smile and the red-haired twins, curious and gentle like oversized playmates. The puzzle pulled itself together piece by piece until only one large hole remained.

Esau!

The sound of the name drove a spike of terror through him and he flinched as the previous night's memories flickered across the screen of his mind. Esau, gaunt and rangy, face like a craggy coffin, eyes like burning coals, tongue like a whip that flayed the sins from his victim's hide. Toby recalled the chilling moment when he first saw the man framed in the basement doorway, the American Gothic farmer without his tools.

"This is the boy?" he had said.

"Yes, Pa," the twins harmonized. Then they backed against opposite walls, leaving Toby propped on the edge of the cot, a vulnerable target for Esau's piercing stare. Esau took two long strides across the room and gazed down on him.

Toby had tried to look up and meet the older man's eyes, but each time he craned his neck, a searing pain stabbed the center of his forehead. Even as he recalled the previous night's events the pain returned, a numbing vise grip that squeezed his temples and made him sick to his stomach. He tried to recall Esau's words.

"The Lord has brought you to me to be cleansed of the devil."

Esau wasn't exactly shouting the words, just speaking with extraordinary emphasis, and it brought to Toby's mind the Sunday morning preachers he heard as he flicked through the channels. Esau towered his full height dressed in farmer's overalls and a plaid flannel shirt tightly buttoned at collar and wrist. The pants were too short—or Esau too tall—and were hiked midway up a pair of work-worn boots. He commanded the room with his presence, legs spread, feet planted, left hand on hip, and the bony finger of his other hand thrust high in the air, indicating the direction of the Lord whose orders he fulfilled.

"The Lord has appointed me to be the captain of His earthly army and through me will rid the world of Satan's corruption. Stand when I speak to you, boy."

The order didn't register until Toby felt the twins each take an arm and raise him bodily from the cot. They weren't rough but neither were they gentle. He swayed lightly and a shower of sparks exploded in front of his eyes. He was paying the price of his fall from the window. The twins backed off once again and Toby was left standing in the center of the room, the top of his head barely level with Esau's chest.

"Do you regret carrying the message of the devil?"

Esau flung the words at the bewildered boy and Toby recoiled, caught his knee on the edge of the cot, and sat down heavily on the rumpled mattress.

"Do you ask God's forgiveness for the trickery and deception you perform in Satan's name?"

Toby cringed on the cot. He inched back toward the wall, away from the venomous words and Esau's spittle-laced perimeter.

"Answer me, boy. Do you seek the forgiveness of the Lord?"

"Y-y-yes, sir."

"Then stand up and pray for His loving mercy," he shouted.

Toby pushed unsteadily to his feet. The shrillness of Esau's command sent another spike through his temple and tears of fear and pain flooded his eyes.

"Well?" Esau ranted.

"I—I—I don't know."

"You don't know what? You don't know that you blaspheme? You don't know that you mock the word of God with your heresies? Answer me, boy. I speak in the name of the Lord."

A fervor blazed in Esau's eyes that even the twins didn't recognize. His fists clenched like rocks and his wiry muscles vibrated like a bow string.

A new wave of dizziness struck Toby and he rocked unsteadily. The verbal battering had taken its toll, but at the same time, it had erased a veneer of inhibition. Now Toby viewed the gaunt inquisitor through an angry mist, one that replaced the aura of fear and intimidation.

"I don't know what you're talking about." Toby's own eyes blazed like hot coals and his voice hit a note he didn't know existed. "Why don't you just ask God if you want to know? You say that you talk to God all the time. Why not ask Him your questions?"

Esau didn't hear the roar that left his mouth and filled the room. Nor did Toby feel the flat palm that cracked his down-covered cheek. He flew across the cot and crashed into the wall, sending one of the Last Suppers splintering to the floor. Amos and Abel flinched but made no move to intervene. Toby sprawled across the cot. The left side of his face flared but he felt no pain. His pupils grew into large black dots and stared vacantly at the ceiling. Esau stood with clenched fists, breathing heavily in short gasps, face wild-eyed and distorted.

"You blaspheme!" Esau bellowed the accusation but Toby didn't hear it. "You dare to mock the captain of the Lord's earthly army?" Spittle rained from the corner of his mouth as he railed at the little sprawled figure. "Do you ask the Lord's forgiveness?" he raged.

Esau stopped short in the middle of his tirade and his face went as blank as that of the boy on the cot. He clutched at his chest and staggered backward and caught himself on the door frame. "Wh-what happened? Why is the boy sleeping like that?"

Amos and Abel rushed to their father's side. "He'll be all right, Pa," Abel reassured him. Amos knelt beside the cot and gripped the boy's slender shoulder. "Wake up, Toby. Pa wants to talk to you some more." He shook gently and the boy responded with a mournful moan. "You're okay, Toby. Please be okay."

"Why is he laying like that? He should be praying to the Lord." Esau's rage-filled face had melted into a mask of confusion as he loomed uncertainly over the cot.

"C'mon, Toby, wake up," Amos pleaded.

Toby blinked and a fat tear ran down his face and disappeared into the rumpled mattress cover. He blinked again and opened his eyes to see Amos's worried face waving and shimmering before finally coming into focus. Then his heart skipped when he saw the farmer's hawklike face materialize next to Amos.

"What happened to the boy?" Esau wanted to know. "Why was he sleeping?"

"You hit me," Toby said, sobbing. "You hit me in the face." He rubbed his hand over the tender skin of his cheek.

"Nonsense," Esau disagreed emphatically. "I'm going to rescue you. I'm not going to hurt you. But you must want to be saved." His voice regained a hint of its former strength and Toby shrank back. "Tell me, boy, do you truly want to be saved?"

To Toby it seemed like a horrible *déjà vu* of the earlier episode. He pushed farther away, sitting with his back against the wall, legs outstretched across the cot. He didn't want to make the same mistake he made only moments earlier, the mistake that was rewarded by Esau's violent explosion.

"Yes, sir," he conceded. "I'd like to be saved."

"It won't be easy," Esau cautioned. "The devil's deep inside you. He must be removed."

Toby's eyes rimmed with unshed tears as he tried to meet Esau's icy stare. Look people right in the eye when you're talking to them, Gramps always reminded him. It took every ounce of young courage to do so now. "How does the devil get removed?" Toby asked haltingly while rubbing absently at his reddened cheek.

"Prayer!"

Esau spoke the single word with undisguised gravity, as if the word itself became the prayer and its healing powers were already unleashed.

"Pa says that prayer's the answer to everything that ails you," Abel interjected.

Esau looked at his son indulgently and a brief spark of pride lighted his face.

"When can I go home?" Toby asked.

"When we're sure that the devil's gone."

"Will it take long? My mom and dad will be worried about me."

"Pa already called them on the phone," Amos blurted out. "He told them—"

"It's time." Esau interrupted his son's response in mid-sentence. He lowered himself to the concrete floor and knelt with his arms hanging limply at his sides. Amos and Abel hurriedly knelt on either side of him.

"Kneel," Esau commanded.

The man was gazing at a saintly picture above his head, but Toby knew the order was meant for him and another wave of dizziness swept over him. He slid off the cot onto the floor, and as his knees neared the hard surface, a barrage of tiny explosions sparkled like fireflies and an icy dagger pierced his temple. His knees touched the floor and the rest of his body followed, slumping slowly until he lay sprawled in front of the three kneeling men like a sacrifice for the Magi.

"It is the devil inside him," Esau said mechanically.

"Amen," the twins responded.

"Lucifer lives inside the boy and his evil presence must be removed."

"Amen."

"It is the will of the Lord that Satan shall depart this boy's body."

"Amen."

"The Lord has appointed these, His unworthy servants, to rid the boy of the evil presence."

"Amen."

"Let us pray."

At this command the twins began to mumble their own exhortations, but Toby didn't hear the droning cacophony. He was having his own revelation. He opened his eyes, stared blankly at the ceiling, and breathed a low moan. Esau read this as a sign that his efforts were taking their toll on Satan's tenuous grip and he increased the volume of his prayer.

"Lucifer, lord of darkness, blasphemer, prince of all that is evil, in the name of the Lord Jesus Christ I command you to depart this boy's body."

Toby's head rocked from side to side and he purred a haunting moan. It was another favorable sign and Esau redoubled his efforts. The twins continued their own humming at his side, background accompaniment for their father's overture. Esau's head felt light, a sheen of perspiration coated his face, and a band of pain girded his chest, but he paid no heed to his physical discomfort.

"Satan, embodiment of sin, in the name of the Lord Jesus Christ, I, Esau, the captain of His earthly army, command you out of the body of Toby Horton."

"Amen," the twins droned.

"Ó istenem, irgalmazz nekem bünösnek. Ó istenem, irgalmazz nekem bünösnek. Ó istenem, irgalmazz nekem bünösnek."

Toby repeated the strange phrase over and over. His voice was flat and emotionless and his eyes were vacant. Esau and the twins cut short their prayers and listened to the meaningless words.

"It is the sound of Satan." Esau thrust an accusing finger toward his captive and the twins shrank back, terrified of being tainted by the proximity of evil.

Suddenly Toby blinked and sat upright, turned his gaze to the three kneeling figures, put his hand to his temple, and shattered the stillness with a soul-wrenching scream. Esau stood suddenly, the twins fell back on their heels, the door burst open, and Hattie came waddling into the room.

"What on earth's the matter?" She saw Toby holding his head and rocking in pain and she rushed past the Manley men to his side. Hattie sat on the edge of the cot, and its metal span groaned under the weight as she pulled the boy close and rested his head against her leg. "What happened?" she asked.

"This is none of your concern." Esau hovered uncertainly over his doughy wife and the frail carrier of the devil.

She ran her hand softly over Toby's head, and he sobbed into her tentlike housedress. "Why did the boy scream? Did you hurt him?" she asked accusingly.

Esau pointed his bony finger at Toby and the crazed look once again passed briefly across his face. "It was the scream of Satan. We have loosened his hold on the boy."

"My head hurts," Toby sobbed. "Help me. Please help me. It never hurt so bad before."

"Satan be gone," Esau shrieked. "Get out. I cast you out in the name of the Lord."

Esau felt a renewed surge of power and confidence. He was hovering on the brink. The prince of darkness was camped on his doorstep and Esau was a prayer away from breaking his evil grip.

"Get out of my house, Satan. Get out of this boy's body." He wrapped one bony hand around Toby's thin arm and wrenched him from Hattie's soothing grip. "Get out, get out, get out," he shrieked and the spittle flew as he shook Toby like a limp rag doll.

"Don't hurt him," Hattie screamed. She pushed her bulk from the sagging cot with surprising agility and grabbed at the sobbing boy. For a few endless moments the frenzied farmer and his wife engaged in a tug-of-war until Hattie finally pulled Toby free and encased him in a maternal bear hug. She turned her back on Esau and pulled the boy into the smothering softness of her ample bosom.

Esau stood rooted in the center of the small room. He watched Hattie soothe Toby as if viewing the scene from a distance. She ran her dimpled hand over his head and Toby buried his face in the soft contours of her chest. She whispered soothing encouragement and Toby choked and sobbed. Esau watched in a daze as a cold layer of sweat coated his body. He swayed imperceptibly, leaning to the right before catching his balance then swaying left. Hattie's broad back became a dark blur and the band around his chest drew tighter—crushing—twisting.

"Pa, are you all right?"

Abel took hold of one of Esau's arms and Amos quickly grabbed the other.

"Ma, something's the matter with Pa."

Hattie turned her head but she kept the massive barricade of her body between Toby and her husband. She saw the fear and uncertainty on Esau's face and wanted to reach out to him but an even stronger instinct drew her to the sobbing boy. "Set him down here on the bed, Abel. Amos, you go fetch a cup of water and a wet washcloth."

Esau raised no objections when the boys eased his long frame onto the rumpled cot. Amos held a plastic cup to his father's pale lips and Esau sipped and nodded his thanks. When he laid the cold washcloth across his father's forehead, a look of contentment flashed across his somber face.

A picture of Christ in the Temple was only a foot from Esau's head. "It's going to work," he mumbled to the picture and the framed figure must have responded with a signal seen only by Esau, because a thin smile cracked his grave face and he lay back and breathed a deep sigh of contentment. "We are winning," he whispered.

"But the boy's still hurting." Hattie broke into Esau's tranquillity with the reminder.

Esau opened his eyes and stared dreamily at the ceiling. "The boy will be fine. Satan is weakening."

Hattie hadn't seen Esau looking so peaceful since before the farm was taken away, and she felt good for him. He was her man and he was a good man. Even during these last few months since he took so keenly to God, she had stayed steadfastly by his side. And he always provided. No one could ever fault him there.

"The boy needs a doctor. He's hurtin' badly, Esau. I can see it in his eyes."

A plaintive whimper and Toby's shaking shoulders attested to Hattie's concern. Esau turned his head on the pillow and felt a pang as he took in the familiar scene. How many times had he watched while Hattie performed the same loving ministrations on Amos or Abel? A strong sense of yesterday added to his serenity. Hattie, the twins, the farm, neighbors chatting, heifers calving, triumphant singing loud and off-key at Sunday service, the twins giggling and laughing, pungent smells of new-mown hay and earthy manure, Hattie, thinner then, washing a scraped knee or wiping a tear from a mournful eye. These thoughts felt good to Esau. They gave him a sense of peace he had forgotten existed and the boy with the devil inside him had made it all possible.

Hate the sin and love the sinner. Isn't that what Christ preached? So wouldn't it be right for Esau to hate the devil but love Satan's unwitting messenger? He harbored no bad feelings toward the boy. How could he? The boy was an innocent, a luckless child caught in the clutches of evil. And the picture of Hattie hugging him to her breast flooded him with a warm memory of better times.

Hattie read the warmth in her husband's face and pressed her advantage. "Can't we call a doctor? Maybe we should just drop the boy off near his home, then his mother could get him to a doctor."

"No!"

Esau rejected her plea but his refusal lacked the rancor of his earlier denial. "I'll have my strength back soon and then I'll get the devil out of the boy. Satan is fearful of the earthly army and he's sucking out my strength. He wants me to stop, but the Lord will give me the strength to overcome him."

"An aspirin then. Let me give the boy an aspirin."

"Please." Toby squirmed in Hattie's arms and directed his plea to Esau. "Please, take me to Mr. Mancini. My head hurts so bad." He tried to be brave but he was powerless to quell the flood of tears that tumbled down his cheeks. "Mr. Mancini can make it go away. Please!"

Toby's face floated in a cloud and Esau blinked to sharpen its definition. First the face belonged to Toby, then it became Abel or Amos. Even Esau had trouble telling the two apart. He saw little tears from skinned knees or hurt feelings. He recalled the time a gang of roughnecks teased Amos because he didn't go to a real school. How could he make the boy understand that it was for his own good? The time the mare stepped on Abel's tiny foot. The tears flowed freely that day too, and Toby became young Abel, and Esau choked back a lump that made his Adam's apple bob like a yo-yo.

"Can we do it, Esau? Can we take the boy to Mr. Mancini?"

Hattie uncurled one thick arm from Toby's waist and laid her hand on Esau's veiny wrist. He felt the essence of her motherhood flow through the contact. In another familiar but almost forgotten gesture, Esau laid his own hand on Hattie's and returned her caress. A spark that had long lain dormant burst back to life. He met her eye and saw the pretty little schoolgirl he had first admired then loved.

"I'm sorry," he said sadly. "I made my promise to the Lord. My work for Him isn't complete as long as the devil breathes inside the boy."

"Please," Toby cried. "Please. I'll help you. I'll pray with you. I'll do anything you say. Please help me." Toby's dark eyes burned into Esau, and he felt a tiny portion of the pain that burned inside the boy.

"No," he whispered. He shook his head in the damp pillow. "The Lord won't allow me to bring you to your friend."

Toby sobbed and buried his head against Hattie's breast.

"But I've had another message from the Lord," Esau continued. "The boy's friend, the teacher called Mancini, he too is an instrument of Satan and he too is a victim. He can help the boy. Amos, Abel, come here," he called.

The twins knelt next to the cot and drew closer to their father.

"If the boy's friend can ease his suffering, then we must bring him here to help him. Find Mancini and bring him to me. He is also in Satan's grip and we can do more of the Lord's work."

Chapter Twenty-eight

❧❧❧❧❧❧❧❧❧❧

"THAT'S A ROUGH ONE, Mr. Mancini. The poor little kid ain't done nothin' to nobody and some crackpot goes and snatches him up like that. The poor kid must be scared shitless."

"O'Neil, I really appreciate your concern and I know that you mean well and I know I'm only a biology teacher, not an English teacher. But I have to tell you that without double negatives and scatalogical references your vocabulary would be on the same level as a protozoan."

"That's good, huh, Mr. Mancini?" the teenager asked with a lopsided grin.

"It's truly exceptional, O'Neil."

"Gee, thanks, Mr. Mancini." He hooked his thumbs in his belt and his chest swelled with pride. "Watcha gonna do now?"

The boy had the irreverent knack of asking the right question at the wrong time. It usually had no answer.

"Watcha think I ought'a do?" the teacher asked, lapsing into the student's colloquial.

Timmy O'Neil rubbed his freckled chin and chewed pensively on his lower lip. "You could always pray."

"Pray?" Mike did some chin rubbing and lip chewing of his own. "Why didn't I think of that, O'Neil?"

"Can't hurt none, Teach."

"No, O'Neil." He sighed. "It can't hurt none."

Mike Mancini had left the Hortons' gloomy kitchen a few hours earlier in a gray mood. He had felt like a bystander, someone whose carelessness had caused an accident and who now had to watch helplessly while skilled hands repaired the damage he had caused. So he had gone to the place where he felt most useful, to the Senior High where the summer smell of floor wax and ammonia temporarily replaced the fragrance of billowing chalk dust and a thousand well-scrubbed students.

There was something uplifting about the empty halls with the waxy floors and open lockers. The musical chirp of adolescent voices still clung to the corners and the colorful rush of milling teenagers danced in the periphery of his vision. This was where Mike was in charge, where he took old knowledge and new ideas and fitted them into the hungry minds of future teachers, parents, and leaders.

A molder of minds.

It was a trite phrase but that didn't bother Mancini. He fell back on it as often as it made him feel good and that was quite frequently. He liked to envision rows of seats filled with lumps of senseless putty waiting for his nimble fingers to work their magic and create mental masterpieces.

Mike loved the school and the students, like Tim O'Neil, whom some of his associates might dismiss as gas-pump material but whom he pictured with slide rule or stethoscope. That's how he saw all of his students, including the T-shirt-and-jean-clad youth who slouched in the desk across from him.

"What brings you to this humble seat of learning, O'Neil? I thought you knocked over gas stations in your spare time."

"Aw yo, Teach. You know me better than that."

Mike did know better and he felt a nick of guilt for his flippishness.

"I came down to shoot a coupl'a baskets in the gym. They been leavin' it open in the afternoons."

"You're going to be a senior next year, O'Neil. Aside from improving your percentage from the foul line, do you have any other plans?"

The boy was thin and gangly with the thick auburn curls and florid cheeks of some ancient tribe on Erin's mist-shrouded coast. He threw a languid leg across the writing arm of the desk, sitting in the chair rather than on it, bending and molding to its curves and corners like molten plastic.

"Plans?" He addressed the question to the ceiling fixture, trying it out as if it were a new concept, a revelation that had some distinct possibilities.

"Yeah. I do have some plans, Mr. Mancini. I'd like to be somebody someday. I don't wanna be a nobody."

His face flushed a deeper red than usual and he studied the torn tip of his tattered sneakers.

"I'd like to be somebody like you, Mr. Mancini."

Timmy O'Neil must have suddenly remembered something urgent, because he uncoiled from the chair in record time, scooped up his basketball, and made for the classroom door.

"See ya, Teach," he tossed casually over his shoulder while doing a showboat dribble between his legs and stuffing the ball through an imaginary hoop.

"See ya," the teacher whispered after him.

It *is* all worth it, he thought to himself. He rubbed the mist from his eyes as the thump, thump, thump of the ball echoed down the empty corridor.

*   *   *

"I'm a little scared, Amos. I hope this is right."

"Pa said that it's okay. It's part of the plan."

"What plan?" Abel wondered aloud. "God's plan or Pa's plan?"

"You shouldn't ought'a talk like that, Abel. If Pa says that it's right, then we got no right questioning it."

Abel wheeled the pickup inexpertly through the city's narrow side streets, a legacy of his driver training behind the wheel of an ancient tractor on the Mankato farm.

Mike Mancini's apartment building was in the middle of a long block, barren, like a brown brick pillbox atop a faceless mound. It had once been shaded by the lush branches of skyscraping trees but they had succumbed years earlier to the fatal ravages of Dutch Elm disease. A blacktop driveway separated the building from its look-alike neighbor and opened into a common lot for the parking convenience of the tenants.

Esau had looked up the teacher's address in the phone book and instructed the twins how to get there. Abel swung the wheel to the right, and the pickup rattled down the drive and pulled up alongside a blue Camaro.

Inside the apartment, Mike eased back in the plush recliner and kicked off his loafers. There was another meeting planned at the Hortons' for the following morning. Toby had already been missing for over twenty-four hours, and by Tuesday morning's meeting, forty-five hours would have elapsed since his abduction. The first twenty-four seemed more like a week and Mike wondered how they must have dragged for Jan and Steve Horton. There was no way that he could understand their feelings, he realized. How could he? His family was his room full of pimply, pubescent kids. They weren't as close as Toby was to Jan and Steve.

Were they?

In spite of the situation, the classroom meeting with Tim O'Neil had lifted Mike's spirits, but that only increased the depth of his plunge when he contemplated the Hortons' plight. He needed a drink—an unusual urge for the teacher. He drank with Clancy at Lindey's or with neighbors at a backyard barbecue but he never *needed* a drink.

He needed one now.

Reluctantly he ejected himself from the recliner and crossed to the tiny kitchen, an apartment-sized refrigerator, a gas stove, and a white porcelain sink with an ell of cabinets bending around the wall.

He grabbed a tumbler from the painted cupboard, two square cubes from the freezer, a heavy hit of Dewar's White Label, and a splash of tap water. He felt guilty, like one of his students slipping under the gym stairs to sneak a smoke. He took a sip, rolled it around his tongue, and let it slide down his throat. It didn't help his mood. He splashed another golden layer of Scotch over the cubes, set the glass on the table within reach, and settled back into the recliner, leaving the bottle open on the countertop. Then the teacher closed his eyes and drifted into a restless sleep.

"What if he don't wanna come with us?" Abel fidgeted inside the small vestibule while Amos studied the confusing array of buttons and mailboxes.

"Toby says he's a good friend and he's the only

one who can make his headache go away. I think he'll come with us."

Amos ran his finger down the row of names as he spoke. Some were neatly typed, others were folded business cards, a few were handwritten. Mike Mancini's name was printed boldly but neatly in blue felt-tip marker. "This is him," Amos exclaimed, a little relieved at the assurance that they were even in the right building. "It says he lives in apartment 216."

"Should we ring his doorbell?" Abel wondered.

Both boys were perplexed. Esau had warned them that the teacher might not want to leave with them. He might even want to call the police, and if he did that they'd take Toby away before Esau could cleanse him of the devil and he'd fail in his mission.

The twins lingered in the entryway, staring wordlessly at the doorbell as if it might hold the answer. They weren't often called upon to make decisions. When they were growing up on the farm their days were laid out for them by the exigencies of the crops and animals, so when things needed picking or planting or milking, some greater power made the schedule. Since leaving the farm, their father had shepherded them here and there, arranging odd jobs and day work, dropping them off and picking them up on a prearranged schedule as if they were helpless children.

"Pa will really be mad if Mr. Mancini doesn't come back with us," Amos said as if to emphasize the gravity of their situation. But before they were pressed for a decision on whether or not to ring the bell, their problem was solved

when a towheaded youngster with bangs like a
sheepdog bounded down the stairs and burst
through the door. He glanced casually at Amos
and Abel, did a quick double take at their sameness, then chugged through the outer door and
hurried down the steps. Abel had the presence
of mind to grab the inner door before it swung
shut.

Mike was easing into a restless slumber when
the soft tapping jarred him to his senses. The
building contained ten apartments and, except
for Mike and a newlywed couple downstairs, all
of them had one or more children. What now? he
wondered. Walk-a-thon, Swim-a-thon, Bike-
a-thon, one of the kids selling chocolate or cookies or pizzas? Mike was a sure thing, an easy
touch, and all of the neighborhood kids knew it.
His small freezer was crammed with six pizzas,
two each from three apartment athletes who par-
ticipated in one of the munchkin soccer leagues.
He loved it, loved the kids, even learned to love
the pizza. So he received a double shock when he
swung the door open and faced the two strap-
ping farm boys.

Amos and Abel pushed in rudely as Esau had
instructed, and Mike sensed from the start that
they weren't selling cookies.

"If this is a burglary, boys, you oughta brush
up on your research." Mike dealt with unruly
youngsters as a chosen career, so he wasn't as
intimidated as the situation called for.

"Are you Mr. Mancini?" one of the redheads
asked hesitantly.

The pair looked strong, physically able to snap
him like a matchstick, but the teacher could read
faces the same way most people read newspa-

pers. These boys weren't mean. The realization pleased him more than it relieved him.

"That's right," Mike answered drolly. "Now that you know who I am, perhaps you'll tell me a little something about yourselves and what brings you here."

The twins looked back and forth, hoping the other would handle the teacher's question. Mike marveled at how identical they were and his thoughts temporarily shifted to genes. The one to his right finally spoke.

"Pa told us not to tell you who we were, Mr. Mancini. He says that don't matter none to you. He says to tell you we got the boy. That's all you need to know."

"You have Toby?" For some reason, Mike didn't doubt it for a second.

"We do," Abel said matter-of-factly. "We all like him—especially Ma."

The boy spoke as if they were discussing some casual mutual acquaintance instead of a terrified little boy who was kidnapped only a day earlier. Mike couldn't hide his curiosity as he looked from one to the other, searching their innocent faces for a clue. What were these boys, slow learners, retarded, naïve, brainwashed? He couldn't make up his mind.

"Is Toby well?" Mike tried to mimic the boy's conversational tone.

"He ain't feelin' too good, Mr. Mancini. That's why we're here."

Mike felt a brick drop to the pit of his stomach. "Tell me about it," he managed to say.

"He says he got a real bad headache. It makes him cry a lot. We all hate to see him cry—especially Ma. She wanted to call a doctor, but Toby says that you can make his headache go away quicker than a doctor can, so Pa sent us to get you."

A headache! Mike had a good idea what caused it. "Why don't you just bring Toby home? That way I could make him better and his parents wouldn't have to worry anymore." Mike felt that it was worth the try.

"Ma wanted to do it that way but Pa won't let her. He says that Toby still has the devil inside him. He can't let him go till he's done cleansin' him." The boy glanced toward the door. "We ought'a be goin'."

Mike looked into the boy's innocent eyes and saw a gentleness that belied his physical strength, like the football player who sold flowers on TV. Still, he wondered what their response would be if he chose not to cooperate. "Wait here while I get my jacket."

Mike went to his bedroom. The twins each waited for the other to follow, but before they could react he was back, pushing his arm through the sleeve of the gray sport coat. He gestured to the door. "Well, are we going or aren't we?"

The twins nodded gratefully, pleased that they didn't have to knock him out.

Mike didn't know what to make of their security arrangements. The boys walked him to the pickup and made no attempt to prevent him from noting the license number. Then they wrapped a yellow bandanna around his head, covering his eyes so he couldn't see where they were going. It was loose enough to peek under but he didn't bother. He still wasn't sure what level of violence the boys were capable of if they got upset, and he wasn't planning to put them to the test. Especially if it would endanger Toby.

They rode in silence for less than fifteen minutes before the vehicle bumped to a jarring stop. Gently but firmly, the twins helped the teacher from the truck, moving quickly to avoid being seen.

"Watch your step, Mr. Mancini. There's two steps to go up." He heard the squeak of a screen door and the rattle of a doorknob. From the bottom of the blindfold he could see a set of chipped doorsteps like one would find in a single home in one of the older sections of the city or its suburbs. He was helped into the house and quickly led down a flight of stairs. It had the familiar basement smell of pipes and furnace and wet cinderblock. Another door opened and a hand on his elbow guided him through, then it clicked shut behind him.

"You can take the bandanna off now."

He did so and his eyes immediately came to rest on: "Toby!"

The boy smiled weakly. "Hello, Mr. Mancini. I'm sorry I got you into this."

Mike hurried to the cot and knelt by its side. Toby was resting with his head propped on a pillow, still dressed in the shirt and slacks that Mike recalled from the studio. He looked pale and his face was drawn with pain, not the little boy with the shining eyes and pinch-red cheeks whom Mike had first met.

"My head hurts real bad, Mr. Mancini. It never hurt this much before. Can you help me again?"

"Sure I can, Toby." He brushed his fingers lightly through the boy's jet-black hair, hoping to cure a portion of the pain with love. It must have worked because a look of contentment flashed across Toby's face.

"We sure hope that you can help the little fella. We don't want to see him hurtin' like that." One of the twins had moved to his side and looked worriedly at the slight form on the disheveled cot. "He sure is a nice little guy."

"Then why did you kidnap him?" Mike shot back angrily.

The twins both jerked reflexively at Mike's sudden outburst. "We ain't goin' to hurt him," the boy said defensively. "Pa says that he's tryin' to save him from the devil. He gets real mad when you say that we kidnapped him."

"Call it whatever you want," Mike argued. "The point is that Toby's here against his will and the law calls that kidnapping."

Mike hadn't heard the door open behind him and he spun on his heel as it slammed shut like a rifle shot.

"The law!" The bellow reverberated off the walls of the boxlike room. "The law that takes my land. The law that steals my cattle and my tractor. The law that takes my house and my barn and gives them to the evil money changers."

Esau was everything that Mike had pictured and a little more. He loomed next to the door, eyes on fire, flakes of spittle flying from his mouth, shaking his fist angrily at the tragic memories. He reminded the teacher of a demented Abe Lincoln with top hat and black coat traded for a face of rage and faded bib overalls.

"That's right," Mike shot back. "That's the same law. It isn't perfect but it punishes people who kidnap innocent children." Mike was on his feet and facing the raving farmer but he wasn't ready for the roar of outrage or the looping swing that exploded on his ear. He stumbled groggily, tripped and tumbled to the floor.

A new stab of pain pierced Esau's chest and he tottered and groped for the chair by the desk. The twins rushed to his side while Toby crawled from the cot to the aid of the fallen teacher.

"Pa! Are you okay?"

"Are you hurt, Mr. Mancini?"

Hattie gasped at the scene that greeted her when she waddled into the room. Esau was slumped in the rickety green chair with the twins hovering attentively but uselessly over him. The stranger, she figured it must be Toby's Mr. Mancini, lay crumpled on the concrete floor with the boy kneeling at his side. The room was boiling with grief and pain and Hattie hesitated at the door, face creased with uncertainty, not certain where she should direct her soothing attention.

Esau clutched his chest and gulped hungrily at the turbid air as the boys stared helplessly.

The teacher uttered a moan of pain and held his hand over the side of his face that was hidden from Hattie's view. Toby bent close to his friend and spoke softly, much as Hattie had done with him the night before.

"You dare accuse me of kidnapping." Esau rasped the words through blood-drained lips. The fire had left his face but the rage still filled his voice. "I do the work of the Lord, He who appointed me to lead His earthly army." The farmer's rumbling voice filled the room, rising in volume as his pain subsided. He shook free of the boys' fumbling attempts to comfort him and rose unsteadily to his feet. With a shaky finger waving at Toby and the teacher, Esau released the pent-up venom of a lifetime of indignities.

"The law tells me I must expose my innocent children to sacrilegious teaching. The law says it will send me to jail for teaching them the way of the Lord. The law allows filth and corruption on the streets of our city. The law allows the devil's evil messengers into our homes. I spit on your law," he shrieked, and he unleashed a weak, wet symbol of his discontent.

Mike Mancini looked curiously at his hand, expecting to see gobs of blood from his aching ear, but it was clean and dry. He shook his head to clear his brain and sat up on the floor, back propped against the cot, arms wrapped around his drawn-up knees. Toby assumed a similar pose. They both listened attentively to Esau's outrage. The throbbing in Toby's head grew with the decibel level of Esau's monologue, but he tried to hide his discomfort. He wanted to understand Esau's words, but their meaning was clouded by the farmer's fervor.

Mike listened with interest. No amount of casual probing could begin to uncover the vivid picture of past injustices that Esau painted. He slid his hand under his coat and flipped the switch on the small tape recorder. That was the real reason he had gone back into his bedroom. The twins never did ask why he needed his coat on such a warm afternoon. Mike understood enough about recording to know that the results would be scratchy at best, but what the man said was important. The same diatribe that could convict him might also excuse his actions.

Esau stepped back a pace and studied the at-

tentive faces of his captive audience. The devil's
helpers. Unwitting, maybe even innocent, but
nonetheless they were the spreaders of Satan's
godless word. "You talk of laws and kidnapping." A hint of sanity replaced the earlier fury.
"What of the laws that fill the streets with wanton women, spreading their foul disease? These
temptresses lure God-fearing men into their
clutches, into their dens of evil. The law knows
them, knows where they go to sell their smooth,
white bodies, knows where they lure their captives. But the law does nothing. The law allows
the filthy traffic."

A new type of ardor seemed to take Esau in its
grip. His angry mien evaporated, replaced by a
dreamy presence. Mike was disturbed by the
transformation. A satisfied grin passed across
Esau's gaunt face. "That's why the Lord asked
me to lead His earthly army. Girls like that have
no place in His plan. Wanton harlots must not be
permitted to tempt the God-fearing."

Esau's rangy body seemed to grow in all directions until its very presence filled the room. A
new glint sparkled in his eye, a look of madness
but lacking the rage that had fueled his earlier
outburst. There was an air of satisfaction and
contentedness. Esau paused and swung his
dreamy gaze around the cluttered walls. Jesus
smiled back at him, pleased with Esau's execution of his duty.

"Girls like Candy must be destroyed, and God
has chosen His earthly army to rid the world of
the likes of her and her tempting ways." His
entire body relaxed and he smiled down at the
huddled captives. Toby was glad he had calmed

down because the shouting hurt his head. He
had absolutely no idea what Esau was talking
about.

Mike stared in fascination and fear at the spent
preacher. He knew all too well what Esau was
talking about. His mind fashioned a picture of a
sweet young girl poring over a biology experiment, turning her eyes away as the fine scalpel
parted the damp skin of the frog's cold belly,
turning white as snow when the colorful entrails
spilled onto the porcelain dish. She was but one
of hundreds who had passed through Mike's
careful hands, but the teacher remembered her,
was fond of her. She had brains and spunk and
love of life. Then something went awry in Debby
Carlson's life. She turned in the wrong direction.
Mike had heard rumors and stories but he tried
to forget about it, hard as that might be. He
couldn't be the conscience of every single kid in
Roseville schools.

But there had been something special about
Debby Carlson, something that convinced the
teacher that his former student would one day
find her direction. She just needed time, needed
a chance.

But she never got the chance. With a sinking
feeling Mike remembered that Debby's street
name had been Candy.

Chapter Twenty-nine

◈◇◈◇◈◇◈◇◈◇◈

THE FARMER'S INADVERTENT confession cast a new light on their situation. He was no longer harmless and eccentric, now he was a killer. Shortly after his rambling discourse, Esau called his clan together and they trooped from the room to pray. They didn't go far, just beyond the door, which they left open. Mike could clearly hear Esau's hearty praises and the twins' droning responses. Maybe they were praying for him. He hoped not.

"Still hurts pretty bad, does it?" Mike saw Toby wince as he helped him to his feet and settled him back in the cot.

"It's worse than ever, Mr. Mancini," he answered. "Do you really think you can make it go away?"

"I'll try, Toby. I can put you into a light trance right away. I think that will work. But I'm not sure what that bunch out there is expecting to happen." He gestured toward the open door. "What did you tell them?"

"Nothing, really. I just told them that you could make my headache go away. I think Hattie felt sorry for me. She's the fat one."

"She sure is," Mike agreed. He tried on a smile for the first time since he left the apartment. "She shimmies and shakes like a whole tub full of Jell-O."

Toby forced a thin smile of his own but the teacher could see that his heart wasn't in it.

"What do you know about them?" Mike asked.

He pulled the green chair next to the cot and straddled it with his arms draped over the back. "Tell me everything that's happened."

Toby told the teacher about the ride from the studio and his conversations with Hattie and the twins. His eyes filled when he told Mike about the abuse he had suffered at Esau's flashing backhand. Mike knew the feeling all too well.

Mike was interested in the twins' background also. It would give him some insight into their nature, and he prided himself on his understanding of human nature. The boys had been dominated by Esau and by God and, in their minds, the two were one and the same. With the right combination of personalities, Esau domineering and the twins passive, it was no surprise the boys obeyed their father's every command without question or objection. They would do exactly as they were told—up to a point. Mike's problem was that he didn't know where that point was.

Toby told Mike about his ill-fated escape attempt and the teacher felt a surge of pride for the boy. He hadn't even been thinking about escape. Uppermost in Mike's mind was easing Toby's pain; getting him out of there could come next. The word *escape* conjured up images of hand-dug tunnels under prison walls, clipped barbed wire, soot-blackened faces, and spinning searchlights on Stalag walls. I'm too old for this kind of crap, he thought. He'd prefer to shake hands with his captors and simply stroll out the front door. But remembering Esau's unwitting confession, Mike thought the idea of escape didn't seem so far-fetched. The farmer was a madman, a killer.

"Mr. Mancini."

The teacher snapped from his thoughts and looked down at the resting boy. "Sorry, Toby. I was just thinking about something. I'll try to hypnotize you now, not too deep, just enough to make you forget about your headache."

"Thanks, but there's one more thing I forgot to tell you."

"What's that?"

Toby pulled the crumpled label from his pocket and handed it to the teacher.

Esau Manley
P.O. Box 1288
Mankato, MN

He read the name and address aloud. "That must be the farm they told you about."

Toby nodded in agreement, and they looked toward the door from which the mumbling prayer session filled the room with an eerie overture.

"Can you do it now, Mr. Mancini?"

Mike prayed that he could ease the boy's pain. Toby was as receptive a subject as a hypnotist could ask for, but in his current mental state, Mike couldn't predict how he'd react. He glanced at one of the wall pictures and whispered a silent prayer.

"Watch my eyes, Toby. Watch my eyes and try to forget about everything else. Think of something nice and peaceful, a winter snowfall, snowflakes big and soft and white floating gently to the ground." He wanted to alter Toby's mood from anxiety to serenity. It would better his chances of success. "Close your eyes now, Toby. Imagine a soft, cool wind against your face and tiny snowflakes landing on your nose. Can you feel them, Toby?''

The boy's sweet smile answered his question.

Mike spoke in a smooth monotone. "It was daytime but now it's getting dark. All around you the lights are growing dim, they're growing dimmer and you're feeling tired. Your eyes are heavy, very heavy. You feel relaxed. Your eyelids are so heavy that you can't open them. Try to open them, Toby.''

Mike watched anxiously. He saw a flicker of movement but nothing more. It had worked and the teacher sighed thankfully.

"Your headache's gone, Toby. It went away and won't come back." Mike knew that was a long shot but he saw no harm in trying.

Toby appeared to be resting painlessly and peacefully. Was that what Esau expected? It's what Mike wanted. The boy was at peace, at least for the time being.

Mike was so absorbed with his ministrations that he didn't notice the absence of the murmuring from the other room. He had been kneeling beside the cot and was startled to see the pair of denim-clad legs at his side.

"Is it done?" Esau looked down at the sleeping boy, head curiously cocked to one side, as if witnessing a rare phenomenon.

"The boy's in a trance. He doesn't have any pain right now. That's what you wanted, isn't it?"

Esau wasn't sure what he wanted. He didn't want the boy in pain. He was sure of that. But what was this about a trance? It didn't sound right—unholy—the kind of thing the fortune-teller did. His thoughts drifted to the turreted home on Summit Avenue and Mme. Chetret and her smoke-filled den and he felt a cold chill creep through his body.

Mike sensed his concern. "It's like a deep sleep. It's not magic or anything like that. Do you want me to talk to him, to ask him anything?"

"Can't I talk to him myself?" Esau asked suspiciously.

"Not while he's in a trance. But I can communicate with him for you." Mike didn't want Toby subjected to Esau's wild mood swings.

"Can he talk while he's asleep?"

"He's not asleep, he's in a trance." Mike sat on the green chair between Toby and Esau. He craned his neck to look up at the farmer, then he returned his attention to the boy on the cot.

"How do you feel, Toby?"

"I feel fine."

"I thought you said he was asleep. Is this more work of the devil?" Esau's suspicion was rapidly turning to anger, exactly what Mike had feared.

"I didn't say he was asleep. I said he was in a trance. It's different. It's like being asleep but still able to listen and talk." He wasn't sure if Esau was buying it. "Doctors and dentists use it all the time."

That seemed to strike a responsive chord and Esau unclenched his fists. Mike felt like he was talking to an angry child ready to launch into a tantrum at the slightest provocation. He turned in the chair and looked up at the man, a hard and long gaze meant to take a measure and to imply a degree of independence.

"What should I call you?" he asked.

The change in the direction of the conversation caught the farmer off guard and he took a moment to reply. "My name is Esau."

"And the boys?" Mike gestured toward the twins with a nod of his head.

"They are Abel and Amos."

Like most Catholics his age, Mike Mancini hadn't spent too much time poring over the mysteries of the Old Testament. He would have liked to comment on the chapter and verse where the ancient names were referenced.

"Why are you doing this, Esau? Why don't you let the boy go home?"

"You know the reason. I told you on the phone. The boy carries the devil in his soul. He must be cleansed."

"The boy has no devil in him, Esau. Toby's a wonderful little boy who goes to church every Sunday and says his prayers every night before he goes to bed. Why do you think that he has the devil inside him?"

"I read what he has done," Esau shouted suddenly. "I read the column of your friend Mr. MacBride."

Mike was amazed—and frightened—at how easily Esau slipped back and forth over the line of reason.

"Fortune-tellers, idolaters—they all do the same kind of devil's work."

The fiery glare returned and Mike felt the man stiffen at his side. He decided to take another tack.

"How long will it take, Esau—to get the devil out of Toby?"

"Satan is weakening," Esau said, as if that explained everything.

"When you are finished, can the boy go home?" Mike sensed the man's uncertainty and it worried him.

Esau's chest ached and he had trouble thinking. Hate the sin, love the sinner. But where did the boy stop and where did the devil start? He hadn't thought about letting the boy go home. Neither had he thought of keeping him. Esau hadn't thought about that aspect at all. God's message had been to get rid of the devil. He didn't provide any details beyond that.

"The boy can't leave until he is cleansed," Esau said with finality.

Mike realized that he was at a dead end. "Then for God's sake let's get on with it." He cast Esau a withering glare then, patience worn to the breaking point, turned his back to Esau and looked down at the peaceful boy. Mike didn't see the vein pulsing on Esau's temple or the flash of rage that transformed his face into a mask of hate.

"How are you feeling, Toby?"

"I'm fine. I want to go to the memory room now."

That's strange, Mike thought. Toby was only in a light trance. In that state he shouldn't even be aware of the memory room.

"What is the boy saying?" Esau's anger at Mike's blasphemy was overcome by his curiosity.

Mike wondered how to handle this one. Many supposedly normal people rebuked his theory, and the present company was anything but normal. What the hell, he thought, might as well go with the truth. "He's telling me that he wants to open another memory, Esau. It's the thing you read about in Mr. MacBride's column. It's what you call the work of the devil because you don't understand it." Mike waited for another of the farmer's outbursts but Toby's clear voice distracted their attention.

"I'm going to the memory room now. It's time to open another matchbox." The words were distinct, without emotion. He wasn't demanding to go but neither was he asking the teacher's permission.

Mike was confused and worried. Hypnotism employed the power of suggestion, but Toby was jumping the gun, taking the lead and racing ahead. The hypnotist should lead and the subject should follow. He reached inside his jacket to make sure that the recorder was running, and he felt the tiny vibrations of the spinning reels.

"I'm in the memory room now," Toby announced.

"What's he talking about?" Esau demanded.

"Be quiet," Mike hissed. "Don't disturb him."

Esau stepped back as if he'd been slapped in the face.

"Are you at the table, Toby?"

"Yes. The boxes are still there. I'm taking the top box."

Mike had led Toby through the sequence in the earlier sessions, but now the boy was moving routinely without waiting for direction.

"Is there a name on the box?" Mike asked.

"Vladimeare. That's all it says. There's no last name. I'm going to open it now and watch the memory."

"How will you watch it? You always used a television before." Mike could feel Esau's suspicious breathing warming the back of his neck,

wondering what tricks the teacher and his possessed pupil were playing on him.

"I don't need the TV anymore. I can see the
memory right over the table in the memory
room. It's easy."

Was he bragging? Mike wondered.

Mike recalled the earlier sessions where Toby
spoke a foreign language. That wouldn't do at
all. It would send Esau over the deep end for
sure. "Remember to speak only English, Toby."

"The memory is coming out of the matchbox.
I'm in a room. It's a very old room."

Esau inched forward and the twins hung close
to his side. He stung from the schoolteacher's
rebuke but he held his tongue in check.

"Can you describe the room, Toby?" Mike
asked.

"It's dark. It's daytime outside but the room's
very dark. There's a little bit of light coming
through the window, but it's not really a window
because there's no glass in it, just a hole covered
by a piece of cloth. The floor's dirty. No, it's not
really dirty, it's dirt. It's hard-packed dirt. That's
what the floor's made out of. And there's a big
fireplace on the wall. I could stand straight up
inside it."

"Is there any furniture, Toby?" The scientist in
Mike was speaking. He hadn't lost sight of their
predicament, but he felt that he might as well
glean what information he could to aid the research. And the question seemed harmless
enough, not the type of topic Esau would find
disturbing.

"There's a table and some benches. Everything's real rough. And there are shelves on the
wall, just boards really. There's plates on them

and some carvings of animals. All the furniture is real low, like the people who live here aren't too tall. The ceiling's low too, a lot lower than ours is at home."

"Is that all?" Mike hoped that the description might help to pinpoint the time frame. He wanted to be able to track the memories through time, to follow Toby's genes across the years and across the oceans and the continents. It was too bad he had to forego the language.

As Mike was thinking his thoughts, Toby stiffened. The peace drained from his face and he became wary, eyes darting wildly about the room, like he was being pursued or afraid that he might be. A sheen of glossy sweat sprang from his brow. Mike didn't like it, not at all. It wasn't the way it was supposed to be. Mike tried to take the mystique from hypnotism, especially when discussing it with the uninitiated. But that was only a front to ease their apprehension. Deep within, he had a great respect for it, the kind of grudging reverence that clever people reserve for the unexplainable.

Now he had an even greater fear. The unexplainable was out of control. Toby was racing ahead. He needed no cues, no prodding, no clever word tricks from the expert. Some other force drove him to explore, and the look on his face told Mike that he was delving into something very unpleasant.

Toby's eyes searched the reaches of the room in response to Mike's last question. They stopped, focused, and filled with a dread that sent a wave of fear that struck the teacher like a physical blow. Even Esau reeled at its icy chill.

Toby locked his eyes onto the ancient vision.

"There's a wooden chest sitting next to the door." A heavy bead of sweat rolled down his temple. The room was cool.

Mike watched in fear and fascination as the boy's pupils grew as big as peas, then shrank to a pinpoint. Then they grew and shrank again as if a strobe visible only to Toby flashed intermittently into his face. The Manleys hung above him, absorbed by the tale, children entranced by a latter-day brothers Grimm.

"Is there anyone in the room, Toby?"

Toby's eyes flickered and the blood drained from his face but he didn't respond.

"Toby, answer me. Is there anyone in the room?"

More silence.

"He don't look too good. I think he's gonna be sick." One of the twins hung over the cot, wearing the same worried expression he'd probably used when watching a newborn colt struggle to its feet. Mike waved a silencing hand without looking up. Furrows of concern worried his face. First Toby had proceeded to the memory room without direction or guidance. Now he was ignoring Mike's questions. Mike no longer knew what to expect. Had his gentle trance turned the boy on or did Toby now control his own "on-off" switch?

"Toby, tell me, what else do you see? I can tell something's bothering you. What is it? Tell me, Toby."

"It's inside the chest."

"What's inside the chest?" Mike reached out for the boy's hand. It felt cold and clammy. Toby jerked it away.

"Her. Some of her," Toby whined. Then he

began to mumble inaudibly, his lips working like those of a palsied old man burbling muffled sounds.

Mike couldn't make out any words but he detected a cadence, rising and falling, starting and stopping at rhythmic intervals. Prayers? And in what language? He could feel Esau's suspicious gaze burning into his back. Toby lay on the cot. Mike sat on the chair by his side. Esau stood behind Mike. One twin stood to Mike's left, the other to his right. Toby's eyes were staring blindly but he wasn't aware of the anxious, curious, or angry faces that stared back.

The tape whirred softly in Mike's jacket pocket. He hoped that the pounding of his own heartbeat didn't drown out Toby's words.

"Her. Some of her."

Mike had no idea what that meant, nor was he sure that he wanted to know. Had Esau caught the words? Probably not and that was just as well.

The farmer's voice rumbled in his ear. "What did he mean, some of her?" An image of Candy with long black hair and bruised neck clawed at some deep recess of his mind.

"I don't know, Esau," Mike answered sincerely. "Toby's seeing something that happened to one of his ancestors hundreds of years ago. If this one is like all the other memories, he's seeing something very disturbing."

Esau muttered something about the devil that Mike couldn't catch. One of the twins whistled under his breath.

"I'm going to open the chest now." Toby spoke softly, the pronouncement sad and grave. "I don't want to do it but I have to do it because I did it then. Now I have to do it over again."

Where was the boy? Mike wondered. Was he actually there, in the darkness of some long-forgotten house whose worm-eaten logs had long since been devoured by the earth that grew them? Was he an actor in an ancient play, re-creating old roles best left unremembered, or was he only a spectator watching the tragic and familiar scene unfold? He seemed to shift from role to role, actor to audience, audience to actor, curiosity to involvement. Did the boy know what was inside the chest? Had he seen it before?

Toby murmured another haunting string of syllables. Prayers? Incantations? "I'm opening the box."

Everyone's eyes were drawn to his face and they watched in horror as it transformed into a mask of anguish. The thin sheen of perspiration became rolling balls of sweat, the sickly pallor bleached to a stark white mask of death, the anxious eyes rolled up into his head, and the onlookers gasped in unison as they gazed into the ghostly sockets.

"Aaaaiiii! Aaaaiiii! Aaaaiiii! Aaaaiiii!"

Toby's back arched like a drawn bow stretched to the limits of its flex. The force of the spasm threw him into the air and he flopped crazily on the cot, grabbing a handful of threadbare sheet, shredding it as he thrashed like someone possessed.

"Aaaaaaiiiiiieeeeee!"

The primal scream filled the small room with centuries of untold agony. Toby finally fell back against the clammy mattress, limp and spent.

The twins had backed away as one would from a mad dog. Even Mike leaned back, a reaction to the shock of Toby's outburst.

But Esau never flinched. If anything, he leaned closer, rooted to the floor, glaring down at Toby with a malevolent stare. Mike could feel the farmer's reaction, the vibrant energy of his hate. What had happened was precisely what he hoped to avoid. If ever the madman needed evidence of possession, Toby had provided it.

Mike had to end the session quickly before things got even worse. "Wake up, Toby. It's over. It's time to leave the memory room. Wake up."

"He is possessed," Esau accused, pleased that the proof was so irrefutable, overpowering. He wanted the boy to be possessed. How else could he fulfill his mission and deliver his promise to the Lord?

Mike ignored him. "Toby! I want you to wake up. Now!"

"There are still more matchboxes," Toby droned, ignoring the urgency of the teacher's tone.

How many more? Mike wondered. Six, seven, eight? How many had Toby counted that first time? A dozen? It all seemed so long ago. "We'll do the rest of them some other time, Toby. I want you to wake up now."

"No. I must continue." The voice was Toby's but the words belonged to someone else. Mike wondered who.

"Toby, don't—"

"I'm opening the next matchbox." His tone was fatalistic. Another new sound, another voice.

"Toby, I don't think you should—"

"The name on the box is Peetur. I'm opening the box now."

"Satan, in the name of our Lord Jesus Christ, I command you to ..." Esau had backed away from the cot and stood by the door. He posed like a crucified farmer, arms spread wide from his bibbed chest, legs firmly planted, fingers splayed, chin tilted toward the ceiling as he made his demands on the prince of darkness.

The twins both shot a worried glance at the sweaty little boy before moving to their father's side where they picked up the prayerful chant. Mike sat uneasily on the chair, the innocent boy bathed in sweat on the soiled sheets in front of him, the wild-eyed farmer with his slow-witted sons to his rear. He didn't know what to expect from either side, but for the time being Esau and the twins were occupied by their self-taught rites of exorcism. In a fleeting moment of frivolous thought, Mike wondered if they'd seen the movie. He doubted it.

"I'm in a city surrounded by high walls." Toby described his newest scene without Mike's prodding.

The teacher snuck the recorder from his pocket and checked the tape. It had completed one side and was stopped. He wondered how much he had missed. With deft fingers, he flipped the tiny cassette and started the other side. The Manleys were too engrossed in their prayers to notice.

"Everything is brown, lifeless. The walls, the houses—everything. It's all the same color as the dirt road. The trees all look dead."

"Do you know where you are?" Mike had to strain to hear over the hum of the praying trio.

"The village is called Dwarkvin."

"Where is it?"

"It is on the plain of Mustafanti."

Mike decided he'd look that up later. He was curious how the itinerant Hortons had traveled through time to the streets of Saint Paul from the dusty plains of Mustafanti, but it would have to wait.

"What's happening today, Toby?" Mike knew the pattern and was anxious to get it over with. Toby had had enough mental trauma for a while.

"Today is the day of the execution."

Mike was almost afraid to ask. "Who is being executed?"

"My friend Jusip."

"What has Jusip done to deserve this?" Mike asked sadly.

Then he noticed that the haunting buzz of prayers had stopped. Esau stood stiffly at his side, boring into Toby with his fiery eyes.

"He has offended the priests," Toby answered. "He has blasphemed so now he must die."

Esau's sharp intake of breath was audible.

"And now I must watch his execution once again." He sighed. "It makes me very sad."

The tape whirred inside Mike's jacket as Toby described the beheading in chilling detail. But there was none of the anguish of previous memories, only thoughtful resignation as the hooded executioner brought the gleaming blade cleanly down and Jusip's curly head disappeared into the waiting basket and his neck gushed forth his life force in a crimson arc.

Toby sighed wearily. "I'm going to open another matchbox now."

Esau had heard enough. The devil was strengthening his hold on the boy, negating the farmer's earlier efforts. "Get away from him," he commanded. "You are aiding the devil," he said harshly.

"Toby, wake up." Mike shook the boy roughly, ignoring Esau's command. "Wake up, Toby. No more memories for a while," he pleaded.

"The name on the next matchbox is—"

"Get away from him!" Esau's roar filled the room and the angry blast coincided with the shower of stars that exploded in Mike's brain. The farmer's bony fist crashed into the back of Mike's head like a hurtling rock and the stunned teacher crashed to the floor.

"I am in a forest. It is nighttime but the moon is full and I can see my way clearly." Toby described his newest memory in a strained monotone, seemingly unconcerned about the violence by his side. Then he moved on to the next memory, one that once again rolled his eyes into his head like egg whites and sent his screams pounding on the thin walls of the Manleys' basement chamber.

One after another—chilling—violent—sad!

All the while, Esau prayed and the tape ran, each terrifying cry from the past calling for increased effort by Esau, and the walls shook from the swells that rose and fell as Toby poured out the torment of generations. And when he'd slump on the drenched cot between memories, Esau would thank the Lord for the successful purge of yet another demon. Then it would start again as Toby resurrected another memory, and he'd tear at the sheets and grind his teeth, pound the walls and wail in pain and terror as he waded through centuries of horror.

Esau prayed and his chest ached but he was

buoyed by the prospect of imminent success. Amos and Abel were terrified. They answered Esau's ravings with the obligatory "amens" but they couldn't block out the horrors that escaped the parched lips of the little boy.

Throughout, the tape rolled slowly around its sprockets in the coat pocket of the unconscious biology teacher as he lay by the cot with a thin trickle of blood seeping from his ear.

Chapter Thirty

CLANCY HAD A full Tuesday morning calendar but Toby Horton took precedence. His secretary had shifted some appointments to his associates and rescheduled others so he could attend the 9 A.M. update sessions at the Hortons'. "Move Mr. Hogan's bowel and scratch Mrs. Elway's hemorrhoids," he instructed in the terse note he left on her desk. Clancy subscribed to the theory that there was humor in medicine. One had only to know where to look for it.

When Inspector Borg first scheduled the meeting, Clancy and Mike had made plans to meet earlier that morning for breakfast. Mike was already five minutes late and Clancy fidgeted with the laminated menu.

"Are you ready to order, sir?" The waitress, looking appropriately cute and perky, stood over him with pencil poised. He asked for coffee while he waited for his friend, and the girl flashed a splendid smile and hurried off to mesmerize another morning patron.

For all of his laid-backness (his own word), Clancy hated to be kept waiting. The Princes of Medicine were the "waitees," the patients were the "waiters." He would have been a terrible patient. The waitress returned with a steaming plastic pot of coffee and a dazzling smile, both of which she left at the booth before wiggling away. Clancy quickly dispatched a cup and poured another, impatiently checking his watch between each scalding sip. Ten past eight and still no sign of Mancini. A typical absentminded professor, Clancy thought with a tight smile. Or maybe that relic of a car that he drove had broken down. It coughed and belched like an asthmatic coal miner when it was in good health. God help it if it caught something.

"Still waiting?"

He bit off his clever retort and ordered a toasted English. The waitress blazed a smile and left. It was a quarter past eight.

The pay phone hung nose high on the earth-tone wall between the men's and women's rooms. Clancy felt self-conscious standing there, like a voyeur who gets off on watching people come and go from the loo. The phone rang five, six, seven times. Even if he was in the shower, Mike would have heard and answered it.

Einar Borg and Teddy MacBride arrived at the same time, parked their cars in the street, and walked the long stone drive to the Hortons' front door. The inspector wore a tan sport coat and dark brown slacks with a matching tie tightly knotted at his throat. He carried a brown leather file folder. His buttoned-down efficiency inspired confidence. He wished that he felt as in charge as he looked.

Teddy MacBride wore a pair of baggy blue-cords, much abused Hush Puppies, and a pale green pullover with a pink pig where an alligator should have been. Next to the inspector, he looked like a bag of laundry.

Gramps was waiting at the door and walked out to greet them, shaking hands like relatives meeting in a hospital waiting room, false smiles and brave fronts, trying unsuccessfully to mask their true feelings. Gramps didn't ask for an update. If there had been any new developments, they would have been told before this. Besides, Steve and Jan should be first in line for any news. Without prompting, they gathered at the kitchen table, where Steve and Jan sat silently, red-rimmed eyes staring morosely at their lukewarm coffee.

Almost two full days had passed since Toby's happy voice enlivened the Horton household, forty-eight hours of gut-wrenching anxiety. Borg had seen it all before but he'd never get used to it. What was worse, he wondered, the dragged-out creeping terror of a missing child or the punch in the gut of a drowned toddler? He had seen it all a hundred times but some things get no easier through repetition. How do you scale grief? he asked himself. Do some people have a higher threshold than others? Does it reach a point where it mercifully numbs the senses, blocking out reality until some later time when the mind and body are better able to handle it? And how should he react to it? He knew cops who could ignore the grief that surrounded them, ones who bulldozed away the feelings like so much flotsam interfering with their investigation. And they were no less successful than Borg. It was all a matter of style, he thought, style and sentiment. Without a doubt, Einar Borg did it the hard way.

"Morning, Jan, Steve."

There was no phony lightness in his tone. They deserved more than that. What right did he have to obligate them to twist their lips into a charade of a smile? But they still favored him with as pleasant a front as they could pull together. For Jan it was a slight upward turn at the corners of her mouth. For Steve it was a withered grin that was halfway to despair.

"Coffee?"

Gramps brought noise and motion to the gathering. The silence needed breaking before it took too firm a grip. Einar and Teddy took the offered cups.

The inspector checked his watch. "The others ought to be here by now." Punctuality was right up there with creased slacks and an empty in-basket on Borg's list of priorities, and he was annoyed and slightly surprised at their tardiness. He expected more from the teacher and the doctor.

"If you don't mind, I've asked a friend to join us, too," Teddy announced cautiously.

"A friend?" the inspector echoed with raised eyebrows.

"His name's Father Gaffney. I thought he might be a welcome addition."

As if on cue, the doorbell chimed. Gramps put the pot down, strode down the hallway, and returned seconds later with the priest.

"This dubious example of the clergy is Father Denny Gaffney. If he prays as poorly as he plays golf, his soul's on the brink of destruction."

The priest waved off Teddy's introduction and circled the table to where Steve and Jan sat. "I hope you don't think I'm an intruding old busybody, Mr. and Mrs. Horton. Teddy explained what you've been going through and I asked him if I might help."

The old priest's smile was the first real ray of light to pierce the gloom all morning. Steve Horton extended his hand and the priest engulfed it.

"Certainly, you're welcome, Father." He eyed the priest apologetically. "But you know we're not Catholic."

"Neither was Christ and He didn't do so bad."

The priest's cheery and irreverent manner helped to disperse the pall that draped across the kitchen. He was a big man with the bloated gut of a beer drinker, a shock of wiry, gray hair, and a belligerent jaw that seemed to defy gravity. Without the black suit and clerical collar he might have been there to fix the sink.

"In spite of Mr. MacBride's unkind attack on my spiritual credentials, I would like to offer a small prayer if you don't mind."

No one minded at all and the big priest planted himself at one end of the table and waved his callused hand in the sloppiest sign of the cross Teddy had ever witnessed.

"I've got a special devotion to the mother of Christ. She's done a couple of nice things for me in the past. How 'bout if we ask for her help?"

Jan Horton couldn't keep the first real smile in two days from lighting her face. "I think that would be wonderful, Father."

"Then let's get on with it."

In what seemed an uncharacteristic gesture from one so rough-hewn, the priest placed his hands together in the classic position and tilted his proud chin to the ceiling.

"Mary, we've talked before." He paused as if giving her a chance to check her files. "I want to thank you for all the other favors you've granted me, and now I have a new one."

Teddy's hands were folded like a schoolboy's on the edge of the table. His eyes were downcast, his expression reflective. Gramps, Jan, and Steve exchanged glances and a spark seemed to jump between them. The inspector sat respectfully.

The priest continued. "These people have a little boy named Toby and he's in a bit of a fix. Our good friend Teddy MacBride tells me they're good people so you don't have to check on that any further."

There was no trace of mockery in his voice, and the Hortons picked up the rhythm of a deeply religious man having a very personal communication. His approach lacked some of the reverence of their Lutheran upbringing but none of the fervor.

"I don't have to tell you what it's like to be a mother. And nobody knows better than you how a mother hurts when her boy's in trouble. So you know exactly how Jan and Steve must feel. Here's the favor I'm asking, Mary. First, take some of the load of anxiety off their backs. It doesn't help a bit and it probably gets in the way of their praying. Second and most important, watch over Toby. I know he's going to come out of this thing okay, because you're looking out for him. You never let me down, Mary. I don't know why you've been so good to me, but I sure thank you."

All during his rambling prayer the crusty old priest had been gazing at the ceiling, looking his intercessor right in the eye. At the conclusion of his request he dropped his chin and lowered his eyes.

"Amen."

"Amen," the others whispered.

The priest nodded deferentially and backed off into the farthest corner of the kitchen, where Gramps poured him a cup. He smiled his thanks and took a small black book from his coat pocket and began reading silently.

Einar Borg coughed lightly. "Thank you, Father. We'll take all the help we can get." He looked uncertainly at the empty places. "Has anyone heard from Dr. Kendall or Mr. Mancini?"

His answer was another melody from the doorbell. This time Gramps led in a perplexed Clancy Kendall.

"Sorry I'm late. I got stood up at breakfast." His eyes did a quick circuit of the table. "Where's Mike?"

"We thought he'd be with you," the inspector answered.

"Well, he isn't. We were supposed to meet for breakfast and he never showed. I thought he forgot about it and came straight here without me."

"Did you phone him?"

"Sure I did. There's no answer. Mike's one of the most reliable people I know. I'm a little worried, Inspector."

Without asking permission, Borg took the phone and absently punched in a number. He identified himself, issued a series of instructions, and replaced the receiver. "I'm sending someone over to his apartment to check. In the meantime let's just assume he had a flat tire and couldn't get to a phone." He could feel the tension returning to the room as swiftly as Father Gaffney had dispelled it.

"Let's talk about where we are," he began. There had been no contact with the kidnapper since Sunday night's phone call. Borg told them that they had tracked down the printer who made up the pamphlets, but the buyer left no address and paid in cash. He was described as a young, soft-spoken man with red hair. It fit Mandikas's description of the boy handing out the pamphlets. It was a weak lead at best since there was nothing linking the pamphleteer to the kidnapper, but cases were solved on thinner threads. Borg advised them that they were still pursuing it.

"Maybe if we offered a ransom," Steve tried.

His contribution didn't please the inspector. "Let's not raise this to a higher level, Steve." He spoke softly but firmly, keeping any hint of annoyance from his voice. "Nobody's asking for ransom and I think it would be a mistake to introduce it. Remember, the man's expressed deeply religious albeit misguided views. He could take serious offense at an offer of ransom."

"The inspector's right," Father Gaffney interrupted from the corner. "I can't read the man's mind, but in a manner of speaking we're in much the same business. The fella's disturbed. Too much God can do that to certain people although I'm certain He doesn't intend it that way. I've met my share of them under my own roof," he confessed.

Borg was interested. "Mr. MacBride's filled you in on everything that's happened, Father. I'd be interested to hear your views."

The old priest walked slowly back from the corner of the kitchen, steepling his fingers and deliberately pondering the policeman's question. "I'm no expert," he acknowledged, "but that's never kept me from preaching, either."

He smiled disarmingly and everyone leaned closer to hear him.

"If I was a betting man . . ." He paused and gave Teddy a thin smile that bespoke an inside joke. "If I was a betting man," he went on, "I'd bet that we're dealing with a basically fine person, a salt-of-the-earth righteous type."

He looked quickly from face to face for a reaction but there was none.

"But even good people sometimes do some pretty questionable things. Lord, I could write a book on it if it wasn't for the seal of confession."

A deep chuckle rumbled from the grizzly man that seemed to start from his toes, echo through his keglike belly and tumble from his lips.

"But I digress." He pulled a chair to the end of the table and sat. Steve and Jan were to his right, Teddy was to his left. The inspector occupied a similar place at the opposite end of the table. The priest carefully folded his hands on the edge of the table and addressed the Hortons. "Most of the people I've met who claim a direct line with the Almighty are basically harmless. I suppose as mental quirks go, that's as good a one to have as any. The problem is that they have a tendency to take themselves too seriously, and when they do that, they cross a bridge between being pleasantly eccentric and rashly unpredictable."

He avoided using the word *dangerous* in deference to the Hortons' fragile feelings.

"I don't speak as a psychiatrist, mind you, but I did spend some years headmastering the seminary and we occasionally had to weed out a few of these super Godly types."

The inspector nodded his understanding. He was pleased Teddy had extended the invitation to the priest.

"When they do cross over that bridge," he continued, "they lose some of the quaint little qualities that make them bearable. Everything they do, from buttering their toast to blowing their nose, they do in His name, His with a capital *H*. It can be awfully dreary." He grew pensive for a moment and allowed a smile to cut across his craggy face. "We had a fella a few years back who claimed to speak to the Almighty every night through the local radio station. He'd lie there with the radio blaring while the rest of the gang tried to cash in on a few hours' sleep. One night, a few of the more irreverent boys rigged a cross and a startlingly realistic figure of the crucified Savior at the foot of the bed. With a little creative lighting and some sound effects they convinced the boy to turn off the radio and whisper his nightly messages into an empty tomato can." He smiled ruefully. "Youngsters can be so cruel. But I digress once again. From what I've heard, I'd say that our man has a Second Savior Complex."

That drew raised eyebrows from the inspector. "A Second Savior Complex?"

"I named it myself. We had a few of them over the years. It's also called the Right Hand of God Syndrome."

"You named that one, too," Teddy assumed. He appraised the priest with a wilting look.

"Of course," Gaffney answered indignantly. "If I didn't, who would?"

The faultless logic stopped Teddy in his tracks so he allowed the priest to continue.

"They aren't dangerous as a rule, at least not to others. They drive themselves unmercifully toward what they see as perfection, and they expect the same from those around them." He glanced between Steve and Jan. "You sure wouldn't want to be married to one of them." The priest laid his hands flat on the table and shrugged. "That's all I know. I didn't mean to go on so."

Borg had jotted down a few notes while Father Gaffney talked. He tapped them with the tip of his pencil as he considered the priest. "You paint an interesting profile," he said.

"Only an educated guess," Gaffney reminded him.

"Interesting nonetheless. And your credentials are as impressive as those of anyone I know."

"That's one of the reasons Teddy asked me to come over." He stepped around the table and laid a large hand on Jan's and Steve's shoulders. "But that's not the only reason."

"I know." Jan smiled up at him. "You pray, too."

"He certainly does that," Teddy agreed.

The trill of the telephone broke the lightness of the moment. Steve picked it up, nodded, and handed the receiver to the inspector. Gramps made the rounds with the coffeepot while Einar conducted a cryptic conversation.

"Thanks, Ellison," he said. "Let me know if anything turns up."

It was obvious that the other end had already hung up, but Einar sat for a few extra seconds with the dead phone resting on his ear, staring curiously at Clancy and chewing at his lower lip. "He's not there," he said simply.

Clancy looked from side to side, not sure whom the inspector was addressing.

"I'm talking about Mike Mancini, Doctor. He's gone. And it looks like he left in a hurry."

Clancy felt his heart skip. "What makes you say that?" It came out like a challenge though that wasn't the doctor's intention.

Borg explained the open Scotch bottle and the untouched drink.

"That's even stranger," Clancy said.

"Why so?"

"Because I've never known Mike to take a drink like that—alone, I mean."

"I'll tell you something even stranger," the inspector added.

Clancy waited as Einar drew out the mystery.

"A little boy from Mike's apartment building saw some strangers around there yesterday, a pair of identical twins with beards and bright red hair."

Once the inspector's surprising announcement set in, it was met with mixed emotion. On the positive side, it verified they were on the right track. The long-shot lead Patrolman Mandikas developed had paid unexpected dividends. The kidnappers now had a face, even though it failed to match their earlier expectations. But the biology teacher's disappearance was ominous, a new level of violence, a new victim.

"Were there signs of a struggle?" Clancy asked anxiously.

"Not a bit. Except for the bottle and glass, everything appeared quite normal."

"What could it mean? Why would they want Mike?"

They all huddled with their own thoughts but no one volunteered an answer. Only Gramps hit upon the truth, but it was one of many fleeting options that raced through his mind and he never voiced it aloud.

"It doesn't make any sense." Teddy scratched his bristly head. "I was the one who got the phone call the other night, remember? He asked for me, not for Mike."

"And the letter to the newspaper," Father Gaffney reminded him.

"So why do they want Mike Mancini all of a sudden?" Teddy repeated.

"He's doing the devil's work," the priest reminded them. "You both are."

"I wasn't aware that I shared that honor," the journalist said wryly.

"Think about it," the priest urged. "You're the lesser of two evils, as it were. You only communicate the blasphemy—Mike Mancini spawns it."

"This is all interesting speculation," Clancy

said impatiently, "but what do we do about it?"

"The same as we've been doing all along," Borg replied. "We were on the right track with the redhead and the pamphlets. This only confirms it."

"And complicates it," Clancy added.

"Maybe. But I'm not so sure of that. Now we're sure that we're looking for a pair of redheaded twins in Saint Paul or thereabouts. We know they've been seen handing out pamphlets on University Avenue. There're also reports of them being seen on Hennepin Avenue in Minneapolis. There can't be too many sets of bearded, Bible-pounding redheaded twins around."

"I have an idea," Clancy said. "Why don't we put it on the evening news? We can ask anybody who knows where the twins live to call the station or the police."

"It's a good idea," the inspector conceded, "but I'm afraid it's a little too risky."

"Why?" Steve asked. "It sounds good to me. We see things like that on TV all the time, runaway children, missing persons, they always do it."

"Missing children are different from kidnapped children," Borg answered. He was getting more help and advice than he really wanted, and he wasn't noted for his patience with amateurs. "In the first place, we don't know what makes these guys tick." He saw Jan eyeing him warily. "They're probably harmless, like Father Gaffney's overzealous seminarian, but we don't know that for a fact. And if they don't fit Father's harmless mold, we don't want to risk doing something to set them off."

Clancy saw the wisdom in the inspector's caution and nodded his assent.

"The other problem is that we may drive them away. Underground. At this moment, we know more about them than they realize. If we show our hand too soon, they may run for cover and we'll lose their trail."

"I surrender," Clancy said. "It was a dumb idea."

"Not at all," Borg soothed. "Under most conditions it would be the way to go. This just wasn't the time."

"But how much longer can we wait to do something?" Jan asked. "What are these people doing? What do they want with Toby?"

"May I?" Father Gaffney asked the inspector's permission to answer Jan's question. "If my guess is right, and I'm basing it on what Teddy told me, our friends are attempting to perform an exorcism."

"Oh, God!" Jan had seen the movie, and the most horrid scenes flashed through her mind.

"Now, now," the priest intoned. "It's not at all what you think. Hollywood has a knack for sensationalizing things, you know. If these people are following the tried and true methods, they're simply saying a few harmless prayers over the boy. At some point in their ceremony they'll congratulate themselves for sending Satan packing and they'll let Toby go."

"Do you really believe that, Father?" Jan asked weakly.

"I think it's a very possible scenario," he replied.

"But that means we do nothing, just sit tight and wait," Clancy argued.

"Not at all," Borg said. "We'll continue tracking down our leads. But Father Gaffney's quite right. This whole episode may come to an end with no interference from us at all."

"Just the same, I'd feel better if we could communicate with the kidnappers," Teddy said. "I'd like the chance to reason with them, to let them know that Toby's memories and Mike's hypnotism are scientific phenomena and not some kind of devil worship hocus-pocus. I think if we could get that message to them, we could end this on a happy note much sooner."

"Quite possibly," Borg agreed. He looked at the journalist suspiciously. "Do you have something in mind?"

"I thought you'd never ask," Teddy answered with a secret smile. "What do we know for certain that the kidnappers read?" He threw the question to the group.

"The Bible," Gramps volunteered.

"No doubt true," Teddy agreed reluctantly, "but not the right answer."

"Ah-ha!" Clancy's eyes lit up triumphantly.

"I think the good doctor's figured it out," Teddy said with a grin.

"Your weekly column," Clancy announced.

"Give that man a Kewpie doll," Teddy praised.

"Of course," Steve said excitedly. He seemed to gain confidence and strength as he absorbed the idea. It would be *doing* something, taking action, and that's what he needed. The inactivity made him feel useless. "That's how the kidnappers found out about the dreams in the first place. I'm sure they read your column."

"And they're probably in the upper intellectual quintile of those who do," the priest added drolly.

"What do you think, Inspector?" Teddy asked.

Einar Borg sat like a buttoned-down inspector doll, tie tightly knotted, every short hair neatly in place, as he mentally sorted out the options, the pros and cons of using Teddy's column. His eyes were fixed on Gramps as he pondered, and Gramps was starting to feel uncomfortable under the silent stare.

"I think it's a good idea," he finally announced. "Properly worded, I think it might be an excellent way to communicate." He turned to Teddy. "How long would it take for you to put a column like that together?"

"Thought you'd never ask that one, either." The newspaperman chuckled as he reached into his back pocket and pulled out a folded sheaf of papers.

Chapter Thirty-one

〰〰〰〰〰〰〰

Saint Paul Pioneer Press and Dispatch
Wednesday, July 2, 1986

MacBRIDE'S MUMBLINGS

A Plea for Toby Horton
Every so often something happens that humbles even this ego-laden scribe, and when these

rare events occur they can be devastating. Such is the situation with young Toby Horton. The power of the press is awesome to comprehend, dear reader, even more so when one sits on my side of the typewriter. I'm able to speak to you one-on-one, like a pen pal, airing my prejudices, venting my spleen, explaining, cajoling, informing you about neighborhood or global gossip, anything that I think is significant. And you, dear reader, mesmerized by my worldly wisdom, devour every nonsensical syllable. Unless, that is, you violently disagree with me, at which time you turn the page to something more enlightening like Steve Roper or Jiggs and Maggie. Well, dear reader, every so often I'm jolted into the realization that not every one of you is so discriminating. Such a realization takes freedom of the press to task because I never know when my column is tantamount to yelling "Fire!" in a crowded theater. I'm sorry to say that Toby Horton's unique powers were the "Fire" to one of my readers.

As you probably recall, Toby is the little boy from Roseville who can dream and describe memorable events from the lives of his father, grandfather, great-grandfather, et cetera, et cetera, et cetera, such dreams being uncovered layer by layer under the gentle hypnotic hand of biology teacher-geneticist Mike Mancini, also of Roseville. Sounds harmless enough to me, exciting too, because it opens another avenue of learning since it's Mike's theory that these tiny memory bits are carried from generation to generation on the genetic chain. And, judging by my mail, you faithful readers out there in newspaperland are as excited as I am. All except one of you, that is. And that's why I'm writing today's column.

It's not for my millions of pen pals who regularly line the bird cage with my heady thoughts. This column is a true person-to-person letter to that one reader who felt so strongly moved by Toby Horton's strange gift that he felt obliged to whisk him away to parts unknown, there to exorcise him from what he perceives to be the devil's evil grip. Dear sir, I have but one request.

PLEASE SEND TOBY HOME

You see, sir, you're mistaken in your judgment of Toby Horton. He's no more a disciple of the devil than I am, although some of my readers may want to delve into that a little further. Now that I've told you what Toby Horton isn't, let me describe what he is. He's a ten-year-old boy, small for his age, who likes pizza, fishing, old Batman comics, hockey, waffles with too much syrup, Sunday school, catching garter snakes, the Vikings, the Minnesota Zoo, and Christmas. He doesn't like spinach, hard rock, fat ladies who hug him, hats except for Twins caps, ice fishing, or dancing. And he loves his mother, his father, his grandfather, his great-grandfather, and his freedom. So he's having a pretty rough time of it right now, sir, since you're keeping him from everything that he loves because you have the mistaken idea that Toby is in cahoots with the devil.

Toby's gift is not supernatural. And it's neither good nor is it evil. It's a natural gift from God, like perfect pitch or coordination or the ability to comprehend the Minnesota income tax forms. So why not let him go, sir? I sense that you're a good man—your motives prove that. Maybe there should be more like you, people with the guts to stand up for what they believe in, to strike out at evil. But this time you missed your target by a mile. You took a wild swing at evil and you hit a very nice little boy whose family misses him and is worried sick. Please, sir, send Toby Horton home.

Chapter Thirty-two

❧❧❧❧❧❧❧❧❧❧

MIKE'S HEAD THROBBED and his body felt like a quarterback's on Monday morning. He was stretched out on the floor, a thin blanket all that separated his aging bones from the hard concrete. A skimpy pillow was tucked under his head but he couldn't recall how it got there. He opened one cautious eye and could barely make out the rectangle of predawn grayness from the window in the bathroom. Every muscle rebelled when he twisted to look up at the boy by his side.

Toby's hand hung limply over the edge of the cot, and Mike could hear his soft sleeping breath and see the slight rise and fall of the covers. Except for the teacher's aching bones, everything seemed so peaceful, so unlike the scene that had greeted him the night before when he regained consciousness after Esau's surprise attack. At the time, Toby's screams had jolted him back to reality. He had jerked upright from the cold floor, like waking from a nightmare only to discover that it was real. Toby was sitting up on the cot, thrashing wildly, white eyes staring zombielike, screaming meaningless gibberish while Esau and the twins shouted incantations one octave higher.

Mike recalled groping his way to the cot and pulling himself painfully to his knees. Esau and the twins ignored him. "Toby, wake up. Toby, stop it," he shouted.

The tiny room was a cacophony of noise with Toby wailing at some ancient tragedy, Mike trying to wrest him from its grip, and the Manleys roaring their exorcism over the din. He felt dizzy, lights sparkled before his eyes, but the stabbing pain in his ear kept him from drifting back into oblivion.

"Mach krishnet vishadon ta pretormon," the boy shouted.

At least that's how it sounded to Mike. He didn't recognize the words or the language but he knew that Toby was reliving another horrible episode along the genetic track. The tape recorder caught every syllable, but that wasn't important at the moment. His well-meaning experiment was out of control. It threatened to take Toby with it and he had no idea what damage was being done in the process.

"Mach krishnet vishadon ta pretormon." He shrieked the strange words with a shrillness that sent an arrow through Mike's brain. Toby slammed the wall, crashing his fist into a glass-covered Francis of Assisi. A shower of glistening splinters rained down on the bed and droplets of

blood flew about the room as Toby flailed at some long-buried memory.

"Toby, for Christ's sake wake up." Mike's lungs hurt and his throat burned from the force of his shout.

It must have worked.

Toby's arms fell limply to his sides and his dark, round pupils floated back into place. A peaceful veil soothed his face, but it couldn't erase the centuries of terror he had relived as Mike lay unconscious on the cold floor. Even the Manleys' doleful prayers were clipped to silence. And the silence was tangible. It had a sound all its own, like the hushed seconds after a crash when the screech of brakes, the squeal of tires, and the ripping of metal settle into a deathly calm, and before the moans and cries of pain and the wails of sirens reawaken the deathly stillness.

"Toby," he said gently. "Are you all right?"

"I'm fine," he said, his tone and expression giving no hint of the turbulence that preceded it. "But there's still one more matchbox to open."

"Leave it be, Toby. You've done enough."

"It's the last one. It's different from the others."

"What makes it different, Toby?"

"It's glowing. It goes from pink to bright red. And it's pulsing. Its sides are bulging in and out. It's like it's alive."

"Don't open it now, Toby. It can wait."

Mike feared for the boy's physical health as well as his sanity. How much can a mind endure? Mike didn't know the answer and he didn't want to find out at Toby's expense.

"I'm going to wake you now, Toby. When you wake up you won't remember any of the memories." As an afterthought he added, "And your headache will be gone. When I snap my fingers I want you to wake up."

It worked, just as it had worked all the other times. Toby's eyes focused and he looked quickly about, taking stock of his surroundings.

"Thank God," Mike whispered and he wrapped his arms around the boy and held him tightly against his chest.

"What's the matter with your ear, Mr. Mancini?" Toby asked through a worried frown.

Mike rubbed a drop of dried blood from his cheek and flicked it away. "Just a little accident. Nothing to worry about."

Mike recalled the events of the previous evening as he struggled to his feet, grasping for the wall and keeping his eye fixed on the dim luminance from the bathroom window. The clatter of plates and scuffling of feet filtered down from the floor above. Mike hoped the activity wouldn't waken Toby, but he had little to fear on that account. The horrible slide through the centuries had exacted a fearful toll and Toby slept the sleep of the dead, exhausted from the physical and mental barrage. With the walls as a guide Mike felt his way to the bathroom. He closed the door soundlessly, laid a towel at the base to block the crack and flicked on the overhead light, wincing at the brightness of the unprotected bulb. He studied his tired face in the cracked mirror. New lines caressed his reddened eyes and drops of blood hung in the stubble of his whiskers. He looked a mess. There was nothing to drink from so he ran the cold water into his cupped palms, sucked it up, and swished it around his mouth, spitting out the rancid taste of fear that had gathered overnight. Then he rubbed some more of the coldness into his eyes and over the painful swelling by his ear.

As quietly as he could, he relieved himself, aiming at the porcelain, missing and sending a wayward stream into the corner where it drew the ire of a listless cockroach. Serves you right, you prehistoric bastard, Mike thought. The insect scurried through a crack, tossing its antennae scornfully at its tormentor. Mike looked up at the window, noticing the shiny metal where the latch had snapped. He couldn't imagine how Toby could ever have gotten through, even if he had been able to open the window. But maybe with my help— It was an option and Mike tucked it away for future use, but he still counted on walking out the front door with the boy at his side, no stealth, no violence. He didn't want to see anyone get hurt. Esau was a very sick man and the boys were no more than pawns in their father's crazed game. Mike harbored no rancor.

But the farmer's capacity for violence frightened him, and Mike had no intention of permitting Esau to exact his anger on Toby. If violence was called for, Mike would find the stomach for it. With a last glance at the mirror, the teacher knuckled the last of the sleep from his eyes, snapped off the light, and moved the towel from the floor. He eased open the door and inched back into the room, stretched the ache from his muscles and lowered himself carefully to the floor. There he waited in troubled thought, staring idly at the ceiling while the morning sun brightened the rectangle above the toilet.

The gentle tapping roused the teacher from a drowsy slumber. He hadn't expected to nod off and the sound startled him.

"Anybody awake?" Hattie eased the door open and a spear of light shot across the floor. She poked her head in like a chambermaid checking for occupancy before entering to make the bed and scrub the shower.

Mike pushed up on one elbow and shielded his eyes from the glare with his free hand. "The boy's still sleeping," he whispered.

"Esau will be along soon so it's time he's waking up." She stepped inside, closed the door, and flicked on the overhead light. Toby made a gurgling sound and turned to the wall. She smiled down at him maternally. "Ain't he a nice little fella? The twins used to be a lot like him. Bright-eyed and full of questions and mischief." She pulled the threadbare blanket over Toby's shoulder and ran her pudgy fingers over his silky hair. "He's a smart one, all right."

"Then why won't your husband let him go?" Mike asked the question with genuine perplexity. "The boy's done no one any harm, his family's worried sick about him, and the only devil around here is in Esau's own imagination."

"Oh, no." Hattie shook her head knowingly. "Esau knows the devil's there. He can tell. It ain't the boy's fault, though. Esau says that it's the devil that does the pickin'. He heard him clear as a bell last night. The poor boy was speakin' in a devil's tongue. You musta heard it, too."

What Mike had heard before being knocked out would be damning enough in Esau's mind, and he could only speculate at what he had missed while he was unconscious.

"But Esau says he got Satan on the run. It won't be long now." She smiled proudly at her husband's accomplishment.

Mike rolled his eyes to the ceiling and breathed a disgusted sigh. It was no use.

"Hungry?" Hattie changed the subject as if the earlier disagreement hadn't taken place.

"Not really."

"You will be. Toby, too. The boy needs to keep up his strength."

"Okay," Mike conceded.

"Got some OJ and Corn Flakes." Her eyes twinkled mischievously. "Or maybe you'd rather have Crispy Critters?"

Mike smiled in spite of their predicament. "Corn Flakes will be fine."

"Coffee?"

"Please."

"I'll be right back. See if you can get him out of dreamland while I'm gone. The boy ought'a be awake when Esau comes." She scratched an itch on her padded hip, tossed a final glance at the sleeping boy, and waddled from the room.

Toby wolfed down his Corn Flakes and asked for seconds. Mike satisfied himself with coffee. It was instant and bitter and it matched his mood. Toby, by contrast, was more like the boy he remembered from that first night on the Hortons' porch, full of life and curiosity. He'd been a captive for almost three days and was getting accustomed to the role, and the presence of the teacher lightened his load. Most important to his mood was that his headache was gone.

"When do you think they'll let us go home, Mr. Mancini?" he asked between spoonfuls. "I bet Mom and Dad and Gramps are worried. Tina, too." Then he remembered one of his greatest concerns. "And I want to know how Greatgramps is feeling."

"I hope we can go home today, Toby. Here's what I think we ought to do."

Mike explained the situation as well as he could, couching his words in phrases that a ten-year-old might understand. But he needn't have bothered. Toby grasped the situation readily and understood Mike's plan and the role that he suggested.

"Let them pray for a while," Mike suggested, "then fold your hands in prayer, look at the ceiling, and recite the Lord's Prayer."

"With feeling," Toby added with a boyish smile.

"With as much feeling as you can muster," Mike acknowledged with an answering smile. "We're going to make that old geezer think that he's chased the devil from here to Timbuktu." He laid a hand on Toby's shoulder and squeezed affectionately. That was how they were when the door crashed open and Esau burst in.

"A fool," he whispered viciously. "They take me for a fool." He waved a folded newspaper under Mike's nose and seared him with hate-filled eyes. "The devil wears many disguises. He comes in many forms." He pointed the paper at Toby like the accusing finger of God. "A little child," he ranted and his eyes squeezed into narrow slits and a wormy vein pulsed on his reddened brow. Toby shrank back against the wall and Mike stepped between him and the frenzied farmer.

"And a teacher!" Another accusation at the end of the trembling newspaper. "A man of trust and honor," Esau mocked in a sing-song voice that terrified Mike by its recklessness. "And now your friend the writer trying to turn me from my mission with clever words. 'Please send Toby home,'" he said mockingly.

He pushed the folded paper into Mike's face, crushing his lip against his teeth and filling his mouth with the metal taste of blood. Mike might have shot out at the madman but for the red-haired twins who stood with arms folded on either side of the doorway.

"But we'll see about his trickery. We'll take the devil's own instrument and turn it into a messenger of the Lord." Esau's attempt at a victorious smile looked more like a death skull, and it sent a shudder through Mike's stomach.

"I don't know what you're talking about," Mike spat through stinging lips.

"I don't know what you're talking about," Esau sang back. It was an unnerving spectacle, a six-and-a-half-foot madman mocking his adversary with a sing-song chant like a spoiled child.

Esau flung the paper to the floor as if it were contaminated and waved his bony finger in the teacher's face. "You know what I'm talking about. You and the boy and your clever friend, MacBride."

Spittle flew from Esau's mouth and Mike turned away in disgust.

"But we'll see who has the last laugh, the messengers of Satan or the Lord and His earthly army."

The man's eyes were glazed and strangely focused and he laughed a shrill cackle that Mike hadn't heard before. Apparently the twins hadn't heard it either, because a look of concern passed between them.

"You're going to write a letter to your friend at the newspaper," Esau hissed. "You're going to help me turn the devil's instrument into an instrument of the Lord." Esau reached into his overalls pocket and withdrew a packet of folded papers. "This is the message of the Lord, schoolteacher. This is God's message and you and your evil friends are going to carry it to His people." He cackled at the irony of it.

Toby huddled against the wall. His initial fear had dissipated and he wore an expression of disbelief. He had never seen a grown-up acting so strangely. Mike was still stationed between the boy and the farmer.

"What do you want me to do, Esau? I'll do anything you say, just don't harm the boy. Harming the boy would be sinful," he tried.

"Don't talk to me of sin," Esau said, sneering. "You'll do as I and the Lord command."

Uh-oh, Mike thought, now they were partners, with Esau having top billing. Given the rapid deterioration of the farmer's stability, Mike wasn't surprised. "And what is that command?" he asked.

"You're going to write a letter to your friend. You're going to tell him to print my message in his newspaper." He waved the packet of papers in Mike's face. "You're going to tell him to do that or the Lord will exact His rightful retribution."

Mike didn't ask what that retribution would be. "I'll need some paper," he said.

Esau tugged a yellow notepad from his hip pocket and threw it on the cot. "Write, schoolteacher," he commanded. He also threw down a large folded envelope. "Put your friend's name and address on this. No tricks, schoolteacher. I'm going to read your letter." He spun and stalked to the door.

Mike was anxious to see the newspaper and find out what it was that set the farmer off, but he didn't dare pick it up until Esau left the room. The man was too unpredictable. For the first time, Mike was seriously worried about their safety. Without a backward glance, Esau and the twins marched from the room. Mike couldn't be sure but he thought he saw the farmer clutch at his chest in the doorway. The door slammed shut and Mike heard the turning of a key in the lock.

"I'm scared, Mr. Mancini. I'm afraid he might hurt us."

Toby pushed away from the corner and let Mike pull him close. Mike was afraid too, not so much for himself but for the predicament he caused for the innocent boy and his family.

"He's sick, Toby. That's why we have to be so careful about anything we say. He thinks he's in charge of all the righteousness in the world, and he takes offense easily." Mike bent and retrieved the newspaper from the floor. "Let's see what Teddy said that flipped his lid."

"A plea for Toby Horton," he read aloud. Then he swiftly scanned the column, lips moving silently as his eyes jerked from side to side. At times, Toby thought he detected a tiny smile as the teacher read his friend's words. Finally he laid the paper in his lap and once again put his arm around the boy. "Please, sir, send Toby home." He recited the final line aloud and gave Toby a quick hug.

"Want to read what Teddy said?" he asked. Toby nodded. "Can I?"

"You're the star," Mike joked. "You read while I compose my letter."

"Are you going to tell them where we are in the letter?" Toby asked. "If they know where we are, I bet they'll come and get us."

"I'm sure they would. Trouble is, Esau said he's going to read it. We don't want to get him so upset that he pops his cork."

"I think his elevator already stops before it gets to the top floor." Toby giggled. "Gramps always says that," he admitted.

"Like he's playing with less than a full deck," Mike continued.

"Or he's got a size six brain in a size ten head," Toby added, and he laughed his little-boy laugh that was so devoid of fear and full of trust that Mike felt a lump like a grapefruit work its way into his throat.

"I have another idea," Toby said excitedly. "How about if you tell them where we are in some kind of code? I read a Hardy Boys book once where they escaped from a castle because they sent a coded message."

Mike eyed him thoughtfully then shrugged apologetically. "I'm afraid the only code I know is the genetic code. And look where that got us," he quipped.

"Another fine mess you've gotten us into this time," Toby followed in an imitation of Gramps's Laurel and Hardy routine.

The more Mike saw Toby's humor and resiliency, the more determined he was to get him quickly out of Esau's grasp. Maybe the boy's idea about a coded letter stood a chance after all. Then he thought again of the risks. Esau was dangerous and unpredictable. Mike suspected that he was more clever than he had first thought. What kind of code would alert Teddy to their whereabouts without tipping off the suspicious farmer? Then an idea hit him. He fumbled in the pocket of his jacket and pulled out a blank minicassette, clear plastic with a gold label on both sides.

"Side 1 Scotch Brand RD30 15 min. recording this side."

The cassette was the type he'd been using to tape Toby's memory matchboxes. If he could get a message on one and put it in the envelope with Esau's papers and his letter, he could alert Teddy and the police. He didn't know the Manleys' current address, but he had their old Mankato address and Mike was sure the inspector could track them down from it. He studied the cassette with interest. It was a little over one inch wide and two inches long and about a quarter of an inch thick.

Mike shook his head despairingly. "Too big," he muttered. "No way I can sneak this into the envelope."

"How did Mr. MacBride know that I don't like to be hugged by fat people?" Toby chuckled. He was absorbed in the column and enjoying it immensely.

"Just a lucky guess," Mike said with a smile. Then he turned serious. "You know, Toby, your idea about a code wasn't all that bad. It gave me another idea. If I could get this cassette into the envelope, I could tell Teddy what's happening." He held the cassette up for Toby's inspection. "But it's too big and I can't think of any excuse to include it that they wouldn't see through."

Toby grew pensive. Mike had seen the expression before, and he could picture the clocklike gears meshing in the boy's head. A smile of discovery spread slowly across his face. "I think I know how we can do it," he said with a hint of mischief in his voice. He explained his idea to Mike, and the teacher could have kicked himself for his stupidity.

"We still need some kind of code so they know to look for it," Mike said. "That'll be your job. You think of that while I'm composing the letter."

"A piece of cake," Toby said cockily. He already knew what he would do.

Before he started the letter to Teddy, Mike slipped the used cassette from the recorder and snapped in the new one. The device was about the size and shape of a pack of king-sized cigarettes. He waited until the transparent leader made one full loop around the empty reel before he began to speak into the built-in microphone. His voice was crisp and businesslike.

"Hello, Teddy, this is Mike Mancini. I'm with Toby and it's"—he snuck a quick glance at his watch—"it's seven-thirty on Wednesday morning, July second. We're being held captive in what I'm sure is the basement of a single home somewhere on the Saint Paul side of town." He paused a moment to collect his thoughts, then he dug the magazine label from his pocket. "We're being held by a religious fanatic and his twin sons. Toby found a magazine subscription label that shows his former address. His name is Esau Manley and his address used to be Post Office Box 1288 in Mankato before he lost his farm and moved to the cities. His wife's name is Hattie and the twins' names are Amos and Abel." He allowed himself a grim smile. "Sounds like the cast from an old Charlton Heston movie. We haven't been harmed but I feel that the man is potentially very dangerous. I believe he might know something about the Debby Carlson case. He thinks that he's God's strong right arm. His boys are big and strong but emotionally immature. They're nice young men but they'll do whatever Esau tells them. I think that Hattie can be swayed. She's quite taken by Toby."

He flipped the switch to the 'pause' position while he considered anything he might have forgotten. Then he snapped it back on.

"Oh, yes," he continued. "The only outside access to the room we're being held in is a basement window on the east side of the house." He rubbed his bristly chin and added, "Get us out of this mess and I'll spring for the biggest steak that Lindey's can stuff on the grill. Oh, I almost forgot. Somebody else wants to say hello."

Toby had been sitting on the edge of the cot working out the final details of his clue. His eyes twinkled mischievously when he saw the recorder poised by his chin. "Hi, everybody," he chirped happily. What a tonic that sound will be for Jan and Steve, Mike thought. "If you got this far, you must have figured out the clue in Mr. Mancini's letter. Let me guess. I bet that Gramps guessed it, right?'' His giggle would further lighten their load. "Way to go, Old-timer. I'm okay, Mom. And I'm taking good care of Mr. Mancini, too. Hurry up and get us out of here. See you soon. Love, Toby.''

Mike snapped the recorder off and gave Toby a playful poke on the jaw. "Is that clue really ready or have you been too busy taking care of me?'' Mike cocked his eye quizzically.

"What do you think of this?'' Toby explained his idea while Mike worked on the cassette. The part of the tape that held the message was wound around the smaller of the two white reels. He slipped a pencil point under the tape that was showing on the front of the cassette and pulled a long loop of it through the opening in the clear plastic case. He carefully unwound about six inches of tape from the unused reel, then snipped it cleanly with a pair of nail clippers. Then he pulled the recorded portion out through the window and he snipped the clear leader where it connected to the reel. He held it up for Toby's inspection. It was about thirty inches long and less than a quarter inch wide and it held the key to their release.

"Is that all of it?'' Toby seemed surprised.

"That's it,'' Mike said with finality.

He folded the tape carefully in a six-inch loop. The envelope that Esau had left behind was heavy-duty, brown, about six by eight inches, the kind with the round hole in the flap for the metal doodad to poke through before it folded flat like the legs of a dancer doing a painful split.

"Hold it open, Toby.''

Toby held the envelope puffed open while Mike carefully inserted the folded tape. It looked like a flattened worm tucked in the crease at the bottom of the envelope. It was barely visible. He laid the envelope flat on the table and ran his thumb along the bottom edge. He couldn't even feel the tape inside. He was confident Esau would never notice it—but would anyone else? As Esau had instructed, he wrote Teddy's office address on the outside of the envelope, then he composed his letter, smiling at Toby's ingenuity as he did so.

There was no polite tapping this time. The door flew open and slammed against the wall and Esau strode in with the twins following closely on his heels. The earthly army was on the march, driven by Esau's newfound opportunity to crush evil and spread His word through the mass media courtesy of Teddy MacBride.

"Give me the letter, Teacher."

Esau's ardent evangelism left no room for time-consuming niceties. The twins were by his side. They no longer seemed harmless as the contagion of Esau's militancy hardened their boyish faces. Hattie filled the doorway looking fat, bland, and only slightly apologetic. If Hitler could mesmerize an entire nation, how big a trick would it be for Esau to buffalo his own family? Mike wondered. From the looks on their faces it apparently wasn't too difficult.

Mike offered the letter and Esau snatched it away impatiently. He held it up to his face and read it word by word, laboriously mouthing each syllable with his drawn lips. Twice he looked over the top of the paper, once at Toby and once at the teacher.

"Give me the envelope," he commanded.

Mike breathed a quiet sigh. They seemed to

have passed the first hurdle. He handed Esau the envelope and the farmer studied the address.

Mike held his breath.

Toby watched anxiously, feeling like he was part of a spy thriller and surprisingly not at all frightened. Then Esau looked inside the envelope. Mike's heart skipped a beat at the moment of truth.

"When can we go home?" Toby cried out.

Esau was distracted from his suspicious inspection and his head shot up, startled and angry. "The Lord will decide your fate," he snapped.

Without further curiosity, he thrust the letter into the envelope, and Mike allowed his anxious breath to wheeze out. A tight little smile of relief worked at his lips in admiration of the boy's audacity. Their eyes met and he thought he saw a similar secret smile curling Toby's lips.

"Here is the message of the Lord." Esau displayed his own sheaf of papers before shoving them into the envelope next to Mike's letter. "Tomorrow the people will read His word." He poked the metal clips through the hole in the envelope flap and spread them flat.

"Take this to the newspaper like I told you."

He handed the envelope to Amos, and Mike saw the boy swell with pride as he fled the room.

"You two will wait," he told the captives. "When Amos returns we will pray."

Chapter Thirty-three

❖❖❖❖❖❖❖❖❖❖

"IT'S BEEN ALMOST three days, Sheila. Can you imagine how they must feel?" Teddy MacBride's face reflected his strain. The usual spark, though not extinguished, was dulled to a warm amber glow, ready to burst into flaming life at the first hint of good news. But there had been none. Thousands of morning newspapers had been delivered and read over coffee and orange juice and eggs and bagels, but the phone had remained ominously silent. At least one crackpot usually tried to reach the writer after every column.

Not today.

Maybe his readers were sharper than he gave credit for. Maybe they *were* leaving the phone lines open for the kidnapper. After all, Teddy *did* say that this week's column was a personal communication.

"Maybe that's one of the reasons I never married," Sheila said huskily. "I'm not sure that I could handle being a mother." She wiped a hanky at the corner of her eye. "My God, I even went to pieces when my nephew had his tonsils out." She tried forcing a smile but it got wrecked by a sob.

Teddy pushed from his chair and rounded the desk to reach out to his secretary and friend. They looked a strange pair, hugging self-consciously and sniffling and smiling bravely, all this between well-meaning words of encouragement that only served to compound their discomfort.

She pushed away and smiled wanly as tears

streaked her powdered cheeks. "But I'll tell you one thing, Teddybear, if I ever do decide to start a family, yours will be the first door I'll knock on."

MacBride wasn't even tempted to blast her with a typical retort. They stood facing each other like strangers, recently introduced, who suddenly realized they were overwhelmingly attracted to each other. Their mutual embarrassment was alleviated by the sudden commotion in the hallway.

"You can't go bursting in there. Give the letter to me and I'll see to it that Mr. MacBride gets it right away."

"I can't, lady. I promised the man I'd deliver it myself."

A few seconds of silence were followed by a cautious tapping. The door inched open and the receptionist peered in apologetically. "I'm sorry, Mr. MacBride."

"What is it, Amy?"

"This young man has something he wants to give to you. I told him I'd deliver it, but he was very insistent."

She smiled resignedly and opened the door to reveal a small black boy with a determined frown and eyes that would melt an iceberg. His bushy hair was level with Amy's waist. He clutched an envelope in his right hand and a dollar bill in his left.

"I promised the man," he explained haltingly. Now that he confronted the awesome specter of Teddy MacBride, some of his earlier confidence drained away. "He gave me a dollar and he told me to bring this envelope straight to you. He told me you'd give me another dollar when you got it." There was a trace of a plea in his last remark.

With a disapproving glare at the receptionist he continued. "He say don't give it to nobody but you, Mr. MacBride."

"That's okay, Amy. Mohammed's a buddy of mine."

The boy's eyes grew wide and he smiled proudly as if to say "Thank you" and "I told you so" in one simple statement.

Amy rolled her eyes at Sheila. "He's all yours then. I have to get back to the desk." She clicked the door shut behind her, leaving Mohammed and his envelope and his dollar bill behind.

"Let's see what you have there, Mohammed."

The boy offered the envelope and Teddy took it from his chubby brown hand. Sheila struggled through her purse for a dollar, and the boy nodded gratefully. Then she took a sugar-covered doughnut from the untouched plate on Teddy's desk and offered it to him.

He shook his head in determination. "Uh-uh! My mom says I'm not supposed to eat any of that junk food. She catch me eating any of that stuff she gonna whup my butt."

"Your mother's right," Sheila said. "Maybe she ought to come over here and talk to the automatic eating machine."

Teddy didn't hear her insult as he unclasped the envelope and pulled out its contents, a single yellow sheet and a batch of folded papers. He adjusted his glasses and looked down his nose at the single sheet. Sheila glanced at him just in time to see the blood drain from his face.

"Get the inspector on the phone," he sputtered.

Sheila gave Mohammed a quick kiss on the cheek and a friendly whack on the behind and aimed him at the door.

"Wait a minute," Teddy shouted after him. "Where'd you get this?"

"A man drove up in a ol' pickup and he gave it to me. He told me I gotta give it straight to you."

"What did he look like, Mohammed?"

The little boy bit back a chuckle. "He look like he wearin' a bright red snow hat."

Inspector Borg asked Teddy to read the letter over the phone, then to hustle down to the station. Teddy tucked the evidence in the baggy pocket of his Harris tweed and hurried from the office. He shouted over his shoulder as he left.

"Call Denny Gaffney, Sheila. Tell him to get his sanctimonious ass to Inspector Borg's office right away."

Borg called the Hortons immediately and, as a courtesy, he contacted Clancy Kendall. The doctor walked out in the middle of an insurance physical, leaving a nervous executive propped unceremoniously as he nervously awaited proctoscoptic probing.

The inspector left his small, sterile office and booted a pair of coffee-drinking civilians from the conference room.

Teddy arrived at the station before the others and handed over Mike's letter. The inspector made a quick transparency and laid it on the stage of the overhead projector.

Dear Teddy,

The gentleman whom Toby and I are staying with has asked me to write this letter to you. He insists that you use your

weekly column to help him spread the
word of the Lord. To this end, he has
drafted a message to be used in place of
your regular column. If you refuse to do
this, he has told us that the Lord will
"exact His retribution."

Toby is fine and he sends everyone his
love, especially Heidi.

Sincerely,
Michael J. Mancini

Steve and Jan arrived next, quickly followed by
Clancy and Father Gaffney. One by one they stood
by the conference room door, reading the short
letter on the screen before finding a seat around
the long conference table. Gramps was out for his
morning walk when the inspector's call came, so
Steve left a note taped to the refrigerator.

By the time Einar reentered, everyone had
helped themselves to a cup of coffee from the pot
at the back of the room and were waiting impatiently.

"We've had a break in the case," the inspector
began without preamble. "As I told some of you
on the phone, Teddy MacBride received a demand from the kidnapper. On the screen you see
a copy of Mike Mancini's letter spelling out the
demands. They're unusual to say the least."

"What do you mean when you say you have a
break in the case?" Steve asked. "Is there more
than what's in the letter?"

"No," Einar admitted. "I'm afraid there isn't.
But at this stage of negotiation, I look at any
communication as a break. It gives us another
shred of evidence, and that's often all we need to
crack it."

"It's been three days," Jan said despairingly. "Why can't they let Toby go?"

Einar shrugged helplessly and pointed to the screen. "You know as much as I do, Jan. It's all up there. The message he wants to print is nothing extraordinary, just the usual fire and brimstone that these types shout on street corners. It pretty much fits the mold that Father Gaffney told us to expect. The man's convinced he's doing God's work and that most of the world is evil and it's up to him to rescue the world from itself."

"May I see the sermon?" Father Gaffney asked.

Einar handed the folded pages across the table, and the priest began to read to himself.

"Inspector!" Steve paused after getting Einar's attention, then he rubbed his hand across his weary face. "There's something unusual about Mr. Mancini's letter."

"Yes?"

"It's the last line. It says 'he sends everyone his love, especially Heidi.' "

"What's unusual?" the inspector queried.

"Heidi! Neither Jan nor I know anybody named Heidi and to our knowledge neither does Toby."

Jan looked up hopefully. "At first when we read it we thought that Mr. Mancini just got confused and he really meant to say Tina. But he's been at our house often enough not to make that kind of mistake. I think it might mean something."

Inspector Borg looked expectantly from face to face but was rewarded by empty stares. Father Gaffney had been studying Esau's scrawled message and hadn't been paying close attention to the conversation.

"A nut case," he said, shaking his head. "Unpredictable and certifiable." His eyes met the inspector's. "And potentially dangerous."

He saw Jan stiffen and instantly regretted his hasty conclusion.

"That being the case," Einar continued, "we have to quickly decide how to handle the demands." He folded his arms across his chest and cocked his head toward the journalist. "It's not in my police power to force you to print the kidnapper's message, Mr. MacBride, but I'd be thankful if you'd consider it."

"Consider it done," Teddy volunteered. "I'm sure I've written worse prose in my day. But I'll have to lead into it with a few lines of explanation."

"Just so you don't insult him or question his motives," the inspector cautioned. "I think this man's close to the edge, and I'm sure you wouldn't want to be the one to provide the push."

"Provide another push, you mean," Teddy said painfully.

Jan reached across the table and squeezed the journalist's hand. "I'm certainly not blaming you, Teddy. So please don't blame yourself."

He laid his hand on top of hers and squeezed back his thanks.

"So where does that leave us?" Einar continued. "We're still looking for a pair of red-haired twins. We're sure that they're not motivated by money. They're deeply religious in an offbeat sort of way. And Mike's note makes a cryptic reference to someone named Heidi whom no one seems to know."

"I wish I knew," Clancy said. "I can't give you the solution to that mystery but I can give you another one."

"Another mystery?" the inspector asked uneasily.

"Another curiosity in Mike's letter," Clancy answered.

All eyes turned to the screen, and Einar began to read the words aloud.

"Don't bother," Clancy advised. "It's in the signature. Michael J. Mancini."

"So?"

"So why would someone named Michael Aristotle Mancini sign his name that way?"

"Aristotle?"

"Call it wishful thinking by his father," Clancy said with an apologetic shrug.

"It sounds to me like the captives are toying with their keepers," the priest said. "It's a good sign. It tells us something about their spirits and it proves that they're not intimidated."

"But what does it mean?" Jan wondered. Some of the earlier gloom had left her mood as she too sensed something mysteriously positive in Mike's cryptic communication.

Clancy sipped at his coffee and grimaced at its bitter taste. "Mike doesn't do anything without a reason. I'm sure that this is his way of trying to alert us to something."

"And that brings us back to the mysterious Heidi," the inspector concluded. "Unless the answer's somewhere in the sermon." He leveled his gaze at the priest. "How about it, Father. Is there anything unusual about the sermon?"

Gaffney spread the papers on the table in front of him and shrugged his beefy shoulders. "It would be more fitting to ask if there's anything normal about it. It's your standard 'right hand of God' raving in all its diseloquent glory. In other words, it's normal for an abnormal person." He curled his lips into a wry grin. "Why these whackos insist on resurrecting 'thous' and 'dosts' and 'begats' I'll never understand. Our captain of the earthly army writes like a semiliterate camel driver."

"But no clues?" Einar probed.

"None that I can find," the priest answered with a palms-up gesture.

"So that brings us back to square one," Teddy MacBride lamented. Then he allowed himself a self-indulgent smile. "Except that my loyal readers will be treated to a guest columnist."

"It looks that way," Einar said.

Before the inspector could continue the discussion the conference room door eased open and Gramps peeked tentatively around the corner. When he ascertained he had found the right room he swung the door open and scanned the anxious faces. Steve's note on the refrigerator had only mentioned there were some new developments without going into details.

"What's happened?" he asked nervously. "Is Toby all right?"

Einar quickly explained about Mohammed and the envelope, the raving sermon and the demands that it be printed. When he mentioned Mike's letter, the inspector gestured toward the screen, where the teacher's neat script stood out boldly against the brilliant background.

Gramps squinted at the brightness and

moved closer to the screen. He pushed his glasses down on his nose and began to read the message through the top of the multifocal lenses. It took John Horton about a minute to read the teacher's words while the others waited patiently. His aging features came alive as he read through the letter. What began as a curious frown became a gleam of discovery and then turned into a deep-throated chuckle that made the others look at him as if he'd stepped over the edge himself.

"That little scamp," he said proudly. "That smart little son of a gun."

"What is it, Pop? What do you see?" Steve asked excitedly.

"Why, Heidi, of course. Where's the rest of it?" he asked impatiently. "Give me everything." He gestured at the inspector.

Einar handed him Mike's letter and Father Gaffney reassembled the sermon and pushed the pages across the smooth tabletop. Gramps snatched them up and studied each page, scanning them front and back before piling them haphazardly on the table.

"The envelope," he demanded. "Where's the envelope this stuff came in?"

"In my office," Borg answered.

"Go get it." Gramps wasn't standing on ceremony or courtesy, and the inspector, sensing the man's resolve, hurried from the room.

"Gramps, just what are you up to? What's all this about Heidi?" Jan asked.

But before John Horton could answer, Einar returned and handed him the brown envelope. Gramps gave it a quick flip, checking front and back and seeming to satisfy himself that all was normal. Then, as the doctor, the journalist, the priest, the inspector, and the parents watched with mounting curiosity, he opened the envelope and peered inside.

The envelope was deep and dark and at first John wondered if he was chasing up a blind alley. Then he noticed the darker streak along the bottom and his eyes sparkled and a wide grin stretched happily across his face.

"What is it, Pop?"

"That little scamp," was all he said as he turned the envelope upside down and tapped it sharply on the polished tabletop. He held the envelope in place on the table and quickly scanned the room, making mischievous eye contact with each of the onlookers.

"Voilà," he shouted and he raised the envelope with a flourish. There, like a flattened worm, lay the folded strip of recording tape.

The inspector was standing next to Gramps, and he leaned close to the brown strip. He poked at it tentatively with his fingertip as if nudging a sleeping insect.

"What is it?" Jan asked. She was leaning over the table, unable to cover the excitement in her voice.

Gramps leveled a victorious smile. "That's for the gumshoes to figure out. We did our part—Toby and me." His eyes twinkled merrily as he shook his head in wonder. "That little scamp."

"It's a section of recording tape." Einar held the long strip by the transparent leader and the brown strand dangled in front of him like a New Year's streamer. "I think it's the kind used in dictating equipment."

"Like the little portable Mike often carries," Clancy added, pleased to be filling in a small piece of the puzzle.

"What's on it?" Jan asked.

"We'll soon find out." The inspector dangled the weightless film like a living thing, careful not to let its oxide-coated surface brush against clothing or door frame as he hurried from the conference room.

Teddy, Clancy, Steve, and Jan chattered excitedly, speculating on the contents of the discovery while Gramps and Father Gaffney quietly read Esau's rambling rhetoric. After a few minutes, Inspector Borg returned looking satisfied and more confident than he had looked all morning.

"We called the people down the road at the tape company. They invented the stuff so we figured they ought to know how to handle this."

"And?" Teddy asked.

"And we're doing a quick splice onto a similar cassette and then we can play it back on this." Borg held up a palm-sized dictating machine. "It will only take a couple of minutes, but while we're waiting I think Gramps owes us all an explanation."

"About what?" Gramps baited. "I should think a little mystery would do you good."

"Don't be cute, Pop." Steve tried to sound reproving but he couldn't pull it off.

"About Heidi," the inspector said. "Who is Heidi and how did you know that something was in the envelope?"

"Ah yes, Heidi. How can I explain her?" he said wistfully.

"Any way at all beats hell out of the way you're doing it," Father Gaffney chided.

John Horton flashed a disapproving look and continued. "Heidi is a secret."

"Obviously." Teddy joined in the priest's sarcasm. "But would it be asking too much to leak out a hint or two?"

"She's a secret elf and only two people in the world know about her."

Jan smiled softly and knowingly. "Is this one of your games, Gramps, one of those secret games you used to play with Toby when he was little?"

John Horton's answering grin told Jan all she needed to know. He turned his palms up in mock surrender. "I guess it's okay to tell you our little secret now. After all," he conceded, "Toby was the one who let the cat out of the bag in the first place. Heidi was a mischievous little elf who always used to hide things." His dark eyes crinkled into laughing raisins. "*Hide-ee*, get it?"

Gaffney groaned.

Gramps ignored it. "Heidi used to take Toby's things and hide them—under his pillow, in a shoe, in a dresser drawer. So we had a little game. When Toby would least expect it, I'd take something like a comic book or a baseball card and I'd hide it. When Toby'd finally miss it he'd come to me with a hangdog look and say, 'Uh-oh. Looks like Heidi's back.' So for a while there"— he scratched at his chin and studied the ceiling— "must have been five or six years ago, whenever Toby couldn't find something he'd tell me that Heidi hid it. Then he'd search around until he found it." He turned to the inspector. "So when he mentioned Heidi in Mike's letter it was a signal to search for something." He leaned back and tugged thoughtfully at his ear. "He couldn't have been more than five years old the last time we played that game. How on earth did he ever remember it?" he mused.

"How did you?" Clancy said with obvious admiration.

"I suppose I just never grew up," Gramps admitted.

"I'll never criticize you again for going through a second childhood," Steve said.

"How could you?" Teddy shot back. "He never left the first one."

The mood was light and charged with expectation when the uniformed policeman returned with the minicassette. He nodded politely to the group and handed the tiny device to Einar. "I think I got it right, Inspector. It's on side one."

Einar briefly admired the man's handiwork and thanked him, then he took the pocket-sized dictating unit and snapped the cassette into place. "Proper procedure would dictate that I listen to this first, but I doubt you'd sit still for that."

Father Gaffney cleared his throat and boomed out. "If I may, Inspector, before you play that I'd like a brief word with a special friend?" He shuffled to his feet.

Einar looked at him quizzically, shrugged, and said, "Make it quick, Padre."

The grizzled priest folded his hands, raised his eyes to the ceiling, and prayed beseechingly. "Mary, please do it again, Amen."

"Amen," Einar echoed, and he snapped the 'play' switch on the recorder.

Hello, Teddy, this is Mike Mancini. I'm with Toby and it's—it's seven-thirty on Wednesday morning, July second.

The inspector instinctively looked at his watch. The tape had been dictated less than three hours earlier.

We're being held captive in what I'm sure is the basement of a single home somewhere on the Saint Paul side of town. We're being held by a religious fanatic and his twin sons.

Another piece of the puzzle slipped into place.

Toby found a magazine subscription label that shows his former address. His name is Esau Manley and his address used to be Post Office Box 1288 in Mankato before he lost his farm and moved to the cities.

Borg was writing rapidly, as was the journalist.

His wife's name is Hattie and the twins' names are Amos and Abel. Sounds like the cast from an old Charlton Heston movie.

Steve allowed himself a tight-lipped smile.

We haven't been harmed but I feel that the man is potentially very dangerous. I believe he might know something about the Debby Carlson case. He thinks that he's God's strong right arm.

Father Gaffney nodded knowingly.

His boys are big and strong but emotionally immature. They're nice young men but they'll do whatever Esau tells them. I think that Hattie could be swayed. She's quite taken by Toby.

Jan flushed and felt a chill.

Oh yes, the only outside access to the room we're

being held in is a basement window on the east side of the house.

Einar nodded in admiration of the teacher's attention to detail.

Get us out of this mess and I'll spring for the biggest steak that Lindey's can stuff on the grill.

"What a guy!" Teddy mocked.

Oh, I almost forgot. Somebody else wants to say hello.

Jan gripped Steve's hand and squeezed so hard it brought tears to both their eyes.

Hi, everybody. If you got this far, you must have figured out the clue in Mr. Mancini's letter. Let me guess. I bet that Gramps guessed it, right?

His little-boy giggle sounded tinny through the miniature speaker, but it was the warmest sound any of them had ever heard.

Way to go, Old-timer.

Gramps's eyes flooded and a lump the size of a softball lodged in his throat.

I'm okay, Mom. And I'm taking good care of Mr. Mancini, too. Hurry up and get us out of here. See you soon. Love, Toby.

The inspector grabbed at the white phone on the corner table and punched in a number. "Gleason, drop everything. We have a break in the Toby Horton case. Write this down. Esau Manley. E-s-a-u M-a-n-l-e-y. His former address is Post Office Box 1288 in Mankato. We're not sure how long he's been out of there. Right now he's living with wife Hattie and twin sons Amos and Abel somewhere around Saint Paul. I need his current address and I need it now."

When he turned back to the table, Einar looked like the primal hunter who had just found a pile of steaming spoor, crouching close to the ground, testing the heft of his flint-tipped spear, and loping softly into the under-growth, knowing that the hunt was nearing the stage of final confrontation. It was the only part of the hunt that counted, the rest being nothing more than preliminaries. Steve recognized the inspector's look from their first meeting, when the trail was still warm and the scent of the prey hung like a living thing over the city streets. He remembered the feline fire in the inspector's eye and the quickness of his step and recalled being thankful that the man was on his side.

As he reconstructed the events since the abduction, Steve realized the investigation would have reached this point of its own accord even without the help of the police, but the knowledge did nothing to dim his gratitude. As he mulled over the thought, the phone jangled by the inspector's elbow.

"Borg," he barked. His face betrayed nothing but it was obvious what was taking place as he carefully jotted a few notes on the writing tablet. He hung up without a word.

"It's 1216 Stanbridge. On the East Side."

"Inspector." The old priest pushed ponder-ously to his feet. "May I do it once again?"

"It's worked fine so far, Father. I'm not about to kick a winner."

Gaffney waved a ragged blessing, prayered his hands, and stared once again at the ceiling. "Thanks, Mary. I owe you a bunch. But there's one more thing and I think you know what it is. Help the inspector this one more time and I promise not to bother you again." He seemed about to end his plea then thought better of it. "At least not this week. Amen."

"Amen," Jan whispered. Her hands were folded at the edge of the table and her head was bowed.

"You know what I'm looking forward to more than anything?" Borg asked.

"I think I know," Gramps said. "You're anxious to make the acquaintance of one Toby Horton."

The inspector nodded. "I wouldn't miss it for the world."

Chapter Thirty-four

〰〰〰〰〰〰〰

IT WAS EARLY afternoon and the sun hung like a molten globe in the July sky. It baked the dying juices from the remnants of early summer flowers and sucked the living color from the patchy lawns. Two young boys pedaled furiously down the street, trailing patriotic streamers in anticipation of the annual Independence Day festivities. Aside from that colorful burst of activity the quiet neighborhood basked peacefully in the P.M. heat.

A green and white Chemlawn truck wheeled around the corner, creeping slowly down the street as the driver checked the stenciled addresses on the curb. From the other direction, a boxy UPS delivery van trundled along. The dusty smell of summer and the angry chatter of a Toro filled the air. The Chemlawn truck rolled to a stop in front of 1214 Stanbridge, and the driver riffled through a stack of papers on the dash. The man at his side checked his watch and glanced absently about the neighborhood. Both driver and helper were clad in the neat green uniform of the lawn-care company. The helper wore a pair of mirrored sunglasses that concealed the feline quality of his eyes. He brought his hand to his mouth as if brushing a wayward crumb from his lips and he spoke softly into the tiny microphone. His words were clearly heard in the UPS truck rolling toward them, finally pulling to a stop in front of 1218.

The helper jumped nimbly from the truck and looked up and down the street in apparent confusion. He walked past 1216, past the parked UPS van, then he retraced his steps. He pulled a crumpled piece of paper from his shirt pocket, studied it momentarily before jamming it back in the pocket. With a final glance at the parked van, he walked briskly up the short driveway to the right of 1216 Stanbridge.

While the lawn-care helper was going about his business, the UPS driver had his own assignment. He approached the front door of 1218 carrying a clipboard and a small parcel. Once there, he made a rapping motion with his fist, missed the door by inches, than stared absently at the house to his left.

While the lawn-care helper was checking addresses, the driver slipped from the truck and casually strode along the left side of 1216. The house had a front door but it didn't appear to be in use, the path leading to it overgrown with weeds and the concrete step crumbling.

The neighborhood was traditional Saint Paul blue-collar, small but proud homes with neatly trimmed yards, detached garages full of snow-mobiles and fishing boats and knotty-pine rec rooms decorated with shelves full of bowling trophies. The Manley home was shabby by comparison, thirsting for a coat of paint and the TLC of a caring owner.

The driver of the Chemlawn truck was Nicky Mandikas in his first venture in plainclothes. The UPS driver was Detective Danny Carr. Einar Borg was the helper and he scratched his head in confusion as he stood in the driveway by the side door of 1216. The sunglasses masked the rapid movement of his catlike eyes as he flicked them left and right. Nicky Mandikas had completed his circuit of the house, and he shot a quick glance around the corner at the inspector. He flashed a grin, gave a thumbs-up sign, and re-treated. Einar took a deep breath and rapped softly on the wooden door.

Hattie Manley had been humming an off-key tune and shredding cabbage when the tapping interrupted her. She rarely had visitors. Esau disapproved of idle chatter, and gossip was sin-ful. Her only company were the likes of people selling cosmetics which she didn't use or those with causes that she didn't understand. But com-pany of any sort was still a treat, so she wiped her cabbage-flecked hands on her housedress and waddled expectantly to the door. Swinging the door open, Hattie confronted the small, tidy man

in the green uniform and the trooper glasses. He
was studying a piece of paper and he looked lost.
He raised his head and she saw a matched pair of
fat Hatties in his shiny lenses.

"Hello," she said hesitantly. "Are you looking
for someone?"

"Is this 1216 Stanbridge?" he asked, looking
back at the crumpled sheet.

"Yes, it is."

"My records show that we're supposed to do
your lawn today. Are you a new customer?"

"You're here to do our lawn?" she said doubtfully. "I don't think Esau called anybody." She
waved her hand at the patchy tufts of grass that
infiltrated the concrete drive. "This is all the
grass we have," she joked.

"It says so right here." He pointed to the sheet
of paper. "This your signature?"

Hattie pulled the door shut behind her and
stepped onto the drive. Einar couldn't remember
seeing such a mountain of a woman. She smelled
of summer heat and cabbage as she bent close to
see the writing on the paper.

"Are you Hattie Manley?" Einar asked officiously as he pulled the paper from her view.

"Yes, I am," she answered with a trace of defi-
ance. Then she saw Nicky as he rounded the corner of the house, and she glared angrily at the
little man in sunglasses. "Nobody here ever asked
anybody to do our lawn. What do you want?"

Einar flashed his silver badge. "Police officers,
ma'am. I want you to step over here and keep
your hands where I can see them."

Hattie faltered momentarily before submit-
ting, and she felt a rush of embarrassment as she

saw the slight movement of drapes in the kitchen window of 1218.

"We don't want anyone to get hurt, Mrs. Manley. You can help by cooperating. I want you to tell me where your husband and your sons are, and I want you to tell me where they're holding Toby Horton and Mike Mancini."

Her eyes opened wide in sudden understanding, and Einar thought that he saw something else in her expression. Relief?

"It was wrong from the start, wasn't it?" she said.

The inspector saw the sadness in her eyes, the physical strain. "Yes, it was, Mrs. Manley."

The farmer's wife slowly shook her head. "They're all inside, downstairs in the spare room." She met Einar's eye pleadingly. "Please don't hurt my man, mister. He don't mean nobody any harm. He don't have no guns or anything like that. He's a God-fearin' man."

The woman was hurt and vulnerable, and a wave of compassion swept across Einar. It took some of the pleasure away from the final confrontation.

"The farm was everything to him, mister. When they took that away, somethin' just seemed to snap inside him. He's a good man."

"We don't want to hurt anybody, Mrs. Manley. We just want to get the boy home safely to his parents."

The inspector stepped to the middle of the drive and waved a signal. Hattie was gripped by fear when she saw a UPS man on her neighbor's lawn make a second signal and the back of a van on the street swing open to disgorge a squad of combat-ready policemen. At another

signal they moved swiftly up the drive with
their ugly weapons held tightly to their chests.
Hattie felt dizzy and had to lean against the
house for support.

"Stay here with Mrs. Manley," Einar ordered
one of the officers. Hattie was surprised to
see the long, auburn curls beneath the peaked
cap.

Einar rattled the orders off in soft, staccato
bursts. "You go to the other side of the house and
stand by the basement window. You come inside
with me and wait at the top of the basement
stairs." He pointed to the UPS man and one of
the combat-outfitted policemen. "Nicky and
Louderman, I want you two to go in with me.
Keep your guns down. I don't think they're
armed and there's no need for a show of force."
As if to contradict himself, the inspector pulled a
snub-nosed revolver from his belt holster and
snapped off the safety. "The three of us will enter
the room without warning. I'll cover the boy
while you round up the suspects. The rest of you
be ready to follow if there's any trouble," he
ordered the last three officers.

Borg took off the mirrored glasses and tucked
them into his shirt pocket. Then he entered the
kitchen of Esau Manley's home with Mandikas
and Louderman close behind.

"Just stay calm, folks. These things are usually
all bark and no bite." The man tipped his cap
back on his head and tried to appear bored by
the entire proceeding.

Jan and Steve smiled wanly at the police sergeant's attempt but they couldn't bring them-

selves to feel as comfortable as he suggested. They huddled on a long bench in the UPS van waiting for the signal telling them Toby was safe. Teddy, Clancy, Gramps, and Father Gaffney were strung out beside them. Einar knew that they shouldn't be along at the arrest. It wasn't proper police procedure. But they weren't in any danger and they had promised not to get in the way and, besides, they were as much a part of the investigation as he was, more if he tallied their contributions. They deserved to be on hand to see Toby and Mike safe home. They sat in silence except for Father Gaffney, who mumbled prayerfully under his breath.

"Lord of the universe, expel Thy enemy from the body of this boy."

"Amen."

"Deliver his evil presence back to the burning fires that spawned him."

"Amen."

"Cast out Satan and his evil works."

"Amen."

"Grant your servants the power to destroy Lucifer and those who preach his word."

"Amen."

An iron band of pain drove hot nails into Toby's forehead and made his earlier headache seem no more than a slight inconvenience. The droning prayers were only sounds, not words, and their meaning failed to penetrate the barrier. It came on suddenly, this most recent attack, at a time when Toby's spirits were soaring in the stratosphere. The innocent charm of his boyish glee had blown away the clouds of fear, raising the schoolteacher's own spirits while layering another tier of confusion in the farmer's muddled mind. The possessed weren't supposed to be happy. The possessed were snarling demons wrapped in borrowed skin. They were masterful actors, but were they capable of masquerading the sparkling eyes and boundless joy that Toby Horton emanated? Esau was confused. But then the headache struck and Toby's playful smile was reduced to a grimace of pain. Esau saw the devil's hand at work and his doubts vanished.

Toby was as gray as death, a shrunken little man stretched mummylike on the narrow cot. Mike Mancini sat helplessly at his side, his own head throbbing to the monotony of Esau's chant. In spite of their predicament, the world had seemed so bright after Amos scampered out with the hidden message, but the joy turned sour when the fiery nails pierced Toby's skull. And now the teacher sat with dimming hope between the pain-wracked child and the wild-eyed farmer.

Mike knew that Toby's agony could be relieved in a matter of seconds, but did he dare? Esau had no doubt that the devil took residence in Toby Horton's body, and he was just as certain that Toby's trance-induced ravings were the devil's double-talk. Mike was afraid to chance the farmer's reaction to a new bout of hypnotism, so he suffered along with Toby and watched helplessly as Esau prayed and Toby hurt.

"I want to open the last matchbox, Mr. Mancini. That will make my headache go away."

Mike ran a gentle hand across Toby's brow. It was as cold and clammy as a frog's belly, and the teacher's thoughts snapped back to his biology class, Debby Carlson's bloated body, and Esau's unintended admission of complicity in her murder. How could he help Toby? What could he do that wouldn't light the farmer's fuse? How much longer could Toby stand the torment without medication or Mike's hypnotic hand? He needn't have wondered.

"I'm going to do it myself, Mr. Mancini. I'm able to do it alone now."

"I know you can, Toby. But I don't think—"

"Shut your blasphemous mouth, schoolteacher," Esau roared. Even the twins glared angrily at the teacher's rude interruption of their prayers. Esau took a giant stride across the room and pointed his trembling finger at the pale boy.

"Begone, Satan," he shrieked. "Get—out—of—my—house."

His rage shook the walls but Toby couldn't hear it. His pain had finally flipped the switch to the numbing pleasure of sleep, and he stood alone in his quiet place with the cold slate floor and the soaring velvet-draped walls, rid of the mind-searing probes and free of the farmer's haunting rites.

Something about the memory room had changed but nothing looked different. The windows high above admitted brilliant bars of sunlight that stabbed at an angle through floating motes of dust before burning fiery rectangles on the cold stone floor. The place still had the same heavy smell of age, sweet and cloying like an empty cathedral. It had the same sound that he remembered, hollow, reverberating with an ancient wail that commanded the fearful respect of the visitor. It was all the same but there was a new presence.

Toby had avoided looking at the table. His gaze swept the periphery, gaining comfort from its familiarity, but for all its sameness, the difference was overpowering. It began as a tiny burst of light that grew and retreated, grew and retreated, like a blossom unfolding its dazzling beauty before curling into a regenerative ball. Then repeating the procedure over and over until the light pulsed like a living thing, breathing deeply, exhaling, breathing, exhaling, breathing—until it bathed the curtained walls with an amber glow before withdrawing into itself. Toby's eyes were drawn to the source of the mystical light show. The last matchbox trembled in the center of the heavy table.

Beckoning.

He squinted to avoid the blinding glare, turning his head to the side so he could keep the object in sight from the corner of his eye. Then the matchbox swallowed the light and he could once again focus his view directly at the table. The box seemed larger than the others. Its sides were bulging round, not the crisp geometry of the earlier memories. It bulged like a bloated frog, as if straining to contain its contents. Toby felt its attraction and was powerless to resist. The glow bathed him in its beauty and he was drawn toward the table, moving effortlessly under the power of the matchbox but not against his will, floating lightly over the bare stone floor like a smoky wraith about to be devoured by a waiting flame.

"I'm going to open the last matchbox," he whispered.

"Get your evil presence out of my house," Esau roared.

Mike struggled to his feet, ready to defend the helpless boy from the raving farmer. Esau towered over him, shoulders heaving, eyes burning with passion, lips flecked with spittle, trembling such that Mike feared the farmer would shake himself free of his emotional moorings.

"I am the captain of the earthly army of the Lord and I command you—"

Einar's entrance lacked the drama usually associated with such operations. There was no kicked-in door, no shouts of "Freeze, asshole!" The door simply opened, no kick, no splintering crash, and two lawn maintenance men and one uniformed policeman quietly stepped inside. All were armed. Mandikas and Louderman tiptoed behind Amos and Abel and gently tapped them on the shoulders. The boys spun and stared in shock at the ugly black barrels that were leveled at their stomachs.

"Esau Manley?" Einar called his name but if the farmer heard it he showed no sign.

"Begon, prince of darkness, I command you." Esau's ramblings were no longer prayerful pleas. Each new demand was a whiplash of frustration and hate. He seemed detached from his own body, possessed by his own fervor, and when Einar moved with lightfooted sureness to the farmer's side and looked up into the feverish eyes, the farmer showed no recognition or surprise.

The inspector slowly replaced his pistol into its holster. Where was the victory? he wondered.

Why did he feel sad? The hunt was over and the prey was captured, yet the success was like that of a desert bird plucking at the bleached bones of a long-dead adversary. "Esau Manley, you're under arrest. It's my duty to advise you that you have the right to remain silent—"

"Satan, prince of darkness, sinner of sinners, keeper of evil, leave this boy, leave my house."

Even as the inspector watched, the spark in Esau's eyes fizzled to a wisp of smoke, but he never slowed the tempo of his prayers, only their vehemence. Mandikas and Louderman ushered the twins from the room with a silent gesture of their weapons. The boys glanced sadly at their father, then they marched obediently through the door without a word being spoken. Einar took Esau's arm and the farmer allowed himself to be lowered into the spindly green chair where he continued his passionless plea, now more a mumble than a demand. He had been hollowed out and he didn't even know it, his praying no more than an automatic reflex, like the frantic dance of a headless chicken. Mike looked at the hopeless man and wondered when the dance would end and the farmer would drop to the dusty farmyard.

"How's the boy?" Einar frowned at Toby. He seemed to be in a trance, features in repose, staring blankly at the ceiling, either not aware of or not caring about the bustle of activity.

"He's put himself into a trance," Mike said worriedly.

"Can we move him? His parents are waiting outside."

"I don't think we should move him right now. Let's give it a few minutes."

"Johnson," the inspector called through the doorway. "Get the boy's parents. Tell them it's all right to come down." He gestured helplessly at Mike. "I can't just leave them sitting outside on the curb wondering what's going on."

Jan was the first through the door. She rushed toward the cot but pulled up short when she saw Toby's dreamy gaze.

"Toby! Oh, Toby." The tears finally flowed unchecked as she knelt by his side and ran her fingers through his tangled hair. The room quickly filled as Steve and Gramps, Gaffney, Clancy, and Teddy MacBride filed past the policeman guarding the door.

"Please," Mike cautioned. "Toby's in a light trance. Most of you have seen this before. There's nothing to worry about, but we have to let it run its course."

"Prince of darkness, sinner of sinners . . ." Esau mumbled the prayer like a fading mantra. For the first time, Jan and Steve took note of him and they saw a pathetic stick figure with aging skin draped carelessly over jutting bones, hollow and beaten. But they had no way of knowing the depths of his despair. How could they possibly understand? One had to be tapped by the personal finger of God and then to fail to carry out His command to fully understand the farmer's devastation. But still he droned on, an empty echo of the man who had earlier filled the room with the acrid smell of brimstone.

Jan knelt by Toby's side, planting guarded kisses on his smooth cheeks while he stared through her. Steve stood by her side with a hand resting on her shoulder, filled with gratitude that they had their son back. Clancy bent close to

Toby and shone his pencil flashlight onto his buttonlike pupil and watched it shrink to a black pinpoint. Gramps stood in the far corner crying silently but unashamedly. Einar Borg conferred with a uniformed policeman at the door, organizing transport for the criminals, victims, and the horde of other interested parties.

Father Gaffney knelt by Esau's side and took the farmer's gnarled hand into his own and joined him in prayer, Esau mumbling incoherent exorcisms while the potbellied priest grimaced on aching knees and whispered thanks to a very special friend. Then he stretched out his other arm and laid his hand over Toby's, joining captor and captive in unlikely communion.

"Why was it me?" Toby's voice was sharp and brittle and it cracked the funereal hum. Everyone except Esau clipped their conversation and turned to look at the frail form on the cot. Mike moved closer, ready to coax the boy through the memory, to examine the contents of the final matchbox in his willing subject's genetic scrapbook.

But Toby didn't continue. He just stared at a vacant point in space. He was watching something, something only he could see. But there was more.

Fear? Humility? Love?

It was all of those things but even more. Even the face no longer belonged to Toby, but how could that be? The small figure on the cot had Toby's glossy black hair, his steel-gray eyes, his soft, full lips. He had all the features that were Toby's. But ten-year-old Toby Horton wasn't capable of the devastating sadness that cried out from whatever ancient soul currently roamed his consciousness. And Esau prayed, at times seeming to gain strength, rising in crescendo before retreating to a mumbling trough.

Father Gaffney knelt between them, his own aches forgotten or neutralized by the swift flow of current between the righteous farmer and the possessed boy. He *is* possessed, Gaffney realized, the farmer was correct on that account. But possessed by what? Or by whom? Who knew such sadness as that which Gaffney saw crushing the breath from the small boy on the cot? Who could ever have known such sadness?

Esau punctuated his prayer with a low moan, and Father Gaffney winced at the lanky farmer's strength as he squeezed the priest's helping hand.

"Why was it me?" Toby repeated.

It wasn't one of his restless memories, not yet at least. There was no thrashing or wailing, no rolled-back eyes. Mike was thankful for that. He was sorry Jan and Steve had had to show up when the boy was in a trance, but at least they wouldn't have to witness the kind of spectacle unleashed by some of his earlier memories. For that reason, Mike left it alone. He wasn't in a rush to coax or question. Instead he allowed the boy to set his own schedule of disclosure. And this *was* the last matchbox, unless there was yet another unprobed level of consciousness. The thought set the schoolteacher's scientific mind spinning but he quickly shut it down, concentrating instead on the specter of sadness on the rumpled cot.

But Toby didn't volunteer more. It was as if the final matchbox was his alone to relive, its grief not to be shared. And the pain in Toby's eyes proved to Mike that the boy was indeed in some other place. And he was suffering. What could be left to regret? Mike wondered. The ten-year-old had already watched through borrowed eyes as parents and pets, friends and lovers suffered their final moments. It was an encouraging statement, Mike thought, that man's most tragic moments occurred when harm befell another. Perhaps mankind wasn't in such a sad state, after all. Or was it only the likes of Toby Horton and his forebears who shared this sympathetic strain? Genes? Maybe that would be the subject of some future research.

The teacher could finally stand it no more. "What do you see, Toby? Why are you so sad?"

The boy's hand squeezed Father Gaffney's, strengthening the connection.

"Today began as a fine day but the sky looks fearsome now."

It sounded rehearsed, as if the story had been told and retold many times over. Instinctively Mike felt inside his pocket to be sure the recorder was running. Then, recognizing there was no further need for secrecy, he removed it from his pocket and set it on the edge of the cot.

"The crowds are festive, laughing, eating, and chatting as if on holiday."

Mike thought he might have seen a hint of a wistful smile but it was fleeting.

"I was bound to duty with my legion, waiting by the hill with the other soldiers. There was no one of authority around so we talked and gambled a little."

Esau's muffled prayers continued unabated but they were less intrusive than they had been, almost a part of the background. Two policemen clumped down the stairs to take him away, but Einar waved them off. He gestured to Gramps to close the door. The inspector was listening attentively to Toby and didn't want to be interrupted.

"It was like a parade, with children racing ahead, families walking together, thieves roaming through the crowds looking for opportunities." He sagged in deep sadness. "It was just like a parade," he repeated.

For an instant Toby's eyes seemed to focus, as if he were present today in Esau's basement, not at some ancient event lost forever in the unwritten pages of history. He fixed his gaze on Father Gaffney's battered face and whispered huskily. "He wanted it that way. It didn't have to be. It could have been different. Why?" he cried. "Why?" A single tear spilled down his cheek like a glistening pearl. "Why did he have to die?"

Another friend, Mike thought. Who was it this time, a father, a brother? The pattern was repeating itself, more grist for his research mill but only more of the same. He was disappointed and wanted the session to end.

"Who are you talking about, Toby? Was he a friend?"

Toby fixed the teacher with a puzzled stare. It was disquieting, as if the past were coming to life, not in the distant narration of an unseen storyteller but here, today. It was actually happening.

"A friend," Toby mused. "Yes, he was a friend."

But what was left unsaid told more than Toby's words.

"Here comes his mother. She's sad. She's losing her only son. How terrible that must be."

Did his eyes fix momentarily on Jan? Mike

looked at her to see her reaction and found himself drawn to the heart-wrenching sadness that veiled her face.

The dam of grief finally broke and tears poured freely down Toby's cheeks. "I helped them. It was my job to do it but I didn't have to. I could have run away. But I didn't. I could have but I didn't. I held him down when they—when they"—Toby choked back a two-thousand-year-old sob—"when they drove the nails through his hands and feet."

Father Gaffney felt the grips tighten on both of his hands. Esau stopped praying and the blood drained from his face and the hate that had filled his face melted into a mask of reverent awe.

"My God, He hurts so much. Why doesn't He save Himself?" Toby turned his head to the wall and gazed at the crucifix. "It's almost over," he wept. "He's looking up to the sky." A new wave of tears burst forth. "How can He even raise His head? He's talking now. He's saying something."

Toby thrust his arms away from his sides, splayed his fingers, and with a toneless stare that stilled the room cried out in a voice edged with triumph.

"Eli, Eli, lama sabachthani!"

The room was stifling with stillness, like the dead space in the eye of a turbulent tornado. Then a strobe of brilliance lit the rectangle on the bathroom wall and a crash of thunder shook the house like a child's toy and the structure shuddered as the whistling gale rattled the windows and ripped shingles from the aging roof.

Toby slumped on the cot, limp and spent. "It is over," he whispered.

Father Gaffney winced at the flow of current

that charged his fingers at Toby's touch, raced
through his arm, his chest, and through his other
arm before jolting the farmer to his feet. Esau's
face was soft with love and his eyes glowed with
the rapture of truth, not showing a trace of the
unrest that had filled his recent days.

Toby brought a hand to his face and rubbed a
knuckle into his tear-filled eye. "What
happened?" he asked. Then he flushed with excitement and his eyes flew around the room.
"Mom, Dad, Gramps," he exploded. "You found
us."

"Father, forgive me," Esau gasped and he
clutched uselessly at his chest and slumped to
the cold floor.

What followed was a tribute to Einar's organization. Paramedics were on the scene before
Gaffney had finished the last rites but they
were too late. No one felt an urgency to add to
the Manleys' sorrow, so Hattie and the twins
were left alone in the kitchen to pray. Gaffney
wanted to console them but he had no time.
Triage, he thought soberly, the battlefield tragedy that forces a surgeon to choose among the
casualties.

A pair of ambulances waited in the driveway,
their blinking lights and screaming sirens thankfully muted. Toby sat on the edge of the cot gathering his strength before testing his legs. He had
declined the offered stretcher, thinking it a gross
overreaction to a mere bout of tiredness. Jan and
Steve sat on either side of him. Clancy, Gramps,
Mike, Teddy, Einar, and the priest hovered in a
semicircle around the warm reunion.

"How's Greatgramps?" Toby asked, a frown of concern clouding his joy.

"He's fine," Steve told him. "He's coming home in a couple of days."

"How's Tina?" Toby continued. "Was she worried?"

"A little bit," Jan replied. "She's anxious to see you."

Toby beamed mischievously. "Somebody must have figured out the clue." He cast a sly glance in Gramps's direction and John Horton's entire being burst with pride and love but his tongue wouldn't work right so he could only smile his answer.

"Way to go, Old-timer," Toby applauded.

Everyone joined in the laughter.

"Are we finished, Mr. Mancini?" Toby wondered.

"Finished?" the teacher said questioningly.

"Your research. The genes and the memories and things. You told me that I opened the last matchbox, remember? Are you finished now?"

"No, Toby," the biology teacher said thoughtfully. "We're not finished by a long shot. This is just a start."

"You never did tell me," Toby continued. "What was in my last matchbox? Who was I this time?"

Jan wrapped a gentle arm around her son's thin shoulders and pulled him close. "We'll tell you all about it soon."

Toby accepted that. Then he wrinkled his face as if flexing his brain to wring out a buried bit of information. "I think that I remember something about this matchbox," he admitted.

"You do?" Mike said in surprise.

"Well, I don't exactly remember any of the dream, but there was something else. A message of some kind."

Everyone watched him. Waiting.

He struggled to dig the flimsy recollection to the surface. "There was a lady." He rubbed pensively at his smooth jaw. "I can't even remember what she looked like." Then he shook his head and smiled regretfully, sorry that he had opened the subject and anxious to dismiss it. "It was nothing," he apologized. "It was probably just a regular dream."

"No, Toby. I want to hear it. It's all part of the research," Mike explained.

"Well, all I can remember is that I'm supposed to say 'I hear you.' I don't even know what it's supposed to mean."

The teacher shrugged and glanced at the others, but no one volunteered. Teddy scribbled some notes.

"Who were you supposed to deliver the message to?" Jan probed.

Toby smiled innocently. "That's why I think it was just a regular dream. I don't even know anybody named Gaffney."

The End?

The end of a book is never really *the end* for a person who reads. He or she can always open another. And another.

Every page holds possibilities.

But millions of kids don't see them. Don't know they're there. Millions of kids can't read, or won't.

That's why there's RIF. Reading is Fundamental (RIF) is a national nonprofit program that works with thousands of community organizations to help young people discover the fun—and the importance—of reading.

RIF motivates kids so that they *want* to read. And RIF works directly with parents to help them encourage their children's reading. RIF gets books to children and children into books, so they grow up reading and become adults who can read. Adults like you.

For more information on how to start a RIF program in your neighborhood, or help your own child grow up reading, write to:

RIF
Dept. BK-1
Box 23444
Washington, D.C.
20026

Founded in 1966, RIF is a national non-profit organization with local projects run by volunteers in every state of the union.